Other books by Randy Thornhorn:

WICKED TEMPER
A Novel

HOWLS OF A HELLHOUND ELECTRIC
Riddle Top Magpies & Bobnot Boogies

THE AXMAN'S SHIFT
A Love Story

Visit Randy Thornhorn online at
www.thornhorn.com

Rosasharn Press
244 Fifth Avenue
Suite C-118
New York, N.Y. 10001
www.rosasharnpress.com
ISBN 978-0-615-96746-2

Printed in the United States of America.

First Edition

for Her

THE KESTREL WATERS

A Tale of Love and Devil

by

Randy Thornhorn

Table of Contents

VERSE 1

A Horny Beatitude

Brother Glenn's mandolin diddled down the mountain railway. The nails of Glenn's fingers danced faster and faster, chasing ghosts on a holy ghost train. He was a brave man, a scared man. It was a dynamite run, night after night, keeping up with his brother Kes when that brother spake in tongues and riddle and criminal lyric.

Tonight, aboard this train, his brother Kes was talking at this nurse. But this Nurse Nightingale, this angel of mercy with her stars and bars, she was damn well distressed by Kes's testament and verse.

"Looney Tunes—" Glenn began as his brother's tongue turned sharp and wicked. "Looney Tunes here—" Glenn said as he saw the train wreck ahead.

Glenn's fingers ran the neck of his mandolin but his diddling did not soothe his situation. Kes had just said a bad thing to this nurse, a hateful bad thing. She might screech at any moment. She might call for the conductor, you never knew. Glenn did know Kes. Glenn knew Kes was unaware of Kes's hand upon her throttle.

"Hey, lady? Repeat after me. Looney Tunes here is Kestrel."

Glenn said it. But did Nurse Nightingale hear it? How could she know where this dynamite train was headed? If she screeched or called for that conductor—well, things would go better if she did not screech. This train was no mystery to Glenn or his mandolin. He knew Kestrel's chords and curves, Kestrel's tunnels through the dark and the light. But Nurse Nightingale did not know the dark-winged Kestrel she sat facing. So, high atop this lonesome train trestle, Glenn's mandolin stopped vamping. He jumped in.

"Don't let Kestrel here salt your tail, lady. Pay no never-mind to that thing he just said. He's got devil in him. And a bad hipbone." Glenn Brass smiled behind dark glasses. "You don't know the half."

"So it would seem, sir," the Nurse said, fidgety, trying to look at Glenn now, not Kes.

"Oft days Kestrel is a one-man freak show. He scares the pee-waddin outa some folk. It's been a long day, a long train ride. He's urgent and needs medical attention."

"Ah. Ah, I see now. I, of all people," she sighed, unruffling her feathers. "Quite forgiveable then."

"And when Big Brer suffers, we all suffers."

"We do?"

"But nobody more than he."

"Brer?" The lady's blue eyes began to tinker. "Did you say *brer*?"

Glenn nodded, diddling his strings again, sweet melody filling the train car.

"Oh, yes, yesss," he almost sang. "Brer Kessstrel. You remember? Brother Rabbit and Brother Fox? That tarbaby stuck in the sticker briar?"

"Aye, aye. From those old fables. Colored folk's fables," she trilled, fondly, relaxing more as she recrossed her legs. A tapering finger checked her nurse insignia, the pleat of her Wave cap. "Aye, I do recall now. Brer Rabbit, Brer Fox. Aye, as if they were fixed in amber. Such wise Negro fables told in the crib, recited in my bygone schooldays."

"Not nearly so bygone as our Brer Kestrel here. He's horngod crazy. I've known him to fall out of bed, besotted, with car keys in his hand."

"Keys?"

"Keys to the kingdom, ma'am. Why, I seen him crank them keys and give the gun to my daddy's coppertop Cadillac. Gun it, flip it, and crash it into the sea."

"A Cadillac? Into the sea?"

"Oh, mama. He loves to make a sound."

"This individual is licensed to drive?"

Kestrel Brass broke in.

"Ain't never had no license," Kestrel spake behind dark glasses. "Ain't never had no license for the things I done."

"Get the picture?" Glenn nudged her with his knee. "Brer Kes needs a doctor's care after a day like this."

"Yes," she said directly at Kestrel, "I think I do understand now. This day has tried you?"

"Ever day tries me," Kes said to the train window.

"Get the picture?" Glenn nudged her again.

Outside their loop, the lady could only flutter her lashes, her nervous breath smelling of sweet tea. Kestrel knew Daddy Malakoff Brass would have her out of her sailor whites and full starkers by now. Daddy worked miracles with women in uniform.

“Gracious,” she chirped, “Well, I will be doing my best to help.”

“Help?” Glenn’s mandolin missed a lick.

“To help shoulder his burden,” she affirmed, her starched sense of duty and her sweet tea scent drifting through Kes’s waking dream. “Yes. I will do just that.”

Glenn went stone-faced.

“You will, will you? You mean, you still can’t see it? Kestrel here is well past his discard date. Lost in his cause. Yet, here I sit before you. This mere minstrel. How about you bear a little shoulder with me?”

“You?”

“Me.”

“Me shoulder *your* burden?”

“Well, sure sister. Sure you can. If you insist. Much obliged. But, listen, you don’t know the half. He is one heavy brother.”

“So, you two? You are brothers?”

“Two bluegrass boys. That’s us.”

“In the beginning—” Kes rumbled to no one, “—in the beginning was the Brothers Brass.”

“Yep,” Glenn said, “there’s love and there’s devil in him. Just you wait and see.”

Kestrel knew better. Or wished he did. He did not like to drive Cadillacs of copper much these days. He did his best loving on trains and in trees. In Kestrel's eyes, both of the two were true.

They were such different ways to love. One love kept moving, like this night train, moving, while the other love stayed rooted in place, rooted like a tree standing by the water. If Kes and her sweet memory had a son, yes, he would sit that brother down and tell him. Spend your love inside a true bird as long as she is no split-tail virgin up a tree. You will thank her for her favor even if forever and a day you be damned.

Yes, you must love a girl like that forever. You will never let her go. A kiss like hers will carry you up the highest, darkest tree then down again.

This was true. Wasn't it?

With such holy riddles chiming, making endless mad melody behind his eyes, Kes had little sensitivity for the silly riddles of others. Besides, this was love, love moving, on a train. Didn't this silly Nurse Nightingale know her ways to love?

"You were born on the sea?" she asked.

Kestrel Brass felt a grin strain his face. His hip ached so bad the train whistled.

"Nope. I was borned up a tree," Kes said.

Mandolin chimed in his head. Oh, yes, Kes almost forgot. Brother Glenn Brass was with them. Glenn was nodding at this lady in white, plucking his mandolin, lapsing into *Life's Railway To Heaven.*

"By the sea, but not on the sea, ma'am," Glenn said. "Borned there, bred there, but never went in no water."

"You never swam?"

"Nope. Never." Glenn hummed. "Hard to fancy, huh?"

"Aye, sir. It is."

"Why? You Navy?"

Kestrel almost spat nickels over that one. Glenn, he was a sly and dry joker. But he did not fool Kes and neither did she. Like movie stars, both Brothers Brass wore dark glasses. Still, any fool could see. They knew a woman yeoman with silver anchors and lipstick in such close quarters. She was an exotic bird, hard to miss. Her lipstick had a baby aspirin scent. Orange baby aspirin.

"Whatcha think, Big Brer?" Glenn kept pondering. "She Navy?"

"No, sir, sailor ma'am. No splashity-splash," Kestrel told her. "He and me, we cain't swim."

She had to think about that.

"Mmmm, but, *what if–*" she began, lashes at half-mast.

Kes murmured "*swim pool, motel*" to the window-glass inside himself.

"What if you were to tumble in some motel swimming pool with nobody to save you?"

"That would be tragic. And unlikely," Glenn said.

"But that's a good question, ain't it?" Kes jutted his jaw at Glenn sitting beside him. "*Ain't that a good question?*"

"Only the finest digs for us, Nurse Nightingale," Glenn told her, "no slop jar motels."

Kestrel kept grinning at the pain.

"Well, darlin, thing is, we just left that Peabody Hotel? Up in Memphis?" Kes slithered a foil wrapper out the window, chewing his Wrigley's, listening to the click-click-clicking, the last red hot kablooms of sunset. "That Peabody has ducks and, them goddamn ducks, they even swim in the lobby. But not me. Never got to swim, no slingshot, never no dog for to hunt. No click-click-click. Had me a mama though. Had me a daddy too."

The white Nightingale rankled a bit, appalled but intrigued.

"A boy like you, never to own a dog. I declare."

"Oh, I got me a good dog now, lady," Kes assured her.

"You do? Where is his kennel?"

"Kennel? She ain't got none. No. No kinfolk we know of. No, lady, and *she* be like *you*. *She* be one fur-beastly white bitch."

"Excuse me?"

"She be a big snowbitch of a hound. Big like a kodiak. Best kept in a box. Like me."

"Where is this box?"

"Back in her boxcar, of course. She is quite secure back there in her boxcar. Harmless. Out of harm's way. Click-click-click."

"Well, I, I, I declare."

"*Au de claire de la lune, mon ami pierrot,*" warbled Kes, "*–open your legs for the love of God.*"

Glenn's mandolin began diddling the old French melody, smoothing the waters.

"At ease, lady. Repeat after me. Don't let the Kestrel salt your tail."

"Yes, well, yes, he is quite *forgivable.* Considering his *circumstance.*"

"I knew a pinhead freak once–" Kes said from nowhere. "Killed a railman for his red lamp."

"Gracious. Well, we must find forgiveness for him too," she said, struggling to keep up.

"Him too? Him who?" Kes shot back.

"Mmmm, this *pinhead,* was it? This freakish fellow?"

Kes was astonished. How entertaining. He leaned into her, hip burning, baring white fang. Yes. He knew her little secret.

"Forgive *him*? *Him*?" Kestrel spake. "Why, you're a credit to your sex, ain't you, your ladyship? I reckon you are ripe tasty."

His dear and darling Bettilia, she always tasted of sweet tea laced with gingermint. Yes, Kes could almost taste her, every minty inch of her.

"Mmmm, well," the Navy Nurse demurred, "all due credit goes to my mother, actually. Her values, her fundamentals."

"I reckon you rear up mornings, tasty, ripe with fresh spitshine."

Glenn hacked loud, stopped playing, thumped his mandolin into the spare seat facing him.

"Up ahead," Glenn squinted, briefly doffing his dark glasses. "Elgar Hill lights. Hurry sundown."

"Glory *be,*" the lady said with great relief. "Home again, home again, jiggidy-jig."

"You live up Elgar Hill way?" Kes asked, wincing, falling

back in his seat. His pelvic felt each click, each jar of the rail wheels.

"Why, yes. Yes I do, young man. Elgar Hill is my home. My lovely home."

"I reckon they got the hardware store?"

"Oh, yes. Hillzabub's Hardware. Lovely old place. Still there standing, all these years."

"Ain't love a nail in the head? A ten-penny nail in the head?"

"Well, I—I don't know as I would put it that way."

"Really, darlin? You ain't never been nailed?"

"Well, I don't—"

"You poor, poor, fortunate darlin."

"Fortunate? Oh, uh, yes, we are daily blessed."

"You been up that Riddle Top? Ole Riddle Top mountain?"

"Why, no. I have not. Riddle Top? Is it far from here?"

"Naw. Naw, it ain't never far from here."

"Thank you."

"For what?"

"For my illumination."

"No need to thank me. Not for that."

"Living and learning. All my life in Elgar Hill. Yet I, of all people, to have never heard one whisper of a Riddle Top. Yes. I will reference my Rand-McNally, mark the co-ordinate. The sea has its pleasures, but I do get lost in a fresh mountain breeze." She lilted, too eager to please to see Glenn roll his eyes behind dark shades. Oh, how she lilted. "I've long felt mountains and sea are like Brother Sun, Sister Moon. Sun and wind, fire and water."

"Up and down, in and out," Glenn deadpanned. "Sonny and Cher."

But Kes—Kes pressed on. Yes, Kes would set her true.

"You get lost up-round that Riddle Top, you best watch out he who you meet—"

"I exercise caution, restraint," she replied, "I chart my course."

"Watch out for that whatnot and that bobnot—"

"For it is better to travel well than to arrive?" she asked, cautiously. "Is it not?"

"You'll do well when you arrive alive, darlin—"

"I am prepared, prepared to help. I do a good turn daily."

"You turns *what*?" Kes spat, pitching half out his britches at the sailor lady. "You turns *what*?"

"A good turn. I do one daily."

"But what about them turns that do *you*, that take *you*, that turns on *you*? Look yonder coming. And you still won't see that hipbroke jag before it will take everthing you dearly elger and what elgerhells you—"

"Elgerhell?"

"Everthing you got worth a give—"

"Elgar Hill? Elgar *Hill*, you mean?" She blinked, her spine rigid.

"Elgerhellzebubba!" Kes blurted, rising from his seat, his hip shooting fire. "Ahkan-dah-lay ah-mo-santee-yah!"

"It *is* a charitable little *town*—" .

"Oh-booger-oom-bay-hipbone-da-*Jeeeeezus*!" Head wobbling, legs wobbling, Kes rose up, teetering over the woman.

She shrank in her seat, her eyes wide, terrified under Kestrel's dark-shuttered and demanding eyes. She must be merciful. She must help shoulder his burden.

"Why, yes, I suppose that's a *perspective*," she squeaked up at him.

Kestrel's arms flew out wild like floppy wings.

"*Booger-oom-bay—*" he belched as a lightning bolt struck inside his Sunday-go-to-meeting suit. His head jerked back, his black glasses and pale face spake up to heaven. "Yes—I, oh yes, I hears you, Lord," he whispered, weak as a ghost. Then lightning struck again. "Booger-ooo-damma-damma-lam-*bone*!"

Hot foam blew from Kestrel's lips. He went limp. He dropped, collapsing face-down into Nurse Nightingale's lap. She *screeched*.

"Repeat after me, lady," Glenn Brass began, slowly, picking up his mandolin again. "Looney Tunes..."

The Brothers Brass stepped off the train and not a lick too soon. They both had earthly matters to attend. The Kentucky Cardinal had arrived three hours late but at least they were alive. The train platform creaked, unsea-worthy under Kestrel's burning hip. He needed a pee, bad. Glenn needed a smoke, just as bad. A sorrowful elderman covered with warts was there with a sedan to meet them, sent by the First Elgar Hill Assembly Of God Church. The Brothers Brass made him wait.

"Don't forget that mighty white hellhound of yours,

brer," Glenn drawled, standing outside the toilet stall as Kes slipped inside.

"How could I ever forget her?" Kes unzipped, listening to his own holy water as his brother smoked and spat loose tobacco. Kes heard both pee and tobacco flecks hit linoleum. There was room for correction. "She's around here somewheres."

"Ain't no doubt about it."

"Book us a room for the night?" Kes sighed.

"Naw," Glenn said. "Half forgot. Half hoping some churchfolk'll bunk us up for free."

"Churchfolk? Half-wit Bible School gals, you mean."

"Yeah. That's what I mean."

"Don't sound like no Peabody Hotel to me."

"A warm bed and a warm bottom with them lights out. You might as well be."

"Them weavers are at you again. You best mind your peas."

"I am weaver-proof and don't you forget it," Glenn said.

"Bullshit."

"That Navy nurse on the train?"

"Yeah?" Kes sighed again, zipping up.

"Did you have to go shoving your nose up her cooze?"

"Well, Little Brer, sometimes you just got to jump in."

The sorrowful wart-plagued man drove his church sedan and the Brothers Brass back over the tracks, through the ripe scat of the stockyards. They skirted the edge of Heathbaugh College where frat boys could be heard drinking and cussing through Kes's open window until, just past the campus, the warm night brought waves of gardenia and the bitter-tar hint of asphalt, the faint sulphur of ironworks nearby. The Jamboree was just a couple of more miles, their driver said. The elder went on about how he was one of their purest fans, fellers, though his voice bespoke little fervor. He was mighty tore up, he said, about not being able to hear them sing tonight. But, after depositing the Brothers Brass, he said, he had to go straight over to the Baptist Hospital where his wife was having a breast removed at nine in the a.m.

Kes and Glenn took pity on him, harmonizing a verse and chorus of *River Of Death* from the sedan's back seat.

Oh, the river of death lies just before me,
Can I find a place where I can cross...

They hummed a few more bars then received the sorrowful man's thanks topped with more blessings. Glenn lit up another smoke whilst Kes settled into his same old melancholia. Kes's sharp ears began to catch gospel chords in the offing and wondered if he would hear Bettilia sing tonight. As always, he hoped he did and hoped he did not. It was a mournful dilemma indeed.

The swarming scent of gardenia gave way to linseed oil, sawdust, old leather, dripping motor pans, and a miasma of summer perfumes, especially Lily of the Valley. The Elgar Hill Full Gospel Jamboree was in full blossom. Butted up against an old National Guard Armory or Masonic Lodge or some damn thing, the big gospel tent flapped in the hot wind as Glenn stuck his head out the window. The parking lot was choked with pickup trucks and outdated sedans with scorched paint. They cruised to a gravelly stop behind the big tent. Glenn and Kes bade farewell to the warted man bound for Baptist Hospital.

"Tell your missus the Brass boys send their best," Glenn told the elder before he backed away.

"Will you sing one for her tonight, fellers? Dedicated to Mrs. Carl Mosby?"

"Why, sure, sure we will, sir," Glenn said with resignation. Even he had grown a bit callous, weary of the endless dedications, the non-stop prayer requests.

"Sang *Bosom Of Abraham* for her, fellers. That's her favorite."

Kes gave a snort then began telling a sick third-grade joke about a skinny gal with sloppy milkshakes. Glenn grabbed his arm and pulled him inside.

The Brothers Brass found their way backstage. All Creation was there. The Speer Family, The Blackwoods, The Holy Mountain Orioles, Reverend Frang and his talented daughters. Sister Rosetta sat on an electric amp tuning her guitar. In a nearby stairwell, Jake Hess leaned into a sheet music salesman, poking at the man's chest with his Pepsi bottle, quoting scriptural wit and wisdom in words Kes could barely decrypt. Bobby Singleton and the Trinity Four were heard onstage, belting out a fierce rendition of *God's Gonna Send Revival,* their quartet crescendos jabbing a hole through the tent-top, through the sky, high above all that clapping, clomping, and stomping from the frenzied flock. Out there.

"Ooooh, you good looking stag, you," Rebecca Frang warbled, twirling her long-nailed finger on Kes's cheek. "Jest look at them booful sideburns."

"Hidy, Becky," Kes said, flashing his shy smile.

"Why don't we see more of y'all at these doings, you booful thang?"

"You know how it is. When I ain't working the road, Mama George just won't let me go."

Rebecca squealed in a way Kes had come to dread.

"That Hard Hearted Georgiana is gonna have to *wrassle me for you*," she proclaimed, clinging at him.

Rebecca was the youngest of the Frang sisters, the prettiest. And she was having her monthly. Kes could tell. She always made herself available to Kes, in words that left little room for Biblical interpretation. Yet Kes continued to resist. Such abstinence took no real effort from where Kes nested in his melancholia. Sucking on a .44 would take a lot less effort than getting it up to bone Rebecca Frang.

"Lawd Awmighty, praise His heaven on high!" It was Preacher Furl Rainey, big and sweaty as ever, pumping both brothers' hands in turn. "Ya'll made it hyere this year. Glenn, my favorite! And Kestrel Brass–still without no dog! I told ever last one of em you was gonna be hyere and hyere you is. Let me assure you, last year's Jamboree you boys was *missed*."

Glenn pulled his picking fingers free of the preacher's big mitt.

"Mama George, she just won't let me go," Glenn said.

Preacher Furl grabbed Glenn's suitcase then led the brothers to a little airless Airstream travel trailer out back. He kept telling them what earthly reward this hot dressing room was and for them to set a spell in it since they had an hour before they stormed the stage. The big preacher blew forth a few more beatitudes then left the Brothers Brass. Glenn tossed his mandolin into the padded booth, turned up his nose at the Airstream's dark innards.

"I hate that blubberball saint. He unwrapped his Jolly Rancher one day when I was nine."

"He's got a bad runny cancer somewheres. A killing cancer," Kes said.

"Really? How can you tell?"

"I can tell. It's a smell. Nothing a moon chant and a buried chicken couldn't cure."

"That sounds Democrat. Brother Furl's Republican. Leave God's plan alone." Glenn plumped the white silk hanky in his lapel pocket. "I'm gonna go wander in the wilderness. Back before you know it."

"Don't get too lost out there. You got four hungry ducklings and a mad housewife."

"I'm just grazing, brer. Grazing on the huckleberries."

"You reckon Bettilia will show up tonight?"

"Cain't never tell. No. Might be some blackberries, gooseberries, a wild cherry or two—"

Kes hmmmphed, sinking into a chair.

"Got anything to read? Make me feel better."

Glenn came back from the door, reached into Kes's bag, tossed the book into Kes's lap.

"Read away, brer. There's a light behind you."

"We'll just vamp."

"What's that ripe smell in here?" Glenn asked.

"You know what it is."

"Yeah. I reckon."

Glenn stepped down out of the trailer, closing the door, leaving half the duet in the dark.

Kes went back to crafting riddles, turning them into song lyrics in his head. Most were too blue or obscene to ever sing out loud anyplace except Indian Lil's house of whores, back in Savannah. He tried not to brood or recline deeper inside himself, but that temptation was about all he had since he gave up the spirits. His hip might be on fire but his loins felt dead, too long dormant, on verge of atrophy. Brother Glenn suffered no such limitation in that area, but Kes also knew there was no real chance Glenn would cheat. No, Gaylenn "Glenn" Brass would flirt with every skirt out there and they would love him all the more for it without him ever posing any real threat of love.

Meanwhile, for Kestrel Brass, all desires had simmered down to one desire. He was only enticed by the possibility he might hear Bettilia sing again tonight—that he might beguile another chance to sing with her the way they sang back at Shelfy Oak Bible College. Back when their lips could do more than caress lyrics together. At least Kes might still harmonize with his Bettilia. At least he could do that much. There was little else he could do with her or for her anymore.

Kes sat thirsting over such things, trying not to brood.

He took off his glasses.

No, sitting here hot, tonight, this trailer did not smell of gingermint. Like so many dressing rooms, this airless Airstream smelled of dead roses.

Kestrel reached for his dop kit. He took out his straight razor, took his whetstone from his side pocket. He sharpened the blade through two more tunes by the Blackwoods out there before he laid the gleaming razor on the table in here, here in this trailer darkness. Kes commenced his nightly negotiations with that straight razor, daring himself not to use it, daring himself to keep giving a damn.

His boogered up damnation couldn't be worth much anymore. But he did have plenty of it to give.

VERSE 2

Bible School Limbo

By the time Mama enrolled them in Shelfy Oak Bible College in 1961, Kes and Glenn had been singing duet for twelve years.

On Shelfy Oak's Invitation Day, Mama George and her boys rode the Nancy Hanks Express up from Savannah to Newdundy, Georgia so the lads could receive orientation. Also along for the journey was Kes's almost-fiancee Chalice. Chalice was a hothouse rose. She and Kes were very serious about each other. At that point in his convolution, Kes was very sincere and very serious about everything. Chalice was serious enough to make the trip knowing she would have to take the train back that evening alone with Mrs. Brass. In the meantime she tried to soothe Kes, who had brought three suitcases and was fighting the jitters over his first day at college. But Mama George felt their education took priority over the boys' singing career, so off to college they would be. She even let Kes pass a year without school—just playing church and show dates—so both brothers could attend their advanced religious training together. When they chugged into Newdundy station about ten that morning, they stepped off the train only to be greeted by the grinning face and flashing eyes of Daddy Brass in his light blue linen suit.

Mama was not pleased to see Daddy Brass. They had not clapped eyes on each other in over six months despite them still being married.

"You are not required or desired here, Malakoff Brass," she spake.

"Aw, Georgiana darlin, let's have none of that," he said, throwing his arms around both boys, eyeing Chalice up and down with lusty approval. "Ain't you heard? This be they first year of high learning in the lap of God. Natcherly, I just had to run up hyere crack o' dawn to make sure my big boys was lined out proper." He spat pine nut, winked at Chalice. "I'll tote y'all over to the big building in my new black Hudson. There she sets all shiny. Motor running."

Mama shook her head slowly, eyes even on the man.

"No, Malakoff. We have a Checkered taxi cab waiting for us. I telephoned ahead for an appointment yesterday. I made a long distance call from home."

"Aw, sure you did, darlin. But I cut him loose and told him to head on 'cause I had you covered. Nice feller. Cracker kid named Toby whose pap used to work River Street for me. His pap's name was Big Toby. Now, lemme tell you, Big Toby was not meant to climb the tree of knowledge, if you know what I mean. But he was a helluva dancer. He drank overly of the goods though, so one day I had to cut him loose too."

"Daddy, you shouldn't oughta done that," Kes injected. "Mama had the situation fully orchestrated to her specifications. She even hired her a private detector to–"

"Don't be a kiss-ass, Kes. I swear you'd shame Honest Abe, you such a goody boy." Daddy Brass looked down, asking sweet Chalice, "Is he always like this?"

Chalice hid her smile, tried not to blush.

"Yeah, but Daddy," Glenn jumped in, "Mama had it orkerstrated."

"Shore, shore she did, son," Daddy Brass agreed. "I just conducted a thrilling new arrangement for her benefit. That's all."

"But, Daddy," Glen persisted, "Mama's taxi man—"

"Now don't you worry about Little Toby. I tipped him well and I reckon he's already working a new fare by now. He's a smart one, that kid. Lots smarter than his daddy. But ain't that the way?"

"Hmmmph," went Mama George.

"Mr. Brass? Ah'm Chalice Dillard." Chalice leaned forward , shaking Daddy's hand, her lips pursed primly. "Please to meet you–"

Kes rallied, aligning his face with hers.

"Aw, yeah, Daddy," he said. "This is my girl, Chalice. Chalice, this is Daddy. Be nice to her, Daddy."

"Don't be *too* nice to her, Daddy," young Glenn advised.

Daddy's possum grin got wider. And wider.

"No, no, noooo, Brer Brass. *Pleeease*, don't make me ride up front with this gal. Not with my goody boy's *best gal.*" Daddy Brass glanced at the Hudson, took Chalice's hand with a courtly flourish, gave it a not-so-courtly tug. "Honey, pleeease don't set up front so I can keep you safe from this boy."

Daddy was slow letting go of her hand.

"Safe from which boy?" Glenn asked.

"Now hear this, Malakoff Brass—" Mama George spake with steely resolve, "—I have fully researched my institutions, had them privately investigated. I have compared and contrasted and settled my final finger upon Shelfy Oak Bible College. I have duly enrolled these boys in Shelfy Oak Bible College after I made all necessary financial arrangements. I have counseled and provisioned these boys for this day. And we will find carriage from this train depot to this day's campus orientation by means decided and provided by Georgiana Brass and no one else."

Minutes later, Daddy Brass's shiny black Hudson was humming down the main street of Newdundy, Chalice alongside Daddy at the wheel, a grim Mama George sandwiched betwixt her sons in the back seat.

"Naw, Kestrel, Glenn—" Daddy Brass was intoning. "—now you know I never cared for this Bible College notion of your mama's. But once a thing is to be done, hell or high water, well, we got to pull together as family. So your daddy did what a daddy's gotta do. I done come up and squared things with these Bible cats. Told em how it was gonna be. And I even wrangled a few extrys in exchange for a sweet treat from you two minstrel boys."

"What kind of treat?" asked Glenn.

"What kind, indeed," Mama said. "What have you adulterated now, Malakoff?"

Daddy Brass could feel her scalding tongue on the back of his neck. But he kept on grinning, spinning the steering wheel with one hand while his other arm stretched along the seat-back behind Chalice's head, tapping his forefinger, often touching, her auburn-red locks. This made Kes feel queer in the belly as he sat directly behind Chalice, watching his Daddy's finger.

"All you got to do," Daddy Brass said, "is sang three little songs after dinner on the ground. Three little boogies and you don't even have to thank this Daddy."

"But we ain't got no guitars," Glenn piped up. "Mama made us leave the Gibsons back home for fear they'd get stole."

"*Stolen*, Glenn—not *stole*," Georgiana snapped. "And it's *any* guitars—not *not* no guitars."

Daddy Brass laughed.

"Don't go popping your cork, little man. I'll git you a gitbox to bang on. Don't you worry."

It did no good for Mama George to argue, but argue she did, with a certain resigned expertise. As it turned out, Daddy Brass knew quite a few of the school faculty from his days selling sheet music for the Sacred Heart Publishing Company out of Nashville. He even knew the college dean, a Brother Abner Pickery, who thought Daddy was one of the most charming fellows he had ever met—an outstanding gentleman, pure of heart. Apparently, Mama George told the back of Daddy Brass's neck, this Dean Pickery had been tucked behind his ivy-covered walls too long. The further education of this Dean Pickery was on her short list, she said. And that is all she had to say on the matter for the time being, until further notice, she said.

Daddy Brass listened attentively, nodding on cue before informing his cargo that he looked over the campus already and had doled out sage advice to a number of teachers. Some found his stripe of insight unsettling, almost visionary, Daddy said, but they came to embrace it in the end. Most notably, Daddy rejected the aging upright piano currently in residence in the choir class room. He told the music director—a Miss Gaudette—that she should give up her girdle, embrace her curves, and he would have a brand new Steinway piano delivered to her from Savannah first thing Monday morning. He would also arrange for a certified piano tuner to arrive later that same day. After touring the boys' assigned quarters, Daddy Brass did a little more mule trading. He got the Dean to move their room assignment to bigger digs closer to the showers with a large picture window overlooking the lake. They would share this new room with a star baseball player named Overstreet whose family owned and operated a distillery north of Atlanta. This suited Daddy Brass a whole lot better, so he just knew it was bound to suit his two big boys who no doubt shared his sensibilities. In exchange, Daddy made a handshake deal with the Dean for the Brothers Brass to perform a brief concert for what was sure to be a receptive crowd of bright-eyed, well-behaved Bible babies, proud mamas, and upright daddies like himself, yes.

When inspired, Daddy was known to quote the poets:

"Yet with a steady beat, have not our weary feet come to the place for which our fathers sighed?" he posed in rich voice.

"That's beautiful," Chalice told him.

"I detest you, Malakoff Brass," Mama said from the backseat.

Daddy smiled in the mirror.

"Now, darlin—is that the kind of Christ-like example you want to be setting for these children?"

"Scuse me, Mama," Kes said. "But Daddy's right this time. It ain't the Christian way to hate—"

"Mind your peas and your own business, Kestrel Brass," she said. "I have paid our way thus far and I am still paying for this journey. One way or another your father will make sure of that."

Daddy Brass laughed in his loud nasty way, pulling a pewter flask from inside his linen coat, thumbing loose the cap. "Anybody up for a jorum of skee? A long pull on a short bottle?"

"Naw, sir," Kes said.

"Naw, sir," Glenn said.

"No, thank you kindly, Mr. Brass," Chalice said.

"You are a living depravity," Mama said, averting her gaze out the window. "And this town is crawling with ants."

"Sure is a fine new car, Mr. Brass."

"Well, sweet thing, the mule makes the man."

Newdundy, and the campus at its heart, may not have

been crawling with ants (that was subject to further inspection), but it was assuredly crawling with kids and kinfolk. Shelfy Oak Bible College was an encouraging array of red stone buildings under hand-split shingle roofs, mostly two and three-story structures dripping with wisteria and tradition. Amidst century-old spreading oaks, every school building and campus dormitory fanned out from the granite-columned administration building—a daunting structure known as King's Door Hall. Daddy Brass parked his Hudson in the reserved Infirmary parking space. There was a small stage with podium set up in the parade field where families and their enrollees were already milling on the green.

Outside the car, Mama George finally regained the lead she demanded all along. Daddy Brass fell back, let her go, hands in his pockets as he trailed along. Mama George found the sign-in table behind the granite columns atop the King's Door Hall steps. They waited in line behind an elderly black woman and a wee white girl in a cornflower blue dress. The line moved slower than any would have liked. Chalice stood there, toes crossed, looking moony and proud whilst Kes looked bored for her benefit, lest Chalice think he was not worldly. Glenn couldn't hide his misery and kept messing with a pimple on his chin. Daddy Brass began cleaning his fingernails with a pocketknife. Mama George found such Daddy Brass behavior to be common as Alabama dirt but said nothing. Neither of them spake for the long hot duration.

There was little for Kes to do but hold Chalice's hand

and survey those on his horizon. He noticed that most of the other boys in line wore sweaters and slacks—not dark suits like the Brothers Brass. In fact, the poor towering lad behind them in line wore a very fuzzy orange sweater that made him look like a stuffed giraffe with a droopy bowtie which seemed terribly old-fashioned to Kes. Not spruce at all. Each time the old lady and wee girl inched forward in line, the Brass clan and this fuzzy giraffe inched forward with them. None of the girls Kes could see were nearly as pretty as Chalice (which made him feel special), that old colored lady's spine was hunched badly (not like his stalwart mother), and the dirty blonde crown of that wee girl was clasped by a plastic barrette shaped like two goldfish tail-to-tail. She never turned around so Kes could not see how the pampered little thing compared to his fine filly. The whole affair took so long that Kes was afraid his folks were going to be forced into conversation again. To make matters worse, when the Brass clan was almost due their turn at the registrar's table, the old hunched lady in front dragged out the proceedings asking question after question whilst plumbing the deep contents of her purse. Finally, she brought forth some cash in a quivering hand.

"Well, I suppose you know your bidness. Here, mister, is the rest of your money I brought ye. I paid half down last week. I be paying the other half now like her mama told me," she said in an unsound voice. "I'll need another of them yeller papers from ye to prove I done paid it. Her mama and daddy is indisposed. But they'll be asking for that yeller paper. Honey, show this man how you can sign your name."

She turned to the little white girl who stepped forward and scribbled on demand. Finally the old lady was satisfied and cleared the way. Kes could not believe some folks were too detained to enroll their own kids and, instead, let the kid's mammy do it for them. Kes felt like he was suddenly surrounded by more privilege than he had ever seen back home on Officer's Row.

Mama George instructed Kes and Glenn to use their best penmanship as each etched his name on the ledger. Malakoff Brass hung back, smiling as he closed his knife, thrusting his hands back in his pockets. Kes was struck by how his daddy acted like this whole show was his idea from the get go.

To prove this point, Daddy Brass was soon leading them all through the hallowed doors of King's Door Hall. But they had barely entered the marbled foyer before Mama George pushed ahead of Malakoff. Malakoff winked back at his boys when she did this, loving every minute of this day. Mama found Dean Pickery in his office helping another family with some sort of dispensation. The wait was shorter this time and when her time came Mama was concise.

"Brother Pickery, I am bound to honor any special arrangements made in the name of the Brothers Brass as a result of their father's dealings with you. But, in future, I would appreciate and expect that any further nuance or necessary adjustment regarding their tutelage here be negotiated through me and me alone."

"Why, certainly, Mrs. Brass. I do hope you are amenable to this afternoon's pre-arranged performance by your illustrious young gentlemen. I believe we will find a pair of worthy guitars over at the music building. I understand your husband has arranged a significant new donation to the school's stock of instruments."

"Sir, you may refer to that man as Kestrel's father or Glenn's father or as Mr. Brass or by his Christian name if you see fit. He will answer to any number of hillbilly vulgarisms routinely voiced by his unsavory rabble of friends. But please never again refer to him as my husband."

Daddy kept grinning.

"Kestrel? Gaylenn?"

"Yes, Daddy?"

"Now, I want you boys to hunker down here. Do right by this here Bible school. Do like your mama says."

"We do not need your stamp of approval, Malakoff," Mama George was quick to say.

"Kestrel? Gaylenn?"

"Yes, Daddy?"

"Y'all still ain't got no wheels, do you?"

"No, Daddy."

"We have a fund for that, Malakoff. We are saving our pennies," Mama said tersely.

"Well, if y'all finish up here at this ivy patch like your mama says for you to, you can have my old copper Caddy to drive around the island back home. I let my coloreds borry it from time to time right now, so it don't get too rusty setting out back of my shop. But I'll set that Cadillac aside for you boys if you study hard here at school."

Kes, Glenn, even Chalice, they were all his after that and Daddy Brass knew it. They might as well be nibbling kibble from the palm of his hand. Mama George struggled to keep her composure.

"Splendid, Malakoff," Dean Pickery smiled. "A splendid gesture."

"Graft and bribery," Mama Brass said. "I will never ride in it."

Dean Pickery donned his Belvedere cap then gave them a personal tour through the campus. The boys could see that Mama George thought the Dean was enjoying himself a bit too much with Daddy Brass. To compound the matter, Chalice was also overly intrigued.

"I never knew your daddy was such a tall man. And so loud," she whispered in Kes's ear as everybody trooped out of King's Door Hall. "I'm proud to finally meet him."

"Yeah, well, there's things I should tell you about Daddy," Kes whispered back. "He's more than meets the eye."

"What's that mean?"

"Shhh. Tell you later."

Chalice giggled, slipping her hand into Kes's coat pocket, finding his fingers in there. Chalice Dillard loved secrets, loved learning secrets, and she loved holding secret hands with Kestrel Brass.

They soon learned that the Dean said "Lord willing" a lot. Lord willing this and Lord willing that. He said it a lot to the other new students and parents he met along the way, shaking many hands, greeting returning students by name. He reminded Kes of a governor or president or one of those door-to-door peddlers Mama was always running off while threatening to call the sheriff.

Amidst the streaming throng of youngsters, one short dough girl with pigtails and a white leather Bible marched up and blurted, "Mister Pickery, I'm so proud to be back! Can I give you a love offering?"

The Dean bowed low like a clerical butler, made ritual presentation of his left cheek, and the pigtailed girl went tippy-toes to deliver her loud smacker of a kiss. Dean Pickery patted her hiney as he moved on.

Dean Pickery led the Brass clan through the dormitory to the boys' newly appointed room. A dour looking round kid with round spectacles was vacating the room, hauling out his duffel and briefcase with no effort to hide his displeasure. Dean Pickery cupped the back of his round head as he slid past them.

"So kind of you, Master Marcus. He that humbles himself shall be exalted. Matthew Twenty-three."

As Daddy Brass predicted, this room was larger and airier than most others, with three beds, a desk with oscillating fan, a hook rug, and the promised high window overlooking a small magnolia-fringed lake. Mama George gave the place her tacit approval. What else was she to do after such an upgrade in lodgings and the lure of a copper hot rod? Afterward, the Dean took Glenn over to the music building to check out guitars while the others went back to the Hudson for the boys' suitcases.

By then, possibly from early onset car craziness, a mischievous side of Chalice had appeared as she clung to Kes's arm—a bottled mischief which saw a possible outlet when Mrs. Brass actually addressed her personally for the first time today.

"Chalice, honey, might you help Kestrel carry this luggage while I spread the blanket for our luncheon picnic?"

"Oh certainly, Mrs. Brass," Chalice replied, demurely dropping her eyes like a pro. "Anything to help."

Chalice and Kes watched Mama George quick march toward the parade field, a plaid blanket over her arm, Daddy swinging the picnic hamper a few steps behind her. Daddy Brass's long legs took one lazy stride for every three steps clocked by Mama George. They seemed an odd match, or no match at all.

Minutes later, back at his new dorm room, Kes had barely stepped inside with a load of suitcases before Chalice fell onto a bed, her skirt swirling up her thighs as she kicked off both shoes.

"Close the door," she commanded with a sly smile and husky whisper.

Obedient, Kes dropped his suitcases, did as he was told.

"I have a love offering for you, Brother Brass," she was saying as he turned from the door. Kes could see she was trying for that same pouty fire Sophia Loren had in that dirty *Boy On A Dolphin* movie they had seen together. And Chalice was made a pretty fair Georgia girl stand-in for Sophia Loren, considering the options around here.

"C'mere," she whispered, even huskier, her eyes heavy lidded.

Chalice was pulling the inner cleavage of her blouse back slowly, ever so slowly, snagging her brassiere as she went, inching the cotton brocade aside–until the rosy edge of her nipple barely crept into view. Then she stopped.

Kes took two steps toward her.

Chalice's flirty smile deepened, she resumed, pulling back her brocade even further, revealing more nipple, and more.

Kes took another step, stopped by the bed. Chalice's free hand reached up, yanked Kes's hand, pulling him down on top of her. Quickly, Kes was kissing her deep while reaching up, trying to pull her blouse back into its proper place, trying to cover up her rosy revelation. Chalice fought him as they kissed, trying to work his hand under her bra, begging for his palm around her breast as more of her buttons popped free. He continued to struggle against this new familiarity, but did not stop his deep-tongued kiss as they both began to giggle inside it, giggling over their familiar tongues of war. Yes, they could both feel Kes's pressing arousal in no uncertain terms. With all the grit of an Olympic-wrestling contender, Chalice threw an arm around the back of Kes's head, pulling him tight, kissing him even harder as she tried to guide his other hand up her leg into the tropical zone beneath her skirt.

Kes *went crazy*, but not crazy like she craved. He broke free of her clutch, her kiss—possessed—his hands were a flurry.

"Behind me, behind me," he whelped.

"Honey—" she pleaded, letting go. He was scaring her.

Kes was suddenly sitting upright on the bed with Chalice still lying there, her clothes asunder. Kes glanced back down at her display then his eyes flew away into far corners of the room.

"You're showing," he said.

"I'm sorry," she sputtered, buttoning her blouse.

As his panic attack subsided Kes gazed back down at her ruffled allure, her pillow-lipped promise. He looked away again, rocking in place.

"I don't wanna be your ruination, girl. Don't let me ruin you."

Chalice was chagrined.

"Dang it, Kes, I'm beginning to think your daddy has x-ray eyes."

"Shush."

"All the sinning in this world is not yours."

"No. Some of it's Daddy's."

"Some of it's *mine*, Kestrel. Mine and other folks'."

That might be true, Kes thought, but he knew better than to believe it.

"I gotta do better'n him," Kes recited softly, rocking, rocking, like holy mantra. "I got to do better. Do better than Daddy Brass. For Mama. For her sake. For Mama."

Chalice sensed Kes coming back to her. She could hear his voice grow gentle again at the mention of his mother. Everything was going to be alright, she told herself. Chalice was soon sitting alongside him on the bed, hands folded neatly in her lap, like the nice girl she was supposed to be and mostly was. She began to praise him, calmly, like he was her baby boy. As she spake, his relentless rocking subsided.

"Well, you're already on your way," she told him, "you and Glenn. Your mama says this first record y'all made of *You Are The Jewel In God's Crown* is selling real good at the tent shows. You're making a name for yourself."

"They do alright, I reckon."

"Before long we'll have a darlin little house with some darlin little babes—"

"If there's money enough."

"You'll cut more records."

"Sacred records don't make real money, honeylamb. We ain't got no contract. Mama George says that recording studio cost us two months of touring and tent show money. It's the touring shows—the playing for folks—is where the real money is. And here I'm fixing to be chained to Shelfy Oak for most of three years."

"Y'all can still do the tent shows come summer."

"Three months don't add up to much. And that's assuming they ain't forgot us by then."

"Not you. You're unforgettable, honey. Kes, tell me that secret you promised. About your daddy."

"Well it ain't so much about Daddy, really. Not anymore. Now it's about me."

"What?"

"About those babes, those little darlin babes—"

"What?"

"Well—"

"Dang it, Kes, you're gonna make me moon looney."

"That ain't funny—"

"I swear, I'll go wolfman on you"—she growled, made claws at him, "—or wolf*girl. Grrrrrr.*"

"Shut up. I'm telling you, it ain't funny. That's my vexation."

"Your vexation?"

He pushed her clawfingers away. She giggled some more, making him edgy.

"I got moon mad blood maybe. A Mexican jumping gene, Daddy called it. But, Daddy, I expect he knows what it really is. It's devil. That's what it be. Dancing devil. Mama said that's why Daddy left. He was ashamed he likely passed his bad blood on to me and Glenn. I feel it sometimes, I swear. That mad gene going boing-boing inside me like a pinball trying to bust out of my head."

Kes could see he was scaring Chalice, but it had to be done.

"Honey," she trembled, "why are you telling me this?"

"My granddaddy, Musgrave Brass. I never knew him. Daddy's daddy. He spent the last twenty-seven years of his life a slobbering lunatic in the bughouse at Tuscaloosa, Alabama. He would eat dern near anything, Daddy told Mama. Thumbtacks, dead rodents, furniture paste, what have you. They say he ate a pay telephone once. I ain't exactly sure how that's done. But it got so bad, they had to keep him away from kids, else he might eat them or their tinker toys. These things were told to me in great seriousness."

"My word, Kes."

"Anyway, Mama tells me there's other ninnies like him going way back in Daddy's family. Word is that sometimes it skips a generation or two. Never more than two. It's mostly the menfolk. So, me and Glenn, we don't know how buggy and boinged-up our genes are. I might be headed into foreseeable despair. So all this baby talk makes me afraid I might eat em or something, someday."

Chalice lay her pretty head on his shoulder, letting him brood. Sometimes Kes just had to brood it out. She counted fifty in her head, she smiled, she gave him a delicate kiss.

"Be brave, Kes. Be brave for all of us. I just know you will be. You're the truest boy I've ever known. I will vow to deliver only girl babes unto you. Or we can adopt. We'll out-boing it with the help of my Tarots."

"Don't let Mama George see them cards."

"What cards?" she teased, batting her eyelashes.

"Yep. I'm hungry. Real hungry. See what I mean?"

She punched his arm as the dorm room door flew open. It was a cackling Glenn with two cheap guitars.

"What in the clear blue Jesus" he hooted as Kes and Chalice leapt up from the bed. "Don't let that Dorm Witch catch you clinched like that. And with the door closed? We'll be expelled before we unpack."

"Dorm Witch?" Chalice gulped.

"Yeah, you know," Glenn said. "Cauldrons. Children. Gospel singers. Garlic and onions. Is it dinner yet?"

Kes lost his appetite. He soon found himself sitting crosslegged with Glenn, tuning two sorry guitars under one of the spreading oaks at the edge of the parade field. Chalice listened with girlish rapture, back to mooning over every little blink and boyish sneer Kes tossed her way. His fevered outburst back in the dorm room was a sour note best forgotten.

Mama George had already opened her grass-woven hamper and laid her blanket with cold roast chicken, her special redskin potato salad, olives, deviled eggs, pickled onions, and thin-sliced cucumber sandwiches spread with cream cheese on black pumpernickel bread. Dessert was gingersnap cookies. Her thermos was full of soft blackberry cider. Georgiana informed Malakoff Brass that it was not in her nature to allow any creature to go hungry so he was welcome to fix himself a plate if he would go elsewhere to eat it and leave her alone.

"Why, thank ye, Georgiana. Your hospitality is number three on the charts," he said warmly, "but I've got to go slap a few asses. Be back later."

"No need."

"It's what I want, Georgiana darlin. Not what I need." Smiling, Malakoff began to sing in rich baritone.

One night of sin is what I'm now paying for,
The things Daddy did and Daddy saw...

Still singing as Mama George bristled, Malakoff Brass strolled away to reminisce with two old friends he had just pinpointed outside the potting shed on the far side of the green.

Dr. Mack Turlington and Mr. Jack Meriweather were former members of the faculty at the Conecuh Zion Bible Academy where Malakoff used to write up frequent sheet music orders, back before the Dawn Of Man. Turlington—the one with the long forelock of white hair—used to host Sunday afternoon get-togethers for the students at his home with the help of his wife, Moira. Malakoff remembered Moira Turlington with strong and fond affection. She was a shapely Irish broad who went a few rounds with Malakoff Brass while her husband was outside on their lawn in Opelika, only a few yardlines away, coaching the boys on the finer points of touch football. Jack Meriweather, the younger, Roman-nosed and handsome history teacher, was a close family friend of the Turlingtons who often joined in the games on those long gone afternoons. This Invitation Day, Malakoff was welcomed warmly at the potting shed.

"My, my, Mr. Meriweather," Turlington said, "I spy the only man who ever skunked me at dominoes."

"Yup. And you still owe me that bass boat you tossed in the pot before our last shuffle," Malakoff proclaimed upon approach. "If I hadn't been so urgently called outa town I would have made you pay up."

"It never happened, Malakoff. And, story was, you was run out—not called out."

"Mack, it's good to see you're still a regrettable liar," said Daddy Brass, shaking his hand, then Meriweather's. "How's the single life treating you, Jack?"

"Real good, Malakoff, real good. Except that I'm married two years now with a baby on the way."

"You always was a slow starter, Jack. Slow start, fast finish. That's what the gals always said."

They all laughed, and shortly after that Dean Pickery got behind the lectern on that stage under the biggest spreading oak and began to drone like an airline pilot reading altitude to nobody in particular. Pickery greeted folks and introduced faculty in perfunctory tones and in no time Daddy Brass felt prompted to take his silver flask out of his jacket. Mr. Meriweather swore he had given up the drink so he took his leave of the two men, going back to his pregnant bride picnicking on the green. Daddy Brass and Dr. Turlington slipped back in the shed, nipping at the flask, drearily watching the festivities out the shed window. Some grey hen from the Newdundy Mother's Club was now up there reading a poem.

"So where's that sweet gal of yours, Mack?"

Turlington took another long pull on the Wild Turkey, his face fallen.

"Don't tell anybody 'round here—but Moira left me nearly a year ago. Went down east to live with her sister. I've got people hereabouts thinking she's off on a mission to Botswana with that new Peace Corps."

"I'm plumb sorry to hear that," Daddy Brass said sincerely.

A few more pulls and Dr. Turlington began to weep.

The old woman finished her turgid verse and Dean Pickery thanked her too. Quickly wiping his brow with a white silk hanky, the dean's words assumed an urgency new to this afternoon's pomp and circumstance.

"Folks, it is now my honored privilege to bless your day with the voices of two young men who have dared to exalt and to excel—to excel as they carry the Lord's banner!" Dean Pickery raised his hand and silk hanky high as others in the crowd raised their own hands in the solidarity of the Lord. "Many of you know these boys and love em already, I'm sure. They've been making mighty music for the Christ since they were youngsters—and they just released their first sacred recording which they have agreed to sing for us today along with a few others, Lord willing. Brothers, sisters, Shelfy Oak scholars and and alumni, please rejoice and make welcome The Brothers Brass. Kestrel and Glenn—come on up here!"

Kes and Glenn bounded on stage, hard strumming in unison, they darted past Dean Pickery and hit the microphone singing full throttle:

To Canaan's land I'm on my way
Where the soul never dies
My darkest hour will turn to day
Where the soul never dies—

Out on the lawn, a beaming Georgiana Brass jumped up, standing on her blanket, clapping in time. After all these years of child-rearing and Holy Ghost revivals, she still loved to listen to her boys. Soon others were standing with her, clapping with her.

No sad farewells, no tear-dimmed eyes—

Kes's high tenor chimed atop the melody of Glenn's rollicking baritone, their young voices like two edges of a whetted sword—slashing, releasing, exultant. Sometimes, when Kes closed his eyes, their voices became a single voice of their own design, a voice that had carried them together since childhood. It was one of the few constant comforts to be found in Kes's worried heart.

The boys sang two more verses then ended to an eruption of applause. This first battle had been won. The folks loved them.

"Thank y'all," Kes said.

"Thank you, folks," Glenn said. "This one is the flip-side of our new recording on our own Angelsprey label."

Earnest, with eyes closed, Kes and Glenn launched into *Life's Railway To Heaven*. And that is when the trouble began.

Life is like a mountain railroad
With an engineer that's brave,
We must make the run successful
From the cradle to the grave—

They were rounding the curve of that first verse when Kes began to hear a new sound: a strange, airy, and eerie harmony—an old droning mountain harmony that wove its way beautifully betwixt the boys' voices. It sounded like the binding, united chord made by Kes and Glenn had birthed a third harmony, a descanting strand so lonesome and mournful, so beautifully true.

Then an acorn fell across Kes's cheek. He did not let that bother him much, he was so taken and fixed on the eerily loving new sound he and brother had achieved that he took no notice really. It was only when they began to climb the second verse and a second acorn fell across his face that he opened his eyes and looked up.

Blessed savior, love and guide me
Till we reach that blissful shore—

High above him in the great spreading oak Kes saw a young girl about his age but small for that age. She was perched on a limb in a cornflower blue dress, her bare feet dangling, her chin and arms resting on a higher limb. She had short blondish hair, looked puckishly cute enough, and she was singing along with them. Hers was the strange new harmony. She must have seen Kes looking up at her but she gazed back down at him without any recognition of this. She shifted a mite with the rhythm and another acorn fell rattling at Kes's feet.

Where the angels wait to join us
In God's grace forevermore —

About the time the boys swooped into the third verse was when a drunken Daddy Brass let slip to a drunken Dr. Turlington that surely he must of damn well known about all those not-so-damn-secret afternoons Turlington's wife Moira used to spend with Jack Meriweather at the Golden Cherry Motel back in Opelika, Alabama—so Turlington was damn well better off without that black Irish wench. She was a fine woman, Daddy said, upstanding or bent over. But she was no more faithful than a wide open box of hot crickets. Hell, everybody else knew about it, so why didn't you?

Soon the crowd on the lawn was applauding again and, without further introduction, the Brothers Brass fell into the tender chords of *In The Sweet By And By.*

There's a land that is fairer than death —

Kes kept glancing up at the kind-of-cute girl in the tree so he did not notice Dr. Turlington weaving his way unsteadily through the sway of folks on the lawn. When all was said and done it was never clear whether he had swiped the pistol from Daddy Brass's coat without asking or if Daddy Brass had handed him the gun. Either was a viable possibility. The only thing sure about that day was the six shots that rang out—*BLAM! BLAM! BLAM! BLAM! BLAM! BLAM!*—blowing Jack Meriweather into the afterlife to the horror of his blood-splattered pregnant bride and all those around them. For all intents and purposes, Invitation Day was over.

There was a lot of screaming and scattering and mamas grabbing their babies. Several men piled on top of old Dr. Turlington, wrenching the gun from his hand.

The voices of the Brothers Brass never did get to finish that song or meet on that beautiful shore. Kes and Glenn began to run from the stage as the tiny blond girl dropped from the tree, landing flatfooted at the microphone where the boys had stood only moments before. Glancing back, guitar in tow, Kes caught site of this and dashed back on-stage to save the girl—but he never got the chance. She took one look at Kes's outstretched hand then scrambled off the other side of the stage, disappearing into the trees.

Kes hoped she would be alright. She was a strange little thing and he worried for her safety with bullets flying hither and yon. Then he remembered his Mama George. Then he remembered Chalice. Then he remembered his Daddy. Then he remembered that a good boy would go see to their safety first.

VERSE 3

Auld Clootie

Late that evening, after all the fuss had died down, Kes slid from the sheets of his dorm room bed. He was careful not to disturb his snoring brother. It was a skill Kes had perfected as far back as those nights when they always slept together as toddlers—something they did less frequently now. Guilt and his chronic good manners led him to gingerly open the closet door and slip inside. He knelt amidst the shoes, beneath the shirts and coats on hangers, and clasped his hands to his forehead.

"Dear Jesus and Lord Almighty," he spake softly, "Please help me to do better and sing better and study better so I can be everything you and Mama want me to be. Please guide me in your path in these days and months coming up. Please let me be a popular man here in this new school. Please help calm Mama's nerves so she can get some proper rest and a good night's sleep, so she doesn't have to take so many naps, Heavenly Father. Please keep Glenn on the straight and the narrow. Please help Chalice to be true and pure for me until our wedding day and our wedding night.

Please help me resist her temptations to the contrary and cast out the devil from our loins. Amen."

He started to get up, then had a second thought.

"And dear Jesus, Lord Almighty, I pray that Mr. Meriweather's soul is at peace with you in Heaven tonight. Help Dr. Turlington in his trials to come. And Lord, please ask yourself: Do they really need to know it was Daddy Brass's gun what did the killing? In your holy name, Amen. And goodnight, sir."

Kes got off his knees and quietly left the closet. On his way back to bed he happened to glance out the moonraked window and noticed movement far down below. Drawing closer to the sash, his hazel eyes narrowed.

There he was again. The hairy beast.

Kes saw a small beast prancing silently, back and forth, upright on his hindlegs along the shore of the campus lake. The strange razorbacked thing reflected to and fro on the dark waters. In an instant Kes knew it was the Satan himself doing a gleeful jig out there amidst those beached red canoes, old Clootie (his Scots grandfather's name for the beast) here in their midst. Yes, the beast had himself a good day today. Yes, it was most definitely he and he was close at hand.

This was not the first time Kes had spied the beast. Kes watched, chilled to the bone and very still, he watched, as the beast pranced off into the trees and out of the moonlight. Gone again, for now. Kes thought about returning to the closet to pay a few more installments into his account with the Lord. Every time he saw that thing he prayed it was a vision and truth revealed to him by the Almighty, and not the early creep of a terrible blood condition festering in his veins, building up steam until it could shovel him from his right mind—tossing him over into unholy madness.

Guilt and good manners kept Kestrel from allowing such disturbances within to disturb his little brother without. But his first night at Shelfy Bible College would be like so many others before, as he lay sleepless till the wee hours, hoping blood and vexation did not overtake him before his work was done.

VERSE 4

Barefoot Savior

The Dorm Witch was known to flog good Christian boys, they said, and burn them at the stake or boil them in her lard vat, they said. She flogged them with a rod of ebony, forcing them to perform acts of depravity upon her withered flesh after cutting out their tongues so they could not tell. Then she incinerated them atop bonfires of cordwood whilst expressing loud dissatisfaction with their services (for she was never satisfied), having extracted the marrow from their souls, condemning them to restless afterlives lusting for horny old women. Where these Dorm Witch torments were conducted unseen was never fully explained. Nor did anybody know where all these boys came from or went, unless it was the few that left at mid-term or never came back in spring. A boy or two had occasionally left Shelfy Oak Bible College without warning due to illness, a death in the family, or dwindling family funds, but they were certainly not enough to satisfy an insatiable succubus or feed a fire proper.

The Dorm Witch was, in fact, the formidable Miss Mertylina Shenk, as Kes would soon discover. None dared call her anything but Miss Shenk to her blighted-tomato face. She wore a floor-length black frock, carried an ebony wood walking stick for rapping dorm doors, and never ventured outside without her little round felt skullcap. It was, therefore, understandable that the vision of her inspired flights of morbid fancy. She was rumored to be older than the old school itself. Another variation insisted she was actually a ripe young tomato once, who gave forbidden birth in the Infirmary to a deformed tadpole child sired during an early Christmas morning encounter with a deranged janitor full of drink. Sometimes this birthing took place in the school science lab and sometimes it was during a wild electrical storm—always at night. Supposedly this now-immortal tadpole child was kept in a special padlocked room in a secret basement beneath King's Door Hall, subsisting without light on a diet of floor sweepings and pinto beans. It was all talk, of course. The kind conjured up by bored, hormone-haunted Bible College students who found themselves far from home and unhappy in Jesus.

Their Dorm Witch was actually a retired postmistress whose job was to make sure all enrollees were in their rooms by eight p.m. and in bed with lights out by ten. In fact, Kes's first personal encounter with Miss Shenk had not been so formidable at all.

"Master Brass?" she posed to him when they chanced to meet in the hall that first week. "Could you and your brother please practice your harmonies a little softer after nine on workaday nights? Some of our boys who have track and pee-tee before breakfast must go to bed early and I know you would not want to rob them of needed rest."

"Uh, yes, Miss Shenk."

"I would add that you harmonize quite well."

"We 'ppreciate that, Miss Shenk."

Kes and Miss Shenk moved on and did not exchange words again for almost two months (when Kes left a jockstrap and dirty socks on his floor). But the Dorm Witch she remained. For those condemned and languishing in stone, every Tower Of London involves a Grand Inquisitor, a specter, or an ogre. Or all three rolled into one Dorm Witch.

Be that as it may, scholastic tedium most often unfolds seamlessly and without redemption. Nothing—not even an Invitation Day killing or the specter of Miss Shenk—could breathe drama into the Brother Brass routine at Shelfy Oak Bible College. Their first weeks were a slow, grinding drudgery. This was compounded by the fact that Kes and Glenn Brass had most recently led more exciting lives as weekend celebrities, of a sort—as stage performers for Christ. They had seen the glare of footlights and bore more than a trace of secular desire in the back of their growing brains. Kes and Glenn had both thrived fairly well in high school—in the relative comfort of their neighborhood and home. They found themselves not so suited to the strictures of daily religious doctrine in dull classrooms and nightly lockdown with a bunch of spooky, glassy-eyed dudes who jabbered on endlessly about the Lord's will—absent or fulfilled—in their various gridiron achievements. These heathens-in-the-making did not seem to grasp that it was old devil Clootie they best be running from, not some dumb and pimpled football linebacker.

The Rowen twins were just such linebackers, oblivious to that which might gobble them up. They were the other two brothers in the dorm. Their room was on the first floor where they resided in stark contrast to the Brothers Brass. They also shared several classes with Kes and Glenn, regularly attempting to strike up miserable conversations about mundane subjects which did not interest the Brass boys in the least. Kes noticed that the tiny girl in the cornflower blue dress was in his Civics Class, often wearing that same dress, but he never quite caught her name. Tilly or something like it. It so happened that the human giraffe—the boy behind them in line on Invitation Day—shared the same class with his not-so-secret girlfriend across the aisle, a comely lass who Kes decided must be the most voluptuous and beautiful (and tall) young lady with golden hair that Kes had ever seen. The giraffe's name was Orville, the giraffe's girl was Lisa. They had both graduated high school together back in Atlanta and now, in the Shelfy Oak evening ritual, Lisa presumably kept to the girls' dormitory on the opposite side of the campus lake. It was far enough around the lake to be formidable, with a patch of woods as a barrier betwixt the two. And it was too far to swim.

Besides, Kes missed Chalice something fierce (along with being vexed by memories of her rosy nipple). Kes was not a good letter writer, but Chalice wrote him almost every day, so he did his best to scratch out at least three weekly pleas of love. It felt sometimes like Chalice's writings were all that kept him from hopping a train home. Yes, this was his cross to bear and Kes pitied Brother Glenn who did not even have the buoyancy of love letters to carry him through each week. Despite these doldrums, both boys tried their best to buckle down and meet the stern standards of the place.

Each morning and evening Kes peered out the dorm window at the lake below, looking for signs of that dancing demon Clootie. Usually he saw nothing but the empty boat dock and two canoes. Some early evenings he saw boys on the dock joshing with each other or the occasional girl or two who dared stroll over from the other side. Most seemed bored by the canoes, though he once saw a kid use one to row out and retrieve his baseball cap, which a stiff breeze had blown out onto the water.

Once, by dawn, Kes saw an old black fellow (a janitor or groundskeeper?) fishing from the dock. From where Kes sat, the fellow reminded him of a gospel organist he once met at a mixed meeting who first told him about arpeggios and a sinister thing called a vamp.

"If you ever has to fill or kill you some time up there in front of the folks, son," the elderly piano man advised, "you'll be needing to know how to play you some vamp—a bit of rhythm to bide your time wid."

Other than vamping black fishermen, Kes detected nothing more along the Shelfy Oak lakeshore in the way of devilish doings. This did not mean he would cease to be vigilant. Mornings, Glenn always beat his big brother to the showers and back while Kes stood intrigued at the window.

Kes was working on the building, as they always sang in camp meetings, building a true foundation. And a strong foundation for the work to be done meant he and brother must be vigilant in all things, whether it be in keeping the devil behind them or in braving the ordeal of this new schooling.

Together, as always, the Brothers Brass knitted their brows as one, hunched their shoulders, leaned inward, each brother toward the other, and learned the tune of the day. Together they learned to vamp. Each day they vamped through morning chapel and prayer, endless prayer, through hours of biblical history and scriptural interpretation. They vamped through gym class designed to sweat out all impure thoughts, then a bland supper in the Barley Cake dining hall, framed by more prayer, then homework in their room, finishing each day with an hour of music and learning new gospel material. Then prayers before bed.

The boys dialed Mama George each Sunday afternoon on the black telephone outside Miss Shenk's room. They told her they were doing fine, just fine, and that is what she wanted to hear. They could hear tremors of ever-festering fear in her voice, though she was obviously doing her best to hide it.

"Are you minding your peas?" her crackly voice would ask.

"You know I am, Mama," the brother would answer with great conviction.

She also sounded odd and slurry at times, with operatic strains of Mahalia Jackson or Paul Robson noodling faintly through the telephone, all the way from Savannah to Newdundy, Georgia. Each brother assumed Mama must still be very tired and still not getting a good night's sleep. It never occurred to either lad at the time that a little yellow pill with sherry wine might be part of Clootie's installment plan. They were still young in so many ways, if not for long. The Brothers Brass had already seen countless jamborees, brush arbors, campgrounds, and all-day revival meetings in contrast to the fresh kids around them. Their world—the world the Brothers Brass had long ago come to know—was bigger than Shelfy Oak Bible College, bigger and more alluring. Time would prove this true. Until then, they vamped.

On his second Saturday at school Kes found time to explore the small lake. He crept down the hollow-ringing stairwell and strolled out of the dormitory to the lake's edge for the first time. It was only then that he learned the lake's name from a small sign as he approached along the footpath to the water. Kes soon decided that, during daylight hours, an early weekend morning like this was probably when Lake Serenity was its most serene and unattended. Most students were sleeping late or the ones who lived nearby were gone home. By mid-morning the place would see more visitors, no doubt, and by mid-afternoon it was probably the busiest it would be all week.

Kes walked the circumference of the shore that second Saturday—starting at the dock and ending at the dock—looking for signs of Clootie's cloven hoofprints. He saw none. There were two little boys with cowboy hats and toy six-shooters who kept trying to skip rocks on the water without much skill or luck. They finally gave up, drew their cap guns and started firing at the water. Both little cowpokes said howdy as Kes passed.

"Howdy," he said back. "What y'all shooting at?"

"Them redskins out there in them canoes," one kid told him before popping another invisible savage.

"Watch out," the other kid told him, "they got fire arrows."

Somebody had to save Shelfy Oak Bible College from being reduced to cinders by a hail of flaming arrows and Kes was not up to the task. So he asked no more questions, heading back to his room for prayers before breakfast. Those little cowpokes could probably tell him when Godzilla would rise from those waves, and they might even mount a worthy capgun assault on the firebreather. But they did not appear wise to the ways of Clootie in the least.

Three more Saturdays would come and go before Kes chose to revisit the lakeshore with more than his bedroom eyes.

"Why you restringing that crappy guitar?" he asked his brother on the fourth weekend morning.

"Aw, I promised I would," Glenn scowled, tightening down a sparkling new G string. "There's a girl singer who needs it for tomorrow's Sunday sunrise service."

"I'm gonna walk the lake for awhile. You're too noisy."

"Good, 'cause you're too Kestry. Can't tell sharp from flat with you in the room."

Kes had been hoarding a fifteen-page letter from Chalice for over forty-eight hours, waiting to find time to read it.

This lazy morning there were no six-shooters holding the fort and Lake Serenity seemed perfect for lingering over her words of love by water's edge.

Walking out over the water to the end of the dock, Kes stepped to the front edge but felt two loose boards beneath his feet. He carefully stepped back from the edge. He sat on the dock, on the steady part, and took twenty minutes reading the first page of Chalice's letter. Kes might not have been enthralled with Chalice's latest trip to Kuppenheim's on Broughton Street to buy sensible shoes for her new job at Krispy Kreme Donuts, but neither was he entirely disinterested. No, but the soothing, mesmerizing way the water lapped against those canoes kept drawing Kes's eyes from the page. The idle dreaminess of those long vessels on the verge, waiting there poised to enter the water, reminded Kes of the years he had spent longing to paddle across that grey-green sea out his bedroom window back at Angelsprey. Alongside Kes, on the dock, lay a rope tied to a piling which was meant for lashing the canoes. But the canoes were not tied or lashed to this dock in any way. If this were really the vast and depthless Atlantic of Kes's childhood, why, the tide could rise up and carry those canoes away. That seemed like an okay thing to Kes—to let the morning tide rise and carry you away into a faraway day, to a faraway place and fathoms unseen. It beckoned like Chalice beckoned on that bed the other day, and his desire to let himself be carried away into the allure and release—to release the tide swelling inside himself—it felt much the same. Then Kes began to think how nice and swell it would be to read his true love's letter while floating in one of those canoes, adrift and rocking gently as if in her loving arms. Surely, that would be safe—Kes thought—safer than being rocked in the depths of Chalice's bosom.

Abruptly, the lonely sailor within him made a decision. The time was now. There was no turning back. His time had come.

Kes folded the letter and put it in the pocket of his pea jacket. He got up and stepped off the dock onto the shore where the two canoes lay with paddles inside. With a surety and fluid motion that felt like music Kes shoved one of the canoes off from shore, leaping into it at the last moment before the bow knifed out across the lake. For the first time in his life, Kestrel Brass was afloat on open water. He grabbed a paddle and found that he instinctively knew how to use it. His heart was not pounding, it was at ease. This felt good, like he was justified in his need to finally do this thing. He felt his mother letting go, releasing him from tooth and nail, his world of troubles falling away with each stroke of the paddle.

Far removed from the shore Kes stopped paddling and began to drift. Autumn was afire on the the lake. The breeze was crisp but not too cold. Above him loomed a leafy patchwork of russet reds and sparkling gold. Off beyond the trees Kes could see his dorm room window. All of the Shelfy Oak dormitories and school buildings filled with all their knotty problems, lessons, cares, and concerns seemed far at bay, barely seen above the wreath of trees which bordered Kes's lagoon of freedom. The sun on open green water was warm, warmer than on shore. Kes took off his pea coat. He took Chalice's letter from the coat then slid forward in the canoe onto his back, resting his head on the seat, using the coat for a pillow. He felt fine and unfettered in a way he could not remember ever feeling before. He could learn to love this life on the sea. Kes returned to his letter, reading it again from "*My dearest dashing Kestrel.*" It was slow going. He was barely into page three when he began to feel drowsy. Truth be told, the Savannah exploits of Chalice Dillard and her new hairdo, new shoes, and developing attitude about Dr. Spock's endorsement of breastfeeding (she disagreed and did not want to sag) began to read like a young bride's textbook, like more school drudgery despite her flirty tone and bright purple ink. Formula was okay, breastfeeding was better—Kes wanted to jot in the margin—but what newborns needed most was plenty of sleep. Even Kes knew that. He yawned.

Kes remembered that his mama referred to Dr. Spock snidely on more than one occasion, saying his book on child rearing was written by Dr. Clootie Mollycoddler and she had tossed it in the trash after skimming half a chapter. With the accepted wisdom that boys in the room under age six have no functional ears or memories, Mama once whispered to a classmate's mother that as soon as the word *circumcision* popped up Mama George knew that Spock book was trash.

Kes looked up and saw the white-striped wings of a black magpie swooping and circling in the high blue sky. Laying the pages on his chest, his eyes heavy, Kes drifted away. across the gentle waters and into his dream. In his dream he and Chalice were naked as jaybirds in his dorm room with sunlight streaming their bodies. They stood only a few feet from each other, facing each other, and she was saying *come on, cowboy* but he could not move his feet. When he looked at Chalice naked and willing he wanted what he saw. But his feet would not answer the call. Looking down he saw that his toy soldier was at full uncircumcised attention. She said *come on, cowboy.*

Looking up Kes opened his eyes and saw the magpie standing on the letter on his chest. A jab of magpie beak and Kes shrieked.

"Beeehind meeeeee!"

Aaaaaaaaak-k-k! Was that him shrilling or the bird?

The magpie and pages flew as Kes's arms and feet flailed, tipping the canoe and himself into the cold lake. He splashed, gulped for air.

"*He-e-e-elp!*" escaped his strangling throat before his head submerged, his nostrils taking on icy water. Kes managed to bob to the top again, mind flashing on how his mother had foretold his doom.

"*He-e-ep!*" he gargled, then sank once more.

He bobbed up briefly once more, catching a glimpse of sky as a wooden paddle hit him in the head. Damn it hurt. Kes felt he was about to black out, into the eternal deep, when he also felt a hand grab his collar and begin to pull him afloat. Amidst his splashing panic, his eyes darted back and saw what looked like that little girl in the cornflower blue dress, tugging him back along the rope.

"Stop your fightin'!" she shouted, pulling him toward shore.

"Wuuuuhaaaaah—" he yelped, swallowing more water.

"Stop yer kickin'!" she demanded.

Suddenly Kes felt the lake bottom beneath him, his feet sinking into mud but his head above water. She dragged him another couple of feet then let go. They both flopped down onto their bellies like beached survivors of a shipwreck crawling ashore. Once clear of the water Kes and the girl flipped over again onto their backs, side by side, gasping for air.

"Thank you—" he finally found the breath to say. "I cain't swim."

"Welcome—" she wheezed, stuttering; "I *c-c*-cain't swim neither."

It took Kes a moment to fathom what he had heard. Finally he recovered enough to raise onto an elbow and look her over proper. Yes, she was wearing that same cornflower dress, soaked to the skin. .

"Then how you come to do that?" he asked quietly, his heaves fading.

"Tied that rope to that extry paddle and thowed it for you. But you wudn't grabbing *n*-nothing but suds. Then I *j*-jumped in. No time to think. Don't know how I done it really. Kinda dog paddled out there then yanked you back. Couldn't of done it without *th-th*-that rope."

"Or the paddle," he added as it occurred to him.

"Yup. Or the paddle."

Kes felt his crown where the paddle had struck him. A knot was already swelling.

"I'm gone have a big ole lump," he pondered.

"You lucky you ain't no lump on that lake bottom. Catfish food. Lest you was borned under the veil."

"What veil?"

"If you a baby borned under *th*-the veil, then you cain't never die in water. That'd explain your good fortune and my being here today."

"I ain't no veil baby, not that I know of. Never heard of such. But thank you kindly. You saved my life, didn't you?"

"Sure did."

"But how did a little ole girl like you—?"

"I'm strong for my size. Always *b*-been."

"That's a good question though—ain't it?"

"I reckon."

Kes could see her budding breasts through the blue weave. She was barefoot, and surprisingly cute up close, from her nose to her toes. Even her fitful stutter was kind of cute. When Kes gave her toes a second glance he saw something not quite right. A toe was missing. There was a gap to the right of her big toe on her right foot—where the second longest toe should have been. He glanced away just as quickly. Things his mama had bred into him stopped him from asking the obvious.

"Where were you?" he asked instead.

"Off there in the trees."

"You hop from there that fast?"

"I'm quick too. You writing a book?"

"Huh?"

"You too full of the questions. Like some talkety jaybird."

"I figure I might figure some things out. If I ask

enough of em."

"I gotta go. I cain't waste all *d*-day at your baptism."

She got up and went before he could stop her.

"*Hey—?*" Kes hollered after her, "where you off to?"

"Homework—" she hollered at a fast trot, not looking back.

"*Who are you, anyways*—?" he called louder.

His plea echoed across the lake. But she was already gone—disappeared by the trees as quickly as their leaves had unleashed the girl to save him. It was all a riddle to him.

Kes sat up, untied his shoes, then slipped them off to pour out the water. His jacket was lost as well as Chalice's letter. He could see a few of the pages still floating out there, soon to sink from view. Beyond the sagging perils of breastfeeding, Chalice's other dozen pages of flirty journalism would remain a mystery to Kes forever. At this moment Chalice Dillard felt far off indeed, and fuzzy in his aching head.

Kes began to feel a chill. He needed out of these wet clothes before he caught the croup. He got up and carried his shoes over to the treeline where the miracle girl had fled. Stepping into the shade in his wet sock feet Kes looked for some sign of her but saw none. He hesitated under an ancient pecan tree and took stock. A few students were over on the quad in front of Kings Door Hall. Beyond this brief band of woods were sleeping lawns, one after another, stretching across the campus then on into the murmuring neighborhoods under a ragpicker's blanket of autumn leaf. Kes heard the faintest echoes of a chainsaw and kids at play, the drowsy small town meditation before Saturday morning business got lively over on High Street.

But there was no wet little girl or clue to where she went.

So the pecan tree dropped a book on him.

A quick rustle of leaf and limb overhead—and before he could look up—a falling object bounced off Kestrel Brass's thick brain for the second time today. He hissed, flinched, dropping his shoes as his hand grabbed the top of his head too late to do any good. With this latest surprise deposit from above, Kes felt like the sky was now out to get him since the lake had missed its chance.

At Kes's feet lay a small clothbound book face down on a smattering of pecans and a gnarled root. He looked up into the branches high above him, from whence it fell. He saw no odd shape or movement up there, only the shimmering breeze in copper leaf and gold. Why would she have been doing her homework up there, he wondered? Kes remembered his daddy telling him how pecan trees that bore fruit always had another pecan tree nearby, like they were married. Kes glanced around, wondering where the other tree was in this tree's life, but he saw no other pecan trees.

Finally, Kes bent and picked up the book at his feet along with a pecan that had survived the harvest. He put the pecan betwixt his molars, holding it there waiting to crack it. Turning the book in his hand, he saw that this was not a textbook for any Bible College course he knew of. In fact, this was not a college text at all. It was an old, out-of-date grade school primer with badly worn binding. This was a book for baby kids to learn how to read, the kind his daddy would have called a hornbook. Opening the hornbook, Kes flipped through the pages, looking at familiar dog, cat, mother, father, house, mule, school illustrations with their simple bold-lettered words beneath. The pictures were all primitive and old-fashioned looking to Kes, in plain black and white, none in color.

Flipping back to the first inner leaf page he settled on a childish, handwritten scrawl:

This book belong two Bettilia Whissler.

VERSE 5

Honeymoon

Dead roses.

Their fresh bouquet, once lost, was worse than the stench of fish or a carny.

Sitting in the dark of this airless Airstream trailer, outside the Elgar Hill Full Gospel Jamboree, all these years after Shelfy Oak Bible College, the fruity rot of dead roses clung unforgiving to Kestrel's flesh. Like the remainders of a dead wedding, Kes could not easily shrug the scent or the memories away. Once they seeped into the pores of his soul, into his aching bones, no waters could wash him clean for many a day to come. None of that gospel and glory banging the drum onstage out there, right now, could cleanse his blood. Not even the clear Christ-powered voices of Jake Hess and The Blackwood Brothers out there, as good as they sang and sounded at this moment (and, damn, they were sounding good) could keep Kestrel Brass from wearing the remainders of a dead wedding.

Hell, Kes was born of a dead wedding. Was that not true?

"We are daily blessed," the train lady said.

But that starched-up Nurse Nightingale back on that train did not know diddly about daily blessings any more than she did about ways to love. Daddy Brass, he knew these ways to love, the winding lines through the pines, through tangled hearts. And, here in his dark dressing room trailer, Kes wanted to forget his lines. Kes did not want to tune his guitar for the show or read this book in his lap. No, he wanted some better, more virginal beatitudes.

He picked up the straight razor again—the gleaming razor his daddy gave him. He licked his thumb then ran the razor's edge, slowly.

In his hand Kestrel held a sharply-honed honeymoon from all this. This was true.

A host of dead weddings had taught Kestrel these true ways to love. He often wished his Daddy Brass had come clean. If only Daddy had bequeathed all he knew on the subject to his only begotten sons before it was too late.

VERSE 6

The Brass Begats

When Malakoff Brass came courting Miss Georgiana Kinoy of Savannah society he was some years older than she but forever the younger soul at heart. If he had realized the object of his affection was a girl with one foot already caught in the bear trap of middle age and about to go crazy from the pain, he might have moved on.

Malakoff Brass sold hymnals, sheet music, and Christian literature to churches and schools. He even went door-to-door when required. It was a trade he had fallen into after a series of livestock jobs and Malakoff quickly found he preferred shoveling tunes to shoveling the newly published product of livestock. Georgiana, at the tender age of eighteen, was already a Red Cross volunteer and treasurer for His Holy Grace Baptist Church in their island community outside Savannah. She also played piano for services Sunday mornings and evenings, along with the Wednesday night prayer meeting. A student of the old shape note method used in hymnals of the day, she was naturally consulted by the church when new hymnals were being considered for purchase.

Malakoff met Miss Georgiana in her Red Cross uniform one Saturday whilst passing the rutabagas at Mrs. Wilkes' Boarding House. Malakoff had accepted a dinner invitation from her pastor who often bought Malakoff's songbooks and spiritual tracts. Georgiana was a mite skittish about accepting his rutabagas (she had never cared for any kind of turnip, white or dark). But she had no choice since she and Malakoff were seated beside one another and the old gentleman on her left was apparently a rutabaga connoisseur. Everybody said they were exceptionally good rutabagas, not that Georgiana was going to try what she had already decided she did not like. But the bowl made its way around the big table five times before the noonday meal was done, so Georgiana had to keep saying thank you to Mr. Brass from Alabama. Malakoff never did find out if Georgiana had ever even tasted a rutabaga prior to this. She implied that she had. Over time, as years went by, he arrived at the opinion that she probably had not.

But she was dark of eye and hair, lovely to look at, and Malakoff saw that she was fine. She found him exotic in her small island world. He, too, was dark. His sideburns were unusual in those days, sported more often by the seamen who came ashore in Savannah and by the long-haul truck drivers who met their ships on River Street. The next day Malakoff and Georgiana sat only one pew apart during the extended revival meeting. In fact, they were again casting eyes at one another at that very moment when the pastor suddenly announced the Japs had bombed Pearl

Harbor. Services were interrupted and, afterward, a quivering Georgiana took Malakoff's arm, telling him she was terrified that those slope-eyed devils would bomb the new Hunter Air Base any minute now. Thus the seeds of fear and love began to intertwine and bloom within sweet Georgiana Kinoy—began to bloom but would not yet harden her heart. There would be time enough for that.

On Tuesday evening Malakoff came to call and found Georgiana and her mother in the kitchen of their grand Queen Anne Colonial home on Officer's Row, a home they called Angelsprey. They were feeding Brunswick stew to a runaway farm boy who had come to their back door begging for chores after he couldn't get work on an outbound sailing ship. Once they got the lad fed they paid him a dollar in nickels and dimes from the kitchen coin jar to sweep all three wraparound porches before they sent him on his way. This left an impression on both gentleman callers. Malakoff was also impressed with the Brunswick stew.

Georgiana was known to fix the best Brunswick stew on the island. She was not shy about her technique. She told anybody who asked, that the secret—besides the chicken, rabbit, and pork—was getting the right lima beans and new red potatoes without overcooking them. She always used fresh corn from the cob along with a hint of all three shades of pepper whilst going easy on the sweet. That, she said, was all there was to it. Yet, try as they might, nobody else ever seemed to be able match a batch of the stew made by Georgiana herself. Georgiana would just shrug and say she never measured anything so she could not explain why their efforts had failed. Some skeptical souls did not believe her. Some were certain she had left something out in the telling for fear of losing her edge in the local Brunswick stew sweepstakes. Still, the doubters were afraid to say it to her face.

On that Tuesday evening, in the wake of the Pearl Harbor attack, the only thing the man and farm boy both said was thank you, Miss Georgiana, before raising their bowls for a second helping.

On Thursday, Hitler and Malakoff Brass both declared their intentions. Hitler might have had the easier row to hoe, he only declared war on the United States. As wartime rationing took effect, Georgiana's Brunswick stew quickly became a weekly staple in Malakoff's diet. Hitler would have to fend for himself.

In the days and weeks that followed, young men made mass exodus from Savannah and her islands. Malakoff had a nagging knee joint wound received during his own Marine stint. This meant he was exempt and turned away when he showed up to reenlist at the recruitment center on Bay Street. These dovetailing tendrils of fate left Malakoff feeling as if the whole damn town and its lovely ladies had been passed to him on a plate too big to fit Mrs. Wilkes' table. This windfall held strong appeal to a Malakoff Brass, who was ready to get off the road and end his days as a traveling peddler. Yes, Savannah and her feminine wiles looked mighty appetizing. But there was also a certain maddening consternation about this new development in his life. Because Malakoff Brass, when backed against the wall, was a hopeless romantic and he was truly smitten at the moment, and possibly forevermore. He knew quality goods when he saw it and he knew he was taking his peach pie at the best table by the sea. All those other Savannah women were wasted, absolutely wasted.

Soon he and tender Georgiana Kinoy were seen together—and seen together often—at prayer meetings, attending some wholesome movie downtown at the Lucas Theatre, picnicking in Daffin Park, or taking long perfect drives in his burgundy DeSoto or long perfect walks on the beach. Lying awake nights in his bed at the motor court, Malakoff was glad he was far removed from his Marine Corps pals and backwoods buddies off in Alabam. It spared him much embarrassment and the loudmouth shaming he would suffer if they could see him moon-calfing around like this. He had even cut back on his drinking, and was about to make a lovesick leap into sobriety. Yes, the girl's pedigree was sobering indeed.

Georgiana lived with her mother in one of the biggest houses on the island, a daunting triple-decker wrapped with porches and great two-hundred-year-old live oak trees on Officer's Row, on the Row's majestic promontory overlooking the sea. This told Malakoff that they were well fixed. This also left Malakoff feeling out of his league, not that he ever let on when he visited their grand home.

Georgiana's deceased father, Colonel William K. Kinoy, was a strict officer, a Scotsman who struggled with over-zealousy but prevailed as a natural leader of the highest calibre. He was also an Evangelical Baptist and a fourth-generation West Point graduate. He could quote Bible the same way he could quote the entire Military Code Of Conduct by rote whilst jotting out long division on a legal pad. He knew right and he knew wrong and, under Colonel Kinoy's command, *broadminded* was just another word for sin. The enemy, on and off the battlefield, was sin, the devil—or *Cloots* as the Colonel oft conjured him from his Scottish roots.

"Stand your ground, hold your water. Fear is the true dagger in Auld Cloot's hand. Not hatred nor malice," Colonel Kinoy would address to new troops. "With fear Cloots will cloud the mind of any man and defeat him. Let you never be his quarry. He must forever remain *your* quarry. Whether he be kraut, yankee peril, or common corrupter of youth. Stand your ground until Clootie is close and locked in your sights. Then cut that devil down."

Only his wife and a select inner circle dared call him Colonel Willy. During his first week in residence in the upper echelon of Officers Row, he sighted a red-tail hawk in one of the oaks—a freak sighting of a winged raptor on an island dominated by gulls, ducks, sandpipers, and plovers. Newly promoted, perceiving the red-tail bird of prey as a divine talisman and symbol of his God-given powers of leadership (and his middle name being Kestrel)—Colonel Willy stood high on the widow's walk that evening, Bible in hand, quoting Job 39:28 to the wind and sea.

"Doth the hawk fly by thy wisdom, and turn wings toward the south," he bellowed from the crown of the roof.

Nobody else knew quite what that meant, but it bore

great import to the crusading Colonel who ordained that henceforth this house—his sanctuary by the sea—would be known as Angel's Prey House. Or, as most came to call it: Angelsprey.

Malakoff Brass had no designs on any Angelsprey House or on Georgiana's inevitable money. His only designs were on Georgiana. Georgiana's mother, Eidla, helped to make the difference since she took a liking to Malakoff right away. He reminded her of her late husband Willy, only nicer, and funnier. Besides, Colonel Willy had wanted sons but never got them. Malakoff Brass wanted her daughter. She could see that Malakoff was a man of great character, quick with a joke, gentle with her only girl, her only child. Eidla felt that he was the breed of fellow who would take good care of her Georgiana since Eidla's health was in decline. More importantly, Eidla could see that Georgiana adored this man as only a young girl could.

"Might I ask your age?" Georgiana asked in time.

"Why, yes, you may, doll. I'm thirty-one years old," Malakoff lied. He lied to her quite frequently. He knew he loved her to the depths of his sorry soul and was afraid of losing her if he told her too much truth.

Things were happening fast in the year 1942. Eleven Saturdays to the day after Malakoff passed her the rutabagas he wed Georgiana in His Holy Grace Baptist Church before a cheerful congregation, then bedded her that night in the upstairs blue room of her mother's house. Georgiana had always dreamt of a honeymoon on the Champs-Élysées, so Malakoff gave her a French Renault sedan as a wedding present. There it sat, sparkling and black in the driveway the morning after their consummation.

This also impressed the neighbors.

Georgiana and her mother were highly revered in the community, so that fact—combined with Malakoff's winning ways, honed by years of music peddling—brought him instant stature and appreciation from the local flock. Malakoff continued to make sales trips out of town a couple of days a week. But he also managed to settle neatly into their society with an ease that surprised everyone, considering his rough edges. He seemed a welcome addition, a dash of hot sauce in the stew.

On New Year's Eve Georgiana gave birth to Kestrel James Brass. Her mother held Baby Kes in her feeble arms only six times in the following months before she passed through the veil into God's arms. Kes was not a year old, only an infant at the time, but he always told his mama that he could remember Gramma Eidla's funeral. His mother had her doubts. In fact, she began to have her doubts about many things. In that year betwixt Kestrel's birth and baby Gaylenn's arrival she began to bristle at certain audacities in her husband's behavior. Why, he acted like he ruled the roost everywhere he went. And he got away with it. Everybody else thought him to be some sort of cat daddy but, yes, Georgiana had her doubts.

Malakoff chose the third month of her pregnancy with Gaylenn—only weeks before her mother's passing—to unload his biggest sockful of guilt. He closed their bedroom door then confessed and apologized with Shakesperean torment for having left his beloved bride uninformed about the strain of mental unbalance that raced through his family. He had never told her much about his clan except that his mama and daddy had lived and died just outside Nixburg, Alabama. Now he was telling her that his pap was a slobbering crazy coot who had to be locked up to stop him from eating his wife's cotton undies and cosmetics when he wasn't exposing toy-truck-chewing perversions to his children. There was no telling what other things he might expose to children. Malakoff's great granddaddy had gone the same route and there were stray uncles going back generations who had carried forth the family tradition. Malakoff said he quit going back home to visit the widows and orphans of this depravity because it was plumb depressing. They gave new meaning, he said, to being eaten out of house and home. Some might say that, to a marginally lesser degree, Malakoff passed this unstable blood condition on to his expectant bride—for she began to come more than a bit unstrung herself upon learning these facts. Yes, Georgiana had always hated sex and found it awkward, messy, but that was beside the point. Their lives together would never be the same. There would be no more babies.

Kestrel was only four when he took notice. Even he sensed something was awry when Daddy Brass started sleeping in the smaller room adjacent to the big blue bedroom. In time, Daddy Brass had moved all of his clothes, guns, cowboy comic books, and other belongings into that smaller room as well.

In Kestrel's mind, the real vexations began when a

coon-tailed kitty cat came sallying up to him on the ground porch one Saturday as the four-year-old boy sat pondering the vast Atlantic Ocean. He often longed to float out across that sea in a bucket with a paddle, but the coon-tailed kitty took his mind off all that. He petted the kitty and kissed on the kitty and rubbed his face on the kitty. The kitty seemed to like it. Soon Kes was covered with itching red blotches, his eyes were swelling shut and he was caught in a sneezing fit. When Mama George found him she was quickly hysterical.

"Don't fret, doll. The boy will get over it," Daddy soothed. "It'll pass."

But Georgiana did not hear a word he said. At Georgiana's insistence they made haste to Dr. Murphy's house that Saturday afternoon so Dr. Murphy could tell her the same thing Daddy Brass had told her. This only made Georgiana Brass angry. To appease her the good doctor gave Kes a hormone shot and a glass of mint tea. By evening the blotches and sneezes were gone.

After that Mama George seemed to grow more afraid. She began to lock up. That is what Daddy Brass called it. He said she locked up on him—in her own mental asylum. She saw figments on the wind everywhere she looked. Besides an ongoing and imminent array of poxes and physical afflictions threatening her family, Georgiana was constantly voicing her concerns over fire hazards, invading hordes of Yankee carpetbaggers, boogermen, sneaky snakes in every crawlspace and attic, and debt collectors at every door—though they had little debt that Daddy Brass knew of.

"Thems just weavels in your melon," Daddy Brass would tell her.

Of course, this just peeved Georgiana and further committed her to proving him wrong. She rarely succeeded in doing so and this only compounded her fears of failure.

Malakoff began to stay gone more days each week and when he did come home he had little kind to say about the sheet music trade or his sales manager. He kept saying they were jewing him around on his commissions. The next time he caught that fat bastard Jim Tucker actually at his desk in the home office Malakoff was gonna pop him betwixt the horns. He kept saying that too. Despite this outward discontent, there were seldom sharp words or raised voices betwixt Malakoff and Georgiana Brass. In fact, Kes could hardly recall his daddy without a big possum grin on his face, even when he was threatening to end Jim Tucker's earthly moment. But behind the closed doors of his parent's lives there was a shift in those muffled tones when they were overheard. The sound of a heart locking up. So Daddy Brass began to drink. Or, better put, he resumed drinking, for he had drunk heavily in the Marine Corps. At first he drank mostly when he was away. But when Mama George smelled him coming through the door with Old Rip Van Winkle on his breath, she said she would rather he drank at home than try to sneak a nip or do it out in public where all Savannah could see. So Daddy Brass began to drink at home. Not much, but enough. He still did his heavy drinking elsewhere, much to Georgiana's chagrin. Kes and Glenn soon realized that their daddy's grin just got bigger when he drank and he liked to hand out shiny dimes more and more the longer he hit the bottle. He would also sit with them for hours on the front porch, reading them his comic books out loud to their amazement and delight. They loved the bright colored pictures and Daddy's booze-fueled array of voices as he read them. Their favorite was a comic called *Long Ago Tales Of Uncle Remus.*

"Brer Fox, you can skin me," Daddy would say in a funny deep voice, "you can snatch out my eyeballs, tear off my ears and my legs, but pleeeeease, Brer Fox, *don't* thow me in no briar patch—"

The boys would laugh then ask fateful questions.

"Daddy," Glenn asked, "what does *brer* mean?"

"Brer means brother. Just like you and Glenn is brothers."

"Why does Brer Rabbit keep begging that fox not to do what Brer Rabbit really wants him to do?" Kes asked.

"Well, you boys remember I tole you about some white folks thinking they owned themselves some slaves around here?"

"Yes, sir."

"Yes, sir."

"Well, see, these is old time stories told just the way them slave folks told em. Sneaky stories about how they outfoxed their masters. And that's a good thing. Right?"

"Right."

"Right."

One night, half-lit and with Georgiana already in bed, Daddy Brass made his boys fried egg sandwiches with loads of black pepper. They both peered over the skillet's edge as their old man instructed them in his special technique, ladling bacon dripping over each egg as it sizzled. Later, the brothers agreed boldly, through smacking lips, that they were finest sandwiches they had ever tasted. Daddy Brass sipped Van Winkle bourbon and grinned bigger still.

Being so close in age, Kes and Glenn seemed to share a pair of handcuffs in everything they did as youngsters. Kes had not begun to boss Glenn too much back then, so they grew, wrestled, ran, started calling each other Brer Kes and Brer Glenn and dreamt together each day.

One thing they did not do was swim in that big Atlantic ocean at their feet. Georgiana had always been afraid of the water after watching her beloved puppy Melly drown when she was six. Her father had tossed the pup into the high tide despite his wife and little daughter's pleas.

"All canines are born with the swimming instinct as sure as a man will kill and fornicate," Colonel Willy repeated before hurling the pup.

Melly had no such instinct apparently. Not yet, she didn't. Colonel Willy was utterly disgusted and offered no apology or consolation to the hysterical females that day on the beach. He shouldered his shotgun, picked up his skeet shooter. He headed back up the hill to Angelsprey House and the uncluttered distraction of his piano hymnal.

"Save your repentance for your prayer bones," he would say.

Little Georgiana had already heard him say it countless times, several years before she figured out that her prayer bones were her knees and her father saved all apologies for God. His sentiment (or lack of it) ripened in her heart over the years, ripened badly like an abused wine.

After that, the little girl—the only child—who had always been so spoiled yet so ignored by her father now refused to learn to swim despite the urgings of both parents. Her father made no effort to hide his embarrassment over this and the fact that she was not born with the proper appendages, hawk-like acumen, and more intestinal fortitude. The one time her mother put her in a bathing suit and tried to force the issue, with the high windy waves crashing the beach, little Georgiana got so hysterical that a swimming lesson was never tried again. Now, years later, she refused to let her own boys learn swimming skills or venture into that ever-pounding surf for fear she would lose Kes and Glenn to some monster sea—or some sea monster incarnate from the briny depths—the same way she lost beloved pup Melly. This agitated the usually easy-going Daddy Brass to no end. He fought for the boys' right to have their horseplay on the sand and splash in the water like other kids they watched endlessly. But Georgiana's mind was fixed and padlocked on this subject. Finally, Malakoff quit taking his morning swims so the sight of him would not further taunt or frustrate Kes and Glenn.

Still the boys managed to do other little boy things despite being in constant struggle with their locked-up mama. They tried to present a united front when faced with her misgivings. Georgiana was horrified when Glenn asked for a kitty cat of his own only two years after Kes's allergy attack. Kes even seconded the appeal—he really liked kitty cats and wondered what happened to the one that made him sneeze. Georgiana would not entertain the notion.

Shortly after, the boys asked for a dog.

"Not yet," she said.

They asked for bows and arrows.

"Not yet," she said.

They asked for a treehouse.

"Never," she gasped.

When she denied that last request, Malakoff rose slowly from his rocking chair, flipped his funny book aside, tossed a queer grin and a wink to his sons on the floor, then left the house. The screen door slammed and his burgundy T-Bird was heard screeching away. Georgiana and the boys sat staring blankly at each other. Old Rip had been left on the lampstand.

Daddy Brass stayed gone that night. When he returned the next morning he had a hammer in his hand. He also had a pickup load full of lumber driven by a colored man they had never seen before. Daddy told the boys the new man's name was Hiram. They watched their daddy lean a ladder against the biggest of the live oak trees—the one whose moss-weeping branches brushed the two upstairs porches on the southern side of the house. Their daddy climbed that ladder and Hiram followed, hauling planks as they went. Soon the rasp of a saw broke Georgiana from her sleep. Daddy never went inside to her all day, having brought his own food and drink. He left at sunset but was back first thing the next morning. Over two days Daddy

Brass and Hiram sawed, hammered, and nailed together the damnedest tree house you ever did see. All the while, Georgiana peered again and again out her kitchen window, afraid to intercede. When they were done, Daddy and Hiram had created a kidhouse wonder. It had four walls, a roof, three windows, and little balcony with its own screen door. Inside were built-in bunkbeds, a table, a floor escape hatch, and Daddy had even outfitted the east window with a spyglass for spying on that wide rolling sea. Late that second afternoon Daddy Brass hung his hammer on the treehouse wall. He climbed down the oak and went inside to Georgiana, who was nervously sipping ginger ale at the kitchen table.

This is what he said:

"Doll, I am moving out. I done quit my job with the Mid-South Music Company near two months ago. Sorry I ain't told you. I can no longer tolerate their wages nor this house. Don't want no divorce. I love you and I love my boys. But I done lost my way and I like it."

Mama did not say a word. None came to her. She was mortified by the thought of being alone, but said nothing.

Daddy turned on his heel, went back outside and hoisted both boys up into the tree house which nestled even with the roofline of the big house. Awestruck, Kes and Glenn cooed and squealed over each neat feature as their daddy stood there somber for the first time either of them could recall.

"Do right by this place, boys," he said with a deep breath. "And do right by your mama."

Then Daddy left them in their rapture. He climbed down the oak for the last time, got his things, and went with Hiram. A few days later they heard Daddy had moved into an old cotton warehouse on River Street, complete with an office, a secretary, and his own bunk. If you phoned his office it was answered by the lush-lipped tones of a certain Mrs. Plum, who was said to be a stunning redheaded grass widow from Corsicana, Texas.

In the years that followed it became apparent to Georgiana and her boys that Daddy Brass had been rubbing shoulders with plenty of both the right and wrong people once he entered Savannah society with Georgiana holding open the door. He began to dabble in gambling syndication and moon liquor running. By the time Kes and Glenn entered middle school Daddy Brass had parlayed both vices into highly lucrative operations under his own thumb, with a fleet of beer halls and distilleries in scattered houses, and a small cadre of lewd men working for him. He was even known to frequent the raunchy jazz joints over on West Broad Street, swapping drinks and lies with the colored folk. Some in white society rumored that Daddy Brass was behind much of the bolitia numbers rackets over there in the colored quarters, but those in the know were quick to point out that most of that action belonged to Bubba Garrity and Sloppy Joe Bellinger. And Daddy Brass was not one to sop his bread on another man's plate. He was well known and generally liked through the region, despite his line of work. Most of Savannah's police force even took a shine to him. They appreciated the fact that Daddy stayed clear of dope and whores, while never rubbing the cops' noses in those doings they were never going to conquer anyway. Besides, in keeping with the natural course of human events, many of Savannah's finest officers were Daddy's best customers. Many were on his payroll.

So it came to pass that Malakoff Brass found his true ministry guiding liquor and loose living to them that liked it. The same way he liked it. As a result, Daddy did thrive and prosper, especially with the waterfront at his feet, Hunter Airfield in his hip pocket, and Camp Stewart out his back door, a few miles away. The good people of Savannah—and the bad—were now Daddy's people, but sailors and soldiers were his bread and butter.

Meanwhile, in a treehouse out on the island, Kestrel and Glenn Brass had begun to sprout wings and sing like the angels.

VERSE 7

Me Magpie Oracle

The pitiful house sat in a strip of pasture at the end of the road. It sat betwixt a pecan tree and an elm. Kes would never forget how bad his heart hurt when he first saw that house or the deep sadness that came over him and never left. How could he know that he would spend the rest of his life trying to forget that place or how poor you had to be to live that way?

Kes's journey that day had not been as easy as he anticipated. He got off on the wrong road out of town before a kid on an English Racer bicycle corrected his path. Kes had to follow a creek over to Highway 149—the road he should have taken in the first place—then follow that highway out to Fuzzy Lick Road, about seven miles beyond the outskirts of town. His feet finally left the asphalt at a tarpaper shack with a tin shed in back that kept barking at him. The sign said **BiG Pups 4 SaLE**. Fuzzy Lick Road was a long rut of red clay passing through shadowy woods, into kudzu-clogged pastures, then back into the woods again, always back into the woods. At the end of that long and meandering mud rut was an ungated gap in a kudzu-choked fence, and beyond that was an open field where sunlight was very unkind to the house that lay there sinking into the ground. Even the pecan and elm, old as they were, looked unhealthy and struggling from their roots. As much as a foot of the house's old clapboard walls had disappeared into the ground in places, sagging from lack of support over countless years, giving up their inches to the earth, season after season. Kes hated to think about the vermin that crawled and snaked around under there now. Recent attempts at beautification sat on the porch in assorted pots. But the recent cold snap had reduced most of the plants and flowers to withered, brown husk. A broad blue straw hat—the kind old country women wore when gardening—hung by the screen door. You know the kind. Kes stopped and stood at the foot of the creaky steps. A pair of cracked leather bootees perched at the porch's edge, laced women's boots from a bygone era.

Yes, Kes suddenly felt very sad and a little afraid. More than a little afraid. What had he been thinking and why would he ever have wanted to come here?

By the time Kes reached these steps he had been walking for over four hours and the afternoon was slipping away from him. Autumn eve would be on him sooner than he would have liked. He was weary, hungry, his feet were sore and he was wearing his brother's plaid pea jacket. The child's hornbook was still under his arm.

After he found the old grade school reading book yesterday he went back to his dorm room. He told brother

Glenn of his near death experience in the lake and the wee girl who had rescued him. Yes, Kes was sure this book belonged to that girl. He was sure it was she who had scrawled her name—Bettilia Whissler—inside the cover. It was Glenn's idea to call Dean Pickery since it was the weekend and Daddy Brass had wangled the dean's home phone for them back on Invitation Day, in case they ever needed special favor.

"In case you get in a tight and need some of Pickery's pull," Daddy said, slipping Kes the number on the back of the Dean's business card. "His pull ain't what mine is. But Pickery must be good for something, else they wouldn't give him the keys to the kingdom."

Now, standing here at this sad house this Saturday with this strange hornbook in his hand, Kes was in quandary. Normally Kes would not have taken such advantage. His mother would disapprove of special favor. But something told him Mama George would appreciate her eldest being saved from a watery grave and make exception in this case. Kes called Dean Pickery and the dean agreed. Normally the dean would not divulge confidential student information such as home address or telephone number but in this case he would make exception. The next morning, after Sunday School, Kes walked over to the dean's big home on campus where he was told by the pregnant cook, Daneetra, that Bettilia Whissler had no phone but here was a paper with her address written in the dean's wife's steady hand. Kes got directions to the address from the cook who lived outside that end of Newdundy herself. At the time, Kes did not think a thing about the cook living out that same way, or that her directions were sending him over to the other side of the railroad tracks that first delivered him and little brother to Shelfy Oak Bible School. But Kes did courteously ask the cook when her baby was due (he was proud of himself for that) before thanking her, then he skipped the big Sunday church service altogether. He had gotten enough churching this week, all week, every week, week after week. His sputtering redemption from Lake Serenity the day before had restructured Kes's priorities for the moment. Surely, that other son of God would understand.

Now Kes found himself standing outside what he believed to be the tumbledown home of Bettilia Whissler. There was not a soul—saved or unsaved—in sight, save for that old Holstein cow ambling this way from up the pasture.

Kes knocked on the door and waited. Nobody answered, he heard no movement within the house. He thought about setting the book inside the screen and leaving but did not follow through. He walked around to the side of the house toward a small barn beneath great maple boughs. A few scraggly chickens were pecking and scratching around a rusty butane tank.

"Anybody? Hello?" he spake to the open maw of the barn.

No answer came as he spied inside and saw an old Mercury sedan parked in the darkness amidst hoes and rakes. It smelled of hay and damp earth mixed with faint manure. The sedan was speckled with bird droppings. He stepped back outside and saw the heifer still loping closer, as if to greet him. Suddenly the cow veered off. She began mooing loudly, starting to trot toward the open gap in the fence where he had entered. Kes's eyes followed her path and saw the figure of an old black woman in a bonnet coming up the road, pulled along by her walking stick. As the bent woman came through the fence—through the gap without a gate—the heifer slowed and turned, trailing behind the woman's trailing skirt.

Kes met her in the front yard.

"What keeps your cow in this pasture?" he asked

"Reckon she's partial to it."

"That makes sense."

"She's got her haygrass, her water."

"That would follow then."

"Yassir."

"But that's a good question ain't it?"

"How are you, young fella?" the gnome-faced woman asked, planting her high burlwood stick for support, her eyes slitting up at him. The stick stood taller than her bonnet.

"Real fine, ma'am. You?"

"Pert fair. We walks that morning service most Sundays. Ethyl gas up to thirty cent now."

"So I hear," Kes said.

"Still, plenty of white folk running up and down the road." Her warbly voice called toward the house, barely rising: "Bit-*teeel*-yee. Git down hyere."

Kes turned and saw a patch of branches rustling high in the big pecan tree betwixt the house and barn. First, two bare feet appeared, then the tiny girl with the missing toe dropped from the lowest limb, landing amidst the squawk and scatter of chickens.

Kes was stupefied. So this little tree rat had been here all along, watching him. She hustled over to the old woman studying Kes and took refuge, shrinking behind her elder's long skirt.

The old lady's verdict must have been good because she smiled suddenly, reached out a hand.

"I be Mambly Elisheba Whissler. This be my girl Beteelyee. And you?"

"How do, ma'am. I be—I mean—I'm Kestrel Brass, ma'am."

"Can we hep ye?"

"I brought this book home to you, ma'am."

"Might as well finish ye words, boy. I ain't just a ma'am. You can call me Mambly like mah girl does. Like ye would ye Mambly and Paply, except they ain't no Paply."

Kes felt he was still not asking the right questions. Mambly? No Paply? He had heard of white men who lay with black ladies and made white babies. But this Miss Whissler looked too gnarled and long of tooth to be this Bettilia's mother, or to have birthed this girl out of wedlock so late in life. Then again, love knows no bounds. His daddy always said that.

Not knowing how to finish his words any other way, Kes held out the schoolbook. Bettilia stepped forward and took it, avoiding his gaze.

"Thank ye, *k*-kindly," she said without conviction. "Just a ole book I *t*-tote sometimes is all."

Yes, there was that touch of a stammer Kes heard in her

talk the other day.

"You're welcome."

"Ain't like I study it or nothing."

"No. Course not."

"How you find us?" Miss Whissler injected.

"Dean Pickery helped. Walked out from town then took the turn back at the big dog sign. I guess they got pups for sale."

"They *always* got dadburn pups for sale," Bettilia said..

"We's mountain folk, wary folk," Miss Whissler added, as if to explain her girl's attitude. "We don't warm up so fast like you ready-made downlander folk."

"Well, I don't know about that, ma'am, er, Mizz Mambly. But I sure appreciate what Mizz Bettilia done—I mean, what she did by saving my life, nearly 'bout."

"No *n-n-nearly 'bout* to it," Bettilia snapped, "You'd be floating with the bloat by now if'n I ain't been there."

"Well, of course, I would be. Wouldn't I?"

"Yep, you would. Is that another of your good questions?" Bettilia asked pointedly. She gave Mambly a sour look. "I swear, you'd think he was writing hisself a goody *b*-book."

"Returning *your* book is all."

"So you *s-s*-say."

"She tole me 'bout your misfortune," Miss Whissler said. "I never learnt that swimming neither."

"So I do say," Kes said to Bettilia.

"We pleased you still with us, Young Brass," Miss Whissler said, eyeing her girl. "*All* of us er pleased."

"And me mostly," Kes said, detecting new doubt in Bettilia about the wisdom of her rescue efforts.

Mambly saw what was going on betwixt them but kept to the high ground.

"Well, the Good Book say, better a supper of herb where love be than a fat ox full of hate. You had any supper?"

"Supper?"

"Young'un your age is gotta eat."

"Yes, ma'am—I mean, Mambly. I mean, no, I ain't had time for supper yet."

"I got crowder peas in the icebox. Conebread in the breadbox."

"I might eat a bite."

And he could too. It suddenly dawned on Kes that he was every kind of hungry. But was his hunger powerful enough to conquer his worst devil—fear—and his fear of that awful, rundown house?

"Well, come on in," Mambly said. "We'll set ye a plate."

Kes turned and went with the old woman who moved past him, question answered.

As he went, he glanced askance at Bettilia in time to see an amazing thing. She smiled. She smiled at him. It was a wee smile, but real, with a girlish glee that took hold of him. It made Kes feel nice yet queer inside at the same time. He smiled back. Then he threw it all away.

"Why was you carrying a kiddy school book?" he had nerve to ask.

Her smile flew as fast as it came.

"Damn fool question."

"Mind them words, mind your manners, Beteelyee,"

Mambly snapped, going inside the unlocked door. "Else I'll cut me a switch."

Newspapers and magazines were stacked high into the corners of the front room, every color of bottle, jug, and can collected in motley groups around a sagging divan, upright piano with broken keys, and scarred rocking chair. It was a very old lady's house. A demented organization was evident, with special piles grouped together and niches for things which must be kept. It might seem a jumble, but it was not litter. It was also a firetrap with an overworked butane heater at the center of the hoarding. There was a path through all this and Mambly led the young ones through it.

Seeing no bathroom, Kes was thankful that they at least had electric. The apparent absence of plumbing and the clomp of their feet on a tired plank floor reminded Kes of a couple of primitive houses the Brothers Brass and their mother had been invited into in years past by Holy Ghost handshakers after North Georgia camp meetings. Handshakers were big on inviting you home with them after seven uninterrupted hours of singing. Mainly, Kes remembered being very cranky and very tired by the time they reached these backwoods haunts. Both times, the houses were in better shape than this, though neither of them had electric like this. But one of those houses, two years ago, more than made up for the lack of electric when a comely widow came to Kes's bed on the back porch after all were asleep and awakened him in ways he had never been awakened before. Throughout that widow's wet and wondrous nocturnal awakening Kes failed to keep old Clootie behind him and had been trying to make up for it ever since. All during and ever after, Kes thanked The Lord that Mama George was four walls away that night, sleeping sound in their host's front bedroom.

Kes could now see that—besides a well-made bed—that backwoods, hand-shaking widow kept secrets well, along with a neater parlor than Mambly Whissler.

Mambly, Kes, and Bettilia shuttled down a short hallway lined with clutter, then into the kitchen where even more clutter almost completely hid the worn and cracked linoleum tiles. Mambly motioned Kes to the table where he took a cane-bottom chair and sat. Bettilia slid into her own chair and stared at him across the bare wood table like he was a cold fried egg.

Kes tried not to notice.

"I know what goody boys is all about," Bettilia said.

"You do?" Kes asked nicely. "What they all about?"

"Same thing rotten boys is all about."

"You don't know half as much as ye think ye do," Mambly told her, "Now git on over hyere else I'll whup ye."

"Goody boys, rotten boys, and they daddies. Daddies and boys, all the same. They been trying to mess wid *m-m*-me all my life. How long they been messing with you, Mambly?"

"Heat up them peas."

Bettilia slid back out of her chair and lit the stove with a wood match from her dress pocket. Kes thought it odd that she would carry matches on her person. Perhaps she was a firebug who lit up barns. That would suit her rancorous personality but would make her a death merchant in this firetrap. Bettilia went to the icebox while Mambly took off her bonnet and coat, carrying them into a bedroom. Bettilia took out a big iron kettle and set it on the low blue flame. Mambly returned, shooed Bettilia away from the stove, took a tin from a shelf above it. The coffee pot was soon percolating, cornbread was on the table.

"Will ye have a cup wid us?" Mambly asked.

"Yes, I would like that," Kes said. He had only tasted coffee once before, at a Krispy Kreme donut stand in Savannah when his mama was off at a funeral. Mama George considered a sugary donut to be trashy breakfast fare for young growing servants of the Lord. And coffee was out of the question. So Kes was eager to try it again.

Mambly set three speckled-blue graniteware cups on the table and filled them with black brew. Soon, they all sat blowing into their cups betwixt bitter sips of the best stuff Kes had ever tasted. No sugar or milk was offered or required.

"Kestrel..." Mambly pondered, cupping her coffee in wizened hands. "Cain't say I've known nobody with that name afore."

"It come from my grandfather. That's what they tell me."

"That's some kind of hunter hawk, ain't it? Kestrel?"

"He ain't no hunter," Bettilia sniped. "He's *j*-just a fool jaybird."

Kes's eyes begged her to cut him some slack, but Bettilia wasn't listening.

"You and ye brer sang real nice at that school-do," Mambly allowed.

"Proud to hear it, ma'am. Thank you muchly."

"Until that feller drilled that other feller dead, that is," Bettilia said.

Kes winced, his mind flashing on the flash of Daddy Brass's gun.

"That'll be 'nough of that," Mambly said.

"Reckon I can sang as good er better than you," Bettilia boasted to Kes. "I'll out-sang a squawking jaybird any day, *n-n-*now won't I?"

"Do it," Kes challenged.

"Just maybe I will."

"C'mon, give us two choruses and an amen then. Two choruses of, well, *anythang*,"

"Ain't likely," she shot back.

Kes began singing.

"I lost my eyes in a blacksmith shop in the year of seventy-six, while workin' on a reee-vaaawl-ver when it was out of fix—" he sang boldly, with lovely vibrato, to prove how easy he could do it, *"I am so sad and loooonely and I am condemned to roam—"*

"Nope. Not today," Bettilia said blithely, her nose disappearing into her coffee cup.

Kes stopped singing.

"Miss Bettilia, did I tip your cow or kick your pup or something? Why you being so mean to me?"

"Aw, she's jist bluff ornery is all. Mostly," Mambly told him. "She's sweet as sorghum once ye butter her biscuit long enough."

"I ain't sure I got that long," Kes said.

"Hmmmph," Bettilia responded. "Reckon I can still out-sang ya."

"I'll have you to know, little girl, that I done cut me a record platter with me singing on

it—"

"—with your brother helping you, ye mean—"

"—with *me* singing some serious *solo* on that record platter. High tenor solo, I'll have you know. One of them new modern forty-five revolving records."

"I'll have you know," she shot back, "that I done played a platter or *t*-two on Mambly's machine and you weren't amid em—"

"—old timey 78 revolvers, you mean—"

"—I been playing them platters all my days and ain't *n*-never come acrost you in the pile."

"Ask my brer how it feels to have one of them old 78 platters broke over his head. I done it to him and I can do it to *you*."

Mambly cackled with laughter. Bettilia screwed up her face.

"I need me some sweet tea, Mambly."

"You dern well do," Kes said.

"This coffee's making sour on my belly," she pushed her cup toward Mambly, ignoring Kes.

"What's your excuse when you ain't got coffee?" Kes pressed.

"In the icebox," Mambly said, still cackling. "Young Brass, you want some sweet tea?"

"No, ma'am. This coffee is fine. I can handle it."

"Wisht we had some *g-g-*gingermint," Bettilia said from inside the icebox.

"Ain't no gingermint for over a month. Be happy with what you get instead of making misery over what you ain't got," Mambly said, here rheumy eyes never leaving Kes. "Hear you and Bit got some lessons together."

"Just Civics class is all," he said.

"She be in the choir-singing class. Figured ye'd be in that'n with her too."

"No, ma'am, uh—Mambly. My mama, she didn't figure we needed it, what with our natural calling and vocation."

"You need it, jaybird," Bettilia said, pouring cold tea in her cup.

"Hesh—" Mambly warned.

"Anyways, Mambly thinks my school day is best spent on things *I-I-*I ain't already too slick with," reasoned Bettilia. She sipped her tea whilst dishing up peas at the stove. "Things like Geogurphy. Pentatuchs. Holy Ghosts. Long division. You know."

"Mmmhmm," slurped Mambly in agreement. "We done worked long hard to git Miss Bit here this Bible College schooling. She's took to it right well."

Bettilia set a plate of crowder peas with green snaps before Kes, then two more plates for herself and Mambly. The old woman told Bettilia to fetch the peppers and fetch she did. Opening the cupboard, Bettilia filled the center of the table with a glass platoon of peppers: long peppers and round peppers, red, green, and yellow, in vinegar-spiced jars of every size, along with some chow-chow and tomato relish. A saucer of sliced purple onion soon joined them.

"Mambly wants what's best for me. I goes with that," Bettilia said, sitting down with her spoon.

"My mama wants the same," Kes responded. "I can go with that too."

"She done her best by me. I'm gone do my best by her."

"You best do your best for yourself," Mambly said. "Both of ye."

Bettilia went on talking with her mouth full of peas.

"So I'm learning all I can about her god—I mean—the God Jehover. She say he's the only one and I believe her. Back where I come from gods is a dime a dozen."

Kes's coffee cup dropped slowly to the table. He had never heard the like.

"What's that mean?"

"Bit, they's a piece of cold chicken hold over in that icebox," Mambly said, apparently ill at ease with the subject. "Set it out for your company."

"Aaaw, Mambly, you know I was hankering on that pullybone!"

"Git the chicken."

Kes smiled as Bettilia scowled. She got up, opened the icebox again, and took the lone piece of chicken back to her chair with her. She sat and looked down at its cold, crisp, black-peppered skin—then slowly slid it across the table to Kes. He quickly picked up the chicken and began to eat it without objection, much to her chagrin. In fact, Kes kept smirking at her as he sucked every smoky morsel off that pullybone. This had a desired effect on Bettilia. She fumed, watching him with envious disdain. After exacting this sweet revenge, Kes even put the bare pullybone in his pocket without breaking it or making a wish.

This seemed to frost Bettilia even more, like this sonny boy had violated some sacred ritual by not even doing what a body was supposed to do as soon as all the meat was sucked off a pullybone. Any fool should know that you split the wishing bone with some other fool right then and there, breaking it betwixt the two to know who won their wish. Any fool should know that much, even a squawking city jaybird from Savannah-wherever-that-be.

Kes paid her no mind. It was not difficult, since the chicken had been delicious. If there had been more, he would have asked for another piece. The peas were good too, with bits of pork fat that were mighty tasty. Before Kes knew it he was sopping his cornbread in the pot liquor on his nearly empty plate. They were definitely the best crowder peas Kes had ever tasted. They might be poor folk, but what they ate was fit to eat.

"You cook a good pot of peas, Mizz Whissler. About the best I ever had."

"I cooked and *d*-doctored them peas, bird," Bettilia sniped. "Mambly might of showed me how, but I can *d-d*-doctor peas and most anything in a pot, and I can pickle okry."

Kes could not stop himself.

"Yeah? And you cook that chicken too?"

Bettilia's eyes blazed and Kes knew his hunch was right.

"Another fool question—" she hissed.

"Easy, *chil'*ren," Mambly said. She fought the temptation to tell Kes how Little Bit here burned every bird she put in the oven until Mambly would no longer let her near one—what with chickens being too scant to let many burn. But Mambly wanted to to keep this war between these kids and stay out of the fray herself. Especially since this Kestrel Brass was turning out to be his own kind of ornery cuss.

"Mizz Whissler—Mambly—you cook as good a chicken as I ever tasted. Yes, I believe that's finest chicken I ever did eat. Even cold. Lotsa black pepper and I like black pepper. And Mizz Bettilia?"

"What?" Bettilia asked, beyond leery.

"You knocked off Mizz Mambly's pea recipe so good I'd like to taste the real deal someday."

"*Chil'ren—*"

"I'll throw you back in that drownin' hole *where I found you—*" Bettilia yelped.

"Anyhow," Kes drawled, "given a go at it, I reckon I can follow a recipe good as you. But then, I ain't still at home with mama to help me. No rubber training wheels."

"I think your rubber's *g*-got *hobnails* in it—"

"Yep, you're a star pupil as pupils go—"

"Let's play nice, chil'ren."

"Daddy Brass, he's a good cook," Kes added. "Of course, all your best cooks are men. Everbody knows that."

"Well, when *j-j*-jaybirds turn to men we'll find out, won't we?"

"You know, Mizz Bettilia," Kes said with a slow grin,

"that's a good question. A real good question. Ain't it?"

"Nobody asked you to come hyere."

"I was bringing you back your book is all."

"So why did you have to bring *you* with it?"

"I been *trying* to express my appreciation in ever way—"

"Yeah, I know *how* you'd like to express that appreciation—"

"—But you won't let me. You just hide in trees."

"Fly your jaypecker home—"

"You got a dirty mind."

"I *read* your mind is all."

"Well that's a sight better than reading baby school books—"

Bettilia squealed, started to leap across the table at him but Mambly's hand yanked her back into place.

"Hesh it, now. Both of ye."

Bettilia eyed the butter knife, Kes's arm went up in defense. Mambly pinched Bettilia's nose to get her attention.

"He's right—" Mambly said, "you got a right dirty mind, sometimes, always expecting the worst in folks. And she's right too, Young Brass. You are a mite short of being a growed man if you cain't see she's jist scary of ye is all."

Bettilia flew to her feet.

"I ain't scary of nobody. And ain't nobody scary of Kestrel Brass."

Bettilia dashed from the room. Kes watched her go with no comment. He wondered how high she would climb while cursing him before she stopped. Mambly's eyes began to twinkle.

"Yep, she be scary alright. She's scary to folks—always has been. If they ain't scary of her, she's scary of them. And she's scary of you, afeared of how you makes her feel."

"How I make her feel?"

"Natcherly. You put that warm sorghumy feeling in her tum. She's sweet on you. Most growed men would know that by now."

"I don't see how."

"How ain't never had nothing to do wid it. *Who* is all that matters."

"But, why me?"

"Why not you? You do pick a good guitar. An you sang a perty tune. Ain't you man enough yet to know what that'll git ye?"

"Appears to me, ma'am, the only sweetness in her is that glass of tea. Besides, I got me a girl. Her name is Chalice, back in Savannah," he mumbled, turning the old woman's question in his mind. "Bettilia, she don't go to Sunday meeting with you?"

Mambly's mind was turning slow too, measuring her thoughts.

"Nope. Nary once since she commenced with this Bible College. That girl never took to churching much. But she knew I was set on her gitting high-tutored at a Christ-abiding school. So I scrapes and saves. All I got left is this land so I get one of them bank mortgages. When the day finally come she tells me it's one or t'other. Either it's Bible come Sunday or Bible five days a week—but she weren't gone do both. She say she'd just as soon stick to Sundays only, like it's always been betwixt us. But she knows how I feel about *that.* So Bible College it be."

Kes heard far off thunder as Mambly's nose flexed upward like a hound.

"Rain on its way, sounds like. Smells like it even more."

"I best be going then. Sure was some fine feast."

"It were our pleasure. Come again anytime."

She rose with him, leading him to the front door. As she opened it thunder rumbled again, closer now.

"Look like ye might git wet," Mambly warned. "Here, take my husband Tinsley's hat and coat. They oughter keep oft the worst of it."

So she did have a husband. And a randy old devil he must be. By the looks of Bettilia, he was a randy old white devil. Kes thought he should protest her offering but he had not felt prone to protest much Mambly Whissler had offered him so far. Kes trusted her for reasons he could not explain. And he was very wary of walking all the way back to town in driving rain. He watched the old woman step around to a hall tree behind the door and return with a long grey slicker and a broad straw hat that looked to Kes like hats he had seen in photographs of places in South America where that coffee came from.

"Don't mind if I do, Mambly. Sure appreciate you. Your concern."

"Bring em back when ye can."

"I will do that. No nearly 'bout to it."

"Hyere, I'll walk ye to the gate."

"No need, ma'am."

"You's company. I'll fetch my stick."

Kes trod slowly with the old woman from the house to the gap in the fence, the gateless gate. As they approached, her walking stick pointed out spots along the kudzu-draped fence where she had erected stripped sapling poles with tiny, brightly-painted bird houses atop them. Kes admired her handicraft and said so.

"I miss me magpie though," Mambly said. "When I were a girl, where I be from, we had the magpie."

"One brings sorrow, two bring joy..."

Mambly had to smile at that.

"Oh me, that be the song. We singed it back there, when we be children."

"Mizz Mambly, you don't never lock your doors?"

"Never have, way out hyeres. Oh, oncet in a while I can tell somebody visits while we gone. Saw some shod hoss or mule hoof around the place I din't recognize a few weeks back. Never knowed nobody to snitch nothing though. If they really needs it, they can have it."

"You're a Christian soul, Mizz Mambly. Not many who say they is really is. Not like you."

"We all got our troubles. I got mine. Plenty of em. I try not to burden Betteelyee with em."

"You figure these folks who visit sometimes, when you're gone, are troubled folks?"

"Ain't for me to say. Who knows what festers inside of folks. Jist yesterday, saw me some queer tracks, almost man tracks, looked like. But live, let live. The world be full of wayfarers."

As the scent of rain rose strong and the rumbling sky grew louder he could not help but glance back at that big pecan tree. He knew that girl was hid high in its dark branches, watching him.

"Ain't she afraid of getting struck by lightning up in there?" he asked.

"Oh, she'll come down directly. Even Little Miss Bit ain't fool enough to ride out a drumfire storm perched in a pee-can tree."

"Well, that's a relief," Kes said as they passed through the fence gap," her being so scary and all."

Mambly paused, eyeing the choking vines surrounding them, then casting her gaze back to the house.

"That little gal never spake a word—not one word—afore she was six or seven year old."

"Dangdang. Is that possible?"

"She still stammers some, but the stutter ain't bad as it were. I got her to talking by teaching her letters and how to read. Teached her how to read with a lot of hep from that old hornbook of mine."

"The book I returned to y'all?" he asked as Mambly nodded. "No wonder she's partial to it."

"First utters I ever heard from her weren't outa no book though. First utter I heard her say was *bobnot*."

"Bobnot?"

"Yep."

"What's *bobnot* mean?"

"I never did know. I've thunk different things, but I don't really know. Of course, it ain't so much what it means.

Only thing what matters is what bobnot means to *her.*"

"Huh?"

"Son, ye ever hear tell of the Kudzu Man?" she asked softly, lost in the faraway.

"Not so's I recall."

"A lot of white folk, city folk, they ain't heared of him. He weren't no white folk."

"No?"

"Folks tell of the lost Kudzu Man and they say beware. Watch ye back. But the Kudzu Man weren't always the Kudzu Man."

"He weren't? I mean—he wudn't?" Kes was a bit lost himself.

"Ye know how that kudzu vine grow thick as creeping leafy thieves and cover everthing like a green-wove quilt, over hills and phone poles and fell-down houses? Well, ye look out acrost them hills and fields of humpity leaf and you prob'ly looking right at that Kudzu Man laying down in the midst of it all—cuz the Kudzu Man be covered in kudzu leaf, that vine sprouting right outer his own green skin. Hot sunny day you might be looking right at his great lumpy knees and elbows but never know it. He jist look like all the rest of that kudzu. He be big, they say. Some folks say tall as a barn. Some say tall as two barn.

"At night when the moon burn dark the Kudzu Man rise up from his sleeping place and he walk the land looking for souls who might hep him. 'Cause he don't wanna be no Kudzu Man. Ye understand? He don't wanna be no Kudzu Man. Never did. Unlucky folk who chancet to meet him some black night on the road turn and run away and say he run away too. But he keep looking. He peep in folk's winders, they say. Ye might look out your own winder middle of the night and he might be looking back in at ye and ye ain't never knowed it. He jist look like a kudzu covered bramble out your winder cuz his eyes and mouth be covered with thickly green leaf so's ye can't see'em. That's why folks be afeared of the Kudzu Man. They think he gone swaller 'em up jist like he's swallered up.

Mambly turned her fierce eyes upon Kes, peering into him as she spake.

"But it was my own pup dog Persiferny tole me that man weren't always the Kudzu Man and Persiferny say she was tole it by her pap. Oncet the Kudzu Man were a real man. A little yeller chinyman. From a fer-off land. A skeered scary man. Same as any man I expect. Only thing is, this little man seen something terrible one day. More terrible than anything you or I can conjure. And this terrible thang come after the little man. So's the little man, he run and run from this fer-off land till he cain't run no more. Then he hide in that kudzu from the terrible thang. He hide there all day and all night and all day and all night again, shaking and trembling, for fear that terribleness would find him and do its terrible ways with him. The little feller hide deep in that kudzu so long, sweating and skin prickling, till that kudzu takes root in him, sprouting plumb outer his skin. It begun to grow on him, making him bigger and bigger till he be nothing but big kudzu arms and long kudzu legs and big kudzu feets. His haid be nothing but a big ball of kudzu with a little skeered brain somewheres inside. By the time he got gumption enough to rise back up and walk outer there he be the Kudzu Man. Forever and a day, he be the Kudzu Man.

"To him it seem like they ain't no going back from what that terrible thang made of him. But he ain't happy with that. Who would be? Would you? So Kudzu Man, he rears up off'n his green-leaf bed come nightfall and walks the roads and peeps in folks' houses. He be looking for someone—that only someone—who kin cut away all that kudzu and find the real man who's still hid in there. Thing is, though, evertime he find somebody who might help him—he turn and run jist like they turn and run. So he never can find him or her what can save him from walking the night forever wearing his fraidy coat of kudzu."

Mambly fell silent.

"Where is your dog Persiferny, ma'am?"

"Snake bit her. She gone now."

Kes chewed on the notion of dog-told tales for a moment.

"That's a powerful yarn, Mambly. Never heard nothing like it before. Almost like one them Bible stories my mama used to tell."

"Ain't no Bible yarn," she spake gentle. "Jist one of them yarns what spins around amongst folks back t'home."

"What kinda snake done it?"

"Copperhead."

Kes did not know what to say to that. His daddy always said a copperhead would make most dogs lay down and die. Not that Daddy always knew what he was talking about.

But Daddy made it sound good in the telling.

"I better go. Looks like a wet walk home for me."

"Looks like. Keep warm, Young Brass." Her withered hand waved Kes on as he began to shift off down the road. "Don't let the same dog bite ye twicet."

"Hope Mr. Whissler don't miss his hat and coat—" Kes hollered back.

"Oh, pee-shaw," Mambly called after him. "Tinsley Whissler ain't gonna miss nothing. He's in the grave since VJ Day of '45."

Rain began to pelt them both as Kes began his long journey back down the soon muddy road.

Kes was not overly concerned about slogging back to his dorm room in a dead man's clothes. Or so he told himself. But he was a bit off kilter when he realized the late Mr. Whissler could not have been the father of Bettilia. So, if Mambly's husband was not the girl's daddy, who was?

Lightning flashed, thunder cracked open the sky. The rain came down, down, with rising fervor as Kes trudged on.

Kes took one last glance back at Mambly as she poked her way to the porch. He liked the old woman. If Bettilia was a riddle, Mambly was a riddle too. But, yes, he felt strangely fortunate to have met this elder Mambly Whissler as he watched her climb those weary steps, disappearing into her desperate house.

Turning away, Kes resumed his journey.

He never saw Mambly Whissler again.

VERSE 8

An Augury of Golden Slippers

Bettilia lit the gas heater. Soon the heater's lattice of ceramic tiles began to glow red, warming the paper-piled room.

"Please fetch me my fester sticks, Bit," Mambly said from her rocker.

Bettilia left the room, returning moments later with fester sticks presented to Mambly's gnarled hands. Quickly, the hickory batons were put to strange work as the old woman rubbed one stick along the other then reversed the process. Occasionally one stick would assume special power and those rheumatic fingers would press a hickory tip to a celestial parchment in Mambly's lap.

Bettilia sat back down on the floor in the heater's glow, her back to Mambly's nightly doings.

"Wouldn't of kilt you to be a mite friendlier today, Miss Bit," Mambly spake, her eyes lost in the fiddling of fester sticks.

"Weren't nothing to be got from it," Bettilia said, her own eyes lost in the fire.

"You don't know that. Now do ye?"

"I know some folks oughter be satisfied by what I already done for em."

"Whatever things you does, you does unto the Lord. Now ain't that right?"

Bettilia sighed. "Yeah. I reckon."

They sat for a spell in clicking silence before the festering sticks paused.

"Ye know, Bit, it wouldn't hurt ye none to purty up your lips and make a friend or two with one of these good boys from the church school."

Bettilia spake to the hot lace of brick before her.

"Good boys like that jaybird, Kestrel Brass, you mean?"

Mambly went back to fiddling. She had an easy, deft touch.

"Oh, him or some other. Long as he be a true-hearted one."

"Never met a true heart in my life."

"Well, you met me din't ye? And I met you."

Bettilia finally threw a glance back at the old woman in the rocking chair. Their eyes met in the flicker.

"But you was differnt. You a rare bird, Mambly," Bettilia said. "And I don't know as much about myself."

"Well, I do. I know ye. We ain't so different," Mambly whispered, smiling soft. "I remember how they was this young Mambly who wanted golden slippers to tuck away for her wedding day. Well, her wedding come and gone, and she never got them slippers. But the dream was the gift, ye see. A good soul don't want to go to heaven so much as they want to carry a bit of heaven with em. They want heaven to touch down here on this good earth."

"Is it? Is it so good?"

"Well, yes, Miss Bit. A lot of this life has good in it. If you'll open the door, let it in. It ain't always there. But it's there." Mambly was never sure how much of these things Bettilia heard, but she knew this girl would never hear them if somebody didn't say them to her. Then, another tugging memory crossed Mambly's mind. "Oh, by the by..."

"What?"

"I saw some peculiar tracks around the place yesterday of the evening. Dirt tracks what ain't familiar to me. Some pockmark tracks outside the winders, some in the ground around the barn. You know who or what they might be?"

Bettilia drifted into the paper shadows.

"No ma'am. Prob'ly just some lost critter."

"Not like any critter I knows. Looked most like man tracks. Nearly. But not exactly man. Hard to read. You seed anythang walking strange hyereabouts lately?"

Turning back to the heat, the fire reclaimed Bettilia's eyes.

"No, *m*-ma'am. Ain't seed nobody."

"Well then."

"Don't worry it, Mambly."

"Don't. Easy word to say. Ye know me."

"Yes. I do, Mambly."

"I got the worried mind."

VERSE 9

Jeremiad

It rained all week and into the next. On Monday Kes's eagle eye found Bettilia Whissler across the room in Civics class, lightning cracking, flashing the windows like this autumn rain spell would never end. Bettilia's pixie-cut hair looked damp at the edges. They never spoke, but Bettilia did squint at him in a kind of recognition. He smiled, waved meekly. Her return wave was fleeting before she snapped open her ring-binder notebook and took up a pencil. To Kes's knowledge Bettilia never looked his way again for the rest of the class. He kept checking. The next day she half-waved again then ignored him for the duration. It became their ritual.

Late Thursday afternoon Kes was passing the choir room and heard voices in song.

She lives across the stormy waters...

Through the small window in the door—as if through a spyglass—he spied Bettilia Whissler—inside, standing third row, second from the left, her voice floating on that sea shanty, that song about the Shenandoah. When Bettilia glanced toward the eyeball in the door it rolled out of sight. By the time Bettilia emerged from choir practice Kes had skedaddled away.

In the course of that week Kes received four letters of love from Chalice Dillard. Kes wrote no letters in return. This was not how he planned it. He had every intention, every night, of sitting down to pour his heart, his mournful desires, out on paper so his words might be whisked away to Savannah shores, into the ravenous hands of his someday-soon fiancee. But, night after night his pen failed to meet the paper, and no pages were sent.

Mostly, Kes kept thinking about Bettilia Whissler.

Kes did not know why. He did not appreciate her personality and he decided she was not even sufficiently cute. She was cute all right, but not *that* cute.

Come the weekend he found himself wanting to return through the rain and kudzu to that tumbledown house and have coffee with that little girl and old woman. He needed to return the hat and coat of course. But Kes could not permit himself to return so soon. It would imply things Kes did not care to imply. Instead, he practiced guitar with brother Glenn. Instead, he fought off impure thoughts with fits of self abuse when brother Glenn was gone to shower, to eat, or sleeping nearby. Instead, he bought a small jar of instant coffee and a paperback copy of *The Warlord Of Mars* by Edgar Rice Burroughs from the T. G.&Y. downtown. With a cup he pocketed in the cafeteria and hot water from the bathroom tap, Kes mixed a black sludge which he drank throughout the day. The brew gave him a wealth of energy as he returned hour by hour to the exploits of one John Carter of Mars—a Christ-like fellow after a fashion—immortal and ready to slay the moneychangers in the temple if need be.

"I still live," John Carter assured the reader.

Despite such Biblical overtones, these activities were worldy things Kes could never have indulged in his mother's house—not to this extent. To Kes, the outer gloom and ever-festering thunder of that weekend provided the perfect storm for his new caffeine addiction, Martian goddesses, and the sins of Onan. This was all a paradox to Kes, since he had once worried over brother Glenn becoming the dope fiend and libertine of the family.

Dark Monday rumbled around again. He spied Bettilia Whissler again in class, still wet around the edges. Despite his forebodings, Kes yearned to go sit beside Bettilia, to ask her endless questions—the kind of questions that were sure to annoy her while providing a tenuous thread—a connection. Kes did not go or sit or ask, but he could no longer deny that he wanted it.

On Tuesday she was missing from class and the rain stopped. The wind rose and took its place.

Bettilia Whissler's desk sat empty. Her name went unanswered at roll call. This made Kes wish he had acted on his desires in some way—not that he knew a way or what way—but some way. His lumpy pinings could find no form or rudder, becoming even more acute when Bettilia did not return to class for the rest of that windy week. By then, Kestrel Brass was in distress.

Friday evening the high winds began to die. This made a lot of kids happy, there was a carnival in town. Talk of carny titillations raced up and down the school hallways. Many had seen the carnival's morning arrival on their way to school—the raising of its tents and rides and odd attractions upsetting while exciting the routine of a small town like Newdundy.

There was no telling how long this weather would hold, so Kestrel Brass took heed. He could not wait another day, not another half day, even if waiting might lead to a fine Saturday walk in warm sunshine. After last class and early supper Glenn said he had a Charlie Louvin song he was hoping they might master in a different key with some flashy guitar work. Kes said no and gave no explanation or apology. Glenn scowled, lying on his bed, twanging in E Minor as he watched his big brother shove a grey slicker and straw hat into a laundry bag then head out the door into the gloaming.

Kes was bundled up with a Shelfy Oak College sweatshirt under his new pea coat, but this did little against the chill seeping into his bones as he made his way past the carnival lights, into the misty countryside. The bar ditches and fields outside town were still wet from a week of heavy soaking. Soon both feet felt numb inside Kes's brogans. He should have dressed warmer. He had never hitched a ride in his life but the thought crossed his mind each time car or pickup truck headlights raked past. None of the headlights slowed. Kes did not hike a thumb. He was either too shy or too polite, he was not sure which. He dreaded the walk back in the coldest pitch of night and knew he would have to hustle to make curfew. Perhaps he could persuade Mambly Whissler to ferry him home in her Chevy if he sprang for the gas using his pocket change. To distract himself from the rising damp Kes spun tales in his head featuring John Carter of Mars slashing red dragons and giant kudzu men whilst spewing verse and invective at these beasts, fiery words straight out of the Book Of Revelation. It was hot fantasy indeed. It helped a little.

After he left the highway Kes entered the long slew of kudzu overhung with tree boughs, a darkling green tunnel with the gateless gap and moonlit pasture at the end. He finally crossed into the open field where the little house sat still and dark beneath a rusty orange moon. His heart sank. Kes wondered if he had come all this way for nothing. The place looked lifeless, dark, abandoned.

Stepping onto the porch, Kes knocked at the door. He waited, knocked again. He got no response. It was still early enough in the evening, there should be some light inside those black windows if anyone was here—unless the old lady and girl had gone to bed at sundown. But no light glowed within. If not for the clay pots and clutter on the porch one might think they had moved. But Miss Whissler was not the sort to be moved out so easily, not with a packrat's lifetime in this nest.

Kes did what he was called to do. He came off the porch and around to the pecan tree. Peering up through the moon-mottled tangle of branches, Kes called up.

"Bettilia! You up there?"

Nothing moved high in that leafy canopy, nothing except the chilling breeze that made Kes bundle his crossed arms more tightly. His gaze dropped again, searching the yard, the barn and field. His bone-deep shivering made Kes consider donning the slicker inside the laundry sack. But, putting the raincoat on to get warmer would mean Kes had traveled this great distance for no cause at all. No, like it or not, he would have to leave the coat and hat, returning to his room without knowing the welfare or whereabouts of Mambly and Bettilia. Kes returned to the porch, setting the folded coat and hat at the foot of the screen door. He shoved the wadded laundry sack in his coat pocket. Before he went, Kes felt compelled to take one last closer look inside—hands cupping his face flat against a window pane. It was too dark in there to see much except vague shapes and shadows and a shaft of moonlight which slashed the back wall of the room, cutting in from a side window.

A face rose fast in front of Kes's.

Kes startled, his heart leapt, he stood his ground.

"Whatcha looking at, jaybird?"

Bettilia was asking inside the glass.

"You," he faltered.

"What *br*-brung you here?"

"You. I was looking for you."

"Well, here I am. You *g*-got your look. Now why don't you *g*-git?"

"Maybe you could just let me in a spell? Mite cold

out here."

"Oh..." Bettilia began to hesitate but jumped over it. "Awright, I s'pose."

She disappeared from the window and the door jangled open. Kes stepped inside, closing the door behind him. The house was iron cold, unheated, but it was better than the bite of that wind out there. Before Kes could speak, Bettilia turned, slipping away fast into shadow, toward the kitchen. Kes followed fitfully, bumping into furniture and door frames as he went. He found Bettilia in the dark kitchen as she pulled a match from her pocket and struck flame. She turned on the knob at the stove, dragged the coffee pot onto the burner. She stood silent, grim, waiting for the burner to light until the match burned her fingers. She shook it out. Turning off the knob, Bettilia turned like a little wind-up toy then plopped onto a chair.

"Butane *t-t*-tank's outer gas," she said flatly. An odd tilt of her head and Bettilia's hazel eyes met the moon outside the window.

Kes stepped sidelong into the room, stopping across the table from her.

"Why all the lights out?" he asked gently.

"Bulbs all *bl*-blowed, I s'pose." She spake as if she were sleeping, murmuring whilst dreaming.

"Bettilia, how—are you *okay*?"

"Fine. Fine as a fiddle hair."

"That's a good question, ain't it?"

"If'n you say so."

"How's Miss Whissler?"

"*D-D*-Dead, I reckon."

"Dead?"

"Yep. Dead. I reckon."

"I best call Mama."

"Why *f*-for?"

"No—I'll call Daddy."

"Why?" she said to the flat windowglass.

"He'll know what to do?"

"Only they ain't *n-n*-nothing *n-n*-nobody can do. Ain't none gonna care. Not about a dead *M*-Mambly."

"Bettilia—?"

"Kes—"

"You got a telephone?"

"Yep. Telephone dead too."

"How long all this been dead?"

"Three days—four. I dunno."

"Where is she?"

"Who?"

"Mizz Whissler."

"Done *b-b-b*-buried."

"You done buried her?"

"Yep."

"Where?"

"Out in the *k*-kudzu. Behind the barn."

"You toted her out there by yourself?"

"Yes, jaybird."

"How'd a little thing—?"

"Done told you. Strong for my size."

"Hell, yeah. You must be."

"That's right," she said to herself. "I must be."

"Show me, Bettilia. Show me where you put her."

Her face turned from the glass, her moonlit eyes beseeching him, filled with quiet hysteria.

"You take a peekaboo outside first—"

"Me?"

"See that they ain't no *b*-boogers about."

Kes did as he was told. He walked from room to room, peeking out each window. He saw nobody lurking.

"Ain't nobody out there as I can see," he told her when he returned.

Bettilia's acceptance and gaze floated somewhere in midair betwixt herself and Kes. She rose slowly, moving from the kitchen to the screened back porch, out the slapping screen door. Kes went with her, down the steps, across the windblown side yard, past the butane tank and the open barn doors with the Chevy inside. Behind the barn Bettila stopped, her hand indicating a narrow rift in the creeping hedge of wet kudzu.

"She's buried in there?" Kes asked.

"Yep." Bettilia squatted before the leafy grave, hugging her knees. "I reckon that makes her the *k*-kudzu woman."

"She told you that tale?"

"She tole me Bible-loads of tales. Ever kind they is. And I *wo-wo*-wove her one or two."

"I know your Mambly was old, but—what took her from us?"

"Death took her, *j*-jaybird. You don't know? Ever harvest leaves some strange, withered fruit."

"But, how'd it take her?"

"Hanged herself from that pecan tree over yonder, din't she."

"Hanged? Mambly done *hanged* herself?"

"I reckon. I come home from school, near dark, wore out from walking. I almost come in the house afore I noticed her. But her Mambly *sh-*shoes caught my eye, them button shoes swinging in the wind. There *M-M-*Mambly were, her head near popped oft, that scrawny *n-*neckbone of hers odd *k-k-*kiltered, jist swinging. Hanged by bobwire, she were."

Kes sank down beside Bettilia, his lips at her ear.

"But—that don't seem like her *at all,* little as I knew her."

Bettilia's face turned and met his without expression.

"Nope. It don't. Do it?"

"Then why would she—"

"Who knows what festers inside of folks?"

"You didn't call the sheriff?"

"Nope. Phone don't work. Besides, no sheriff gonna resurrect her or do a dang thing. I mean, she's jist another old colored lady. Ain't she?"

"And your electric is cut off too?"

"Yep. Maybe she din't pay the bills. Who knows."

"Who knows?"

"Or maybe *he* cut the wires."

"He *who*?"

Bettilia bent forward and began crawling into the kudzu, the leaf quickly engulfing her. Kes watched, barely discerning her shape now, as she lay down, curled like a baby alongside the narrow grave. If he had not seen her crawl in he would not have known she was in there, under there. Kes scooted into the edge of the kudzu and whispered in at her.

"He who?"

Her voice floated out at him—

"Feller I seen."

"Seen where?"

"Poking around the place sometimes when he think we'uz off from the house. He din't know I was spying him from up that pecan tree."

"When was this?"

"Aw, must of been a month or more back. He come around two times. Peeping in winders."

"He do anything else?"

"Nope—just peeping in the winders."

"You recognize him?"

Kes heard her rustle inside the kudzu, like she was gathering thoughts under there.

"Nope. Nope. Stranger."

"What he look like?"

More rustling.

"Oh, I dunno. Just a wayfarer is all. A burnt feller."

"Burnt?"

"Yup. Like a long fried weasel in boots. On muleback. His face was scarred pert bad."

On a mule? Kes remembered what Mambly said about her troubles, and about hoof tracks around the house.

"You reckon *he* kilt her?" Kes asked.

The kudzu heaved a long, troubled sigh.

"Nope," her voice said soft.

"Well, you seen sign or tracks of *anybody else* since then?"

The kudzu did not answer. Kes leaned his face closer, asking gently of the kudzu leaf.

"Anybody else since then?" he repeated.

Her voice came out, but barely heard.

"Nope. Not nobody."

"What then?"

"Reckon she done hung herself is all."

"Bettilia?"

"Yuh?"

"You say a prayer over her?"

"Nope."

"You don't say no prayers."

"She did. But I don't."

Kes sat back on his haunches, pondering the narrow grave. Then he stood. Somehow, this did not seem right to Kes—that this kindly old woman who had treated him so well, welcomed him in and fed him, had been laid to rest without words or song over her passing. Kes's good heart dwelt at the edges of this dilemma until, without decision, he began singing in tender eulogy.

Where dost thou at noontide resort with thy sheep
  To feed on the pastures of love?

Divinely, on perfect cue, her harmony emerged. That uncanny, bewitchingly plangent sound joined with Kes's timbre, coming from the girl in the kudzu.

Say why in the valley of death should I weep
Or alone in the wilderness rove?

Their voices entwined through ghostly chorus on cool night air until they resolved their voices together, in completion of their song. There was long silence before Kes spake.

"Bettilia—?"

"Huh?"

"Got any eggs?"

"If any chickens be left, we *g-g*-got eggs."

"Good."

"If'n some egg-sucking black hellhound ain't *g*-got em."

Since that scenario had never occurred to Kes, he refused to dwell on it.

"Would you like a fried egg sandwich?"

"Mmmm—yes. I would."

"Well, then, I'll fry you an egg."

"How so? We ain't got *n*-no gas?"

"Matter of fact, you do. I noticed when we passed your butane tank. Somebody just turned off the gas valve is all. Let's go fry you an egg."

"I sure would like a fried egg sandwich."

"I sure would like to fry you one. So why don't you come on out of that kudzu and help me find a skillet?"

For once, Kes did not have to ask twice. Out of the kudzu she came.

VERSE 10

Black Cat Begats

After Daddy Brass moved out of Angelsprey House on Officer's Row, Georgiana Brass began to feel the burden of guilt. Being the center of the cosmos as she knew it, Georgiana felt she and she alone was responsible for this fracture in the family unit. Except when it was all Daddy Brass's doing, that is. Yes, Mama George had been remiss in the spiritual vigor of her own home. So she began attending her beachside Baptist church with a renewed and addictive fervor. Every time the doors were open Georgiana was in the sanctuary. She read the Bible to her boys for a dedicated hour each night before bed. She told them they should embrace the gospel as the unerring word of God and testify to others, asking one and all if they too had supped at His table.

"Have you accepted the Lord Jesus Christ as your personal savior?" Georgiana instructed. "That is the righteous catechism, the good and Godly question—the only worthy introspect. All else is flotsam."

Trapped together in their big house on this little island

outside Savannah, the sons of Georgiana Brass were left with little escape from such righteousness.

But the Brothers Brass resisted her will in other ways. Try as she might, Georgiana could not get them to speak properly at all times, as she did, or erase from their vocabulary the slovenly influences of their father or their other less-cultured classmates with their low country gullah aberrations. For Kes and Glenn it was fun to play hillbilly. They played it until it wasn't play anymore, until they became what they aspired to be. It was release. When they spake they oft spake in tongues, tongues of the backwaters, the tongues of those who would soon be their most devoted flock. And those folks liked to hear their gospel talked that way. It was also a slang-powered rebellion, an openly sly subversion of their mother's polite society and total dominance. Only in fits and spurts could Georgiana prevail on that front. She might make her boys behave—or else. She might keep them from cussing outright or swimming in the deep green sea. But she could not make them enunciate or bring them to forever abandon ain't, wudn't, prob'ly, nearly 'bout, or the lure of the double-negative. Their taste for rough tongues wore her down. In time, Georgiana all but surrendered, nearly 'bout.

To compound matters, little Glenn developed an early habit of toying with his mother's mind and the minds of others, expressing twisted thoughts and tangled words with a straight expression just to test their mettle, to see where it took them.

"Howdy," little Glenn would say when introduced to his

mother's church circle. "Mama, Kes, and me are like two peas in a pod."

It often took a moment or two or a question or more before the victim got wise. Glenn's sly enjoyment of his playful put-ons drove his mother and others to regular distraction when his innocent mask and manner wasn't provoking laughter in all around him—his mother included. What was a Mama George to do?

In contrast to little brother, Kes was more of a mystery to her. Kes was a brooder, wandering off alone in the big house, to some dark corner where he could wrestle growing demons he dared not share.

Kes knew that dice games, betting the bolitia numbers, and drinking hard spirits was wrong. His mama told him so. His pastor Brother Dub told him so. His schoolteacher Miss Oglethorpe told him so. So he did not indulge in such things. Not that Kes had many opportunities for such indulgence whilst still wearing short pants and a burr haircut. But he did spend long summer days in that tree house with Glenn. They played games, drew on the walls in crayon, took turns trying to shove each other out the windows, and spent endless hours looking through the spyglass, across the swelling waves of the Atlantic. They could see the regular trail of sea traffic, the trade ships with fanciful flags, the tugs, and the occasional sloops sailing into the estuary of the Savannah River. Kes also swore he saw great sea beasts, pirate vessels, bare-breasted mermaids, and Nazi submarines on a regular basis.

"Thems just weavers in your melon, brer" Glenn told

him. But Kes swore all to be true all the same.

If Kes had also told his brother or anybody else that he often spied Satan himself—hairy, hunchbacked, and prancing cloven-hooved on the beach—he suspected Mama George would have him back to see the doctor or the preacher or both. That prancing devil went by the name Clootie. Kes knew for it had come to him in a dream once when was running high fever. Or his mama told him. Or his dying grandmother. He was not really sure after a while. But Clootie he was and Kes feared Clootie coming closer to their home or climbing this tree to snatch the Brass boys away. Kes had once felt safer from Cloots with Daddy Brass at home. But now his daddy was gone—or might as well be—to Kes's thinking. Only by accident, by repetition, did Kes discover a sure and secret—though temporary—reprieve. Singing songs at play in their treehouse seemed to ward off that Clootie and keep him at bay, for now.

Georgiana did not like or approve of their high oak haven, but she bore it. And, in return, the tree bore her fruit. It was from the high perch of that treehouse that Georgiana first heard her sons sing a psalm in a natural, unforced brotherly harmony.

Little birdie, little birdie, what makes you fly so high?
It's because I'm a true bird, and do not fear to die—

Kes had often sung little songs to himself as he toddled around the place, but she had never before heard their voices entwined in such pure and sacred communion.

Georgiana would never forget that first childsong.

Little birdie, little birdie, come and sing me a song,
I'm a short time to be here and a long time
to be gone—

When the boys finally came down from their treehouse that afternoon they found their mother sitting on the edge of her bed in tears.

She felt their talent was God's gift and even she could not deny it, despite her fears. She rang up Brother Dub who, upon hearing them sing *Oh, How I Love Jesus,* agreed that they needed expert guidance commensurate with their gift. He too made a phone call and the brothers began vocal training with an old fellow named Thorley Ricks who had sung with several gospel groups professionally, including The Trinity Four and The Joyful Gents. Twice a week Georgiana drove the boys into town where they spent three hours with Mr. Ricks in his parlor on Chippewa Square. All who heard them from that time forward were entranced by the way Kes's tenor naturally found sterling passage atop Glenn's soothing baritone. Georgiana was not the last woman who wept from the sword of her boys' voices in song.

Even Daddy Brass was quick to admit that they sang "real pure-dee sweet and purty." The first time he heard them warble *Whispering Hope* during one of his return visits home, he pulled out his wallet, gave them each a fiver for the show, then offered to hire a hillbilly band, hook them up with a promoter, and stake the whole shebang to a string of one-niters on the summer carny circuit. He suggested they call themselves The Big Brass Balladeers. Only he mispronounced "Balladeers."

But Mama George was having none of it.

"These two young men are *psalm-singers*, their voices born to serve the Lord, Malakoff Brass," she said. "And His will be done."

When she came back from the kitchen a few minutes later and caught Daddy Brass teaching them the words to *Doodle Hole Blues* she told him to leave her house forthwith and take his nasty ten dollars with him. The boys stood agape as Mama George yanked both bills from their hands and threw them at their father. Daddy smiled.

"I knew a little gal who was very, very nice," he sang from his belly, putting on his hat as he scooped up the money. *"She got to doodle once but she want to doodle twice—"*

Later, after he had left, Kes and Glenn found the two fivers tucked in a notch of the oak tree. The next day, while Mama was at a Daughters Of The Confederacy luncheon, they bought themselves bottles of Chocolate Soldier, a bagful of jawbreakers, two squirt guns, and fourteen Action comics which they hid in the treehouse.

The boys' first public performance outside church was in a revival tent at the Exchange Park Fairgrounds. Billed for the first time as The Brothers Brass, they wore matching dark blue suits Mama had sewn herself. Everybody said they looked adorable. By then the boys had honed a six-song repertoire which they often sang with their eyes closed due to stage fright. That night they opened with *On The Jericho Road* and closed with their brotherly arrangement of *I Shall Not Be Moved.*

"*Just like a tree standing by the water,*" they sang, "*we shall not be moved—*"

They were very well received. The preacher passed the plate and they made twenty-eight dollars and forty-nine cents. Sitting on the front bench in that tent that night, their Mama George's head and bosom swelled with pride and promise.

This debut performance led to the Brothers Brass doing guest spots for several months on a local fifteen-minute gospel radio program sponsored by the J.F. Goodson Coffee Company. They became local household names. Listeners loved those little boys and the mail flooded the station.

"We're working on the building, it's a true foundation, we're holding up the blood-stained banner for Our Lord—"

And working on the building, Mama said, meant building their repertoire of song, a little bit every day.

"Can Kes and Glenn come out and play half rubber wid us," the neighbor boy would ask.

"Not at this time, Peabo," Georgiana would tell him. "These boys need practice and have more compelling things to do than swat at some loopy half-a-ball with a broomstick. A sound presentation requires constant cultivation."

"Can they come swimming wid us later den?"

"Of course not."

The Brothers Brass began to appear often on weekends at churches, tent revivals, and the occasional bluegrass or gospel jamboree. They began to make some money. At the churches and revivals they accepted love offerings from the congregation, which was often over fifty dollars. Once in Charleston they came home with almost two hundred dollars. There had been some high-rollers at that camp meeting—high rollers wearing strange hats who sifted in with even stranger women from the Shriner's convention across the street. There had been much weeping, repenting, and one blubbering chap from Biloxi even wrote Mama George a personal check. At the big jamboree shows Mama always negotiated their fee in advance. She always accompanied them and she never let either boy out of her sight.

At times it felt to Kes and Glenn like little of their lives were spent out of their mama's sight. Life outside their home or godly vocation was no different. In the beginning, Mama George walked them to grade school six blocks going and was waiting to walk them the six blocks back when the bell rang at end of day. Later, Mama George drove them to middle school whilst the other kids took the bus. She was taking no chances. By then rock'n'roll came flying out of passing car windows like a big string of Black Cat firecrackers. To their mama and the other landed gentry, it was as if all those joints and clubs on West Broad Street had spilled their boogified grunt and grind into the living rooms and laps of sleepy white Savannah.

Mama George allowed no television or radio in her house; she said her boys' music was solace enough for her world. But even she could not escape this rise of jungle jigaboo music in the streets, shrubs, and trees around her home. She took note that this musical upheaval coincided with Glenn's grades beginning their steady slide to mostly Cs and the occasional B.

Bombabombabomba baby baby little baby—

Elvis wanting to play house with his sex and swagger scared the pee-waddin out Mama George, as Glenn would one day say.

Well, you wear low dresses, the sun comes
shining through,
I can't believe my eyes all that mess belongs to you—

She never let on, even to herself, how much that Hillbilly Cat evoked the swagger of one Malakoff Brass, if the Hillbilly Cat was an uglier, louder, middle-aged man with a belly. That Jerry Lee creature, Little Richard, Screaming Jay whoever—they were surely baptized at Malakoff's altar. Fortunately her havens of home and church protected her from too much brutality. She did not know about the transistor radio in the treehouse, the radio secretly purchased with funds dropped in buckets from Holy Ghost-guided hands. If the tree dwellers kept the volume low they hoped Mama George would think the taunting tinkle came from somewhere farther off, down the street, from some pack of unwashed heathens nesting outside Officer's Row.

Even without that little tree radio Kes and Glenn would have heard. They could not help but hear the wail of Elvis—

then the Everly Brothers—beckoning them from bedrooms and shop windows.

Yes, the Everlys. The Brothers Everly. Phil and Don. Kes and Glenn never spake of the Everlys—no, not even to each other. That is how palpably those other brothers' path beckoned and haunted. Anytime *Bird Dog* or *Cathy's Clown* warmed the transistors in their treehouse, the Brothers Brass fell silent and rapt, the air betwixt them thick with implication. Not that Kes or Glenn could foretell a way—outside of their juvenile fantasies—to gain any footing on that path. For them, that path ended before it ever began. That path had a jagged and bottomless Mama George they could never leap over. If the Everly Brothers had ever registered fully on Georgiana's radar, she would have been absolutely undone. Mercifully, she never took proper notice of the popular brother act, thereby sparing her heart from such mortified terror. Mama George's boys had no place in this dreadful rocking and rolling, she told herself. People who played beastly trash like that did not even want her boys. Mama knew what they wanted. What they wanted was as plain as dogs rutting on the front lawn, wasn't it?

What she did not know was that little brother had started dropping aspirins into his RC Colas when they made play dates and Kes was not about to tell her. Georgiana was beside herself most of the time as it was and—for better or worse—the Brothers Brass were becoming so caught up in the fervor and condemnations they heard at their own performances (condemnations of those radio devils) that the two were like young perch on salvation's trot line. For them, the smoky allure of boogie and bop were fated to be echoes of sinful ecstasy that enticed as much as that wanton sea outside their door—always there, but just out of reach, forever denied them. For, first and foremost, the Brothers Brass were good boys who must set good examples for all the other youths who came with their families to hear them. The Brothers Brass must deny all sinful urges lest they risk drowning in perdition whilst pulling all those other boys and girls down with them.

"Why, their little souls are in your hands," she told them. "Don't you understand?"

So they became strange boys, boys whose young lives moved both inside and outside the daily rhythms of other Savannah teenagers. In other ways they were not so strange. A Brass boy's rhythm was vamped with Jesus, restless pride, love of music—and even a tart twist of vanity. But his rhythm did not vamp outside the hormonal storm soon raging in all boys their age. As it turned out, there were quite a few pretty girls—pretty girls like Chalice Dillard, the island mayor's daughter—who fancied strange boys with enough spending money for a Bubble Up soda or an ice cream. Mama George did not dole out extravagant amounts of anything to her sons, but she did provide them a three-dollar-a-week allowance, which they had certainly earned. It was good money for a high school kid in those days.

The first major skip in their rhythm track came when Kes marched up to Mama George and Glenn waiting on the school sidewalk after the last bell.

"Mama, y'all go on without me. I believe I'll walk Chalice

home today," Kes said, shrugging toward the pretty redhead with bangs standing over his shoulder. "I'll come straight to home after."

Proper introductions were made. A shy Chalice took Mrs. Brass's hand whilst Mrs. Brass failed to muster a cogent rebuttal in her overtaxed brain. Her fear of sex—that red horned demon—had returned to roost, having shape-shifted from a hairy male beast into a pretty young redhead with bangs.

"You two use the crosswalk, no jaywalking," Mama George called after them as Kes and Chalice walked away, not daring to hold hands till they were out of sight. "And, Kestrel, you've still got leaves to rake and porches to sweep before supper, don't forget. And supper is at six sharp, as usual. So don't shillyshally."

So, for the first time, Glenn walked home alone with his mother. It was a very quiet walk. Glenn was afraid to ask obvious questions about his brother's new interest and Mama George was afraid to comment on any of it for fear she might give Glenn ideas of his own.

Kes first met Chalice in Sunday School, then later they shared Algebra Class together where they began passing notes to pass the tedium. She was a budding beauty, proper and polite in public, and this made it difficult for Mrs. Brass to express disapproval over such wholesome puppy love, especially since Chalice's family was so high profile and approving of Kes. The young couple went to the occasional movie, driven by the mayor himself. They did nothing but hold hands for almost four months before Chalice let him kiss her. In time, Daddy Brass caught wind of the situation but went easy on any teasing of his son on such a ripe subject. Still, Kes felt oddly compelled to steer Chalice Dillard clear of his daddy. And Kes never took her up into the treehouse. Chalice refused to go.

Meanwhile, the random Miltown pill or codeine with a trace of sherry wine helped Georgiana Brass through the adolescent days and nights to come when the imminent threat of red-banged sex became too difficult to bear otherwise.

Then, as if boogie music and puberty weren't enough to rattle her nerves, February 5, 1958 gave Georgiana and the entire island something bigger and even more threatening to worry about. In the wee hours of the morning a crippled B-47 bomber was forced to dump its payload—a two-and-a-half ton hydrogen bomb—into the waters just off the coast before making emergency landing at Hunter Airfield. The presence of an H-Bomb in the silt and murky shallows within earshot of Georgiana's bedroom window was enough to turn her into a nerve pill junkie, and it did. In years to come Mama George got her painkillers from two—then three—unsuspecting doctors in the city. They were little yellow pills which she chewed two at a time, downing them with ginger ale in the morning, sherry wine at night. She liked to practice moderation. Sometimes, to keep things interesting, she combined them with a green capsule a fourth doctor prescribed. For over sixty days the Navy and Air Force searched and dredged offshore without ever finding the bomb. Then they made the official proclamation that their efforts had been fruitless—but there was no need worry, they said. They said the bomb had not contained its detonating device, despite its innards being stuffed with four hundred pounds of high explosives and enriched uranium. Later they proclaimed it to have been a dummy bomb on a training mission.

"Horseshit," Daddy Brass said to Georgiana when he heard that one. "The U.S. gubment don't spend two months and a few hunert thousand dollars hunting for no dummy that cain't blow."

Leave it to that man to salt her wounds.

Georgiana just knew she was going to be a Fifty-Foot Glowing Woman very soon or blown sky high through those pearly gates to her Maker. Two weeks after her government left her sitting on a slow ticker, the medicinal powers of Mama George's little yellow nerve bombs were tested to the limit when she received word that her beloved Aunt Zazu was on her death bed. Then Kestrel Brass had sass enough to ask for a car.

"It's a '52 Cranbrook with good tires. Only sixty-six thousand miles," Kes said. "Tom Burly down at the Pure Oil station says he'll let me have it for three hunert fifty dollars cash."

"It is *hundred,* Kes—not *hunert.* Sometimes you boys' language is just atrocious. And your father is spiteful help with the example he sets." She tossed a sheet over the upstairs clothesline. "I suppose you know your little brother is scoring a D in Problems Of Democracy? His teacher just telephoned."

"Yes, ma'am. Three hundred fifty dollars is all he wants."

"He wants to be *bribed* to make decent grades?"

"Not Glenn, Mama—Mr. Burly. Three hundred fifty is all he wants for the Cranbrook."

"*All* he wants. That is a lot of money."

"But it's *my* money—ain't it, Mama?"

The clothespin snapped like a death sentence. She was slow to clip her next pin on his damp linen trousers.

"Oh, me ... Kes," she spake carefully, moving the length of the upstairs porch to the other end of the line, away from him. "Wouldn't you rather have a nice new Schwinn bicycle? Instead of somebody's hand-me-down?"

"Bikes are for little children," he said, following her. "Me and Chalice, we—"

"Chalice and *I*—"

"Chalice and I—"

"Why the great capitals of Europe are teeming with adults of every age and persuasion peddling their bicycles to work, to shop, running this errand and that—"

"I've got my license now and—"

"Perhaps that was my first mistake."

"—and I figure it's time I had a car of my own for doing my own business and taking Chalice to the library or to the Lucas for a show."

"The library is a healthy walk away, good for heart and mind. And Mr. Dillard told me he does not mind driving you children to the picture show one bit. It tickles him no end."

"You fail to grasp the situation, Mama."

"You know I have to leave you boys on your own tomorrow morning. I must journey all the way to Nashville. I only hope Aunt Zazu will linger that long. But when I get back—well, if you insist upon driving, perhaps I could steer my way clear to lend my car for your little outings with this girl."

"Mama, you fail to grasp—"

"She is a darlin girl, in her own special way. Yes, I'll just loan you my car."

"I want my *own* car, Mama. I want that Cranbrook with only sixty-six thousand miles on her. Bought with my *own* money. Money me and Glenn *earnt*."

Georgiana dropped her clothespins into the basket at her feet. Slowly, she walked to the porch swing and sat. She began to quietly weep.

Kes was unprepared for this. He had heard his mother cry from somewhere behind closed doors, but he had never actually witnessed her tears. He moved to the swing and sat beside her.

"I'm sorry, Mama. I didn't mean to get ugly with you. I'm sorry I raised my voice—"

"I don't have it, Kes," she blurted.

"Don't have it? Don't have what?"

Georgiana looked out across the ocean, floating elsewhere in her mind.

"Daddy used to say I was useless as tits on a bull," she said.

Kes did not take long to digest this.

"He shouldn't of said that, mama. That's just wrong."

Her face got longer as she turned back and met Kes's eye.

"I don't have the money to give you. I would not want to if I did, but I would. But I can't because I don't have it."

"Don't have it? Where is it? Is Daddy keeping it?"

"Of course not. I would never give him access to your funds."

"Well—where did it go?"

"Most of it is spent," she sniffled, pulling a hanky from her smock. "It gets spent week in and week out."

"Spent for what?" he asked, his eyes darkening, pity giving way to anger.

"These clothes, upkeep on this big dreadful house I've come to hate, food on the table, the replacement for that cracked commode upstairs, the new divan forced upon us when the old one collapsed. We are house poor, Kes. My father had a military pension and some stocks that went sour. He did not leave us with as much as you might think."

"Why don't you just sell it, Mama?" Kes could not believe he was saying this, this was the only world he knew. But he said it. "Buy something we can afford."

"Oh, I can't do that. Angelsprey is my father's house, your grandfather's house. You never knew him. But I could never sell Angelsprey. Still—it is fiscal torment, day after day, week after week. I told myself I would to set aside half of everything you boys earned for your higher education and your future. And that money would be yours. But I have failed. I have failed to do that. I have failed my family, my boys. Life's kept pecking at me. Like a gobbler pecking for a penny here and a dollar there till most of it is gone come end of each month."

"I'm sorry, Mama," he said, laying his hand on hers. "I didn't know we were house broke."

Georgiana wanted to laugh at his accidental joke. She

needed to find gaiety in his slip of tongue, but gaiety was nowhere in her. Her eyes fell, aching to hold his hand like a lover. She fought back the urge.

"People think we are wealthy. We are not. Oh, I have money enough in the bank for us to keep going, barely. But never enough it seems. So we are not broke, not really." She looked up at him, finding her steel again. "We are not broken."

"Of course we're not, Mama. We are not broken..."

"That is why, Kestrel—that is why I cannot give you money for a vehicle. Your money. I dearly wish I could. It would worry me sick, to see you behind the wheel. But I do wish I could."

"You ain't failed us, Mama."

"Don't say ain't, dear."

"Glenn and me, you helped us find our calling, our truest path."

She smiled weakly through her tears, then touched his cheek.

"I don't know what I would do without you," Georgiana whispered.

"There's just one thing I still don't grasp, Mama."

"What is that, my darlin?"

"Daddy Brass—don't he give you any money? I mean, money for *us*?"

Georgiana's well dried up. She stopped crying, stopped smiling, and withdrew her hand. Wiping away her last errant tear, she slid the hanky back into her smock pocket.

"I will not discuss that with you," she spake, finally. She

got up and returned to the clothesline.

"But I, I don't—" Kes fumbled, rising after her. "Daddy must give you *something.*"

"That is betwixt me and your father. Now let this rest. I will do my best to set aside funds, a little each week, so we can acquire a vehicle. In your name. It is unlikely to be this Cranbrook you crave. Someone is sure to snatch up such a prize before we have sufficient capital. Perhaps, by next summer, this can be arranged." She turned back to him, steady now. "Would that be alright, son?"

Kes could not help but smile, his venom sapped away.

"You're the original peach, Mama." He leaned down, kissing her forehead.

She did not kiss him back. Kes barely noticed. She never kissed him or anyone else anymore. The last kiss he could remember from his mother was when he wore peejays with footies.

Kes went downstairs, then out to the street. He was heading over to the park to hunt up Glenn who he suspected was playing half rubber with that gang that was always there. Kes had just landed on the old brick pavement when he heard her song. It was a woeful old song she sang, her soprano drifting soft down through the leaf and dripping moss. He knew her voice. Yes, it was his mama's song.

The key's in the mailbox, the same as before,
But no one is waiting for me anymore,
The end of our story is there on the door,
A cottage for sale...

VERSE 11

Friends by Shame Undefiled

Kes and Bettilia ate their fried egg sandwiches in silence by the light of a hurricane lamp. Afterward, Kes asked if she needed money for the electric bill.

"Nope. Don't worry your silly *p*-poke about that," she said. "I nary had electric in my life till Mambly got it four *y*-year ago."

Then she told him it was best for him to leave now. Kes found it all very odd and wondered how she could live with no electric and no telephone and it occurred to him that he might not see her at school anymore since Mambly Whissler was dead, buried, and sung over. But he did as he was told. He left her there alone, inside that house on the pasture.

After his late night visit, a lonely weekend passed. Kes looked for her at school on Monday to no avail. Tuesday also passed without a Bettilia spotting. He had almost resigned himself to her permanent absence when, on Wednesday in civics class, Bettilia Whissler's name was called and he heard her answer "yes." He looked across the room and there she sat at her desk. She was wearing her cornflower blue dress. She smiled at him sweetly. Very sweetly. Then she began taking notes, ignoring his ever-present gaze. Class passed like winter sorghum with Kes doing a poor job of taking his own notes or keeping his eyes off her bowed head and scribbling hand. When class was over, she left without uttering another word. Kes wondered how she had squared her long absence with the school. She seemed to be a very capable girl. He liked that about her. Yet she also troubled him with a lonesome and longing he had never felt before. And he realized for the first time how much he wanted to go with her, wherever she was going.

That night, Kes told little brother Glenn about Bettilia's current predicament, or most of it. Well, just part of it really. In fact, he left out the big stuff. He didn't mention old Mambly's grave or the part about the burnt stranger Bettilia saw snooping about before she found her old Mambly hanging in the wind. Kes was not even sure if that burnt man ever existed or was just some wayfaring figment of Bettilia's imagination. Kes also neglected to inform brother about his nagging desire to tag along with this girl wherever she might go. Besides, this desire might be an urge which would pass but, in the meantime, leak its way back to the shores off Savannah to Chalice Dillard.

"But Bettilia, she's stuck alone out there. No phone, no electric," Kes told Glenn. "A sorry circumstance if you ask me."

"Where's her old woman?" Glenn asked.

"She don't know and she won't tell a sheriff. She ain't

got no birth certificate and—young as she looks—she's afraid they'll put her in a orphan home."

"Yeah. They probably would at that," said Glenn.

Glenn found Kes's tale quite occupying. He even expressed desire to meet this Bettilia Whissler.

"Whatsay you and me pack our insterments of destruction out there and follow up on her," Glenn offered.

"Why would you wanna go all the way out there, brer?"

"That's how Mama raised us, right?"

"Watch out, brother," Kes said wearily. "If you don't mind your peas, you'll wind up hymn leader in a leper colony."

"Well, maybe we can sing a smile on her face."

Glenn had always been a kind soul at heart. And Kes could think of no reason—or desire—to drag his feet about it.

Saturday morning found the Brothers Brass marching down Fuzzy Lick Road, warm sun and a guitar on each brother's back. Behind them, there were still plenty of **BiG Pups 4 SaLE** and there had been two massive white dogs sounding shaggy warnings up and down inside the fence-line of that farm back there. It was the kind of crisp, apple-fresh day when the brothers could not keep from singing. So they sang as they walked. They sang *Tenbrooks And Molly*. They sang *The Old Rugged Cross*. They kept singing about clinging to that cross until they rounded a curve of road and heard another soul singing. Their own voices fell away as they approached the frail house in the kudzu, as they listened to her contralto voice floating toward them on the autumn air.

O, you Shenandoah, I long to hear you,
Away you rolling river...

They found Bettilia Whissler singing to herself in a nappy red coat, scattering feed for the chickens. She eyed both boys with a wisp of smile, stopped singing, and flicked some grain in their direction.

"I reckon I ain't scary enough," she said.

"Do what?" Glenn asked.

"The meat-eaters ain't scary of my noises."

Glenn cocked his head but Kes took her in stride:

"Reckon you remember my brother Glenn. Glenn this be Bettilia Whissler."

"Oh, yeah," Bettilia said. "You the other bird whose screeching drives growed men to kill. They ever figure out where ole Doc Turlington got that pistol from on Invitation Day?"

"Okay, brother, we can go now," Glenn said, dead serious.

Kes stopped and eyed the sky, shuffling in place.

"Naw, I don't read newspaper much," he mumbled.

"Me neither," Glenn agreed, wondering if Daddy ever got his gun back.

"Welp, you ducks had already strangled two tunes in their tracks that day. Weren't no need to finish off a third."

Kes looked blankly at his brother.

"See what I mean?" Kes asked.

His brother nodded.

"You always this ornery?" Glenn asked Bettilia.

"Pretty much," she answered, her face lighting up. All in

all, she seemed glad for their company.

"Bettilia," Kes said curiously, "you sure do talk country when you're t'home. But you talk good and proper when you sound off in Civics Class."

"I talk one way at Bible school," she replied, a bit testy. "That's for benefit of others. I talks my own way when I'm on my own."

"Yeah," Kes said, "I know what you mean. We does that too."

"Yeah, we does that too," Glenn echoed.

"Yeah, you sure does, don't ye?"

Behind them, Kes and Glenn heard a motor roar against rattling iron. They turned in time to see a police sedan come bucking through the fence gap, then ease up the road to the house. Both brothers looked back to check Bettilia's take on this.

But Bettilia was not there. She had flown without a kick of dust.

Kes returned his gaze to the Newdundy sheriff's sedan—but not before he saw that goosey fear cut loose inside Glenn as Glenn backed off slow.

"Oh, my clear blue Jesus..."

"Steady on, little brother," Kes said. His even timbre halted Glenn's retreat. Any sight of a cop got little brother goosey these days.

The sedan stopped. A jowly, Conquistador-looking man got out with his high cheekbones and sheriff's badge. His skin was dark, his hair white and trim. He wore a pith helmet, like he walked straight out of one of Kes's Tarzan Ape

Man books. His aftershave on the breeze said he just left the barber's chair. The sheriff took a few steps toward the porch before squinting sidelong at the boys in the yard.

"Morning, boys."

"Morning, sir," they piped back in unison but no harmony.

"Miss Whissler be to home?"

The brothers tried not to look at each other or let their faces betray secrets.

"Not so's we can tell, sir," Kes said.

A dark thumb nudged up the safari helmet, the man gave them the once over.

"I'm Sheriff Puck. She know you all out here?"

"Well, sir, funny you should ask that. Mizz Whissler invited us out to sing for her, sir."

"Yes, sir, we come to sing," Glenn injected.

The Sheriff moved toward them, his jowly jaw clenched. He made no effort to hide his suspicion.

"I know you. You them gospel tune boys over to the Bible school. Ain't you?"

"Yes, sir," Glenn told him.

"I'm Kestrel Brass, sir. And this'n is my brother Glenn."

"Please to meetcha," Glenn offered the Sheriff, humbly. But the Sheriff was not ready for any of that.

"You come to sing, you say? How come she ain't here to do the listening?"

"We was just asking the same ourselves, sir," Glenn said, stepping forward, showing preacherly concern. "It ain't like her at all."

Kes marveled at his brother's newfound grit. One would

think brother had known Miss Whissler's knee.

"We ain't in no hurry," Kes added. "Thought she might show up soon."

"Yes sir, Sheriff Puck," Glenn agreed. "We thought she might show."

"I suppose she took that gal of hers with her?" the Sheriff posed.

"Aw, her," Kes said. "Yes sir, I s'pose she did at that."

"You sure about that, boys?"

Kes held the man's eye, in a kindly way.

"Ain't no girl as I can see. Sir."

"Don't that girl go to school with y'all?"

"Yes sir, Sheriff," Glenn said, "I reckon she does. Ain't got no class with her though."

And that was the truth, for a change. Glenn had no classes with Bettilia.

Sheriff Puck studied the ground at his feet. Slowly, he took the .38 revolver from his holster. He dropped open the pistol's chamber, pointed it up at the sun, then spun it. He removed a spent shell casing from the revolver, tossing the empty brass on the ground. He plugged the vacated chamber with a new cartridge from his belt, slapped it shut, then spun it at the sun again. Satisfied, apparently, the sheriff returned the gun the to its sheath.

The brothers stood hypnotized by this display.

"Well, they was long lines at the Piggly Wiggly this morning," the Sheriff said, looking less skeptical at last. "Freezer bin croaked on em yesterday noon and they lost a goodly bit of beef. Bad news on a Friday. You shoulda seen the flies. Coulda been worse. But they's a carnival in town. Carnival man come by and took the bad beef for their animals. Freezer's back on line now though. New condenser coil in from Augusta." The Sheriff finally smiled a little. "Hell, I hear they had to rattle Ole Tom Turlington out of bed at three a.m. He runs cattle up Jasper County. He got em enough chuck and chops to git through the weekend. Looked like half of Newdundy lined up long and early outside the Pig when I drove by. Your Miss Whissler and that little gal are tied up in that mess, most likely. Late getting home."

"Yes. That would do it," Kes agreed.

"Sure enough would," Glenn said.

Sheriff Puck returned to his police sedan and opened the door. Before he got in he gave Kes and Glenn a last appraisal.

"Don't you boys mess with nothing round here."

"Oh, naw sir, we wouldn't do that," Kes professed.

"Not a chance, sir," Glenn said with a head shake.

It felt good to tell the truth again.

"And if you see Miss Whissler—" the Sheriff continued, doffing his helmet, tossing it inside on the car seat, "—tell her she needs to come pick up a hunert dollar check from the newspaper office. She entered that little gal's name in the Tribune's Ghost'N'Goblin lottery and she come up the winning ticket. They been trying to call Miss Whissler all week. They say the line's disconnected."

"Willikers," Glenn whistled. "One hundred bones. What I could do with that."

"You and me both, son. Man can't make a living with all these pale pink socialists in D.C. I voted Ike twicet, but he ain't worth a flip."

"We'll tell Miss Whissler, Sheriff," Kes said. "If we see her."

Yes, Kes knew he would tell her. If he saw her. That was the truth too. Wasn't it? He was not so sure—what with Mambly Whissler being dead and all. He felt things getting shaky again.

Sheriff Puck did not seem to notice or care. The Brothers Brass stood shoulder to shoulder, watching as the Sheriff drove away. The police sedan bucked back through the gap at the gateless gate before being swallowed by a bend of kudzu.

Suddenly, a hard *strum-m-m* of guitar strings rang across Kes's and Glenn's spines and they whirled around.

There stood Bettilia, magically reappeared. She had popped back up like a jack-in-the-box in her nappy red coat.

"You birds handled yourself real good there. Come on inside and I'll boil up coffee. Also got some right nasty cheese you might go for."

"I got a pocketful of rock candy," Glenn offered, a bit off kilter, still recovering from his recent re-encounter with law enforcement.

"That's real fine," Bettilia said with a winsome smile at Kes. "I'm right fond of rock candy."

"You can buy a dump truck of rock candy with a hunert bucks," Kes said, smiling back.

But Bettilia was not biting. She turned on her heel and headed for the house. The Brothers Brass unslung their guitars, following behind her.

"If you don't mind my being nosy," Glenn said as she led them through the front door, "how long you reckon you can fend off folks like that Sheriff and such before you're found out?"

"Ain't got no answers, Glenn-bo," she cracked without looking back. "Just coffee and cheese."

"But what about that hundred?" Glenn persisted.

"They'll wait, Glenn-bo."

"The hundred bones?"

"You betcha."

With that, Bettilia skipped ahead, disappearing into the kitchen as Kes snagged Glenn's shoulder from behind.

Glenn stopped and looked back at him.

"You're getting better," Kes said. "With cops, I mean."

"It's just like picking a guitar long enough, brer. They do pay off."

"What pays off?"

Glenn wiggled his left fingers.

"Callouses."

After Bettilia made coffee they sat on the front porch and sang. The brothers started out singing but soon she joined in. They picked back up with *Molly And Tenbrooks*—but by the time that horse race was run Bettilia was harmonizing right down the middle betwixt Kes and Glenn. Then they sang some slower songs. They sang *Wild Mountain Thyme, I'm A Good Old Rebel,* and *Knoxville Girl.* Glenn quickly began to realize what Kes already knew: Bettilia Whissler had one of the most unearthly, beautiful girl voices he had ever heard. She veered betwixt alto and soprano, going wherever her ear led her, and her ear seemed to know no wrong. What neither brother nor she could have fully known until that morning was how naturally her uncanny voice melded with Kes and Glenn across the full spectrum of their repertoire. With Bettilia, their voices found chords they had never raised and—if asked—would have sworn they had never heard in their young lives. Why, Bettilia sang as if she was a little lost sister, a lost sister now found.

Eventually, Kes and Bettilia's voices fell away as they listened to Glenn sing solo in a warbly falsetto he outright owned:

In prison cell and dungeon vile,
Our thoughts to them go winging,
When friends by shame are undefiled,
How can I keep from singing?

Glenn finished with a delicate finger-picking flourish on his guitar then looked sheepishly over at Bettilia. She beheld him with fresh wonderment.

"You ain't bad," she said.

"Oh, yes, I am," Glenn replied.

VERSE 12

Wilderness of Brass

Before Mama George left for Nashville she left strict instructions.

"You young men are to be inside with the doors locked by eight p.m. each evening," she told them as they loaded her luggage into her aging French Renault. "You'll take supper with Brother Dub and Duchess for the next few days—I should only be two or three days. Duchess will look in on you time to time. You know how to fix your own Maypo cereal of a morning. Your school cafeteria dinners are paid for. I wish you both could accompany Mama. But with mid-semester exams coming up I do not want to take you out of school. Kes must have the grades to enroll in Shelfy Oak Bible College in fall."

"Dang it, Mama," Kes said. "I don't wanna go off by myself. I wanna wait for Glenn."

"This is not the time for that discussion. I'm running late. I will try to telephone whilst I am at Aunt Zazu's. We shall see. Long distance telephone charges are so frightful. And there will be legions of family in that house till after the funeral. All needing to telephone no doubt. Yes, legions of callers." Mama George turned Kes toward her, peering into him. Her voice was stern. "There will be *no* young ladies in *this* house whilst I am gone."

"Yes, Mama," Kes said.

"Yes, Mama," Glenn echoed.

Georgiana looked over at Glenn and smiled. It had never occurred to her to direct that at little brother. Glenn slumped against the fender with a cocksided grin and ran fingers through his hair with a rebellious James Dean flare he had adopted of late. This did not please his mother. Yes, she had noticed his adopted changes of late. Her face went sharp on him.

"Stand up straight, Gaylenn Brass. You are not the Tower of Pisa."

Glenn got sober, stood straight, obliging her until the little black Renault drove out of sight, his mother at the wheel. Then he slumped against the oak tree and gave his big brother a sneering grin again. Kes grinned back, even bigger.

It was an epic moment. It was elation like they had never felt or shared before.

The Brothers Brass had never been free of their mother's gaze for an entire day, much less for multiple days and nights. Nor would they have guessed the depth of heart Mama George felt for her Aunt Zazu, who a young Georgiana visited summers as a girl—a girl who was nursed through the big red measles by her Aunt Zazu. All the brothers could think was God Bless Aunt Zazu and her whiskery chin. This creaking relative Kes and Glenn barely remembered from two visits so many long years ago had just awarded them a brief but sweet liberty.

Of course, there was a not-so-small whirling dervish in Kes's loins which would have liked having Chalice over to the house in days to come, to test his spiritual resolve on the divan or even in his bedroom. But that urge had been foreseen by more than his mama. Mr. and Mrs. Dillard had been notified by Georgiana Brass of her imminent departure, so the Dillards kept a close eye on their daughter while her young man's mother was away. Chalice had to come straight home from school and Kes had to leave their front porch by suppertime. This gave the lovebirds little time to nuzzle before Mrs. Dillard called Chalice to the table and Kes was remanded to the preacher's house for his soulful serving of bread and gravy. At least the brothers got to watch Jack Benny or The Colgate Hour or some good western television program after supper at the preacher's house. Unlike Mama Brass, Brother Dub was considered very progressive in his views on television. He had bought one of the first Zenith sets on the island and his antenna was the tallest. Apparently it never occurred to Mama Brass that her boys dining at the preacher's table could lead to this electric wedge of corruption while she was away. Still, Dub and Duchess limited the boys to one hour of TV before sending them home. Kes even managed to feel a little guilty but giddy each night after those stolen glimpses of flickering comedy stars, cowpokes, and Lucky Strike ads.

But not Glenn. Glenn was guilt-free, giddy or otherwise. Glenn Brass blazed his own trail that week. This was Glenn's moment, he knew it, and he grabbed for the brass ring.

Mama George left on a Tuesday morning. Tuesday evening Glenn and Kes came home from supper with the Dubs, locked the door, then sat up playing Parchessi and drinking two six-packs of RC Colas until almost three in the morning. Kes suspected Glenn was slipping aspirin in his bottle when he made trips to the bathroom—which was often—at that rate of RC consumption.

On Wednesday evening they repeated the routine only Glenn said he was beat and wanted to go to bed early at nine o'clock, a decision Kes found very odd. How many shots at late-night Parchessi did little brother think they were going to get? Time was wasting.

When Kes got up the next morning he noticed that Glenn's bed was empty. He went downstairs and started heating water for Maypo. About five minutes later Glenn came through the kitchen door in jeans, jersey, and tennis shoes.

"Got up early. Went walking the beach," Glenn told Kes, keeping his head low. Kes thought little brother looked a bit ragged like he had not slept at all.

"You beachcomb any nakey mermaids?" was all Kes asked as Glenn ignored him and headed upstairs to shower for school, leaving no sand on the stairsteps. Kes was trying not to boss Glenn so much—at Mama George's request. Kes's overly-noble sense of decency and fair play kept his mouth shut as he scooped a half cup of Maypo.

Mama George telephoned promptly at eight-thirty on Wednesday night. Kes took the call, afraid to tell her that Glenn had missed supper or that little brother was still not home. He asked his mama a lot of featherbrained questions about her trip and the state of Aunt Zazu, stalling against that dreaded moment when she asked to speak with Glenn. Mama George told him Aunt Zazu had rallied a bit at the sight of Mama—her favorite niece—and had not yet passed. Kes took this news excessively well. The old woman was not even dead yet. So Mama did not know how many more days before she would be home. She asked Kes a lot of questions about his school work and personal hygiene, then—as she began to digress about Mrs. Dub's use of oleo in her Mexican cornbread—Brer Glenn came bounding in from the frigid night. He was out of breath and Kes eyed him warily as Glenn took his turn on the phone.

"Where you been keeping yourself, Gaylenn?" Kes asked after Glenn hung up.

"Don't call me that. And mind your own bee's wax," Glenn told him without a backward glance as he tripped up the stairs. Glenn looked a bit wild and unsteady, if you asked Kes. There was not much else to go on. Glenn was not slurring his words or anything as exciting as that.

On Friday the H-Bomb exploded. The Martians landed, the world cracked open, and the Brothers Brass went flying.

The first quakes began toward the end of Kes's last class. He was sitting through one of Mr. Standhope's numbingly long lectures on the local island ecology when it occurred to Kes that he had not seen Glenn in the halls or lunchroom all day. That was a bit odd, he thought, before setting that thought aside. Chalice had Pep Club after school so Kes came straight home without brother or girlfriend. That was odder still. It was a good thing he came straight home alone in time to hear the first explosion. Kes heard the parlor telephone ringing, ringing, as he came through the door.

"*Kes?*" the line crackled, Glenn's voice shaky at the other end.

"Brother?" Kes snapped. "Where are you?"

"H-Hinesville. You know, just outside Camp Stewart?"

"What are you doing down there?"

"Well, the deal is—they got me in jail down here."

"*Jail?*"

"They gimme this one phone call."

"They? The police?"

"Yeah, you know, the Hinesville po-lice."

"But, how—?"

"It'uz them rascals I been skidding with over at the park. We been running round some this week. I, uh, I reckon you might of noticed."

"Yeah. I reckon I knew something was up."

"Anyways, we cut school today. Started out bumming smokes down on the pier. Then a ole boy named Geetsy had his daddy's car, so we drove into town, to West Broad, to get us some brew and smoke some new kind of cigarettes."

"Brew?"

"We wanted to get some beers—alright? Not to get all liquored up or nothing. Just a few beers, alright? Well, we found some. We also found these three Army boys from

Camp Stewart who needed a ride home. So we give em a ride. Anyways, we got pulled over by the M.P.s. They're saying we was drunk. They kept the soldier boys and turnt the rest of us over to Hinesville sheriff."

"*Damnation*, brer." Kes said. It echoed off the kitchen walls, back at him. Nobody had cussed so loud in this house since his daddy left.

"Anyways, do you know when Mama's gone be back? I want to get out of here and come home. My head hurts bad."

"I don't. I don't know when she's coming home. That is–I expect she'll have to come home quick now. I expect I'll have to call her."

"Yeah. That's the only way I see to go. Mama's gone crucify me."

"Yep. I expect she will."

"My head hurts real bad, Kes. And I broke my Timex."

"They's plenty more wristwatches in this world, Glenn. You sit tight. I'll call Mama George. She'll pitch a fit, but I reckon it has to be done."

"Okay, Kes."

"Okay."

"Kes—?"

"Yeah?"

"I'm pert near scared. Ain't got no pee-waddin left in me."

Kes hung up the phone. He began to calculate how long it would take Mama George to get home and down to Hinesville while Glenn sat in that cell. No matter how he figured it, Kes was sure Glenn was looking at another day in jail—at least one more day—before he got bailed out. And with Mama George there would be no end of hell to pay. Suddenly it occurred to Kes that neither he nor Glenn had considered calling Daddy Brass. They were used to going to their mother when in need. Besides, she would only blame Glenn's drunken ways on Daddy Brass's daily ways and hold it against both Glenn and Daddy all the more, now and forever. If Daddy Brass bailed Glenn out and Mama George caught wind of it (and it would be just like Daddy to let it slip from an unsober lip) she would probably never let them see their grand old man ever again. Kes had come to know his mama's mind. And that was a growing knowledge too shudderful to ponder. So Kes moved on, he moved forward. Slowly he began to vamp a plan.

Kes picked up the phone again and called Daddy Brass's office. The phone rang and rang with no answer. Finally he hung up. This was getting more thorny by the minute. He wasn't going to tell Daddy the whole story. But he did need to reach him. Yes, Kes began to vamp him a plan.

Kes could not ask anybody here on the island for help. If Glenn's current plight became common knowledge then took flight over Savannah society—and beyond—his mama would be mortified and their sacred singing dates were likely to dry up faster than Mama's kisses. Folks seemed to tolerate and even appreciate that two fine youngsters could sing the Lord's message while their daddy was such a hellraiser. The way it looked so far, the boys and their gifts seemed like the Lord's redemption from the sins of the father. Right now, the Brothers Brass set a fine example for those cutup kids in the flock. But one of the Brothers Brass being a cutup, hellraising, jaildog himself while still a sophomore in high school? That was an example Kes knew most of those upright mamas and daddies would choose to live without.

Since Mama George had not meant to be gone so long, Kes had only four dollars and thirty-seven cents in his jeans. But Mama George had almost thirty dollars hidden in her Nabisco tin in the kitchen. She didn't know Kes knew, but Kes knew. How he was going to replace it would have to be dealt with later, before Mama got back. Time was wasting. Kes donned his old bomber jacket and caught the last afternoon bus into Savannah. Kes sat on the front seat so he could pester the greying bus driver.

"You ever get thowed in jail, sir?"

"Not that I recall," the driver said.

"If I was to get thowed in jail, what do you figure it'd take to get me out?"

"You fixing to get thowed in jail?"

"No, sir. But what do you figure it'd take to spring me?"

"Well, being the age you is, your daddy'd surely have to come down and sign you out."

"My daddy?"

"Yup. Your loving daddy. Or your mama. If you kilt somebody they'd be a heap of bail money involved."

"Oh."

"You fixing to kill anybody?"

"No, sir."

"That's a relief."

"Mister, have you accepted the Lord Jesus Christ as

your personal savior?"

"Why, yes I have. You?"

"I reckon." Kes slid forward on the seat. "But that's a good question—ain't it?"

An hour later Kes stepped off at the bus stop on East Bay and Abercorn in downtown Savannah. His nerves were jangling, made worse by the cold nip in the air. Spring was late this year. Kes jaywalked across Bay Street in the waning light, dodging another bus and a cute freckled nun on her bicycle. Then he walked down the Drayton Ramp to old River Street with its long string of brick-faced warehouses facing the trade waters of Savannah River. A passing Norwegian steam tanker named *Tanahorn* gave two long horn blasts to greet him. In all these years Kes had never visited his daddy's office or seen the trappings of this crusty street where Daddy Brass did business. He turned right, walking west for three blocks without any luck before he doubled back, going east from where he landed on the street. Finally, he found a two-tone copper and black Cadillac parked in front of a door with this sign:

M. BRASS FREIGHT & CARGO LTD.
= SAVANNAH, GA . =

Kes knocked softly on the door. No answer. He knocked harder. No answer still. He tried the handle. It was locked. He peered through the small window alongside the door of the four-story warehouse. Daddy Brass seemed to run a spiffy ship. The clean glass panes sparkled in stark contrast to the ungodly big cockroach nestled in the rusting window frame. Kes could not know that this ogre of a cockroach had just landed with a load of bananas from Costa Rica and was as much a stranger to this street as he.

"Might I help you?" she asked.

Kes turned and saw a shapely redhead in her middle years and high heels expertly navigating the brick pavement. She bore keys and an alligator-skin purse. The cockroach hissed in his ear and Kes knew she was one Mrs. Plum. Yes, even Kes knew of Mrs. Plum. And Mrs. Plum was a much different kind of redhead than Chalice Dillard.

"Uh, no, ma'am," Kes stuttered, "I mean, yes, ma'am."

This redhead sized him up like a stray calf. Kes had never seen such violet eyes.

"Are you Kes?" she asked, smiling faintly.

"Yes, ma'am."

"I'm Mrs. Plum."

"Yes, ma'am."

"Come on in."

"I come looking for my daddy—"

"Yes, of course you have," Mrs. Plum said, unlocking the door.

"I tried to call. Nobody answered."

"I was just over to Lady Sho-Fine gitting a poo and wave."

Kes held back a bit as she turned the lock then led him inside. It was a small, heated front office. Closing the door, Kes took quick stock of the place. The wood-paneled room was to be expected—with two file cabinets, a Mercantile Bank calendar, a steam radiator and guest chair. Mrs. Plum set her alligator bag on the desk.

"He said he was off to Rothchild's," she was saying, "to buy Blondie Boy Bichét a new pair of shoes. That was nearly two hours ago." Without missing a beat she pulled off an earring and put the phone to her ear, dialing with a pencil to protect her long ruby nails. "Hello? Biddy-Sue?" she cooed into the receiver. "This is Roberta Plum. Is Malakoff over there shoe-shopping?"

Kes heard the faint crackle of Biddy-Sue's voice on the other end of the line as he studied a framed yellowing photograph on the wall behind Mrs. Plum's desk. It was a picture of a St. Patrick's Day float. Perched atop the crepe and tinsel was a younger Daddy Brass waving, grinning big, beside a slightly-blurred and waving young woman with longer tresses than Mrs. Plum but who looked a lot like Mrs. Plum nonetheless. To the left of the old photograph was another glass-glazed door into the dark warehouse. Through the glass, the leaking light of the office revealed the faint reflection of barrels, kegs, crates, a hand truck. Kes wanted to see more.

"He say *what*? How long ago? On Blondie's Army scooter? My, my. We 'ppreciate it, Biddy." Mrs. Plum hung up the phone, arched a perfectly-lined brow. "They bought a new pair of Buster Browns and left Rothchild's at least an hour ago, Biddy says. They was heading over to Bo Peep's."

"Bo Peep's?"

"Bo Peep's Pool Hall. I'll call over there—" she said, reaching for the phone again.

"No, ma'am. I'd rather go on over. You know. Face to face. Where is this Bo Peep's?"

"Just four blocks down Drayton, sugar. Across from Christ Church. Can't miss it. You want I should walk you there?"

"No, ma'am. I'll do fine on my own. Got personal business with my daddy."

"Why, sure you do."

She looked at him with wistful composure as Kes backed bashfully out the door.

"Can't thank you *enough*, Mizz Plum," he stammered.

"Tell Bo and them that Roberta sent you."

Mrs. Plum was right, of course. Her directions were true. Kes would come to realize that Mrs. Plum was right more often than not. You could bank on her. Kes sprinted the four blocks down the darkening Drayton Street and easily found the pool hall. The bright neon helped. As he approached the glowing den he heard rough voices, the hard clacking of balls. Painted on the front window was a cute fluffy sheep with *Bo Peep's* stencilled across her belly. Bo Peep's fluffy sheep was leaping over a Give To The Red Cross sign propped betwixt the glass and Venetian blinds.

Kes went in, stepping into the clacking racket.

He had heard about pool games and pool dens, of course. Many a preacher had evoked them whilst the Brothers Brass waited in the wings or a nearby pew. But Kes had never gone wading into the smoke-filled cacophany of them. He had never even seen a pool table before. Suddenly, now, Kes was faced with a cluster of such tables, hustlers, and fat gamblers. There was also a lunch counter, cigar case, and a vast blackboard with lots of sports teams chalked on it. Kes's rosy-cheeked arrival went unnoticed by most of the men within who huddled or bent over their wooden cue sticks, taking aim across light-puddled fields of green felt. The room ran long and deep with low-country bantering so loud none of the clientele heard the door rattle closed behind Kes.

A staggeringly tall cook in his mustard-streaked apron was clearing a dirty plate and cup from the the lunch counter. He caught Kes's eye instantly. This cook did not miss much from his lookout post atop broad ebony shoulders. Kes felt like a landed house fly, about to be swatted.

"What can I do for you, suh?" the unsmiling cook asked.

"Are you Bo?"

Without a blink, the cook turned, hollering through the kitchen door. "*Mr. Wolfie.* Somebody out 'chere for you."

Out of the kitchen came an impish man in an open-necked white shirt and blazer, a wad of money in one hand, a wad of paper chits in the other. He stopped behind the beer taps, front teeth mincing his chewing gum, making a swift but thorough appraisal of this eager lad shifting foot to foot.

"I'm here," he said to Kes.

"You Mr. Bo Peep?"

"I am that."

"This your pool hall?"

"The sign says it is. Some might seek a second opinion."

"It's a very nice pool hall, sir. Nicest I've ever seen."

Mr. Peep shrugged.

"It ain't bad for a Jew-boy from London, England."

"No joke? You're a Jew?"

"Shhhh. Didn't you see Christ Church across the street? I just bought em a new roof. You'd scandalize the city, son, if they was to disown their own roof."

A rack of pool balls broke loud throughout the hall.

"Only Jew I ever knew was Jesus. But he ain't no ordinary Jew."

"So they tell me," Bo Peep chuckled.

"Anyway, Mizz Plum—uh—Roberta sent me."

"That's some good company you keep, youngster. I admire your budding instincts."

"I don't really know her too well."

"Shame."

"I was looking for my daddy. Mr. Malakoff Brass?"

"Mal Brass? You *his* boy?"

"Yessir—"

"Sure 'nough. I might see some resemblance. Sure. I hear you sang real pure-dee sweet and perty. Zat so?"

"Some say I do, sir. Mizz Plum say Daddy Brass come over here. Was wondering if you've seen him."

"You sure you ain't no taxman? No jealous husband?"

"Uh, no sir. I ain't neither of those," Kes said, missing the joke.

"Sure. I seen him. He had hisself a plate of roast beef and a jolly big glass of sweet milk. Slid out a little while ago saying he was off to jazz it up."

"Jazz it up?"

"That's right. That means he was headed over to West Broad for some hot nuts and booger down."

"West Broad? Is that a street, sir? Or some*body*?"

Even the cook got a kick out of that.

"Yes, yes, a street it is" Bo said teasingly. "A helluva street. Where coloreds of all colors make merry. Buncha clubs over there yo daddy is known to frequent."

"Can you tell me how to get there, sir?"

Kes watched as Mr. Peep's gum-chewing slowed. Peep and the cook cut quick eyes at each other.

"That's way too far to walk, son. Boy your age ain't got no bidness there by hisself anyways."

"Got personal business with my daddy. Face to face."

"Well, I can understand that. Sometimes a boy just got to go face to face with his daddy. I can follow that."

"Yes, sir. Mr. Peep?"

"Hello?"

"You don't talk like no Englishman I ever heard."

"And you don't talk like no Malakoff Brass. Tell you what. I ain't too busy. I'll run you over there myself in my limousine."

"Ain't no call for that, Mr. Peep."

"Yep, that's just what I'll do. We'll take my car." Mr. Peep beamed bigger, gum going again. He winked at the cook as he came around the counter to face Kes. Then the smile dropped, a bit of meanness replaced it. "But how we know you really is who you say you is, Mal Brass's boy?"

The tall cook looked darkly foreboding.

"Good question—" Kes stammered.

"How we know you ain't some sneaking imposter—some Chi-town hit job come to eradicate Mr. Brass?"

"Sir?"

"I think I better hear some perty bell tones outa you so's I know you ain't pulling my pulleybone."

"Y-You serious, sir?"

"Oh, yes, boy. I am serious as a dead man's suit."

Kes cleared his throat, ill aware that most of the pool hall had fallen silent and was watching him.

"I am so sad and loooonely, and I am condemned to roam ... I am a blind fiddler, and I'm a great long ways from home..."

Mr. Bo Peep laughed loud with the rest of room, slapping Kes on the arm.

"That'll do. We just funning you. Let's go find you daddy."

Mr. Peep led Kes through the kitchen past a simmering pot of corn cobs and red potatoes to the alley where a car was parked. Mr. Peep's limousine turned out to be a Bel Air Coupe. Minutes later the Bel Air turned onto West Broad Street from Congress Lane. Several blocks south, the bars, joints, and domino halls began to flourish and the faces got blacker. Kes saw all manner of colored folk dressed to the nines, laughter and night-life spirits filling the neon-lit sidewalks. Hot music came sifting through the chill, its echoes shifting and co-mingling as Mr. Peep cruised into a raunchier, more garish stretch of town that Kes had never laid eyes on. If his mama had ever seen this place, she was not telling.

The car pulled to the curb.

"Hear lately old Brass fancies the Delta 88 Club hyere."

They got out and Kes followed Mr. Peep's jaunty step inside. The club was dim, loud, and crazy in the heat of rowdy folk of many hues. Kes had never seen the like. A six foot chocolate lady in a tight green sequin dress and the brightest red lips Kes had ever seen brushed her bosoms against him, *smooching* at him as she passed on out the door. The power of her florid green perfume would remain in Kes's soul for the duration of the night, perhaps forever. There was a boogie band on stage with barrelhouse piano and doghouse bass. The piano player was barking a message out the side of his mouth.

Big-legged woman, better keeeeep yo dresses down—

Couples danced with arm-flinging abandon. Kes hurried to keep up with Mr. Peep who was moving toward the bar like he was Kes's personal pathfinder. Yes, it was a good thing Mr. Peep was with him. Kes did not want to be the only white jellybelly in this swirling hopper of multi-colored beans. Yes, Kes felt fear, he must admit. And exhilaration. He liked that music they were making up there. He liked it too much.

Law, you got the stuff to make a bulldog hug a hound—

By the time Mr. Peep reached the people-packed bar rail, Kes kept thinking about that fleeting chocolate woman—thinking how she must have strut halfway down the street by now. Yet her green perfume was still dripping into Brother Brass's loins.

"Hey *Peachy*. Hidy-*doo*," Mr. Peep hollered above the din to the green-visored barkeep who flashed big Chiclet teeth. "I hear you cleaned our clock on that third race last Sunday."

"Yez, Mistuh Bo, I believe I did. I believe I did and might do again," the barkeep roared back.

Mr. Peep reached across and shook the man's hand.

"Good for you. Say, maybe you can help us out. We looking for ole Mal Brass—this boy's daddy."

"I see, I see, Mistuh Bo," the barkeep said, nodding and smiling at Kes.

"He been in hyere today?"

"Naw sir, not today. Ain't seed Mistuh Brass since last Saturday afore our weekly prayer meeting."

"He packing his railroad Bible?"

"All fifty-two psalms, suh. He likes his draw poker."

"I figures they was fifty-three psalms," Bo winked, "the way he plays it."

"Might try over to the Blue Dice. Heard Mistuh Brass was making some book over there."

"He best not be. They's my best customers. I'll have his hairy hide."

Both men laughed, then Mr. Peep and Kes went across the street to the Blue Dice Club. Daddy Brass was not be found in the strange sweet smoke of that joint either. The jazz trio made soft blue sounds that confused the boy.

The three-hundred pound lady behind the Blue Dice bar tipped them toward the Pickalilly Bar And Grill. As they approached the Pickalilly a long sloppy fellow pitched out the door, followed by a flying Stetson hat. The fellow's face landed on the sidewalk, he twitched once, then did not move. Mr. Peep trotted ahead, grabbed the drunk by his belt and collar, dragging him off to one side so the door was clear. Kes felt sorry for such a sad human husk. He could see that this drunkard was toothless and unconscious as Mr. Peep placed the Stetson back on the fellow's sagging head.

Kes glanced up, looking in the window, and spied his six-foot-two Daddy Brass holding court at the bar. Daddy was raising a glass betwixt the belly of a great purple-black bruiser who stood nearly seven feet tall and a pretty young man who looked almost white. Kes was beginning to feel very small in this new tall world. Even out here, beyond the glass, Kes could make out the bull-notes of his daddy's familiar voice as it rose with a tumbler-filled hand to make a toast.

"Right there he is," Kes said to Mr. Peep.

Mr. Peep returned to Kes's side, looked through the window and saw.

"Uh-huh. Let's go pick his bones," Mr. Peep said, stepping toward the door.

"Uh, Mr. Peep, if you don't mind I'd just as soon go speak to Daddy on my own."

Mr. Peep softened.

"Why, sure, sure you would, son. I can noodle that."

"You sure been every kind of help to me, Mr. Peep," Kes said, shaking the man's hand. "I cain't thank you enough. Din't have to do it but you did."

"Now, Mr. Peep—he was *my* daddy. Here on, you call me Bo. Or Wolfie. I cop to either one. Besides, you really think I let little lambs wander these woods on their own? Come rack some pool sometime or run a number. We could use you. Ain't got no jukebox."

"Well, Mr. Bo Wolfie, I ain't got no idea how to play pool. But Mama says I'm a quick study." Kes hesitated as a thought crossed him. "Is there gambling involved?"

"Not the way we do it."

"Well, then I'd like that. I'd like that a lot."

Pulling away, toward his car, Mr. Bo Peep glanced back through the bar window.

"You tell Big Brassworks in there I got my eye on him. And long odds."

As Kes slipped into the club he heard Daddy Brass howl above the howl of *Wang Dang Doodle* on the jukebox. Kes almost slipped back outside when he heard that—and might have if he had not been afraid Mr. Peep would see and think him a callow kid. For a moment, he stood inside the door, listening to the black folk and bartender laughing around a four-sided bar in the middle of the room. They were laughing with and at Kes's very own daddy.

As usual, Malakoff Brass stood armed with attitude, taking no prisoners:

"*Sooooo,* Blondie Boy here tells me if I want a ride on his new motor-sickle it's gonna cost me a shining new pair of Buster Brown shoes for them teensy, tiny toes of his. Penny weejuns he wants. You got that? That's weeeejuns. Limey green ones. Well I tells him only a perfect pussy would wear loafers wid pennies in em and I'd ruther settle the deal with a whup-it-out contest. The long and the short of it. Right there on the pool table. So Blondie Boy come back at me with a few reams of Elizabethan law which entitles him—he say—to the right of proxy. A stand-in. A designated hitter. And, sure 'nough, little Blondie's swordsman of choice is big ole Bugga here, who everbody knows is hung like a damn long-eared donk. Of course I had no choice but to plead genetic disadvantage—"

Kes was circling the bar at safe distance when Daddy Brass cocked around, arms wild, and saw him. Their eyes locked as Daddy Brass slowly set down his drink, his bourbon landing near an abandoned set of dentures. If those false teeth had bitten him, Daddy would never have noticed.

"Blondie, boy, you done slipped me one too many," Daddy Brass said soberly. "I look acrost the way and I sees my number one son standing middle of The Pickalilly on Broad Street. One more sip an it'll be Abe Lincoln with titties in a grass skirt."

Kes stepped up to the plate, up to his Daddy.

"Daddy—I come to talk to you."

The high yellow Blondie Boy smiled at Kes. He seemed nice in his new lime and shiny shoes.

"We just friends," Blondie Boy said.

Kes nodded at Blondie.

Daddy nodded at Kes.

"You gotdamn right about that, puddle duck," Daddy Brass said, beginning to bellow again. "You come to talk to me. But how the hell did you come here?"

"City bus mostly. Then a Mr. Peep drove me over from his pool hall."

"Wolfie? *Wolfie's here?* Where is he?" Daddy asked, his eyes searching over Kes's shoulder.

"Mr. Peep went on back. He said I could handle it from here."

"Did he now—"

"Yes sir, he said he was watching you with long odds."

Everybody laughed and Kes wondered why.

Daddy suddenly slid his tumbler hard past his companions, cutting a cavernous grin as he laid that broad hand on his son's chest. His hot whiskey breath began to burn Kes's eyes.

"You the sight to behold, Kestrel. I hoped we might split a jug one day. But then, you ain't of age yet, are you?"

"No, sir. And I ain't got time to be splitting things right now anyhow."

"Why, I was jist telling this girly—" Daddy's forelock of black hair flipped in Blondie's general direction. "—Oh, by the ways, this here's Mr. Blondie Bichét and the biggun is Bugga Higgin. Y'all, this be mah first boy. This be Kestrel Brass."

Kes nodded again as the yellow fellow blinked hello. Behind fair Blondie, the mighty bruiser named Bugga tipped his glass a notch.

"We juz friends, mon," said the Bugga, with deep Caribbean lilt.

There was one more man in attendance.

"Oh, and this here is Saint Peter," Daddy said.

A silver-haired gent sat farther up the bar in his pinstripe suit, with no drink, saying nothing. His somber, cocoa-colored face watched behind a veil of freckles.

"So, I was jist explaining to these conkheads," Daddy Brass said in lewd abandon, "that I ain't racial prejudiced. But I wouldn't wanna *foller* one of em."

Bugga and Blondie laughed again. So did most folks within earshot of this. But not the silver-haired gent.

Suddenly, a louder ruckus cut through the ruckus.

"I don't gib a good guddam whud yewz thanks. Gimme another fugging shot o'Jack afore I cut yo lights!"

All heads cranked as one to see another pop-eyed drunk. This drunkard stood caddy-corner across the squared bar, weaving and waving a big stiletto knife in the barkeep's face. The drunk's voice reminded Kes of that negro chap Rochester on the preacher's television—if Rochester was a jowly two-hundred pound woman in a rumpled housedress and Marcelle wave who conversed with Mr. Jack Daniel more than Jack Benny. The vested barkeep, an onyx-faced Buster Keaton, kept cool and kept his distance.

"Now, Tippystaff, you best put that knife away," the barkeep cooed. "I ain't giving you no more to drank. You done past your limit."

Tippystaff's knife sliced across the bar as the barkeep took an easy step back, just out of range.

"Git another jolt *in that glass* afore I *cuts* you," Tippystaff raged, spraying spittle. "And I wants to know whar my running buddy Jeebo done went. He be standing besides me jist a drank or two ago—"

Just as suddenly, Daddy Brass cut through it all.

"Say, Tipstaff!" Malakoff barked. "What's that greasy muck hanging from your *snoot?*"

Tippystaff jerked her big head around, her bleary eyes trying to focus on Daddy Brass.

"Huh? Whud yew says?" this Tippystaff slurred, obviously addled by such a question.

Daddy Brass smiled like the king cat.

"You got some kind of nastiness hanging out your nose."

Tippystaff started furiously rubbing at her nose to remove whatever it was, all the time hefting the stiletto's sharp point aloft with her other fat hand. The barkeep still kept his distance, kept his cool. Tippystaff stopped rubbing and blinked across the bar corner at Daddy Brass.

"It gone?" Tippystaff asked.

"Nope, something goobery there alright," Daddy said, shaking his head. "Come 'ere and lemme git a good gander."

Tippystaff's load lurched around the corner of the bar toward Daddy Brass, leading with her stiletto, roughly rubbing her nose some more. She reached Daddy and stood unsteady before him. Again, Tizzystaff stopped gouging and rubbing.

"Did I gid it?" she asked.

"Uh-uh. Nope," Daddy Brass said, showing great concern as he squinted at Tippystaff's snoot. "I reckon you need to get our your snot rag and blow that honker something fierce."

Tippystaff commenced rubbing her nose again, then something slow took root from the words she had heard. She stopped rubbing and reached her free hand in her dress pocket for a rag that may or may not have been there.

"You looking fer Jeebo? Jeebo Cooks?" Daddy asked at that instant.

"You guddam right I is—" said the fumbling Tippystaff.

Daddy grinned bigger.

"Well, there he is, up taking a whiz on the ceiling—"

Sure enough, Tippystaff looked up at the ceiling in search of her lost buddy. In a flash, Daddy Brass sent a huge right fist crashing into Tippystaff's jawbone. Daddy snatched the stiletto from Tippystaff's hand as she fell, slipping the knife into his own coat pocket. Tippystaff had barely unfolded on the floor before Big Bugga Higgin grabbed the scruff of Tippystaff's housedress and began to drag her tonnage toward the door.

Kes watched as Bugga pitched his soggy cargo out onto the pavement, then slammed the door shut. It suddenly occurred to Kes that the toothless man Mr. Peep propped up outside with his Stetson was surely named Jeebo Cooks. And those would be Jeebo's false teeth smiling back now over the lip of the bar.

"Much obliged, Mistuh Bugga—Mistuh Brass," the barkeep droned.

"Ain't nothing to it, J.P.," Daddy winked. "This ole roundhouse of mine needs the workout."

All grins, Daddy turned back to face his bewildered son.

"Daddy—I cain't believe you'd hit *a woman* like that."

"Aw, Tipstaff ain't no woman, son. He jist likes to dress up that way."

Something about this Tippystaff now being a fat man in a dress boggled something loose in Kes's brain. So he blurted it out.

"*Daddy, I was wondering if I might could borrow your car.*"

The words had barely cleared Kes's throat before he heard a loud clanking *smack* on the bar. He looked down and saw Daddy Brass's big mitt slide the keys at him.

"Parked outside my office. The two-tone copper Caddy. If you bust her up jist give Oglethorpe Auto a rang and they'll come git her."

Kes was stumped as his daddy's tumbler of bourbon rose from the bar.

"You—you ain't gonna ask me no questions why or what for?" Kes questioned.

Daddy took a little sip, holding Kes in his sights.

"Naw, son. If you come this far on your own I figure you got good reason and gumption enough to go the rest without any guff or bullshit from me."

Kes felt like the whole big easy room was watching him, smiling soft, waiting for punchlines they knew but he did not.

"Gee. I sure appreciate it, Daddy."

Daddy Brass tucked a fiver into Kes's shirt pocket.

"This'll stake that taxi back to my office to pick her up," Daddy said, then hesitated. "How you fixed for grease after that? I ain't asking what you might need any funding for or what you up to, understand?"

"Oh, I'm good," Kes lied. He had no real clue as to how much money he might need.

Daddy Brass pulled a roll of bills from his pant pocket. Unlooping the rubber band, he thumbed off a hundred-dollar Benjamin.

"If you got the devil to pay, he'll want extra red-eye on his biscuit. He always do," Daddy said as he poked more mad money into Kes's shirt. "So how's that little brother of yours?"

"Oh, he's just fine."

"Good. Good. Saint Peter? Cash me another check. I'm running shy."

When Kes came out of the club he felt like a new car with new paint coming off the assembly line. He was doing all right so far. He had never hailed a cab before, but that's the sort of thing that came easy to a high roller like Kestrel Brass. Kes walked almost two blocks through a stream of colorful folk, his eyes searching the street.

A wiry little brown dude in his checker-banded cabbie's cap slipped out of a phone booth, studying his racing form. He happened to look up as Kes passed by.

"Kid? Cab?"

"Oh, you betcha, sir."

"I'm parked by the fire escape."

The cabby led Kes around the corner, into an empty alley. Before Kes could ask anymore questions, the cabby and another fellow Kes never got a good look at slammed Kes's face into the brick wall. They took his wallet, ripping the cash from his shirt pocket, leaving him lying in the shadows, spitting blood.

A half hour later, with the help of the telephone booth and some yellow pages, Kes was in a Miracle Seven taxi cab headed back to River Street. The old driver took no outward notice of Kes's sorry condition. This was West Broad on a Friday night.

Collapsing in the back seat, Kes took off his shoe. His fingers searched inside, then fished out the hundred dollar bill. Yes, his daddy was a wise man, telling Kes not to carry all his bankroll in one place. But that was small comfort now as Kes swabbed the blood off his jaw with his shirttail. He was suddenly more scared than he had been all day. That other cabby—the one back in the alley—had just clobbered him with a message from on high. Kes was not in a state of grace after all.

His daddy had swept away the last hurdles which might have allowed Kes an excuse for not making the biggest leap. But Kes's good judgment was obviously iffy at best, it came in fits and spurts. With his daddy's car and cash, Kes could now land flatfooted across the desk from the Hinesville sheriff who had brother Glenn locked inside that drunk tank. That reality was actually within his grasp. With a good tailwind, Kes might even skid into that tadpole town outside the gates of Camp Stewart inside the hour.

Yes, he was definitely picking up speed but he knew

goodness was not hitching this ride. The faster things got the more Kes was sure he was headed for an even bigger, even badder crash with lots of screeching mamas and shattered dreams. An unsupervised high school kid with a bankroll and big flashy sedan was sure to set off any sheriff's radar. Tomorrow morning's headlines were flashing before Kes's eyes: UNHOLY BROTHERS BRASS CROON JAILBIRD TUNE.

Buzzing down Broad Street, Kes zipped up his bomber jacket, hoping this cabby could break a hundred dollar bill. And before Kes could figure out a way to pump up the brakes on rocketing fate, the cabbie counted out change, kept a tip, and dumped Kes out on River Street right beside the copper Cadillac. Kes was fumbling in his crotch pocket for the car keys when lush-lipped Mrs. Plum stuck her tawny head out the door.

"Can I help you with that, sugar?" she asked.

"No, ma'am," Kes said. With a meek smile he unlocked the door and got in fast, hoping she wouldn't see his battered face in the dark. He felt Mrs. Plum's eyes on him so he rolled down the window a crack and spake to her again. "I got urgent personal affairs to tend of a serious nature. My daddy has loaned me his car."

"I allowed as much. Drive safe. Remember, the traffic laws are for our own protection."

The big Cadillac roared to life as Mrs. Plum closed the door and returned to her desk where she was eating a cucumber and cottage cheese sandwich. She had just taken another slurp of Tab cola when the door squeaked open again.

"Mizz Plum?" Kes said, stepping inside slowly.

"Yes, sugar?" She set down the Dixie cup. "My Lord, look at you. What happened to your face?"

"Oh, nothing big. Took a tumble on the Drayton Ramp. But, Mizz Plum, that's not the thing—"

"Yes, sugar? What's the thing?"

He was starting to sweat, so he unzipped his bomber jacket.

"I need somebody I can trust."

"Most of us do from time to time."

"I mean, I need somebody I can trust with the truth."

"I knew what you meant."

"Mizz Plum—?"

"Yes, sugar?"

"Will you be my mama?"

"Say what?" she blinked.

"Will you be my mama? For one night only?"

VERSE 13

A Scarlett in Uniform

Kes explained brother Glenn's Hinesville predicament quickly and found himself surprisingly not so surprised when Mrs. Plum immediately agreed to his plan. Best of all, she immediately agreed to leave his daddy out of it. Kes had nursed an odd feeling from the moment he first met her that Mrs. Plum was game and could be trusted. He sensed that Daddy Brass would not keep somebody so close to him as he kept Mrs. Plum if she and her backbone were not true.

Mrs. Plum told Kes she had just the number for this trip. She went back in the warehouse then reappeared minutes later wearing a Sherwood green business dress and sensible shoes. By the time the Cadillac pulled onto Coastal Highway 17 with Kes at the wheel Mrs. Plum was pinning her auburn tresses up into a respectable bun.

"Only thing, ma'am," he was saying, "I'm just hoping they don't ask you for no driver license or I.D.—"

"I already thought of that," Mrs. Plum said. "That is why my purse will stay in the car. If they ask for identification

I'll say I ran out the door without it because I was so very, very flustered by your brother's—my *son's*—telephone call from inside the walls of the Hinesville jail."

"Yeah, that might work."

"Maybe they won't ask for it at all, sugar."

"I surely appreciate you for this, Mizz Plum."

"Call me Roberta. Cryminitly, I feel like I know the woman. Like I could pen her memoirs. I've taken enough calls from her and stuffed enough of your Daddy's checks into envelopes with her name on it over the last ten years. I licked so many stamps for her till she feels almost personal. It gits plumb intimate, after a while."

Kes did not know what to think when he heard this—hearing somebody he hardly knew talk in such a way about his mama. And if what Mrs. Plum said was true, how could Mama George be so hard up for money all the time?

"Not that any of those checks *ever* clear the bank," she continued, as if Mrs. Plum could read Kes's troubled mind. She flipped open a compact mirror and began wiping off most of her makeup with a hanky.

Kes's throat cleared. He decided to roll the dice again.

"If you don't mind me asking, Miss Roberta—how did you come to be working for Daddy Brass?"

She did not answer right away. Most of her makeup was removed when Mrs. Plum clicked the compact shut. Her gaze drifted out through the glass of her window to the draperies of Spanish moss sweeping past.

"Oh ... I married a Navy boy down in Galveston when I was real young with him heading into the war. After the war was over he come back but joined the Merchant Marine and stayed gone near as much as before. The company of women did not appear to be something he highly prized. Maybe it was just me he didn't prize. About all he ever gave me was a drugstore wedding ring and a monkey pod coffee table from Honolulu. He'd write letters from time to time. Short letters that got shorter. Finally they stopped coming altogether and so did he. Couple of years passed. It got real lonely there for awhile with me and my Walgreen's ring. I've always been a faithful cuss. I was working as a toll booth operator over in Port Arthur, out by the strip joints and petroleum plants. The air smelled nasty all the time. Bum-crack of the world if you'll excuse my French. One day your daddy comes through singing his song and backing up traffic for fifteen minutes. He liked a woman in uniform, he said. I decided to commute my wedlock to time served. I needed some fresh air."

"Ever find out what happened to your sailor?"

"Nope. He must of sprung a leak and drowned. But I still fancy that monkey pod table. It's real slick."

About forty minutes later, as they were pulling into downtown Hinesville—or what there was of it—Mrs. Plum took the Walgreen's ring out of her purse and put it back on her finger. It was well after dark in the tiny town. The short run of shops and the cafe were closed. Kes saw a few scattered troops from Camp Stewart, and even one girl. Obviously, there was not much to do in this downtown on any night. Even on a Friday night like this, any soldier with wits and any paycheck left at all would be up the road in

Savannah if he could swing the transport.

Mrs Plum was also unfamiliar with Hinesville, so Kes anxiously pulled to the curb when he spotted two MPs. While asking directions, Kes could see that both the military policemen were busy eyeing Mrs. Plum while only half grasping Kes's very good questions. But Mrs. Plum ignored their greedy eyes, choosing that moment to slip back into her sensible shoes. She seemed accustomed to such crude appraisal. The older MP finally managed to point the way to the police station four blocks down and one block to the left.

Kes steered the Cadillac into the gravel lot and parked betwixt two patrol cars with cherry-red lights on top. He and Mrs. Plum both caught a shared breath for a moment as they watched two junior high girls—one brown, one pink—enter the station beneath the freshly re-painted HINESVILLE POLICE DEPARTMENT (and "Law Enforcement Center") sign.

"I'll try to keep you shy of any trouble, Mizz Plum."

"Try hard, sugar."

For a moment, from the way Mrs. Plum reviewed the flanking patrol cars, Kes thought she might be about to back out of this deal. She proved him wrong when her car door was the first to open. She slid smoothly from the Cadillac, marching for the door without a backward glance. Kes had to scramble to keep up.

Inside the station two deputies laid back lazily at their desks, one with his boot propped up betwixt his typewriter and Ritz box. A telephone kept ringing but neither deputy was rustling any khaki to answer it. As Kes and Mrs. Plum stepped inside, a starched man of middle years stepped from his inner office, a sheriff's badge on his white shirt pocket. The Sheriff was having trouble with his Zippo lighter, flicking sparks from the flint wheel, trying to get a flame. The two teenage girls were first to snag his attention. He did not wait for word one out of their open mouths.

"What you two doing here?" the Sheriff demanded, finally lighting his Roi-Tan, teeth clenching its plastic tip. "How many times I got to tell you Jackson girls don't go traipsing these streets after dark like little dirt-road whores? And stop pestering my deputies."

"Pleeease, Sherf, it's differnt this time," the brown girl said.

"Yessir, Sherf, this time it's super FUBAR," the pink girl said.

"It's always differnt, it's always FUBAR," he barked back.

"Mmmm, yessir, that's right, sir," the brown girl said, "but this time, Sherf, Diddy took off with granmommy's purse, all the corn willies and saltines, and Pedro."

"Pedro?" the Sheriff squinted. "Who's Pedro?"

"Pedro's granmommy's pet ducky. Diddy's been gone long time. Since this mawnin. We hongry and want our duck back."

"Well, see," the Sheriff said, mulling this as he lay his cigarillo in a tin ashtray atop the file cabinet. "I cain't be chasing no corn willies or ducky wuckys. Her purse, you say?"

Both girls began nodding with great fervor.

"Ain't your grandma still dead?" the sheriff asked.

The two kept nodding without detectable remorse.

"Yeah, well, you got my condolences, girls. That daddy of yours, he still pulling his disability checks? From V.A.?"

Both girls shrugged.

"So what's in this purse your daddy took?" the Sheriff asked.

"Lawd owny knows," the pink sister said.

"Uh-huh. Lawd owny knows."

Kes and Mrs. Plum approached the bald deputy behind the nearest desk, the one who looked like a stubby thumb in seam-popping uniform.

"S-Sir?" Kes said as the deputy pulled his sleepy gaze of the teenage girls. "I'm Kestrel Brass and this is my mama. We come to get my brother Glenn you got locked up back there."

Mrs. Plum served a prim smile to the deputy. The officer gave this new pair of visitors dim appraisal . His eyes kept darting back to the girls murmuring to the Sheriff. Finally, the deputy studied the blotter on his desk.

"Gaylenn? Gaylenn Brass? One of them drunks they picked up this afternoon? That boy?"

"Well, sir, we just call him Glenn," Kes said. "But, yes, that'd be my brother."

Behind his deputy the starched Sheriff edged closer, listening sideways, until he was close enough for Kes to see a speck of ketchup (blood?) on his badge. As the Sheriff edged away from her, the brown sister was back to talking louder about her lost duck Pedro, but the sheriff did not seem aware of her words anymore.

"Uh-huh. I reckon your brother be about sober by now." The bald deputy circled something on his day book with a ballpoint pen. He cocked his head at Mrs. Plum. "You his mama?"

"Yes," she said softly. "I am Georgiana Brass."

Hearing his mama's name tumble off Mrs. Plum's lush lower lip unsettled Kes. He skipped a groove but kept playing the show.

"W-We call her Mama George."

This mattered not to the deputy, more interested now in his ballpoint pen as he clicked it in, out, in, out.

"We'll let the boy go this time with a warning. These snots start running wild at his age and next thing you know they's fresh meat on a chain gang."

"Yes, sir. I mean—no, sir. My brother, he won't run like this again. My mama, she'll see to that."

The deputy nodded slowly then spake at the boot beside the other typewriter.

"Jerry—bring that Brass boy out here."

The boot came off the other desk, knocking over the Ritz box as Jerry, the younger deputy, got up shedding cracker crumbs—but the Sheriff *snapped* out his forefinger at him—pointing for Jerry to stop. The young deputy stopped, stood, watched.

"Hold that phone *just a datburn minute,*" the Sheriff spake.

"Whatcha think, Sheriff Argle?" the bald deputy posed, arching his neck to see the Sheriff.

The Sheriff stepped up behind him, studied the blotter for a moment, taking it in his hands. Scowling, his eyes connected what he saw with Kes and Mrs. Plum.

"You and your brother—" the Sheriff said to Kes,—"you any kin to that rum-running Malakoff Brass?"

It seemed an improperly placed question, a trick question with a built-in, self-incriminating booby trap. But Kes could think of no other answer than the one he gave.

"Well, yes sir."

"So you admit it?" the sheriff said with faint glee.

"Yes, sir. I ain't gonna deny my daddy."

The Sheriff became one big yellow-stained grin.

"Who bunged up your face?" he asked.

"Nobody, sir. I took a tumble on some bricks."

"Well, I'll be butt-kicked. Malakoff Brass's boys," he gloated to his deputies. "Hell, I bet Ole Brass got his young brig rat and them soldier boys liquored up hisself. Corrupting the cradle and our U.S. Armed Forces. I think maybe we best pull this Daddy in here to answer a few pointy questions before we go giving up custody of his kid. No need to be so knee-slapping quick on the draw. If'n he's anything like his old man, that drunkard kid back there is another blight on society."

Kes's guts began to churn as he braced for the big crash he had seen coming slow for hours. Suddenly Mrs. Plum stepped forward.

"Excuse me," Mrs. Plum said icily. "Are you Sheriff Pearce Argle?"

The Sheriff's red-specked badge puffed out a bit.

"Yes, Mizz Brass. That I am. Retired Artillery. Church deacon. Scoutmaster for our local troop. For good boys who uphold our community standards. Any more questions?"

"Your son is R. J. Argle? Lives over in Midway?"

"Affirmative, Mizz Brass. He's my eldest. Just made lieutenant in the Georgia Patrol."

Strange mirth moved across Mrs. Plum's face.

"Yes, Sheriff Argle—you should most definitely call my husband in for questioning. It is the only right thing to do. This requires a full and proper investigation. You might begin by asking him to show you the small zippered-leather book he carries everywhere inside his coat pocket. I doubt he will deny its existence. He is not the best of scribblers. His hand can be a bit demanding. But the taxman can read it. Malakoff is real good about his taxes. You see, after being wounded, awarded, and discharged from the United States Marine Corps, he became a circuit salesman for the Sacred Heart Publishing Company out of Nashville. They were very demanding. More demanding than the Corps, to hear my husband tell it. They required he keep scrupulous records of all expenses and transactions. Full names. Dates. Exact and to the penny. In black ink, not blue. The man can be unruly at times. Even reprehensible. But he has carried that work ethic forward in everything he does. Everything. So, absolutely, I suggest—no, I *implore* you to pick up that telephone and get Malakoff Brass down here, inside your tiny little office in your tiny little town and do so without delay. I know he will insist upon full disclosure and do anything he can to clear his son's name. You will find him quite charming, with firm resolve that his son's name never be associated with any nefarious or illegal activities you might rightly or wrongly associate with his father. And while you've got him in your hot seat, Mr. Sheriff, you be sure to ask Malakoff Brass why your eldest son's name is the third name on the first page of his little leather-bound book. The one he carries at all times. Yes, the very first page. In black ink. Not blue. Rodney, isn't it? Officer Rodney Jim Argle? My, it is a small world. *Is it not?* And you may rest assured my husband will spearhead this crusade to publicly and loudly maintain your highest community standards. Those high standards will be upheld here. Tonight. For all this tiny world of yours to see tomorrow *morning*, when a new day will dawn on *you*. In fact, there is not a doubt in my mind—Malakoff Brass will be *hellbent* on it. So, please, let me give you his unlisted number."

The room held its breath while the two goggle-eyed girls made soft sucking sounds. Sheriff Argle stood frozen before Mrs. Plum for a full three seconds before he broke free from her ironclad gaze. He slung the blotter back on the desk.

"Hell, *I ain't waiting around for nobody,* I got Masonic tonight—" the Sheriff spat "— Jeff, cut that Brass kid loose."

"Right, Sheriff," Deputy Jerry obeyed, hopping to.

The Sheriff snatched his cigarillo off the file cabinet, grabbed an open box of Ritz crackers off Deputy Jerry's desk. He shoved the Ritz box into the pink girl's hands then tromped into his office.

"But what about our Pedro duck, Sheriff?" the sister cried.

The Sheriff's door slammed shut.

Mrs. Plum snuck *a smooch* at Kes. Kes fought to contain his rapture. This was his night to get smooched at.

Minutes later Deputy Jerry produced a lousy-looking, red-eyed Gaylenn Brass. Mrs. Plum rushed over, kissed Glenn's cowlick and began administering guilt.

"Look at you, *son*" she snipped, trying to tame his hair with her hand. "Mama's gonna salt your tail when we get home."

Glenn tried to pull away—he was about to wail about this strange woman—when brother Kes grabbed his arm. Quickly, Kes and Mrs. Plum shuttled Glenn out the door to the car, putting on a good show with no encore for the deputies' benefit.

"You gone done it now, little brer—" Kes spake loudly for all to hear, "—Mama's gonna keep us *both* chained in the yard till Scarlett sells the farm."

Hinesville and Camp Stewart had faded far behind the copper and black Cadillac by the time Glenn finally surfaced from his clouded brine long enough to renew the issue.

"Who are you, ma'am?" he asked betwixt sour belches from the back seat.

Kes explained as Mrs. Plum reached back over the front seat and squeezed Glenn's hand for a moment. This strange woman gave him a tinged but comforting smile and even from inside his hangover Glenn began to get the picture.

"Thank you, Mizz Plum," Glenn mustered. "Ain't nobody ever done nothing like this for me before."

"You are very welcome, Glenn Brass. I feel I've known you boys for years."

By now Kes's eyes were dancing on the highway ahead, awestruck, lovestruck, afraid to even look at her.

"Mercy *yes*, Mizz Plum," Kes told his hands at ten and two on the wheel. "You were *Joan of Arc back there* with sword and hatchet. A mighty winged miracle woman, I swear. I can see why you and Daddy—I mean—I see why Daddy keeps you close."

"Yes, well, be that as it may, sugar, you two must never forget one thing," she said without sentiment. "It is your mama he loves."

She took off the Walgreens ring, returning it to her purse.

VERSE 14

Clear Blue Jesus

They were soon back in Savannah, returning Mrs. Plum to the office on River Street. Glenn moved to the front seat. Mrs. Plum told them they should take the Cadillac on back home, back to the island.

"I'll have one of your daddy's runners come retrieve the car in the morning. Ya'll stay sweet now," she chimed soft, bent at the car window behind a drape of red hair. "Stay sweet and stay sober mostly."

Mrs. Plum was looking Glenn over closely when she said it. He got the message.

It felt sorrowful somehow, watching her go back into that office alone. Both brothers waved as Mrs. Plum returned a little toodle-loo with her long ruby fingernails before closing the door.

As they drove up the ramp to Bay Street, Glenn said he was thirsty enough to drink kerosene from a gas cap. Kes drove to the Hires Root Beer stand where he finally put a minor dent in the money Daddy Brass had given him. Kes paid for two root beers to go and a slaw dog for himself. Glenn was still too queasy for solid food. By the time Kes's slaw dog was gone they had cleared Victory Drive past Williams Seafood and were headed out over saltwater to the island.

"You okay, little brer?" Kes asked. "Did they work you over? Did they put the boots and blackjacks to you?"

"Naw. Naw, nothing like that."

"Hmmm. That's good."

"Don't sound so disappointed. What about you? How'd you git so bungfaced?"

"Oh, just a little fall from grace is all. With bricks at the other end."

Gazing out across the waterways, Glenn and the big V-8 began to open up like the marshland.

"I reckon you saw this coming..."

"I reckon. Way you been acting up."

"Kes—"

"Huh?"

"I kilt a girl once."

"Stop it."

"Yep."

"Stop messing with me. Been a long day."

"A wee little girl."

"You ain't serious—" Kes creased his brow, darted an eye at Glenn scratching his ribs while looking very serious indeed.

"Yup. I kilt her. See the saw, she said. See the saw."

"See the saw?"

"See how I kilt her with the saw. Remember when we was

still pipsqueaks and Mama took us to sing at that King's Harvest festival a ways up north in some hill country? You'd remember better than me. We met some deacon's truck at a crossroads, then Mama followed them farther back in them hills, up to a place called Cooga Ridge—or something like that. Mama could never of found that place on her own, even with a map. We stayed with some elderly Hard- Shell Baptists. That's right. They asked us up to the festival, offered us beds for the night in their old house by a schoolyard. Schoolyard with a low rock fence around it. And me no more'n eight or nine years old. I'll never forget it. The show was later that evening, so Mama put us down for baby naps in their back bedroom. She left the window open. The weather was ripe. After she put us down, you dropped right off. But I couldn't sleep. Then I got an idear. The kind of idear a nine-year-old kid would get."

Glenn was avoiding his brother and everything else in the world except the brooding marshland out there. Kes listened, both hands glued to the wheel.

"I slipped out that window that day, to go play in that schoolyard. I reckon I thought I'd slip back in with nobody the wiser. So I unlatched the screen. Before I knew it, I was over in that schoolyard monkeying on the jungle gym. And that's when I seen her."

"The girl?"

"Uh-huh. Itty bitty little girl. Setting off on the rock wall next to a patch of trees. Dirty blond hair, mouth needed wiping. Who knows how long she'd been watching. She says hidy and I says hidy back. She told her name which I still cannot recall. I told her mine and she starts to tell me about this teeter-totter she knows about. A teeter-totter not everbody knows about. I look around the yard, I sure don't see no teeter-totter. She asks if I want to see it. I says yes. She rolls off the fence to the outside, motions for me to come with her into that patch of trees. Sure enough, in a spot inside them trees was an old rusted teeter-totter, hid from view. Like it used to be part of the schoolyard but got left behind long before when they rebuilt the fence or something. I never could figure it, but you can figure what happened next, Kes. She asks do I want to play and she don't mean doctor. Before I knew it we was both teetering and tottering. I went down, she went up. She went down, I went up. See the saw, she said. See the saw. Only, I must of got bored or something. Short attention span. I ain't changed much. Anyways, perty soon I come down and stayed down, holding her high up in the air. She was giggling a lot up there. I remember that. See the saw, she said. Then it happened."

"What?" Kes asked.

"She smarted off at me. She said something I still can't remember to this day. But—whatever it was that spurred me—I rolled off my teeter-totter seat and let her drop. She dropped hard. She bounced off'n her seat and her head hits a rock or the totter or some damn thing. She didn't move or giggle after that. I remember looking down at her a real long time. She looked like a little ragdoll that had been thowed away. Wudn't nothing I knew to do about it." Glenn looked across the carseat, locking eyes with Kes. "So what did I do?"

Kes shook his head slowly, steering down the causeway, not knowing or if he wanted to know.

"I climbed back in that window and lay down until Mama come to get us from our naps," Glenn said, scratching, "in time for the show that night. That's what I did. I even dozed off finally. You slept through it all. When I woke up it was like that little gal had never been real, like she was just a quarrelsome dream. A dream I never told nobody about. I got up from that nap, started tuning my guitar. Later, after the show, I sneaked back out into them trees, to see that see-saw. She weren't lying there no more. No ragdoll. Nothing. No sign she'd ever been there. So, back then, I told myself for sure she was not real. But now—now I know she is."

"Was," Kes said.

"Is. She is real. Now more than ever. Sometimes, after all these years, I'll have a day or two that I forget what I done. Then I remember. Then I feel bad for letting myself forget. Bad because I can't remember her name she told. Bad for letting her drop without even knowing why. One thing I do know. No little girl like that could have anything to say as bad as what I done to her. But, bad as I feel, I ain't never felt bad enough to tell Mama or no preacher or police. I'm still afraid. So I reckon I got more to suffer."

"You just told me. Not that I'm much redemption."

"I did. Didn't I?"

"Yes. That's worth something. It must be."

The whir of marsh grass and these small revelations made both their hearts heavy.

"I just hope somebody found her right quick," Glenn mused. "I'd hate to think she stayed lost. Hate to think she had folks what loved her who didn't know where she was or how she was. Somehow, she didn't look very loved though—*Kes, watch out!*"

A giant dog *dashed* in front of the Cadillac—across the causeway—Kes fighting the wheel, dodging the dog. Tires screeched rubber, kicking up mud as the Cadillac skimmed the soft road shoulder—

"*Hold on*—" Kes yelled.

Swerving hard, the Cadillac regained the road as the big mottled hound galloped on, disappearing into the marsh.

Kes and Glenn's hearts pounded.

"*Christ*, we almost *lost it* back there—" Kes exclaimed.

"*Damn* that dog—"

"*Damn* this *day*—"

"Glad I ain't got nothing to erp."

"A trucker flipped his cab and *drowned* in that marsh water last month," Kes said.

"Yeah, I remember—"

"Okay, brother, that does it. Before one of us winds up dead today, you best know the rest of that story."

"What story?"

"This damn story you started," Kes closed his eyes, opened them, gathering his wits, trying to breathe normal as he drove. "We almost got lost as that little girl, is what I mean."

"I *know it*. Dog damn near did us in."

"No, Glenn, I'm talking about that King's Harvest show.

I never knew about your little see-saw girl, but you're right, I do remember that King's Harvest show. And I'll never forget the next rainy morning driving back, while you slept through it all."

"All of what?"

"You was conked out in the backseat. Mama had told them Hard Shell Baptists she could find her way back out of them hills without any help. Well, I don't know how or what happened, but Mama got more lost than I ever seen her. We was driving in circles and snakes. It got to where they was nobody nowhere to be seen. No houses. Nothing. Just hills, woods, crooked road. Mama started to cry. Never seen her so scared or wore out. Then I started to cry with her. I wanted to help her so. I didn't know what to do either or no way to save us. And then—I'll never forget it—we passed a tattered feller, some packrat on a slow mule. He was bent, bad. His face, eyes—he was all scarred up, looked to me—when we passed him, like them good-as-dead firemen we sung for in the state hospital. That pack mule was hung with clinking bottles and tin cans. Mama was afraid to stop to ask that feller the way. We drove on. Well, it weren't two minutes later we saw some Burma Shave signs, then a highway Mama recognized. Then we was out of there. Mama never mentioned it again. I think she wanted to shut that scary lost trip home out her mind. And you—you just slept back there, in the backseat, dreaming about your lost little ragdoll through all that scary."

"Well, I'll be damned," whispered Glenn, a peephole opening in his brain.

"No. You ain't damned just yet. And I don't think any good would have come from you being dragged into any mess over that poor little see-saw girl. It was something what couldn't be undone. It were an accident, really. It ain't like you was the Wolfman or she was the Lindbergh baby. She was just a kid's mistake."

"Maybe," Glenn mumbled, scratching his chest with frenzy. "But I had a little talk with cellerphane blue Jesus back in that jail cell. Lemme tell you, Kes, that was a terrible place. Terrible. Cockroaches after me. Mattress smelled like old pee mixed with new. If I had a shotgun I believe I'd a blowed my nose wid it, rather than face Mama. And then that cellerphane Jesus showed up."

"*Cellophane whoozus*?"

"His rippling skin, his sweet spirit, it was all there in blue cellerphane. He slipped right through them cell bars with his blue cellerphane beard and long cellerphane curls. Long cellerphane whanger too."

"You saw his *whanger*?"

"Well, I caught a long glimpse of it through his cellerphane robe when he sat down beside me on the bunk. You shoulda seed it. Or maybe not. I could kinda see all through him, you see. And he made a crinkly sound, like cellerphane does, when he sat down beside me and laid his clear blue hand on my heavy, heavy shoulder."

"Did—did he say anything?"

"Sure. Sure he said plenty."

"Okay. Okay. So what did your cellophane Jesus say?"

"He told me I was chose jist like you was chose. That we

was chose together. The Brothers Brass. That we was here to sing his word and whup the red rubber devil and not to throw it all away on liquor, half rubber, and go-to-hell living. An he told me, in his soft crinkling voice, not to go the way of Daddy Brass."

"What did you say to that?"

"I said no sir, I won't throw it away. And, yes sir, thy will be done."

A tuck-and-roll epiphany struck Glenn, his hand falling down, stroking the leather upholstery he sat on.

"Kes—how you come by this fine-decked car of Daddy's?"

"Daddy Brass lent it to me himself," Kes said with a sneaking smile.

"You tell him about me?"

"Nope. He didn't ask no questions."

"Oh. Well that was nice of him. Clear blue Jesus would approve, I expect. I'll be sure to tell him. Daddy could use a good word or two."

"Your clear blue Jesus say anything else?"

"Well, since you ask—yes, he did. He said my big brer Kestrel would come emancipate me. And you did."

"Yeah. You looked overdue for emancipation alright. But I cain't emancipate you from yourself."

"Don't you worry. I'll roll the stone rest of the way. That Jesus—he give me the backbone and hindlegs to go forth in a clean and godly manner, like Mama's always preached. He give me something else too."

"What else he give you?"

"That cellerphane Jesus—he ain't all gentle, you know.

He give me kind of a pox in the perverts for good measure. He told me take heed of them weavers in my melon. He give me the pox to remember by."

"Now you're losing me, little brer. You're just drunk sick. But otherwise you look plenty healthy from here

"Yeah? Well, look at this—"

Glenn pulled up his shirt. A rippling mass of red welts covered Glenn's chest, erupting down his rib cage like he had been blistered on a hot grill.

"*Christamighty, Glenn* . What did all *that*?"

"Brer, I'm gonna ask you to watch your language from now on. Well, for a little while anyway."

"But, *Christa*—"

"Truth be," Glenn said blandly, "my perverts—I mean, my privates—is worst of all. But I ain't gonna show you them. He just give em to me where the rest of world cain't see but where I'll know it. To remember Him by. This all come blistering and bubbling up right after that celler-phane Jesus slipped back out the bars of that hateful jail. I'm hoping it'll all go away, directly."

"If it was me it couldn't go away directly enough."

"It did before."

"*Before?* When?"

"When I kilt that little gal. You and Mama never knew that either, cause I dressed myself in the closet before the show and took my bath behind closed doors that night. But that was the first time this pox took me. Even then, I knew it had something to do with the killing I done. I knew my Bible well enough by then. Pox was gone the next day.

But I've always known it was still in me, just under my skin, crawling, waiting to pop back up—hot red and snarling outa my sorry soul." Glenn smoothed down his shirt. "That Mizz Plum was real nice."

Kes kept shaking his head, watching for new dogs in the road.

"Uh-huh. Real nice. Smart too."

"Not much like Mama though."

"Nope. Not much."

"Thank you, brer. Kestrel—I mean—you been nice too. What with everthing you done for me this day."

"Don't fret it, Brother Brass. Folks like ours—well, you and me, maybe we're chose and maybe we ain't. But no brother nowhere ever chose folks like ours."

VERSE 15

The Crack of Bones

There was one of God's chosen crickets chirping on Dean Pickery's windowsill. No morning could ask for a more blessed omen. Yes, that chirping was so lovely, so lyric. The Dean nipped more than a nip of cherry soothing syrup before returning it to his bottom drawer. His cherry red lips smiled at the wee cricket. With enough cough remedy and the good Lord willing the Dean would find inner peace in a very few minutes.

"Willa?" the Dean asked, pressing his intercom button. "Are you a superstitious sort?"

"Why, no sir," his secretary spake from the intercom speaker. "That would be ungodly. It's like witchcraft isn't it?"

"Do you believe in luck?"

"Well, yes, I suppose I believe in luck. Lord willing."

"How you feel about crickets, Willa?"

"Crickets? I never thought too much about em," the speaker crackled.

"My mama always said a cricket was a sign of good luck."

"Mine too."

"You won't forget to stop by the Rexall over your lunch hour will you?"

"No, Dean Pickery. I won't forget. You about out of your medicine again?"

"Hold my calls, Willa."

"Yes, Dean Pickery."

The Dean swiveled back around to see the cricket. Yes, perhaps this was his lucky day, Lord willing. He was not the superstitious sort either. But he could use a little luck right now. Here he sat, first thing of a morning, greeted with this unfortunate reminder that Newdundy Hot Shot Pest Control was wayward, remiss, and overdue. Then, he would have to contend with lunch at the Rotary with Mrs. Pickery. And, finally, this God-given day required mandatory attendance at tonight's meeting of the Board Of Trustees where that goddam Piggly Wiggly man Bevin Brooks kept calling for an audit of the college accounts. Yes, and that, sir, was going to take a lot of crickets.

Dean Pickery knew he could not forestall this intrusion and insult to his fiscal management of the school much longer. A good CPA would uncover certain irregularities in the official ledgers, no doubt, and those weren't even Dean Pickery's private ledgers—the *real* ledgers. Yes, Bevin Brooks was a twice-divorced alumni who had never done a damn thing with his life but peddle tomatoes and chops while fornicating with half his cashiers. Bevin Brooks had no higher calling like Dean Pickery's. Only Dean Pickery's lengthy tenure and his high esteem within the local community had allowed him so many years of grace without proper review of the ledgers. A younger and less tenured man's gambling debts and fiscal malfeasance would have been exposed long ago.

The Dean leaned forward in his chair. Chewing the corner of his art gum eraser, he studied the cricket's legs as they rubbed and twitched. The infernal chirping made Pickery's head throb even worse than before he downed the BC Powder and bi-carb. Shouldn't that codeine syrup have done its wonders by now?

Come to think of it—and the Dean had thought about it plenty—none of Malachi's peace or equity was to be found here. No, a younger Bible college dean would never have been permitted the luxury of accumulating such a heavy financial burden or be so heavily indebted to one Malakoff Brass. A few too many games of boo-ray and high stakes poker, a half dozen bad ponies at long odds—and that younger dean would have been sent packing years ago or, worse, delivered unto a Georgia state chain gang. A fledgling administrator would have been detected after embezzling no more than two or three thousand dollars, instead of sixty-six thousand. Arrested at that stage the backsliding cad would be sure to face up to two years in striped britches, hacking weeds in a bar ditch. One or two years at most—but no more than that. Why, when you looked at it that way, Dean Pickery was a victim of his tenure and long loyal service. And now, all bets were off. A man could die behind bars for misappropriation of sixty-six thousand dollars. Unless, of course, he woke up one day to a lucky cricket.

Yes, Dean Pickery was the fortunate pilgrim. Wasn't he? With age and experience came privileges and perks, allowing a tenured man time to braid a longer rope for his rafters.

The Dean laid his eraser on his knee, wondering how such a lowly cricket could have risen to such a lofty perch. He was about to flick the cheery cricket off its perch—when he saw the girl. Young Bettilia Whissler was walking down the sidewalk two stories below his office, her schoolbooks clutched to her chest. Dean Pickery had some words for that young lady—words that had waited patiently for several days. Now this God-given moment was sprung upon him. It was not in the Dean's nature to let such an opportunity fly out the window. Besides, he was feeling better now. Much better, younger, full of life and cherry cough syrup. It felt fine to be a man of hope and charity and cherry cough syrup. He flicked the cricket and grabbed his Belvedere cap.

Dean Pickery felt mighty spry as he skipped painlessly down the stairs then out into soft sunlight. Picking up his pace, he drew alongside little Miss Whissler who looked unsurprised at his sudden appearance. She did not stop walking, nor did he.

"Why, you are Miss Bettilia Whissler as I recall?" he said, short of breath.

"Reckon I am."

"And how are you this blessed day, little Bettilia?"

"Oh, *f*-fair enough, I suppose," she said, feeling nagged by this horsefly in his flat, funny cap. "You got the croup or something? The creeping crud?"

"Why, no, honey. I'm fit as a fiddle. Why do you ask?"

"Aw, you smells like that cherry *c-c*-cough serum. Sure you ain't sickly like?"

"No, honey," Dean Pickery insisted, his voice notching higher, "Look, we need to have a little chat—"

"My Mambly says folks been knowed to drank that Rexall serum for the pure pleasure of it. Fills their heads with fairy fog, she say."

"Now, you see—your Mrs. Mambly Whissler—she would be the purpose of this little chat. The precise purpose. I have been trying to reach your sweet caretaker for weeks now, regarding your scholastic records. You've missed several days—"

"She'll be joyful to hear from you, I'm *sh-sh*-sure."

"That's just the point, though. Slow down a little. Your Mambly does not answer her telephone and the postal missives I've sent have gone unanswered. Miss Bettilia, you hearing me?"

The Dean grabbed her arm. They both stopped and stared at each other. Bettilia could see he was half lit. She knew all about half-lit men and full-lit men.

"I wouldn't know piddly about that," Bettilia mumbled.

"Say now," the Dean said, with a ruddy, growing grin. "I sense a certain frost in the air betwixt us, young lady. How about a little love offering?"

Pickery bent, offering his cheek. Hackles rose on Bettilia's neck. Her hand closed. Such offerings had passed her way before.

"How about a little *love offering* this morning?" his red

lips smiled in her face.

Bettilia *slugged* the old bastard, hard. Then she ran.

Kestrel Brass was crossing campus, fresh from breakfast in Barley Cake Hall, when he heard a howl. Across the green, he spied a bareheaded Dean Pickery huffing along as fast as he could in his three-piece suit. Pickery was chasing Bettilia. She was outracing the old bastard with little effort.

"Git your beee-hind back here, young lady—" the Dean wheezed. *"I'll bend you over my knee."*

Bettilia disappeared into the trees.

Kestrel dropped his book satchel and went chasing after them. As he ran he snatched the Dean's cap up from the sidewalk. He caught up to the Dean, overtaking the old man with little effort. Kes landed square in front of the Dean, stopping him in his fat tracks, under the pecan tree. Dean Pickery was short of wind, short of patience, and fully enraged. His bleary red eyes shot into Kes's eyes for a split-second before he tried to push past the boy. Kes snagged Pickery's coat sleeve, stopping him.

"Dean Pickery?" Kes asked, his own blood rising. "You dropped your hat."

"*Thank you—*" the Dean sputtered, fitting the cap on his head.

Kes had to snag him again, so he couldn't get away.

"Dean Pickery? You after Bettilia Whissler?"

"Yes, Kes, *I dang sure am,*" he exploded. "I need me more of *that little bitch.* I'll *wear her out—*"

Kes grinned a little.

"I seen her. She's up taking a whiz in that tree."

Sure enough, Dean Pickery looked up in the tree. Sure enough, Kestrel Brass sent a right fist *crashing* into Dean Pickery's jawbone. Kes had always been stronger than he looked. A treehouse will do that for you. But even Kes was a bit surprised at how effortlessly Dean Pickery went reeling, unfolding and landing flat-backed on the pavement. Kes heard the crack of bones beneath all that settling flab. It was a sickening sound, like cell bars clanking shut. So Kes did the next right thing to do. He turned and he ran.

Bettilia was not hard to follow. Not at first. Kes jogged quickly after her, into the grove of trees. He saw a pile of schoolbooks scattered on the ground, then one button-down shoe, then another. After that, her trail grew confusing. The brown grass was groomed low. There were no footprints he could detect or follow as Kes slowed in his pursuit. He began to wander amidst the trees. Dean Pickery would soon come to his senses back there and begin to make trouble. Time was of the essence. Kes stopped and listened closely to the flutter of autumn leaves whispering to him. Then he spied a bright yellow-gold speck in the polyglot of colors on the ground. It was a gold hair barrette on a red maple leaf at the base of one of the great trees. The barrette was plastic and shaped like two goldfishes tail-to-tail. Kes snatched it up then peered high into the tangle of maple limbs.

"*Bit-teeel-yaaa-a-a-a!*" he shouted, expecting no response. He got none.

He knew what he had to do. Kestrel Brass had been climbing trees all his life. He pocketed the barrette, then took purchase upon a big knot of the tree's trunk with one foot. His fingers bit into the bark like it was a rock face on which he gained slow ascent. Finally, reaching for the lowest branch, he began to heave himself upward, gaining speed as he went, He climbed and he climbed.

He knew Bettilia would be high up. She was. About two stories up he finally saw her dangling feet. Breathing hard, Kes's arms and legs flexed higher still until he flopped onto a great limb adjacent to the limb where Bettilia was perched.

She showed no surprise, she looked out through the trees.

"Well, hell now," he said, blowing hot clouds. "We might as well steal a gun, a car, and a po' boy sandwich and just—just *hit the road.* I hear Panama City is full of sin and sand. I can tell all them wicked folk how I used to sing songs for Jesus."

"Wonder what he be thinking of *n*-next," Bettilia said, dreamy, as if she didn't hear a word Kes said, as if she and Kes always met in trees.

"Who? Who be thinking of?"

"Ole Dean Pickery."

"Oh," Kes followed her gaze to the far sidewalk below.

Through the leaves they saw the old man sprawled on the sidewalk pavement down there. Nobody had found him yet.

The chapel bell started to ring. *Bong, bong, bong.*

Dean Pickery raised his head. Blinking, lost, his wits were slow. Suddenly, he leapt up and looked around. His coat was badly rumpled, torn at one elbow. The Dean turned on his heel and began marching fast back to his office, gaining vigor as he went.

"He'll be making phone calls, I expect," Kes said. "Or calling out the dogs."

"Maybe not. He might wanna *l-l*-lay low till he *s*-sobers up. He don't want no questions about why I whacked him."

"Why? did you whack him?"

Bettilia tossed a maple seed and watched it twirl to the ground.

"Kes?"

"Yeah?"

"You ever see a calf stuck outside a *b*-bobwire fence, on the other side from its mama?"

"Don't believe I have."

"Happens all the time. A calf slips through them wires somehow, then be too *d*-dumb or scary to git back through to mama's tit and warm belly. They is the most lonesome looking little things you ever seen. Most times you can chase that calf and the calf will *t*-take the plunge. It'll hop back through the bobwire to mama and everthing's okay. But not always. And they's not always somebody there to help that calf back through.

"One time they was this old *m*-mama *c*-cow up the road from me and Mambly. The mama cow had her jist born calf what hopped outside Mr. Hurd Mayfield's fence. It had come one o' the *c*-coldest nights of the year. Frightful, bitter *c*-cold. I come along and seen it next morning. Calf was curled on the ground, froze dead. But the *m*-mama cow was still standing on t'other side of that bobwire, freeze and drizzle hanging out her snout, like she'd watch over that froze calf forever if'n she had to. Finally, *M-M*-Mr. Mayfield, he come and led her away. I come back by later and the froze calf was *g*-gone too. No *t*-telling what that old farmer done with it."

Kes had no words for a story like that. He studied Bettilia's faraway face. Her eyes were sad and lost in the leafy shadows.

"I always wish't I had some *k*-kind of mama," Bettilia said, "way back when I was a child. Any mama, I guess. But especially a *m*-mama like that. Even if they led her away after I froze in the cold."

"But I thought Mizz Whissler was your mama."

Bettilia smiled a mite.

"You know better than that," she murmured.

Kes supposed that he did know better, and had all along.

"But what about a daddy? Did you have a daddy?"

"Yeah. I had one, you might say. Kind of like I had Mambly for a mama. Only Mambly was good and my *d*-daddy was *n*-not. *N-N*-Not."

"You don't recollect your own mama?"

"No. *N*-Not really. I think he took me when I was real little. Weeks old maybe."

"But he weren't your real daddy?"

"He was real enough. Too real to believe. I used to hide from him, from everbody, up here."

"Up here?"

"In these trees."

"You wearing me out, girl. You make me work for everthing. So how you come by Miss Whissler? She your mama or mammy or whatnot?"

She did not answer him.

And then she did.

Her head turned, she looked straight into his eyes. Kes felt giddy, weak, hot-wired. Bettilia's voice came dry, hardly heard under the breeze.

"Mambly come down from *th*-the hills. Running from a *horned man.* Not much older than I be *n*-now, she were. She lost a child afore it was borned, cause she had sickness in her womb. Her first feller died of black lung she say. She settled in these parts. Married Mr. Whissler. I remember her saying she always wanted *gold slippers* to git married in, but never got em. Mr. Whissler was just a poorly janitor for this school. He moved her into his *h*-house. That house. She told me the years passed and they was happy enough, though she missed having babes to raise up. Then Mr. Whissler, he passed *t-t*-too. She weren't an old woman then. But she weren't a young one neither. Mr. Whissler, he weren't just a janitor. He was also a mule man. He bought and traded and finally left her a fairly pot of *m*-money when he died, and almost a hunert acres. She weren't the kind to remarry, agey as she were. Taught first grade school, in the *c*-colored school, for awhile afore they retired her. Then I come along."

"You come along?" Kes asked, his head against the

tree trunk. It made him feel closer to her sitting on the other side.

"Yep. I come along after my daddy *d*-died. I lit out when I was eleven, twelve, *th*-thirteen—I dunno. I don't know how old I be exactly."

Kes could not conceive such a thing.

"Bettilia?"

"Kes?"

"Can I come over and set next to you? I can't hear so good from over hear, what with this wind and the tree rustling."

"I reckon," she said.

He knew it sounded feeble. Yet it seemed to be enough of an excuse to suit Bettilia. And that made Kes feel better about where things were headed. Wherever that might be.

Carefully, Kes rose to his feet on his limb then climbed around to Bettilia's limb. She scooted over to make room for him. He settled in beside her.

"So, a body can not know how old they are?" he asked.

"This body can."

"Hmmm. I guess I never thought of that."

"I ain't from them same hills as *M*-Mambly. Hills I'm from is way farther *n*-north somewheres and up in the backcountry. Near Riddle Top mountain."

"Riddle Top?"

"Mambly, she said she heared of Riddle Top, once *m*-maybe, in a dream she had. Or from the horned man what come after her. That meant something to me. Most folks ain't *n*-never heared of Riddle Top."

"Horned man?"

"Anyways, that *d*-daddy dies and I ain't gonna *st*-stay around that place on my lonesome. So I walked and hid for miles till I spied a freight train. A freight train what come choogin through them pines. It slowed. Then slowed some more. I climbed up in a boxcar. And then we was gone. I rode all night, into the next day. I waited till them hills was *m*-most behind me afore I hopped off. When I hopped I landed in a burnt tobaccy field. Woods all around that burnt tobaccy was burnt too. It was late *s-s*-summer. Somebody must of got careless or got mean. Never seed so much burnt ground in my day. But at least I was outer them hills.

"So, I commenced walking. Lord, if I didn't about walk my dern toes off. Sure enough, I begin to see a green bud here and there, until I'm walking in green woods what weren't burnt. I'd eat me some wild blackberries and gooseberries, but I remember being thirsty as all git out. I kept looking for sign of a crick, but weren't no cricks to see for the longest time. Then I spy the smokestack of a cotton gin and—afore ye know it—they's a *b-b*-big drive-in picture show screen. Din't know what it was then. Looked like a big ole empty sign in a pasture full of iron posts, fer as I knew. Then I seen a water tower. It begins to look like a *t*-town up ahead so I steers clear. Didn't need no high sheriff or orphan home snagging me. Not after I come this far.

"So I kept to the back roads, hungry and hard up for a drank of water. Next thing I know I'm sneaking through the *k*-kudzu and the cows, up to a house with a windmill. Even back then I knowed a windmill meant *w*-water. Then I sees Mambly for the first time. She was throwing out feed for her chickens. She was plumb funny to look at. But I weren't in a laughing mood. I come around back of the coop, peeked around the corner and cotched sight of a *w*-water trough. Mambly's got her back to me, she's a goodly ways away. So's I crawl over to the trough thinking I'm no more noisy than a noonday shadder. I was good at being quiet. I didn't talk none back *th*-then. So, real quiet-like, I start sucking water. She told me later I sounded like a spent coonhound. Well, you know the rest. Mambly, she turns around easy as you please. She give me the squint eye. And I was too *t*-tired to run. We was together, ever after that. She took me in. She didn't ask too many questions. Not at first. She fed me, got me good clothes. Over the years she'd parcel out a query or *t*-two, but without no push. And she took no insult when I din't answer. Folks around here din't ask no questions neither. None of em wanted me. So they believed whatever fib she told em about a busy mama and daddy I never *d*-did have. They took her money. They let me into their schoolhouses. I weren't like I was some colored kid who might cause trouble. I kept to my own self, and so did Mambly. I reckon Mambly liked things the way they was, never having no *b*-babes of her own."

"So you become her babe."

"I reckon."

"You miss her?"

"Like the night don't never end, I miss her. Something fierce."

"Yeah. Life must be fierce if you ain't nobody's babe."

"Well, Mambly always said she had to ready me *f*-for the day she wouldn't be here no more. She said that was the most important job for any Mambly. To give ye what ye need to go it alone. She said I had a running start on most of em. I din't know no words to tell her how far out ahead of em I really was. Mambly said, if anything was to ever happen to her, she din't want *n*-no fuss. No townfolk or no funerals. I was to just put her away, real peaceful and quiet, she said. And keep on gitting ready."

"Gitting ready?"

"Gitting ready. For what was next. For the coming of the day."

"For the Judgment Day?"

"Aw, I already seen that one, I expect. But they's always another day, after that. And whatever or whoever *c*-comes, I'll be ready."

Kes reached over and took a fallen twig from Bettilia's hair. Bettilia did not seem to mind.

"So, how did your daddy come to die?"

"Rail spike fell on his head. Kilt him."

"Dang. That must of hurt his feelings."

"I wouldn't know. Doubt he felt much at all. He never did feel much at all. Besides, he was too dead to feel *d*-diddly and he damn well deserved to be."

"Did—did he mess with you?"

Bettilia tossed another whirly maple seed.

"I ain't got words for what he done to me. It was his nature. I can still hear the click of his hobnails on my bedroom floor. I took to the trees mostly."

"What was his name?"

"I don't—" she faltered. "Don't make me say it. I ain't *g*-gonna. Just saying his name, it can still make him too real to me."

The maple seed blew sideways. The wind had begun to whip around. Their shared perch on the limb, the entire mass of maple tree, had begun swaying and rocking like a great creaking ship at the sea.

"You know, Bettilia, " Kes said, "Even if ole Pickery gets over it, you're gonna have to drive yourself to school and into town. Winter's coming on. You'll have to learn."

"Aw that Mercury sedan in *th*-that barn ain't been running for three years now. Motor's froze up. Mambly kept forgetting to put oil in the crankcase."

Kes got a clearer picture.

"You mean you both been walking to town and back all this time? Through fair weather and foul?"

"Been afooting it everwheres. I don't mind really. I'm strong for my size. Like I said. Walking and weather don't jug me none."

Kes shook his head.

"I wondered why they was so much dust on her," he said.

"Mizz Mambly?"

"Naw. On the Mercury sedan."

"Kes, it's pert near quarter after *n*-nine by the King's Hall clock. I gotta git to Civics class. At least till I find out if Pickery gives me the boot."

"Yeah, me too. Bettilia?"

"Yeah?"

"I like you."

"I reckon I like you too, *j*-jaybird."

"And I worry about you. What with your Mizz Whissler gone. You out there all alone with that man prowling at your windows. After what happened to Mizz Whissler, her being hanged and all. Ain't you afraid?"

"Not really. I got Mambly's squirrel rifle. And I ain't seed nothing of *n*-nature boy or mule since that one day. Probably jist another *m*-mule man, looking for ole dead Mr. *Wh*-Whissler."

"Well, I wish you'd get that phone hooked back up. At least do that much. So's you could call if you really needed help or anything. You call me and I'll come running. I'll hop a horse or steal a car. Be there lickety-split."

He was so earnest she had to laugh a little. Bettilia even looked kindly toward him, gentle into his eyes. Kes felt the wind blow right through him.

"Yeah, I just bet you would," she said. "C'mon let's git outer this tree."

"Sure enough."

Kes hoisted himself up until he was standing on the limb. He took Bettilia's hand, helping her to her feet. High in the branches of the maple tree, their hands held longer than need be. Their eyes met with soft smiles.

Finally, Bettilia released Kes. She reached past him to grab another limb on her way down to the ground. Bettilia must have jostled the limb they were standing on. Kes must have been caught off guard from the wind blowing through him or from her touch or unsettling thoughts of Chalice or Dean Pickery or Mama George. Whatever it was, something must have upset his grace notes and inner balance.

Because, as Bettilia brushed past him, Kes fell from the tree.

VERSE 16

Brief Thanksgiving

By Thanksgiving, an icy lacework spread across the marshland docks. The long deep damp of winter settled over the island, seeping into Kes's broken leg and broken arm. From where he sat at the laden and colorful table, the brittle skin of a roasted duck had never looked so cold or so stuffed with misery.

Kes gave thanks for the headache that split his skull every morning. He gave thanks for the crackling and popping of his bones every time he shifted his hip in this rosewood chair. He gave praise when his mother looked at him like he was a crippled amputee trundling the sidewalks on a roller board with a flat-iron in each hand. Should he thank her for teaching him how to chronically break the Ninth Commandment with her, himself, and everybody else? Hell, your mama or your daddy lied to you first, before anybody else in this life, didn't they? Who better to teach you the fundamentals?

"Here, honey," Mama George said. "Let me slip this little pillow behind your hip. It will ease your back spasms.

Mmmmhmmm. There you go."

Kes leaned forward and let Mama George fit the pillow betwixt him and the back of the chair. Despite her best efforts to keep him comfortable, Kes hated her best goddam rosewood chair. Wasn't that the truth? But, goddam, wasn't he thankful for it? Couldn't he count his goddam blessings? Mama George said this chair was a family heirloom—which translated into "this chair is weak and rickety." But it was the only "nice" chair in the house that allowed the cast on Kes's left leg to jut out sideways whilst he hooked his elevated arm cast on the left handle of the chair's back. In this double-odd cantilevered position Kes managed to hunch over his plate, chewing some chewy wild rice. Chalice's daddy, the island mayor, had even given Kes the bent rosewood cane hanging on the other handle of this chair, so he could gimp around in proper style. Another family heirloom, or so they said. So wasn't Kes blessed?

Every year Mama George laid out oyster stuffing, mushroom and giblet gravy, and marshmallow-clotted fruit salad. All three repulsed him, but Kes knew he should give thanks for something. What was he really thankful for? Wasn't he overjoyed by the goddam gift of life?

"It's kismet, isn't it?" Aunt Jewell asked. "Divine kismet from the good Lord above. Tis the good Lord's bounty we receive and—*look here*—his bountiful blessings include wild rice on this blessed day of thanks. Not white rice. Wild Indian rice. Dr. Greever sat me down and told me in no uncertain terms. No more white rice with sweet milk and sugar of a morning. It backs me up, he says. My diverticulitis will no longer tolerate white rice. Yes, Georgiana, yours was the hand of His kismet when you set this wild and bountiful table."

"Gee, Mama," Kes said to his spoon, "I reckon that's why them rats got into your white rice. So you'd throw it out."

"Aunt Jewel?" Glenn asked. "I thought kismet was what you got from that Araby god, Allah. He ain't a Baptist god is he?"

"Both of you mind your peas," said Mama George, returning to her chair. "Jewel? Would a dipper of duck gravy help it pass easier?"

The insane itching Kes felt under both casts was aggravated by Aunt Jewell and Uncle Bee Joe sitting across the table. They didn't have to do anything to aggravate him. They only had to be here. The old couple had driven down from their home in Beaufort to spend this Thanksgiving day at this table.

"Come to think of it," Glenn pondered, "the South Caroliny flag does look a bit like that Araby flag, now don't it? With that sliver of moon and all?"

"Mind your peas, Glenn, Mama said."

Aunt Jewell and Uncle Bee Joe had never been favorite family to Kes. In fairness, Kes felt no particular like or dislike of them. Oh, Aunt Jewell brought too much to a party—chattering on and on—while Uncle Bee Joe didn't even know there was a party. But they were nice people as people go. Their greatest sin, in Kes's book, was their boring ways of just being. By just being here, Jewell and Bee Joe made Kes want to climb deeper inside himself to hide, where he could sweat more inside his plaster and fester over this infernal itching, which meant Kes needed somebody to make him forget about himself. His brother was doing his best to help.

"Yeah, Aunt Jewel, I know you and your sweet teeth," Glenn was saying, "I remember you used to put sugar tea in my baby bottle till mama got wise."

"Mmmhmm, I do recall," Mama agreed.

"Glenn Brass, there is no earthly way you could remember that." Aunt Jewell was getting a bit testy.

"Rot yer teeth," Uncle Bee Joe grunted through the tines of his fork.

"I'll have you know I was raised on sugar tea in the crib," Aunt Jewell advised the table. "My grandmother Elvy said sugar tea helped soothe and settle a child's tummy."

The only thing soothing this cold sweat in Kes's innards was the warmth of gravy and the lyric hum from his mother's throat as Mama tried to validate all who sat at the table without her uttering too many words. Mama George was always a bit cautious and phony and started mmmhmmming a lot when company came to call.

"Mmmmhmmm," Mama George kept trilling, with a slight, bright uplift to the second note of her vamp. Most of the time she ended on a B Sharp. Yes, Kes's trained ear knew a B Sharp when he heard it.

"I spoon a little wheat germ on my scramble eggs," Uncle Bee Joe said from out of nowhere. "Keeps me from backing up."

"Mmmmhmm?"

"I like fried eggs," Kes muttered. "Fried egg sandwiches."

"Loads of black pepper," Glenn agreed.

"Yeah, brer. Loads of black pepper."

The boys had just finished breakfast that morning when Daddy Brass came breezing through the kitchen with a hummingbird cake in each hand. He left his Hudson idling in the driveway. Mama George was still frantic at the stove—so frantic she did not bother to show her usual displeasure upon Daddy's arrival. Daddy Brass presented his peace offerings and made a loud announcement.

"Georgiana, I will not be staying for no duck eggs or duck dinner. Now don't grab my leg or beg me. I will be at the downtown mission today, scraping turkey soup from cans to feed them hungry staggerbums, orphans, and a destitute widder or two."

"Malakoff, that is a plain and pagan lie," Georgiana said without lifting her head from the oven. Her bread pudding never set up to suit her and she was anxious to get her birds in behind it.

By now Kes and Glenn knew one of their Daddy's hornswaggles when they heard it. But his high humor and brave voice still cheered his sons, briefly jarring his eldest from the grievous suffering he nursed with such Kes-like earnest.

"How's Mizz Plum these days, Daddy?" Kes asked wickedly.

Daddy Brass's eyes got wise, narrowing at Kes.

"Why, she's just fine, son."

"Wish her Happy Thanksgiving for me," Kes said, pushing the envelope.

"I'll wish her," Daddy said, his voice soft.

"How do you know Mrs. Plum?" Mama George asked Kes, pulling her head from the oven to do it.

"So, Georgiana, my darlin—how you come by these two prime ducks I see on your cutting board?"

"Stop poking those birds, Malakoff. No telling where those fingers of yours have been. Deacon Arthel Dodson gifted us with those ducks. He drove all night back from his Caddo Lake hunting trip, over in Texas. Knocked on that door at crack of dawn."

"Did he now?" Daddy said. "Well, I'll just have to buy that sneaking Arthel a new Mossburg shotgun and gift him with the business end of it. It's the least I can do when a good church deacon takes such fine care of my wife and children in their hour of need."

His hand was on his heart when he said it.

Mama George was unimpressed. She slid the ducks into the oven and thanked him for the hummingbird cakes. Daddy Brass made crazy cross-eyes, shot his pistol finger at the boys at the table, then his grinning gus was gone.

There was no telling where or with whom Daddy was spending Thanksgiving dinner. None of them knew and only his boys wanted to know. Mrs. Plum was only one of many possibilities and, yes, Mama George had left such concerns far behind her and long ago.

"Kestrel? How do you know Mrs. Plum?" she repeated after Daddy was gone.

"Mama—your peas are gonna scorch—" Glenn said.

"Oh, piddle! My crowder peas—" She scurried back to dim the gas flame and add water to her pan.

Neither boy could remember a holiday without scorched crowder peas. Yes, they had learned that lesson well. You had to mind your peas.

With their mother piping commands from the kitchen, their morning commenced without much enthusiasm or Thanksgiving spirit. Due to his new infirmity, Kes was mostly consigned to tending pots at the stove while his mother rolled pie crusts, chopped celery and onions, and measured out her spices. Glenn got the worst of it. He had not complained much since his big brother's crackup, even though it meant little brother had to take up a lot of the slack around the house. On this morning, Glenn brought in firewood, salted all the steps and stone paths, cleaned gutters, cracked pecans, then swept the parlor and dining room. Kes propped his plaster against the stove and stirred a wooden spoon. After he finished the dining room Glenn came in the kitchen and took a look in Kes's pot.

"That's some well stirred giblets you got there, brer Kes."

"Just don't seem fair, do it?"

"The fair is over on Montgomery Street, every year," Mama said from inside the pantry. "You both know that."

"Yes, ma'am," Glenn said, with a Daddy Brass grin. "I do know that."

"You two go upstairs and put on your good clothes."

Glenn went clipping up the back stairs from the kitchen, Kes followed slow behind him. Kes's heavy left foot had just swung onto the top landing when he heard his aunt and uncle's car ease into the drive.

Now, with afternoon half gone, this great godawful holiday feed was dragging worse than Kes's left foot. He tried to keep his head low and his fork moving to hurry things along .

"You oughter seen her," Uncle Bee Joe was drawling. "Your Aint Jewell here let that water hose get loose from her and it was whupping around, splashing her Sunday-go-to-meeting dress, her cat Blowsy. Blowsy took off up the flagpole. Yup. That water hose was soaking down me, my short-sleeve shirt, shoes, and my brand new copy of the *Grit* that I ain't even read yet. I know I'll never forget it. Memories, memories."

"Mmmhmmm."

"Great story, Uncle Bee" Kes said, breaking the Ninth again.

"When do your plaster casts come off, Kes, honey?"

"Eleven days, Aint Jewell. They cut em off Monday after next." That's right, Aunt Jewell, eleven more hellish fucking days.

"And your fiancee? What's your girl's name? Where is she this Thanksgiving?"

"Chalice. She took the Greyhound bus to Americus. Her grandma lives there. And we ain't engaged yet, exactly."

"That reminds me rightly of that snake," Glenn said.

The room got quiet.

"What snake?" Aunt Jewell asked politely.

Mama George and Uncle Bee Joe looked over at little brother. Kes looked down at scorched crowder peas.

"Aw, it was just last Labor Day weekend," Glenn allowed, unfolding in his chair. "Hotter than tick fever and I was over to Van Horne Street, coming back from a game of half-rubber in the park. I saw a big, long nasty snake wriggle like a long water hose outa the grass, across the road and into a culvert. Scared the pee-waddin outa me."

"Really?" Uncle Bee Joe asked with grim concern. "What kind of a snake was he?"

Glenn blinked.

"I don't know. Just a snake."

"Well," Aunt Jewell pondered, creasing her brow, "I wonder where he come from..."

Glenn shrugged.

"I wonder where he was going..." Uncle Bee Joe said, chewing on that long-gone snake.

"Wonder where he is now..." Aunt Jewell posed, the weight of the world on her shoulders.

Glenn tossed his napkin on the table, rolled his eyes.

Kes let little brother squirm over the great dilemma his snake tale had created. Kes took another slice of duck, pouring gravy with his good hand. He had discovered in the last weeks that he had been hiding a nasty, wicked temper his whole life without knowing. He felt cheated, resentful of this cocksucking kismet.

Kes was not all that anxious to go back to Shelfy Oak Bible College. Not that he could dare go back. But this was not the wellspring of his newfound anger. What was that Nat King Cole song? *A Blossom Fell*? Well, for Kes, a new and heartaching bloom had fallen away. It was the sense of fresh bloom he felt back in that tree with Bettilia, before the fall. After he fell, they said, he was unconscious for a few minutes. Kes did not remember the fall or hitting the ground. He had tried to imagine it, conjure it up, pry the memory to the surface. He imagined a great cracking sound from inside himself as wind burst from his body upon hard impact with the cold and unforgiving earth. But, no matter how he tried, he could not remember it. All he remembered was standing in the tree with the sweet mint tea scent of Bettilia's breath. The next thing he knew he was coming around and saw people racing toward him from across the campus lawn. Apparently, Bettilia shinnied down the tree, checked him out, then ran like wildfire for help. A couple of teachers strange to Kes bent over him and cooed words of comfort until the ambulance arrived. Kes tried to speak but could not, only sputterings. He caught glimpses of a sober Bettilia standing off behind the growing crowd of medics, faculty, and kids. Everybody kept shushing Kes when he tried to speak, telling him to take it easy and everything was going to be fine, just fine, don't you worry. They hefted Kes into the ambulance and took him away. He had not seen Bettilia since. He had not seen Old Clootie since that day either. But Kes didn't need Cloots to know he was going crazy.

Kes wanted to reach Bettilia, of course, to talk to her and tell her it was okay. Nobody could say he had not tried. Miraculously, Daddy Brass himself drove Mama George up to Shelfy Oak to retrieve Kes—he drove her in his new Hudson and she agreed to ride with him. Such was the level of their concern and despair. Nobody asked many questions at first, they could see Kes was hurting too much. Daddy Brass drove them back to the island and carried his eldest son up the stairs by himself, despite Kes's heavy casts. Daddy Brass laid Kes gently on his old schoolboy bed.

"You lucky that head lick didn't knock out the last of your brains," Daddy told him.

"Doc said it was just a mild concussion," said Kes.

"Too bad. I always wanted me an idiot kid for a conversation piece over to the Pickalilly Club. You know? A kid to catch Palmetto bugs and crack em. Suck their heads. Help keep my storehouse clean."

Daddy almost got a laugh out of Kes, but Kes felt too cheated. He wanted to telephone Bettilia, to find out her situation. In the days that followed, he tried to telephone but her number never rang through. Over and over the woman said the line was disconnected. Then Chalice came calling, day after day. Then the letter came from Dean Pickery saying that Kes would not be able to return to school this year due to all the time he would miss and "other matters of delicate nature." Mama George kept asking Kes what "matters of delicate nature" might mean. Kes kept breaking the Ninth and telling her he did not know to which matters Dean Pickery referred. So Mama George started calling the Dean's office. Strangely, Dean Pickery was always away from his desk or otherwise indisposed when she telephoned. Kes was angry, relieved, and he figured it was just a matter of time until the truth came out. He was in no mood to speed up the process.

Then Glenn showed up with his luggage and all Kes's dorm leavings. Glenn had found his own way home by Greyhound bus, declaring to all who asked that if his big brother was not going back to that Bible College then Glenn was not about to linger there longer himself.

"Mama, I don't care what you or Daddy or anybody else has to say about it," Glenn informed her in a toughed-up voice. "I ain't going back there unless Kes does."

"I ain't going back," Kes said, staring at the floor.

"Well, see Mama? That's how it is. Me and Kes, we ain't going back."

Glenn had danced on Mama George's last nerve. And Kes had danced on it too—or would have if he could still dance. Mama knew that Daddy Brass had triumphed once again. She wasn't sure how Daddy had done it. But she felt his peculiar will behind all this as surely as if he had been there to flip Kes out of that tree.

Mama Georgia's nerves had simmered down in time for Thanksgiving, had simmered so long she might scorch at any moment. But, just like her singing sons, she could still put on a happy and harmonious show. By the time Georgiana was setting sweet potato pie and pecan tarts on the Thanksgiving table, soft sleet had begun to streak the frosted windows of the warm dining room.

"Where's them hummingbird cakes, Mama?" Glenn asked.

"Oh, we don't need so much dessert on the table, Glenn. I'll give those cakes to the woman who cleans the church. She's got eleven children."

"I do like a good hummingbird cake," Aunt Jewell said.

"Uncle Bee Joe, your sweet potato pie?" Mama asked. "Big slice or little?"

"Big," he said.

The conversation had moved from long-gone snakes to how soon Kes would regain mobility and be able to pick a guitar. Kes was not all that comfortable with this topic either—especially when their small talk veered too close to the events leading up to his injury. But he did relish being back on stage playing some revival and camp meetings. He had gone from feeling cooped up in a stifling dormitory—chained down by Bible college in general—to feeling like a prisoner in a plaster cell block back here in his own home. He had finally learned to navigate his way downstairs so his mama did not have to bring him meals. He flatly refused her suggestion that he sleep on the parlor divan until the arm and leg casts came off. He was not about to be the center stage freak in a freak show. Chalice visited every day after school. Kes did not know how to keep Chalice away or why he wanted to. He did not know what to tell her or even how he felt about her. So he gave her a kiss now and then, keeping up appearances. This only made matters worse, tweaking at his temper. No wonder he felt edgy all the time, goddam it.

"I was just climbing a tree," he told his Aunt and Uncle, his fork picking apart a pecan tart. Those pecans looked like sections of his brain being picked to pieces.

"Sakes alive, young man," Aunt Jewell fawned, "what were you doing up a tree before morning classes?"

It was the same question Mama George posed again and again, almost daily. "In fact, what were you doing up a tree at all?"

"I've been doing finger calisthenics," Kes muttered. "Keeping my fingers nimble. Wriggling em and working em around so's I can get my chord progressions back fast soon as they saw off this anchor. I'll be guitar-ready before you can spit."

"Yeah, and I've wrote a couple new songs. Kes and me been harmonizing on em."

After dessert, Mama George and Aunt Jewell cleared the table as Uncle Bee Joe and the boys moved into the parlor. Actually, Uncle and Glenn moved, Kestrel Brass lumbered. Loudly. He felt like a slow-thudding pile driver on the hardwood floors of this house.

Once the three settled in the parlor with a lit fireplace it was the idle chit-chat that lumbered. Neither boy had ever had much to say to Uncle Bee Joe. What little Uncle Bee Joe did speak he spake sluggishly through clenched teeth and briar pipe smoke. Sickly sweet pipe tobacco was not a popular aroma in this house, not with Mama—not even with Mama's boys. Uncle Bee Joe's runaway tale of the water hose was the most wordage her boys had ever heard out of the old man in one sitting. Apparently Uncle Bee Joe thought it particularly worthy of his time and effort, because he began to expand upon the tale some more.

"Ye know," he puffed, "I like to never got that faucet to stop leaking. Took two rubber washer and a pipe wrench..."

The boys felt welcome relief when they heard the giddy

voices of Mama and Aunt Jewell re-emerging from the kitchen. When the two women appeared in their winter coats and hats, pulling on gloves, the boys' spirits sank again.

"The radio says a big winter storm is on its way," Mama George told them. "They say the worst will make landfall shortly after dark."

"Kismet," Aunt Jewell said, pinning her hat to her hair. "It's a good thing we'll be home before then, though I hate leaving y'all so soon. I do so love to visit brother Will's old Angel's Prey House. I know Bee Joe feels the same. But those Carolina roads are bad enough without an inch of ice on em."

"We are toodling over to the church real quick so I can show Jewell the new Wurlitzer organ," Mama George said. "Y'all should come go with us?"

Kes hesitated, trapped by the choices on his plate. He did not care to stay here tugging words out of Uncle Bee Joe, but he also had no desire to wedge his plaster baggage into a car or go calling on churches or windy organs for idle distraction. He suspected his brother felt the same. Uncle Bee Joe stared out the window as if he never heard the question. Aunt Jewell stepped in again.

"*Bee-e-e-e?* Whyn't you come drive us over?" she pled. "Then we can drop Georgiana back off here before we journey homeward. We'll need to leave earlier if we're going to beat this storm to our door."

"Aw, I reckon," Uncle Bee Joe drawled, rising through his pipe smoke.

Kes and Glenn felt reprieve.

"Come see the Wurlitzer," Mama urged the boys. "Delivered new this week. You've never heard such pipes of glory. Better than any in all the churches where we've performed. Well, except for First Baptist Atlanta. But our little island Baptist bake sales and paper drive did not go unrewarded. It's a Wurlitzer."

"That big cashier's check from that anonymous donor helped, I reckon. Huh, Mama?" Kes asked cynically."

She did not answer.

"I better stay here, look after big brer," Glenn said. "He might take a spill or need a bullet to end his doddering days."

"I'm good," Kes agreed. "This fire here needs me."

The windows were dripping sleet by the time Mama George got back from the church. Glenn opened the kitchen door for her and waved goodbye to their aunt and uncle out in the car before they drove away. Kes stayed staring at the fire in the parlor, a *Boy's Life* in his lap, glad to be excused from such duty.

"Kes, Glenn," Mama said, "I must go lie down. Aunt Jewell has given me a dreadful headache betwixt the eyes."

"Yeah," Glenn laughed. "BC Powder oughta put Aunt Jewell on their signboards."

"Go lie down, Mama," Kes said.

"I believe I will lie down. Can you boys make yourselves sandwiches for supper? There's plenty of leftovers in the Frigidaire."

"We're able, Mama. Glenn knows how to spread up my

sandwiches just right. Just the way I like em."

"Yeah, big brother. Someday I'll tell you all them secret nasties I smear in your sandwiches."

That's when the lights went out.

The house went dark. They stood there, lit only by the fire's glow and the dimming grey light of stormy windows.

"Oh, kiss my foot," Mama said. "Georgia Light and Power. I was afraid of this."

"Flashlight's in the pantry—" Glenn said, and he was gone, banging back through the dining room to the kitchen.

"Son, those are my heirloom chairs you are abusing in there," Mama called after him.

"Hmmmph," Kes grunted, tossing the old *Boy's Life* magazine into the flames. "Them chairs might be kindling to keep us warm before this night's over."

"I had better go show your brother where the candles are kept. We will need to conserve those flashlight batteries."

"Yes. You've always been the conservative one, Mama."

"Kestrel, I swear, I don't know what you mean by that."

And she didn't. So she stuffed her gloves in her coat as she left to go find Glenn. Minutes later Glenn and Mama George returned with lit candles in two of Mama's silver heirloom candlesticks. The windows were darkening as the storm and an icy dusk began to cloak their house on Officer's Row. Kes glanced out a side louvered window at the house next door. He could see candlelight shifting in a window frame over at the Dodson's.

"Glenn, I told you to stop switching that flashlight on and off like that," Mama George was saying. "You'll wear out the switch and batteries both."

"Yes, Mama, okay."

Glenn flopped into the overstuffed wingback chair with his lit candle and dark flashlight. He set both on the lamp stand beside the phone. Glenn lifted the phone receiver, listened, then set it back on the cradle.

"No buzz. Phone's out too."

"Just think, little brer," Kes said with a wicked grin, "if we had those electric Stratocaster guitars we been wanting we could sit here and bitch, bitch, bitch about not being able to pick em."

Glenn tried not to laugh out loud but failed.

"Kestrel Brass, I will *not* have that language in this house," Mama Brass hissed. "You're too old to spank. But I won't have it. What kind of trash have you been consorting with to learn raunchy words like that?"

Kes and Glenn both looked up at her, knowing the answer, saying nothing. Mama George did not need a psychic.

"And *that* is why he was banished from this house," she snapped at their unspoken words. "I must lie down. Georgia Light and Power. No telephone. Merciful grace. I told my mother we might as well live in the Congo."

Mama George's candle left the parlor, glowing into the foyer. Glenn watched her candle go.

"Banished?"

"You know where your blankets are," her voice echoed from up the foyer's wide staircase.

Sinking back into his chair, Glenn cocked an eye at Kes. "Banished? I thought he walked off on his own."

Kes punched his arm cast with his right fist, grimaced, then sank back into the cushions of the divan, his eyes in the fire.

"He did. He did the leaving," Kes said.

"Right," Glenn said, "I don't know as I could do it. I don't like alone so much."

"Sometimes alone goes better."

"If you say so. At least you got Chalice. You know how to pick the peach."

"You reckon?"

A little later, with the storm raging after dark, Glenn went and got his Martin guitar. He strummed a few tunes by the firelight as the brothers toyed with some different harmonies. But their hearts weren't in it. The long day had sapped them both, especially Glenn, who had borne the brunt of the day's hard labor. Somewhere around nine o'clock he decided to go to bed early.

"Here, since you're single-handed," Glenn said, "you keep the flashlight."

"Okay. Thanks. You ever wonder if this old house of ours was ever haunted?"

"Hell, I know it is, brer. Always been. And you its biggest haint."

"Goodnight, Gaylenn," Kes said.

"Shuddup. And goodnight."

Glenn went upstairs, leaving Kes to ruminate in the ebbing glow of the parlor fire. The house was getting colder. Kes felt his heart and bones getting colder with it. He had put on a decent performance at the dinner table, but he wasn't sure his left hand would ever be able to make chords again—not like they once had. Kes had never been a great guitarist, but he was solid enough to drive the rhythm against Glenn's flourishes and fancy fingerwork. Surely Glenn must be fretting over that too, just a little. On the other hand, Kes realized, ever since Glenn's short stint in the Hinesville jail, little brother did not seem to let much fret him. Glenn would still flutter a little every time a police car went past, wherever they might be. Kes felt it through some other chord they shared. But, these days, he seldom displayed anything like the bottled panic Glenn fought in the nights after they dropped off Mrs. Plum at Daddy's warehouse on River Street.

As the flames of the parlor fire danced lower and lower, Kes looked into the red embers and remembered Mrs. Plum's tawny hair. Where had Mrs. Plum spent this holiday, he wondered? With Daddy Brass? Or alone? Kes felt like he had spent his holiday alone, so he knew how that went. He also knew he didn't have what it took to get up and get another log from the porch to feed these dying flames. So, he grabbed his cane. He considered tossing it on the fire. Instead, he went upstairs with it, slowly.

In the chill of his bedroom, Kes kicked off his shoes, switched off the flashlight, and lay on the bed in his clothes. He arranged the covers to suit him. His mama would harp about it if she caught him that way in the morning, but it was hard enough to get undressed with her there to help him. Without her it would take Kes a half hour of grief and tangled curses. He could hear brother Glenn already snoring down the hall—snoring loud enough to hear through two closed doors. So brother would be no help. And Kes was not about to revive Mama George and her scoldings. Kes knew he would hear enough from her in the morning about his poor linguistic choices and sorry Thanksgiving attitude.

Under a Roy Rogers bedspread, Kes lay for a long time, listening to the storm against the glass, counting his blessings. He was thankful that Chalice had been off in Americus all day. He was thankful that Aunt Jewell and Uncle Bee Joe were gone too. He hoped they hadn't slid off the road. He hoped they weren't drowning in a flooded culvert. But he was thankful they were gone. He was thankful that this goddam Thanksgiving day was over. And, more than anything, Kes was thankful he did not have to return to that goddam Shelfy Oak Bible College after this Thanksgiving holiday was done.

He drifted off to sleep with these blissful thoughts of thanks filling his noggin.

Kes wasn't sure how long he slept. But it was hours later when he awoke to the sound of a horn honk and a car's headlights in the leaves outside his window. Kes's head rose from the pillow. The sleet was still thrashing the glass, the room was dark arctic cold. Now someone was pounding on the kitchen door downstairs. The pounding stopped, then started up again.

"Kes? Glenn? What time is it?" Mama George's voice was outside Kes's room, up here in the hall. "Is somebody down at the door?"

Kes heard the kitchen door rattle open below him then slam shut. Faintly, he heard the muffled bull tones of his father.

"Too humping cold to stand out on that porch all night—"

Daddy Brass's voice reverberated through the walls and up the stairs as Kes heard his brother's door open down the hall.

"Who is it, Mama?" Glenn's groggy voice asked outside Kes's door.

"Don't be simple, son," Mama's voice said. "You know very well who it is. The man has no decency."

Kes tossed off the blanket, sitting upright on the bed. Mama George and Glenn were creaking down the stairs together. He could hear their murmurs as he switched on the flashlight. Kes's feet were cold. He tried to work his feet into his basketball shoes, but the shoes kept flopping over, refusing to cooperate. He gave up, grabbed the cane by his headboard and pulled himself up until he could balance on his good foot . Kes opened his door and lumbered out onto the landing. The voices were heating up down there.

"—And why couldn't this wait until in the morning, Malakoff?" Mama George was demanding.

"Aw, baby doll, you know how it is. Sometimes this ole world just don't rotate on Georgiana Time like it's supposed to—"

Working his plaster leg and cane down the stairs, Kes heard Glenn laugh at their daddy's boozy, booming insolence. Kes always felt better, strangely better, when Daddy Brass was back in the house. Daddy always brought a lot of gladness with him.

"Lower your voice, Malakoff Brass. Kestrel is sleeping."

"Better wake him up then," Daddy Brass's voice bellowed up the stairs. "Y'all got any eats around here? We hungry."

"Don't be asinine," Mama's voice said. "We've got enough food to feed Cox's Army."

Kes heard the refrigerator door click open; he heard his daddy rustling around inside, shifting jars and cartons. Kes dropped down the last few steps into the kitchen, minding his sock foot and cane, careful not to fall. Glenn and Mama George stood there, holding their lit candlesticks, their expressions curious in the flickering, guttering light. Both looked at Kes like he was some odd fellow they had never laid eyes on before.

From behind the open Frigidaire door, Daddy Brass's head appeared, grinning over the top. He was drunk alright.

"Just the man I wanted to see," Daddy Brass said.

"Hi, Daddy," Kes said, amused but bewildered. "What's going on with you?"

"Well, son, the way it is, ye see—I got somebody here you might oughta meet." Daddy blew out a laugh and closed the Frigidaire door.

Behind it stood Bettilia Whissler and a big white puppy dog.

VERSE 17

Candlelight Stiletto

"Will someone put that animal outside?" Mama George said.

"No," Bettilia said. "She'll freeze out *th*-there. She's staying here with *m*-me."

Bettilia looked straight into Mama George's eyes. This was non-negotiable. Mama George could see that.

"Aw, Georgiana darlin," Daddy said, tossing a tube of bologna on the table. "Leave that puppy dog be. She rode all the way out from town and left no mess in my Buick. She never talked politics, the Pope, or run down my driving skills. Neither did this little girl. That's more than I can say for some around here."

"She come this far with me. I ain't gonna leave her scary *n*-now," Bettilia said.

Mama George pulled her housecoat tighter, buttoning another button, looking from Bettilia to Daddy Brass then back to Bettilia again.

"I'll put on coffee," Mama said, heading for the stove. "Don't waste that flashlight, Kestrel."

The big puppy sat like a little polar bear with a tip of tongue sticking out, ignoring them, staring bright-eyed at the bologna on the edge of the table.

"Bettilia—how did you get here?" Kes asked, switching off the flashlight. He hobbled over to Bettilia on his cane. His plaster casts intrigued her.

Daddy Brass dropped cheese and Rainbow white bread on the table beside Glenn's candlestick, then fell into a chair with a squeak and a chuckle.

"I told ye," Daddy said. "They rode out here with me. Georgiana—you got any good fall tomaters?"

"Yes, Malakoff," Mama said, scooping coffee. "I have tomatoes from Mrs. Frayberger's garden. How much have you had to drink?"

Daddy took out his stiletto pocketknife. The blade shot out.

"Well, darlin, that's hard to say. A coffee cup or two. At least. Girl—you want tomater on your sandwich?"

"Yes sir," Bettilia said. "I'm real hungry."

She gave him a little smile.

"You oughta be," Daddy said, slicing bologna on the bare table. "Ain't no cheesebooger shacks open on no Thanksgiving. Don't seem right, now do it?"

"Glenn—get your father a plate to slice that on," Mama said.

"Yes, ma'am. I reckon your pup dog's hungry too."

"I reckon she is," Bettilia said. "Thank you *k-k*-kindly."

Glenn went to the cupboard, taking out five china plates only recently returned from their Thanksgiving table.

"I won't be eating," Mama George said as she lit a flame beneath the coffee pot.

Glenn put back one plate, glanced down at the white pup, then took out a large china bowl. Mama George scowled at him. She turned and tossed a tomato at Daddy Brass. He caught it and winked at her. She didn't like that.

"But how did you hook up with Daddy?" Kes asked Bettilia. "I been trying to reach you. Where you been? How you come this far?"

Bettilia gazed up into his eyes.

"You and all your riddles."

"How did you come by the pup dog?"

"Them riddles gonna *b*-bite you back someday, jaybird."

"But that's a good question. Ain't it?"

Bettilia shuffled to the table and sat across from Daddy Brass who was now slicing tomato on the plate Glenn gave him. The pup dog went with her.

"She showed up on River Street, knocking on my office window. I was hard asleep on the floor," Daddy said. He speared a slice of tomato and bologna together, dropping them on another plate beside a slice of cheese. With the back of his pocketknife hand, he slid the plate over to Bettilia.

"Thank you kindly," she said.

"So, as ye all know, I ain't the sort to leave no orphans or darlin beauties out in the rain and cold," Daddy allowed. "I let her in. What else was I to do? She says she come looking for one Kestrel Brass and I says I happens to know one. She says, you do? I says, yep, and I know right where they keep his hide hid. Well, you can just imagine how our little chat meandered from there. Next thing I know, I'm tipping back another cup so's I can see clear enough to drive all the way out here through these gale force winds. Hell, I feel like Santy Claus or sumpin."

Bettilia opened the Rainbow bread, took out two slices and slowly built her sandwich by candlelight, wind and sleet shivering the window behind her. Once done, she sat and stared at it.

"I didn't know where else to *g*-go," she said. "After you fell out of that tree and they come got you, I slipped away and back to that cold dark house. Without no Mambly, or you, it got mighty empty out there. Mighty empty and alone. I couldn't see going back to that school."

"Me neither," Glenn blurted.

"*Glenn—*" Mama snipped, pouring coffee into a mug.

"Sorry, Mama," Glenn said as he set a china bowlful of oats and scorched crowder peas on the floor for the eager white puppy. Daddy chortled, took a big bite of sandwich.

"I didn't know *n*-nowhere else to *g*-go..."

Glenn sat down betwixt Bettilia and Daddy Brass and began piecing together a sandwich of his own.

"I got to *th-th*-thinking, Kes, how you had never had you no dog," Bettilia continued, her eyes shifting down to the white pup. The pup's nose was busy crunching in the bowl. "So I went down the road and got you one."

"Young lady," Mama George said, setting a mug of steaming coffee in front of Daddy Brass, "we have not been introduced."

"I'm Bettilia Whissler, ma'am."

"Oh, I'm sorry, Mama," Kes said, inching toward the table on his cane. "This is Bettilia. From school."

"That much I deduced," Mama George told him. "So, Miss Bettilia, you saw Kes fall from his tree?"

Bettilia took a wee bite of sandwich, chewing it, swallowing.

"Yes, she did. You could say that," Kes said.

Mama George returned to the coffee mugs on the counter, dropped her shoulders, then cocked her head back toward the table.

"Well," she said to Bettilia. "What did you see?"

"I seen him *f*-fall," Bettilia said, taking another bite, avoiding Mama George's eyes. "I seen it all."

"What do you mean—you saw it all?" Mama asked evenly.

"I mean," Bettilia said, looking up at her, "I was in the tree with Kes."

"Oh, sweet Jesus," Daddy Brass guffawed, spewing bits of white bread. "Let us pause and give thanks."

Kes jabbed Daddy Brass's leg with his cane.

"It ain't like you think, Daddy," he said. Kes pivoted around toward the stove. "Mama, it ain't like you think. Is it, Bettilia?"

"No. No, I reckon not," Bettilia sighed.

Mama George was watching the dog eat from her good china bowl.

"How big will she get?"

"Big as a horse," Glenn said thickly, his mouth full of sandwich. "If she's anything like them dogs she come from."

"They get perty dern *b-b*-big, ma'am," Bettilia said.

"She'll be wanting to do her business pretty soon after she eats," Mama George said. "Won't she?"

"Yes, ma'am," Bettilia said, petting the crunching pup. "I expect she will."

The big white fuzz face lifted from the bowl. The pup looked up, batted her eyelashes, panting at Mama George.

"Well, Bettilia Whissler," Mama said to the dog, "you can spend the night in my old bedroom upstairs, the one I grew up in. I'll put newspaper down on the floor of the bathroom—the bath my old room shares with my master bedroom." Mama looked over at Kes. "The big bedroom I sleep in now."

Kes understood his mama. He understood that she still didn't understand. He lowered himself into the chair betwixt his father and brother, across from Bettilia.

"Thank you, Mama," Kes said, leaning his cane against the table. He studied the side of Bettilia's soft face in the candlelight, her fingers lacing over and over through the white fur at her knee.

"Malakoff, you will sleep on the parlor divan," Mama said. "This coffee is ice cold by now. It's late. Or early. No telling what time it is. Bettilia, I'll go up and fix your room. You'll need extra blankets. Finish your sandwich. Then I will show you where to find what you'll be needing."

"Thank you. I won't stay long, *m*-ma'am," Bettilia said sincerely, their eyes meeting again. "I'm sorry to trouble ye so."

"Why it's two-thirteen in the morning," Daddy Brass

yawled, picking his teeth with his thumbnail. "Wanna take my Elgin ticker up with you, darlin?"

"No, Mr. Brass, I do not," Mama said, then started up the kitchen stairs with her candlestick. "I will send Glenn down with your bedding."

Daddy Brass picked up his mug, sipping from it as he watched Mama George go, her glow disappearing up the stairwell. Suddenly, he kicked his head back, drained half the mug, set it on the table. His smile fell on Bettilia.

"Whatever you do, little gal—don't take any highhanded horseshit off her," he said.

Glenn snickered, popping the last bite of his sandwich. Kes still sat staring across his empty plate at Bettilia.

"Oh, she seems alright to me," she replied gently. "Not a lot of folks would weather all this so *w*-well."

Kes watched Bettilia take two more bites. She gave the rest to the white pup then carried her plate to the sink. He was almost surprised to see Bettilia and the white pup head immediately for the kitchen stairs.

"Bettilia?"

She and the dog looked back at quizzical Kes.

"You got busted up perty bad," she said. "I didn't realize how bad. We'll *t*-talk it out in the morning."

Bettilia went up the dark stairs, disappearing with the white pup fumbling up the steps behind her.

She had barely left the room before Daddy Brass and Glenn were leering back at Kes, their grins coming at him from both sides. Only then did Kes notice the fierce alcoholic fumes coming off his daddy.

"You know what, son?"

"What?" Kes replied.

"I never did like me no duck samwich or no duck dinner neither."

"I like both," Glenn said.

"Gotdamn Arthel Dodson and his gotdamn ducks." Daddy belched into his mug, then blurted: *Shitfire*—"

"What? What?" both sons demanded.

"That little white fuzztail never told me her name."

VERSE 18

Sisters in Morning

Kes looked out his window the next morning and saw something he had never seen and never expected to see. Bettilia was laughing.

Bettilia ran around and around the great sunlit oak, splashing puddles beneath the treehouse, the big white puppy goofy and galloping after her. The pup yapped, Bettilia giggled, Bettilia laughed. Bettilia ran down toward the seashore, laughing, toward the next hint of storm out there—approaching over the water—laughing, Bettilia ran back toward the house, laughing. Her bare feet splattered as she zigged and zagged, threading uphill through the live oaks, the clumsy pup barking and chasing after Bettilia's lovely laughter.

The lights were on in the empty kitchen when Kes came downstairs. The welcome, bitter-bright coffee smell met him there. Kes hobbled to the stove and poured. A kitchen chair was missing. Kes found Daddy Brass out on the side porch with a steamy mug, balanced on the chair's hind legs. Daddy was enjoying the girl and dog show, watching them laugh and play.

"She's a frisky little bit, ain't she? Almost cute too," Daddy said.

"Which one?" Kes asked, leaning his back against the house. He was tired of standing up and tired of never being able to sit comfortable. "When did the lights come back on?"

"*Hey, there little Tilly,*" Daddy shouted out. "*You gonna freeze your toebones off, running around out like that.*"

Bettilia came running up to the porch, one of her tiny toebones already off and missing, but Kes didn't care a whit. The pup came with her, big clumping paws kicking up rainwater.

"I'm used to the cold," Bettilia said, catching her breath, eyes happily darting betwixt Kes and Daddy Brass. "But I ain't no Tilly. Ain't never been and don't wanna be."

"I git you," Daddy said, grinning.

"Malakoff is a strange name," she said, shading her eyes with her hand. "Ain't never heard of no Malakoff."

"Go tell that to Mrs. Brass upstairs," Daddy said. "She'll like the gist of that sentiment."

"What's it like in all that sea water down there?" she asked, eyes sparking at Kes.

"Deep and wet, I suppose. Why? You wanting to go in it?"

"Naw. I still cain't swim," she said. She wasn't sure why that still made Kes look so pleased.

The big white puppy bounded onto the porch, dipping her big white head, pouncing on Daddy Brass's feet.

"*Sister—*" Bettilia scolded, "—get down from there."

The pup leapt back off the porch, landing beside Bettilia.

"What's that you call her?" Kes asked.

"Aw," Bettilia hesitated. "You can name her whatever you want. She's yourn after all. I just been calling her Sister. I always wanted me one."

"Sister," Daddy mused over his shoulder at Kes who looked pleased and pitiful with that plaster cast and gray china cup.

Their eyes met, Kes smiled.

"I like it," Kes said to Daddy. "Ain't never had me no sister."

"Me neither," Daddy Brass allowed, turning his beaming mug back at Bettilia. "My mama raised up seven boys and nary a girl in the litter."

"I never knew that," Kes said.

"Son, that's just one of multiple things you don't know. Like you didn't know it was almost six a.m."

"With that sun sitting up there like that? It ain't no six a.m."

"It was when the lights cut back on."

The kitchen door rattled open beside Kes as faint thunder rumbled in off the sea.

"*Sister.* Hungry?" Glenn hollered, coming outside with a black iron skillet full of Thanksgiving scraps, the screen slapping shut behind him.

"That's a *f*-fool question," Bettilia said, watching the pup—Sister—jump back on the porch to greet Glenn. "You almost as bad as your brother."

Glenn set the skillet down. Sister went at the scraps, tail whisking the air.

"It's been said. You ain't the first," Glenn admitted, petting the dog. "Telephone's still dead."

"So," Daddy posed, clearing his throat. "Miss Bettilia. We might as well git down to it. Where's you mama and daddy?"

"Dead," Bettilia said.

"Yeah? I know how that be," Daddy said. "Both mine have passed over."

"Bettilia—you wanna see the treehouse?" Glenn asked, ready to go.

"I been *g*-gandering at that treehouse since I come out this morning," Bettilia said. "Show it to me."

She and Glenn wasted no time. They headed up the side yard together to the big oak. Kes felt a twinge of green envy. He had wanted to be the first to show the treehouse to Bettilia, back before Bettilia even knew there was a treehouse at Kes's house. Sister kept scarfing leftovers from the skillet while Daddy and Kes watched Glenn lead Bettilia up the tree. Glenn climbed the plank rungs up the trunk to the treehouse, talking every rung of the way as the sky darkened over their heads. Bettilia followed Glenn fast like she might overtake him.

"She ain't just frisky. That little gal is strong," Daddy Brass said.

"It ain't no secret," Kes said, sipping his brew. "She'll be the first to tell you."

"I still don't know how she found my office in the middle of a winter storm."

"Did Mama George get up and make the coffee?"

"Nope. I did. I don't sleep much these days, older I git. Except when I'm asleeping it off."

"Yeah."

"I reckon your mama's still in bed with one of her spells."

"I reckon."

The pup kept crunching and lapping at the skillet. A cold gust of wind hit the porch, arriving just ahead of the bruised underbelly of clouds coming ashore. The sun had quickly disappeared. At the back of the side yard, all chatter from Glenn and Bettilia up in the treehouse had stopped. This bothered Kes more than it should have.

"What you figure we gonna do with her?" Daddy asked, setting his empty mug on the boards of the porch.

"Mama?"

"Naw."

"The dog, you mean?"

"Naw. That little gal up that tree yonder. What we gone do with her?"

"That's a good question. Ain't it?"

Suddenly, Sister looked up from her skillet dog dish. She looked around. Daddy and Kes could tell she was looking for Bettilia. Sister went to the edge of the porch, whimpering as her thick white snout sniffed at the whirl of ocean air, then her snout turned, looking up the hill at the biggest oak. She whimpered again, hesitating before she dropped awkwardly off the high porch and started walking up the side yard.

"Watch this," Daddy said, like he had seen it all before.

Sister's stumpy white legs trudged through the puddles

up to the great oak—the spreading oak that held that silent treehouse up there. The big pup stopped at the foot of the tree and sat betwixt the tangle of great roots, looking up into the tree, waiting. Little Sister voiced no more whimpers of woe. She looked up into the limbs and leaves and she waited.

She did not wait long before the kitchen door rattled open again. Mama's voice came through the screen.

"Gaylenn Brass—" she snapped, "—stop using my good skillets and chinaware to feed that cottonball beast."

The transistor radio clicked on up there in that tree, *Jingle Bell Rock* trickling down from the leaves.

VERSE 19

Railman's Cap

"Morning, Mama," Kes said to the voice behind the screen.

"Morning, doll," Daddy Brass said to the woman behind the screen.

"Malakoff, that will be enough of that," Mama George said, squeaking the screen door open a notch, poking her head out. Dressed and ready, she took quick stock of the situation. "Good morning, Kes. If this gathering wants breakfast you had best come inside and help make it happen. We are due for more rain. *Gaylenn, remove yourself from that tree—*"

Mama George took her skillet back inside, cleaned it, then began frying pork sausage. Daddy Brass rolled a batch of his buttermilk biscuits, cutting them with a tin cup. He slid the biscuits in the oven while Mama made sausage gravy in the skillet. Outside the wind rumbled and raindrops began to tap the glass again.

"Is my good kitchen chair still outside?"

"Unless it walked off on its own," Daddy told her, adjusting the oven dial.

"We're out of eggs," Mama announced, "They all went in my bread pudding yesterday. Biscuits and gravy will have to do until dinnertime."

"Mizz Brass?" Bettilia asked, approaching the stove with caution. "What can I *d*-do to help?"

"You can set the table, dear."

"I don't mind biscuit and gravy," Glenn said, dragging in Daddy's abandoned kitchen chair. "I'll take four. I like biscuit and gravy."

"I'll take three," Kes said, standing with his plaster wedged against the china cabinet. "Biscuits and warm sorghum beats out bread pudding any day."

Mama George shot Kes a withering eye. Her wooden spoon scraped the skillet with implied threat. She knew exactly what Kes meant. Kes meant that his Daddy's biscuits beat out *her* bread pudding. It all came down to raisins, Mama George decided then and there. Kes had never been partial to raisins, yes, raisins must be the origin of his prejudice.

Kes reached down and opened the china cabinet drawer for Bettilia, showing her the sterling Stradivari silverware.

"Bettilia, please use our everyday plates in the cabinet over here, and the flatware in that drawer by the sink," Mama said. "Glenn should have known better last night. And Kes should know better now. Glenn—take your guitar off the table."

"Yes'm," Bettilia said, trading unspoken thoughts with Kes before she changed course and began mumbling to herself, leaving the fine china and silver alone. Kes couldn't take his eyes off her.

"Bettilia can sing, Mama," Kes said.

"Ain't that right, Bettilia?"

Bettilia hid her face, trying not to blush, looking for a stool and wishing Kes would shut up.

"That's some gospel *truth*. You oughta hear her sing, Mama," Glenn said, hanging his guitar on a coat hook by the door, looking outside. "Listen to that rain, will you? Another dang deluge. Looks like nightfall nearly 'bout."

"I've still got a good ham purchased at IGA for Thanksgiving, before Arthel's ducks were gifted yesterday," Mama said, still stirring, scraping. "I will put the ham in the oven for dinner at noon. Glenn, take two dollars from my purse. After breakfast I want you to go over to the market and buy the biggest cabbage head they have. That should leave you enough to purchase a proper plastic dog dish."

Daddy pulled his pan from the oven. At the kitchen counter, buttering the hot biscuits, he winked at Bettilia as she slid the step stool alongside him to reach the upper cabinet.

"I hear that sumbitch is going after the mayor's seat this next island election," Daddy said to Mama.

"Yes, Malakoff. Arthel Dodson is running for mayor."

"He'll lose."

Sister lay under the table, her tail sweeping the floor, soulful eyes watching the commotion of feet, still uninterested in politics. Bettilia began setting the table with plain plates of different colors.

"I think I got follered here," she said to a little girl inside her, "maybe."

In the kitchen commotion nobody heard her mumble this—except Kes—who kept watching her every move. He didn't know what to make of what he heard. He watched Bettilia circle the table, her head down, carefully placing a fork, knife, and spoon: all grouped together to the right of the plate. It occurred to him that Bettilia had never set a proper table before. His mama was a stickler. His mama would notice, Kes knew that.

Kes caned his way over to the table and sat down alone as Bettilia went back to get juice glasses. While Daddy handed the glasses down to her from the cabinet, Kes quickly rearranged the silver at each plate, the fork on the left side, the knife then spoon on the right.

"Nope. He's too jellyfish. Nixon man," Daddy was saying. "Ain't nobody gonna vote for no Arthel Dodson."

"Hush, Malakoff."

"Would you?"

"Of course not."

Bettilia came back with two glasses of apple juice. Before she could set the glasses down Kes knew he'd boogered things up. Bettilia was quick to notice the switch Kes had made with the silverware. Kes saw the fleeting realization, the embarrassment in Bettilia's eyes. He should have left the silverware be. Nobody would have said a word about it. Mama George would not have mentioned such a thing under penalty of death. And now Bettilia would think Kes was ashamed of her—when the flip side was true. How could he fix that? How could he do it fast?

"Kes, will you ask the blessing?" Mama George said, scooting up to the table with Daddy and Glenn.

Bettilia set the two apple juice glasses on the table then went back to get the other glasses. Returning, she sat down betwixt Glenn and Mama George, avoiding Kes's hangdog gaze.

Kes had no choice really. He asked the blessing.

Glenn was forking into a biscuit before Kes could say amen. Daddy's fork was close behind, followed by Bettilia's spoon in the gravy bowl. Mama George sipped apple juice, watching Bettilia, trying not to get caught at it.

"Who spooked off my sunshine?" Daddy Brass asked, chomping biscuit and gravy, watching Mama watch Bettilia.

Kes shut his eyes, breathing deep, hearing the roar of rain, asking silent prayer for this girl's forgiveness. Then his eyes opened, he picked up his fork.

Bang. Bang. Bang. Somebody was at the back door again. All eyes looked up from the table.

"Christ on a crutch—" Daddy blurted "—in *this* rain?"

"Malakoff. Your *language.* These *children."*

He was already out of his chair.

"Yeah, darlin, and this damn *door."* Daddy's finger hooked a window curtain. "Well, hell. If it ain't your green-eyed duck hunter."

"Whatcha mean?" Bettilia asked.

Daddy opened the door.

"Hello, Arthel," he said. "Git in here outa that rain."

Arthel Dodson stepped inside wearing his rain slicker and a dripping fisherman's flophat. He was square-faced and Texas-sunburned.

"Morning, Malakoff. Georgiana. Morning, folks," Arthel said, nodding at the table.

"Good morning, Arthel," Mama George said, rising from her chair. "Sit down and share some breakfast with us. I'll fix you a plate."

"No, thank you, Georgiana," Arthel said, "I don't want to mud up your kitchen. And I'm so full I'm afloat in toast and grits."

"So you outa eggs too?" Glenn asked blankly.

But Arthel Dodson had no time for such confusing and idle query.

"Malakoff, could I have a word with you? Outside?"

Daddy arched his brow at Mama. She sat back down.

"Why, sure, Brother Arthel," Daddy said, amused but wary. "You bet. Anything for our future mayor."

"Aw, cut it out, Malakoff," Arthel Dodson said. "Besides, we're just island folk. And you are now Savannah gentry. Or so I hear."

"Don't you believe it, Arthel," Daddy said as they stepped outside, closing the door. "Don't you never believe it."

Sister yapped from under the table.

"*Sister—shhh—*" Kes said, reaching for his second sausage. "Wonder what that's all about."

While his Mama sat watching the door, her mind on the two men talking through the door glass, Kes slipped his second sausage under the table.

The men's voices were indistinct, just murmurs under the drumming of the rain, the ringing of forks and knives on plates.

"Who's *th*-that feller Dodson?" Bettilia asked.

"Our next door neighbor," Mama told her, dabbing orange marmalade on a biscuit. "He's a very nice gentleman. A deacon at the church."

"That's right, Bettilia," Glenn said with gravy on his mouth. "A church deacon and a politician. What more you need to know? Huh?"

"Gaylenn—"

"Yes, Mama?"

The door blew open again, letting in the wind and the sound of Arthel Dodson's feet clipping down the porch steps. Daddy Brass stuck his head inside.

"Glenn. Could you come help me out?" Daddy said. It was not a question. He had strange hue in his face, trying to keep pleasant.

Glenn blinked, wiped his mouth quick with his napkin. "Okay, Daddy, sure."

"What's going on?" Kes asked, a little scared. He was about be left alone with his mother and Bettilia.

"Y'all finish your breakfast," Daddy said through the door. "I need Glenn to run me an errand."

Glenn slipped out onto the porch. Daddy Brass eased the door shut, but he let the screen slam hard behind them.

Inside, Mama George flinched in her chair.

Outside, Glenn turned to his Daddy.

"What?" Glenn asked, but his Daddy was already gone.

Daddy Brass hustled down the steps, out into the rain, calling back at the porch.

"Stay put, son," he hollered.

Glenn watched Daddy Brass jog out through the pounding rain to his Hudson parked beyond the treehouse oak. Daddy opened the passenger door, leaning inside. From the porch Glenn heard the glove compartment click open and closed. Daddy dashed back through the rain.

Inside the kitchen, Kes grabbed his cane, struggling out of his chair with a clatter.

"Kestrel, what are you up to?" Mama George demanded as she poured herself more juice.

"Be right back," Kes said, already hobbling from the table.

Bettilia and Sister sat perplexed, watching Kes's cane and plaster casts rumble into the formal dining room, headed for the front parlor.

Outside, Daddy Brass came up the steps, out of the rain. He strode quickly down the long long side porch, toward the front of the house. By the time Daddy reached the front corner and stopped, Glenn was already headed after him. Daddy didn't want to conduct his business outside the kitchen door. That much Glenn could see already.

"I want you to run on over to IGA like your mama said—" Daddy Brass told Glenn as he approached. Daddy's clothes were soaked, his hair plastered, face dripping.

"Okay—"

Daddy took a snub-nose revolver from the pocket of his pants, flipped open the cylinder. He spun it, checking the chambers, then gave Glenn a nod.

"Yep. I need some shells."

"Shells?"

The gun went back into Daddy's pocket. He had his wallet out now.

"I'm gonna stay here, look after this bunch. Here's a twenty spot," Daddy said, handing a crisp, newly-printed bill to Glenn. "Take my car. The keys are in it. Git your mama that cabbage head. Then go by the hardware and get me a box of shells. Tell Marv Deetz that I need .357 cartridges. Hollow point. I'll take .38s if that's all he's got, but I'd ruther have my .357s."

"Damn, Daddy. What's going on here?"

Daddy Brass gave Glenn a steady size up, rain dripping off his brow.

"We've got company."

"I know we do."

"Naw, we've got other company. Arthel Dodson looked over here this morning and saw some trampy feller looking in the winder at us while we was fixing breakfast. Arthel said the feller looked scar-faced, long old coat, railman's cap, he said."

Glenn's eyes went wide, looking up and down the porch.

"Where'd he go? That stranger?"

"That's the question, ain't it? And what's he armed with? Don't say nothing to them in there just yet. But Arthel said the feller tramped off fast down the back street when Arthel flipped his porch light on."

The parlor window slid open with a *slap*.

"What's going on out there, Daddy?" Kes spouted from

inside the window screen. “Where’s the fire?”

Daddy Brass reeled, his right hand fast back inside his pocket, until he saw Kes’s face inside the window.

“Boy, you better *git* your clumsy butt back to that table and tend to them *women*,” Daddy growled at Kes. “Ain’t they enough for you? I’ll let you know when this is any of your bidness.”

Daddy Brass started back down the porch, dragging Glenn with him, out of earshot from that nosy Kestrel.

“Who you think it is, Daddy?” Glenn asked as they moved.

“Well, son, your Daddy’s got hisself some enemies—”

“I know that.”

“And one or two of them of ‘em can still fog a mirror—”

“Yeah?”

“But I got me a hunch.”

“Okay.”

“I don’t think this one come looking for *me*.”

Glenn knew what that meant. He didn’t have to ask. The twenty dollar bill went in his shirt pocket.

“I’ll be back quick as I can.”

“Take your time. Everything is lovely. Lovely as can be. We don’t wanna upset nobody if we don’t have to. Now do we?”

“Tell that to Kes,” Glenn said.

“I’ll tend to Kes. Don’t worry. Anyhow, with this rain raining buckets like this, it shouldn’t be too hard for me to keep that gal and that dog inside till you get back. Then we’ll see how things play out, won’t we?”

“Yes sir,” Glenn said, starting for the steps, toward the

Hudson. ".357s?"

"That's right. .357s. And, hey, don't fret it."

"No?"

"That old rail tramp could just be some peeping creep. My hunches ain't always right."

Glenn put on a brave face for his daddy before he ran through the rain to the car. He hopped in the Hudson and found the keys in the ignition. The engine boomed with power the moment Glenn cranked it. He worked the pedal, revving the motor. As he was shifting into reverse he looked up and saw Daddy Brass shouting out to him from the edge of the porch.

"*Don't forget—*" Daddy was saying, the rest of his voice swallowed by the rain and the V-8 motor.

Glenn rolled down the window.

"What?"

"*Don't forget that little bitch's bowl. Git a good'n*"

"I won't—I mean—I will."

"*Stainless steel.*"

Glenn nodded, backing out of the drive. As he pulled away he saw Daddy Brass had his snub-nose pistol out and flipped open again, shaking empty shells into his broad hand.

VERSE 20

Ther Button

Chalice kept the package in her lap all the way back from Americus, Georgia. It rained most of the way. At Cordele a hefty woman in three-inch heels wiggled on and squeezed her polka dot dress into the seat beside Chalice. The woman reeked of too much Estée Lauder and beer and she quickly passed out, snoring, her platinum head and big body falling against Chalice's shoulder. Every time the woman would snort and slump deeper against her, Chalice's arm was quick to protect the red-ribboned cargo in her lap. The rain began to let up around Little Ocmulgee. The drunk woman finally slumped the other direction and fell into the aisle of the bus, which was advantageous in the end, from Chalice's point of view. The bus driver pulled over at the next stop outside Claxton (Fruitcake Capitol Of The World) and made the drunk woman get off. She tried to complain but could not rise to the task.

"Lady, if you care to pursue it, just telephone that number on the back of your ticket. My name's Rafer. My driver number is three-six-four-nine-four."

She asked him to repeat that. He did. She still didn't write it down or seem to grasp his words. They left her head sagging on the Greyhound bench outside a Phillips 66, her overnight bag betwixt her three-inch heels.

When Chalice finally stepped off the bus at the station in downtown Savannah she was extra careful not to jostle the box, which wasn't easy with all the folks jostling Chalice in their hurry to get off and go.

"Who's that pretty present for?" her daddy, the island mayor, asked on the way to the car.

"Oh, shush. You know who. I'm tired and I can't stand the teasing, Daddy."

"And your trip?"

"Dreadful," she said, "I thought I was gonna wrinkle up and die an old maid on that bus. And Grammy Dillard kept calling me Chelsa all through turkey dinner."

"Chelsa?"

"I swear, Daddy, your mind has gone soft as Grammy. Chelsa was that colored girl who used to come by mornings and help Grammy with the house."

"Oh, mercy. Of course. Chelsa. Sad Chelsa. Well, I'm afraid your mother may be going the same way as your Grammy, and faster too," Mayor Dillard said, motioning with the suitcase in his right hand. "I parked the station wagon down and around the corner, safe under a street lamp."

"You worry too much, you worry wart. And I think Mother's getting better, don't you? Now that they changed her prescription. Anyway, I tried to call y'all. I tried to call Kestrel. This morning. Last night too."

"No phones till an hour ago or so. No lights most of the night. Brother Dub is calling it an Old Testament storm, and it sure enough was that."

"Dreadful. Simply dreadful."

"You know, Chalice honey, Brother Dub tells me that new youth pastor just arrived from Birmingham late Wednesday. You should meet him."

"Oh, I'm sure to get around to it. What's Mother making for supper?"

"I'll heat some Chung King. You like Chung King. He's real handsome, your mother says. If that's the fellow she's remembering. Hard to tell these days."

"Who?"

"Robert Straw. The new youth pastor."

"I'm sure he'll excel at whatever youth pastors do."

Mayor Dillard's remainder of smile turned into a hard jot. He unlocked the station wagon for her.

"Let me set your package in the back seat," he said.

"Oh, no, Daddy. It's most fragile."

"Well then."

"But my Kes will be beaming for a week once he sees it."

"Well good."

Mayor Dillard looked both ways, even though traffic could do no more than crawl the tight corners of Old Ellis Square. He went around and got in behind the driver's wheel, taking the Bible off the dashboard.

"Chalice, honey," he began, engaging the clutch, "haven't you noticed that Kestrel seems a bit, well, out of step with the Word these days?"

"No," she said, looking straight ahead, the present back in her lap. "He's in a lot of bone pain these days. That's all. His bones will heal. So will he."

"Kes is not exactly courtly at you of late," her daddy said, cranking the ignition. "He never telephones on his own."

"Chung King. I can't wait. We haven't had Chung King since, well, the day before I left for Grammy's."

"I don't know. Kes just seems kind of sharp and kind of—out of kilter."

Chalice smiled to herself but did not look at him. She kept her eyes straight ahead, beyond the windshield. Mayor Dillard had no choice. He put the car in gear and headed home. Under the endless canopy of Spanish moss, the station wagon slowly wove around one ornate garden square after another while Chalice watched the the gothic balconies and ironwork pass by out her window. She breathed easier and began to cheer up when they finally turned left on Victory Drive, heading out toward the island.

"I hope we get back with time to spare before suppertime," she said. "Please don't drive like a nudgy old lady, just this once."

"What's your hurry? Another Greyhound to catch?"

"No, darlin Daddy. But I would like to stop by Angelsprey—the Brass's house—before we go on home. If you don't mind."

He sighed behind the wheel. Chalice looked at the present in her lap, thinking how Kes would soon be the only fellow she had left. She felt her daddy letting go. Letting go of her, of her mother, letting go of everything he ever had.

"No. No, I don't mind," he said.

The storm had passed, but the porches were still dripping in the dark. Bettilia had never seen so many porches piled on top of one another, stacked like three frilly, drippy petticoats. She could hear Kes thumping around on the porch above her head—thumping around while Sister's big paws thumped around him and his cane. It had been a long night and a long day and they were due for a long talk. Bettilia knew she could not avoid that talk for much longer.

"Land o'goshen, which one of you heathen left the front portico door *open?"* Mama George's voice sounded from deep inside the house. "And you've tracked *mud* all over my clean foyer floor."

"Not me, Mama," Glenn's voice said back there in the kitchen.

Bettilia found Daddy Brass toward the back of the first floor side porch in a rocking chair. She saw how his rocker was cocked toward the street behind the house, the only street approach to Angelsprey. Bettilia also saw the pistol Daddy Brass slid from his lap and into his pocket when he heard her approaching behind him.

"Take a looksee, little gal," Daddy said. "Gale wind and gullywashers all afternoon. Old Cedarweed Drive here was the river of no return. And now she's just a glitter slick in the dark. The last of the glass with no more bottle."

"You're right *f*-funny, Mr. Brass," Bettilia said, her

hand on the arm of his chair. She felt safer, standing this close to him.

"I'm jist Daddy Brass around here. Don't call me mister unless you come with a court order."

"Okay, well, Daddy Brass, you're right funny sometimes."

She noticed how his eyes never stopped slitting up and down the street, how he studied the shadows across the yard like they were doors of knowing.

"Ever hear of a feller name of Swinburne?" he asked, still drifting.

"Naw. Is he serving *p*-papers on ye?"

Daddy chuckled soft, then spake ever softer to those shadows.

"*From too much love of living, from hope and fear set free, we thank with brief thanksgiving, whatever gods may be. That no life lives forever, that dead men rise up never, that even the weariest river, winds somewhere safe to sea.*"

She was impressed.

"I didn't know you was a *s*-singer too. Did you pencil that down or just make it up right here?"

"That's poem, not song."

"Same thing. Where I'm from."

"Hell, it was that Swinburne feller what wrote it down. Before either of us was borned, gal."

"Oh," Bettilia pondered, drifting out into the shadows with him. "Nights back where I *c*-come from, after long rain like this, that's when I'd see them willer wisps."

"Willer wisps?"

"Yeah. Far off lights in the woods, *m*-moving in the trees, like ghosts."

"Where is it you come from, Miss Bettilia?"

"Hills. On no map to speak of. Hills, far and away."

"You ever holler out to one of them willer wisps? Ask em what fer?"

She looked down at him and he up at her.

"Naw, sir. I didn't really *t*-talk back in them days."

"Well, some weren't raised to talk much. I talk too much."

"Naw, sir. I mean, I didn't talk at all till after Mambly took me in. None at all."

"Hmmm," Daddy said, setting his hand on top of hers, giving it a pat. "Maybe you didn't have too much to tell just yet. Maybe you just hadn't seen enough yet."

"Oh, I had lots to tell. I seen *t-t-t*-too much. But I did not tell none of it. I never have."

Daddy didn't ask. He took his hand back, lacing it into the fingers of his other hand, letting them fall on his belly.

"That's awright, too. Everthing in its time. And some things ain't fit to tell. Don't I know it. Another thing I know, I like you, little Bettilia Whissler."

"I like you too Daddy Brass," she said, then got bear caught again, shy. She had never felt so many safe folks around her at one time. "Anyway, Daddy Brass, I'm supposed to tell you—I mean—Kestrel asked me to let you know this Mizz Plum telephoned from your office. They's a *sh*-shipment you need to sample, she says."

He shifted in the rocker. Bettilia heard the pistol in his pocket when it hit the arm of the chair. Daddy acted like he didn't hear, but she knew he did.

"I'll give her a call back in a few," he said. "Comes a time, I reckon, when a body has to tend to bidness. I cain't sit out here on this island forever."

"Yes sir. I mean, no sir."

"I'll be in directly."

"Yes sir. I reckon I ought go have a talk with Kes."

"I reckon so," Daddy said with kind eyes. "No life lives forever, dead men rise up never."

"N-No?"

"No."

After Bettilia went back inside Daddy Brass took the folded brown strip of paper out of his shirt pocket and read it again. He had not told Glenn or anyone else about this rough bit of butcher paper he received forthwith this morning from good neighbor Dodson. Arthel Dodson said the tattered tramp—the one with the unfortunate face and railman's cap—had dropped the paper on the lawn in his hurry when he first went skittering off after Arthel flipped on his porch light.

"That sneaky peepster must have realized he dropped this," Arthel told Daddy as he handed over the ragged note, "because he started back to pick it up. But when he saw my head stick out the door to holler at him—the fellow turned, hustled back down the hill. Lost sight of him after that. Left this in the grass, though."

"You're an educated man, Arthel," Daddy said, scrutinizing the message after he unfolded it. "How would you decipher this?"

"I don't. Looks like grade school stuff to me, Malakoff. I couldn't make up or down of it."

The brown paper strip had been folded in fours and soaked through when Daddy first looked at it—the ink was spreading, the letters running together. But the crude hand-scrawled print was easily legible even then. Now, tonight, as Daddy turned the near dry paper over and back and over again in the dim light, the words still asked more than they told.

WHo GoT THeR BuTToN

It was like some elementary challenge or a puzzling paper snippet from a child's game. A troubling question with no end mark. It was likely worthless, meant nothing. Or it could engender great troubles should the wrong person read it.

WHo GoT THeR BuTToN

Daddy Brass took out his WWI trench lighter, the kind of lighter that would do the job in a heavy fifty-mile-an-hour blow, the kind of wind they'd been having for the last day and a half. Now, with the storms passed over, there was no wind to speak of tonight. As Daddy Brass watched the flame quickly blacken and devour the rough message he never doubted or questioned his decision. Fear doth blight you, he sang to himself, a worried mind can make a life not worth living. He knew that, yes, he knew it too well. Some things were not fit to tell.

The Dillard station wagon crept up Cedarwood Drive, tires crackling and rumbling over the red brick pavement.

Before the car even pulled to the curb, Chalice had already seen Daddy Brass sitting up there in a rocker on the dark bottom porch. Chalice smiled. She had always liked Daddy Brass. Everybody liked Daddy Brass. Everybody except Mrs. Brass, that is.

"I'll just be a jiff," Chalice told her own daddy as they squeaked to a stop.

"You want me to go in with you?" Mayor Dillard asked, idling.

Chalice noticed how Daddy Brass leaned forward in his chair up there. She could see the shape of him studying their car.

"No," Chalice told her own daddy, "I'll be real quick about it. I'll let Kes open his gift after I'm gone."

Chalice already had her hand on the door latch when her eyes lifted upward, up from Daddy Brass to the porch above him. On the second story porch was Kestrel. Chalice could easily see the white plaster of his leg and arm casts leaned against the white railing of the second story porch. And Chalice saw the girl. She could easily see the girl in the moonlight. A cute little girl talking with Kes, talking with such gravity. The girl's hand rested on Kes's arm, his arm that was not in a plaster cast.

Chalice could also see the other man looking down at Kes and that girl. The stranger looking down at them from the third porch of the third story of Angelsprey—the porch above Kes and that girl.

"They've got company," Chalice said in dead tones. "Let's go, Daddy."

"You sure?"

"Yes," she said, sliding the red-ribboned package under the car seat.

"Who's that visiting up there in that railman cap? He looks worse for wear."

"I don't know, Daddy. They've got company. Let's go."

Mayor Dillard did as his daughter beseeched. He engaged the clutch, eased away from the curb, sneaking away, down the wet brick road, leaving Angelsprey and its strangers behind.

VERSE 21

Belated Raindrops

Daddy Brass had begun to doze in the rocking chair, lulled by the soothing stillness, the constant dripping from the thick trees and high porches, the distant steady tide of the ocean. Mrs. Plum called to tell him he was needed back on River Street at his storehouse to okay a new shipment. But Daddy knew he could not leave. Not just yet. Mrs. Plum would have to sample that business herself. Daddy was not worried about her. She was able.

He was dozing in the rocker, the pistol in his lap, when he heard, then saw, a station wagon come slow through the oaks and dripping moss of Cedarwood Drive. The car stopped with its lights on, down the hill below the house. Daddy waited for someone to get out. The car was not familiar to him. After a few moments the station wagon drove on, disappearing in the tangle of streets behind Officer's Row.

The street, the night, they settled again into the rhythm of waves and random raindrops. Daddy Brass began to settle again too, his head nodding off, when he heard the clopping sound. And the clinking.

Yes, it was the clip-clop of hooves. Daddy had been raised with that sound in his ears. He had grown up sweating in hot corn and cotton fields behind that steady rhythm of muscle and heavy hoof.

Daddy came awake, alert, on the edge of his rocker, his .357 Magnum pistol in hand. The echo of the hooves and clinking, clanking, was coming from the same direction the car had come, like an afterthought from bygone times.

Through mottled moonlight, the swaybacked mule appeared. The mule was defeated, decrepit, head hung low as it passed. From the empty saddle, stringers of bottles and cans hung clinking and clanking with each inevitable, beaten-down step the mule took on the bricks. The riderless mule passed by, passing up the street, disappearing as the station wagon had disappeared, as Daddy Brass rose from his rocking chair.

He slid the pistol into the front of his belt. He went down the steps, taking the steps quietly. He did not want to wake those sleeping in the house. He slipped through the wet grass, down the hill, and into the street. He looked both ways, then went after the mule.

VERSE 22

Radioactive

Reeeeeerrreeeeeeek.

A loud squelch of feedback blasted from the P.A. speakers. Faces winced, hands and fingers flying up to plug the ears of the fairground crowd. Then the men, women, and cotton-candy smeared kids laughed when the Governor was almost run over onstage by two stagehands racing to control one of the amplifiers. Sonic order was restored, the stagehands returned to the wings, the Governor started tapping on the center stage microphone.

“Is this deal still working?” he asked as he tapped. His voice ricocheted over the nodding heads, he smiled at the loosely segregated sea of black and white faces. “Sorry about that, y’all. That’s *mawdren tecknawlgee* for you. And I regret to inform you that our scheduled performers will not be appearing here tonight—” The crowd groaned as the Governor tossed a sly wink stage left.

“Now, now, folks, they can’t help it. They’d love to be here. You prob’ly heard. The Broadway cast of *Damn Yankees* was supposed to dance and prance for y’all but they took one look at our fireworks tonight, turned around, and took off running back up north where they come from."

Most of the crowd pealed with laughter, overloaded with pride and appreciation.

"That goddam show closed two years ago," Kes muttered.

"Hell, none of them know that," Glenn muttered back.

"*Damn yankees*," Chalice giggled to herself, "that's *funny*."

The Governor was waving his arms in the air, trying to quiet the crowd, a magnanimous grin on his face. His head cocked, his gaping grin cocked with it, he pointed hello to a gaggle of high school girls on the front row, then went back to calming the clatter with his hands.

"But we don't need them, now do we?" he hollered into the microphone.

"*Noooooooo*—"the fairgrounds shouted.

"We sure don't, folks, because our homegrown boys done got em beat tonight. Here they are, back onstage for the first time in over a year. Give a big Savannah hand to Glenn and Kes—*the Brothers Brass."*

Hoots and howls and a wave of applause hit the stage. So did Glenn and Kes. The Bonafide Beat Band went into a rollicking vamp, heavy on the bass and drums. The Brothers Brass ran out from stage left, swinging their guitars like tommy guns. They were already strumming hard in unison when they landed center stage, their voices flanking the microphone.

I'm traveling down this lonesome road oh how I
hate to go

The wind and storms are raging high and it's
awful cold—

Out in the frenzied audience, Mama George stood and frowned. She had sworn to one and all that her boys would never play secular music. They would always be gospel boys, she always said.

My mind drifts back to you sweetheart and I
love you so,
Now you've gone and left me here to travel this
lonesome road—

Yes, the way they played it in their new shiny suits and bolero ties, this song was veering too close to that rock and roll. Mama George was pleased but not pleased. She was ecstatic to see her boys back onstage again, with Kes's arm healed. But she would have preferred a different venue, with a more reverential psalm to kick off their career revival.

All I do is roam around and look for you my dear,
I know I'll search ten thousand miles,
Oh, how I need you here—

Kes and Glenn's voices fused together into a driveshaft of song, a shaft that shot like a guided missile, galvanized and true, over the sea of shining faces. The Brothers Brass found each other, as they always had, as one and at one with their purity of purpose, the surety of their sound.

They sang with their hearts about to burst. At last they were back where they belonged, lost in the ecstasy of the moment, where time stood still and a single note was all eternity—where time was a funny thing.

Their opening number ended with deafening thunder of applause and big smiles all around, onstage and off. Then the Brothers Brass ran through a royal flush of songs. They sang *Radio Station S-A-V-E-D,* which greatly pleased their mother, she even began to relax in the sway of the crowd. Their voices rambled through *Knoxville Girl* and a new song Glenn wrote called *Mercy Is Mine.* They sang a couple of other tunes that were a blur to both brothers, lost in that moment. Kes's cramping left hand, so long out of service, gave him a little trouble on the chords of *Where The Soul Never Dies*, but the joy of life center stage and the joy of the words carried him through:

To Canaan's land I'm on my way,
Where the soul never dies—

For the half an hour or so they were up there Kes even forgot about the eternal ache in his hip. They finished with a rousing rendition of *I Done The Devil Like He Done Me*, the crowd cheered, drowning out the carnival sound, the bellowing of beasts beyond the fray. Kes and Glenn ran from the stage with their guitars.

In the wings Chalice was clapping and jumping in place.

"Oh, my Lord, y'all burned down the barn—" she squealed as Kes came at her out of the spotlights, into the shadows. "*Radioactive, y'all.*"

"Thanks, Chally," Kes said. Their eyes locked fast before he slipped on past her to grab a drink of water.

Dripping sweat, beaming, Glenn came off the stage, strolled right up to Chalice and kissed her full on the mouth. She threw her arms around his neck and he lifted her off the ground. Then he kissed her again while the crowd still cheered.

"They'll be wanting that encore," Kes hollered to his brother, betwixt gulps.

"Damn right they will," Glenn said, his sleeve wiping away lipstick. "Didn't I tell you?"

"Yep. You told me."

The stomping, the clapping out there, it got louder and louder, just as the brothers knew it would. They had returned with glory and vengeance. The Brothers Brass were back, that hungry crowd out there wanted more, they gave it to them.

"Let's go," Kes said, then the two strolled back out into the flood of lights to the center of the stage.

The people went crazy at the sight of them again. They loved these boys.

"Folks—folks," Glenn stammered into the microphone as the crowd quieted down. "We can't tell you what it means to be back up here, sharing these good times with you all. We love you."

The people applauded, loving them back, loving them in waves.

"Folks," Kes said, leaning into the microphone, idly

strumming. "We wouldn't be back here tonight if it wudn't for all the strength we've wrought from the fire of love and faith we've been blessed to receive from when we was baby boys, the greatest gifts we could ever hope to receive—all thanks to our mama and our daddy." Kes held back a moment, waiting for the roar to subside. "But, more than all the mammon gold and silver, all the diamonds, all the jewels in this world—we've been watched over by angels—and blessed by the good Lord above. Yes, folks, it's He who's seen us through." He waited again, till the howling fell away. "And right now, we'd like to share another little blessing with y'all. We'd like to bring somebody special out here to help us with this next song. A young lady who has also been blessed with a beautiful voice and a heart of purest gold—"

"Folks," Glenn's voice rose, throwing a beckoning arm toward the wings, "please give a big Savannah welcome to *Miss Bettilia Whissler!"*

Bettilia stepped from behind Chalice and came strutting out of the wings, into the bright lights of the stage. A spotlight hit her. She wore a champagne satin dress, her hair was coiffed and piled high, she walked nervous in two-inch heels. Her lips wore a soft ruby rouge, her eyes wore shadow and dark mascara.

Bettilia managed to make it to the microphone without teetering over, smiling, her face frozen with fear.

"Cryminitly—" she trilled under her breath so only the Brothers Brass could hear. Kes put a hand on her shoulder to steady her.

Mercifully, Glenn was already plucking the opening chords.

And they sang.

My life goes on in endless song,
Above earth's lamentations,
I hear the real, though far off hymn,
Above the new creation—

Bettilia had little time to waver. She took the leap, her voice found its natural path. Once again, Bettilia's haunting alto made eerie passage, harmonizing down the middle of the stream that flowed from the Brothers. Together, the three wove a wondrous sound unlike any most folks, including the Brothers Brass or Mama Brass, had ever heard. It made folks pause, their hearts in their throats, suspended, listening, afraid to breathe for fear they would break the spell.

Through all the tumult and the strife,
I hear the music ringing,
It sounds an echo in my soul,
How can I keep from singing?

By the time the trio finished, their voices fading into final accord—those faces out there were awash in tears and bliss and exhalation. Something magic had happened, a transformation in the crowd, as if all those present this night—for a few minutes—had been part of a communion, a common soul, sharing in a rare moment of ethereal repose.

When their song was done, this gift was not taken lightly.

As the last note of Kes, Glenn, and Bettilia's spectral harmony resolved—there was a hush, like silent rapture falling with no parachute. Then the crowd exploded, bigger than anything Kes or Glenn or Mama had ever heard at any revival meeting.

It took Bettilia a moment to realize what was upon her. It scared her, this loud and raucous outpouring of clapping hands, whistles, and praise. She had never been at the center of anything much, and certainly never at the center of a storm of love like this.

A lambasted little smile burst upon her face, tears almost welling in her eyes. Almost welling, almost she cried, though she had never cried in her life. Kes and Glenn were grinning down at her. Before she knew it, each brother had her by the elbow, leading her from the stage, waving goodbye to the folks. It was over, for now.

Backstage, they were met with hugs and handshakes from a host of well-wishers, other performers, local luminaries,and stagehands. The Governor gave all three big bear hugs, starting with a startled Bettilia. Waiting for his moment, a sharecropper stepped out of the shadows to gift Glenn with a jar of his wife's fig preserves. A couple of FFA girls closed in on Kes and asked for his autograph. The youngest girl's mother got Kes to sign her Bible. There was endless praise and countless thank yous.

Amid the glory and backslapping, Chalice touched Bettilia's arm. Bettilia turned, blinking up at her.

"You did really good," Chalice said, tears in her own

eyes. “Y’all were beautiful. Together.”

Bettilia would have blushed but she had been blushing for five minutes. She searched for the words.

*“Th-*Thank you, Miss Chalice. Kindly. I cain’t never thank you e*n-n-*nough for helping me with my makeup, my hair, and all.”

“Oh, you’re so welcome. I’m no singer. But I do know how to eyebrow pencil pretty well.”

Bettilia knew no more to say. Words were never easy for her.

“Well, I’m obliged.”

“Bettilia?”

“Yes?”

“All this time and I never got around to asking you. Who was that man who came with you, to the island? Is that who brought you?”

Bettilia went stiff, glancing about nervously.

“Daddy Brass? He drove me to the island.”

“Oh, I thought I saw another man, a stranger at Angel-sprey. A little ragged looking. Right when you got here.”

“Oh. Can we *t-t-*talk about it later?”

“Why, sure, honey. We’ll talk about it later,” Chalice said, turning to go, then, “Bettilia?”

“Yes?”

“Be good for Kes.”

Bettilia knew not what to say to that either. Kes wasn’t even hers, nor was she his. Not really, not in any way that Bettilia could understand. She gave Chalice an uncertain nod before Chalice walked away.

Another hand touched the back of Bettilia's neck and Bettilia *jumped*. She whirled around.

It was Mama George. And Mama George hugged her for the longest time.

"You were even better than I foretold you'd be," Mama whispered in Bettilia's ear as she kept hugging, eyes closed, as if in prayer.

When Mama finally let go of Bettilia, Bettilia felt better again, back in the dazzle of it all.

"I couldn't have done it without *you*," Bettilia said. "I couldn't have done any of this—not without you."

"Look at you. You look beautiful. Lovely. Like a tiny China doll."

"Oh, *st*-stop it, Mama. I couldn't curtsy or pour a pot of gingermint tea until you taught me how."

"Yes, my darling. But you were a fast learner. Have you been reading this week's scriptures I left by your bed?"

Bettilia went a bit stiff again, but less so. She was getting the hang of things.

"Sure, Mama. You know I have," she lied.

Fortunately, like Galahads, the Brothers Brass swooped in to save her again.

"Hi, Mama," Glenn said, giving his mother a quick hug before relaying to Kes, who took over, hugging her also."

"Mama," Kes asked, "What you over here telling this girl about me?"

He was only half joking and Mama George knew it. They all knew it. Mama just smiled and kept her mystery.

"I was telling her how divinely inspired you three were tonight. You sang like the angels. Yes, like angelic reception. And Kestrel, your guitar, you played as expertly as ever."

"Well," Kes said, his right thumb kneading on his left wrist, "my hand still cramps me some."

"No matter, son. No one could tell. Not even me. And I'm your eldest fan."

"Thank you, Mama. I doubt you're really eldest, but you're our longest fan," Kes said, sincerely, before his eyes fell back into Bettilia's eyes. "But Bettilia—she was the knockout punch tonight."

"That's right, brer. She's all they'll remember. Dang," Glenn joshed, "I wouldn't of wanted to follow her."

Bettilia poked Glenn's ribs.

"Like you wudn't in on the deal," she teased back. "I just wished Daddy Brass could have been here *f*-for the show."

Mama George became quickly distracted, unlatching her purse.

"I'm sure he's somewhere on the premises," Mama said, coldly, rustling inside her purse for who knew what. "Off the rails as always."

"He's a businessman, Mama. The County Fair is big business for him."

"I'm sure it is, Kestrel."

"Let's go find him—" Glenn blurted, "—tell him how it went."

"My time is better spent than spent looking for that man," Mama spake into her purse. "There were booking agents out there tonight. Booking agents and music people wanting to speak with me about *our* business. *Your* business. Besides, there's no telling where your daddy is right now."

"I know where he is," Kes said.

The freaks and strippers were far removed from the gospel tent, on the other side of the midway, behind the cotton wagons. Chalice refused to go there.

"I might be nineteen, but my mama would wear me out," she said.

"Bettilia? You wanna stay here with Chalice?" Kes asked.

"I ain't staying here with nobody. Not even you, if you was to stay. I'm *go-go*-going."

Kes, Bettilia, and Glenn made their way through the neon sights and clanging sounds, past the ferris wheel and spookhouse. The Brothers Brass shook more hands along the way, received more good tidings.

"Will you smell that popcorn?" Kes growled. "I ain't had a bite to eat since supper last night. Been too nervous all day."

"I wudn't," Glenn bragged. "I ate two corn dogs before the show. Lotsa hot mustard."

Bettilia lit up.

"Yeah, Glenn give me a bite of one. It weren't half bad."

"I can't wait to get Chalice up in that there ferris wheel," Glenn boasted with a hint of lust.

"You ain't getting Chalice Dillard up in that wheel, little brer. I figured you to know that by now."

"I ain't?"

"Nope. She's afraid of heights."

"What's a *f-f*-fairy wheel?" Bettilia asked.

They cut through the arcades on the midway, then through the line of cotton wagons behind the main thoroughfare. Bettilia took serious interest in the Hellzabub's Human Zoo tent. (*"A Gallery Of Flesh & Blood Freaks!"*) But she did not like the looks of the cigar-chewing woman in hobnail boots and dirty overalls with an upended hoof betwixt her knees outside the freak show entrance. Hammering iron shoes onto a mule, the mean-eyed woman seemed to sense Bettilia's distaste. Bettilia avoided hobnail boots and hurried to keep up with the brothers as they pressed on until they reached another tent. This sign invited them to *Step Inside and See "Catahoula Becky"*. Kes spake with the garter-sleeved ticket man at the burlesque tent. The man let them pass for free through the canvas portal into darkness.

At first they only saw a round pimply butt hiked up in the spotlight. *Moon River* oozed from a record player. With her backside to her audience and bent over, high heels spread wide, the stripper's rubber snake hung around her neck and dragged the floor.

Neither brother nor Bettilia made any effort to avert their eyes as they slipped along the inside edge of the tent, past country boys and factory men on wooden folding chairs. The mostly naked, big-bosomed woman rose up, turned around, and tried to twirl her tassels slowly, trying to evoke something erotic out of a moony tune too romantic for this venue. The flopping snake wasn't much help, detracting from the effect. Still, there were a few half-hearted whistles. The running commentary from the close, smelly bunch took on new life as the stripper bent backwards this time, swaying, spreading her legs further for maximum exposure..

"Damn, so *that's* where I left my John Deere tractor," one chucklehead spouted.

Her rubber snake fell off on the stage, her long breasts hanging off each side of her ribs.

Bettilia looked at the woman, then at the record going around and around. Glenn looked at the woman and tried not to laugh. Kes just looked. Kes even felt a certain kinship with the raven-haired old girl up there. She reminded him of a farm woman he once met—a Holy Ghost handshaker at a camp revival up in Burton, Georgia, back in the hills. In the glare of the spotlight, the stripper looked straight at Kes for a moment, but did not seem to see. A man's hand reached up and tucked another bill in her g-string.

"She's familiar," Kes said.

"I think she's half-drunk, big brer. She'd have to be."

"I had me a record player once," Bettilia muttered to herself.

Kes and Glenn found Daddy Brass right where Kes predicted, in a shanty attached to the back of the tent, surrounded by cases of moon, Canadian whisky, and a light-bulb-framed makeup mirror. Daddy sat in his sock feet at a card table playing faro with a few friends, some ragged soldiers, and a tattooed midget. Daddy's boots lay beside him in the sawdust.

"How y'all like that burleycue out there?" Daddy asked,

barely lifting eyes off his cards. "I've road tested ever one of these gals."

"Hey, Daddy."

"Hey, Daddy."

Kes recognized the big black man in the bright toucan and tiki god shirt who held the deck of cards across from Daddy. He was the towering bruiser Kes could never forget from the Pickalilly Lounge.

"You next, mon. You ready?" he asked Daddy as Daddy's face said yes.

"How'd your show biz comeback go?" Daddy slid two twenty-dollar bills into the pot. He drew a card from the thirteen in his hand, flipped it face down on the table. "Easy on me now, Bugga, you big Jamaican bastard."

Bugga started flipping cards face up, back and forth, into two piles.

"You, mon. Me, mon. You, mon. Me, mon—"

"They was a good crowd, Daddy. We went over real well," Kes said, watching the cards pile up.

"You, mon. Me, mon—"

"You boys know Bugga Higgin, don't you?" Daddy asked, eyes glued to Bugga's huge hand, flipping down hearts then spades then diamonds then spades.

"You, mon. Me, mon—"

"Oh, yeah, hidy Mr. Bugga," Kes said, nodding at Bugga. Glenn joined in. Bugga glanced up, flashed them a big white smile.

"You, mon. Me, mon—"

"Blondie. You meet my boys?"

The golden Blondie Boy Bichét who sat beside Bugga extended a soft hand, each brother taking it in turn.

"So very nice. So lovely to make your acquaintance. We just friends," Blondie Boy purred.

"Yes, we've met," Kes said.

"You, mon. Me, mon—"

"Say howdy, Saint Peter," Daddy said.

Old Saint Peter sat glum and freckle-faced in his pin-stripe suit and said nothing. The tattooed midget watched him do it.

"*Gotdamn it, Bugga,*" Daddy Brass barked, pitching all his cards onto the table. "A fine fucking game. How'd you do that?"

Bugga and Blondie Boy laughed along with the four disheveled soldiers at the table.

"The trey wins," Blondie Boy chirped. "Ain't that how it goes? The trey wins?"

"Naw, the big house wins," Daddy said, glowering at Bugga. "The house *always* wins."

"Ain't that what you taught us, Daddy?" Kes asked, confused by the game. "The house always wins?"

"Shuddup, Kes," Daddy Brass said.

"Yeah, Daddy?" Glenn agreed.

"You shuddup too."

"But that's a good question, ain't it?" Kes contemplated the top of Daddy's head, standing behind his chair with his brother.

Daddy kept glowering at Bugga. Bugga and the rest of the table got seriously quiet, afraid of what Daddy Brass might do next.

"Why you play spade queen, mon? I told you never play no spade queen. Unlucky."

"Yeah, boys, it's a good gotdamn question," Daddy said. "And it's a good gotdamn thing you boys come by yourselves. I wouldn't want my next play to upset the ladies."

"But Bettilia's here," Glenn said, then realized she wasn't.

"Where?" Daddy rumbled, disgruntled, but his head turning to see.

Bettilia was not with them after all. Kes stepped back into the dark show tent and found her still watching the striptease, watching *Moon River* going around and around.

"Bettilia?" Kes whispered at her.

"I had me a record player once," she told him, as he took her hand, leading her away.

As Bettilia stepped into the attached shanty in her champagne satin dress and two-inch heels, Daddy Brass's mood changed. He took a long draw on her, gazing up and down.

"Do I know you?" he asked, merriment teasing the corners of his mouth.

"Oh, hush," she said through red-rouged lips.

"I'm hungry," Daddy said at her. "Y'all hungry?"

"I sure am," Blondie piped in. "I could eat a sailor boy's shoes."

"Not you," Daddy told him, putting on his boots. "You can stay here and let these sorry bastards fritter away at *your* grandkid's college fund."

Looking at Blondie Boy, Daddy suddenly burst out in a loud laugh that shook the shanty. The brothers and Bettilia missed the joke as old Saint Peter whispered something in Blondie's ear. But no matter. Daddy stood up, took his white linen coat off the chair. He threw an arm around Bettilia. She looked tiny beside him, dolled up like a little girl who had gotten into her mother's wardrobe.

For some reason, Kes didn't mind Daddy's arm around Bettilia—not like he minded when Daddy had done the same with Chalice. Bettilia did not seem to mind either.

"Gentlemen," Daddy Brass told the table, "I will be over at the Pirate's House eating oysters with my prodigal sons and daughter. You all can just stay here and eat all this stink off Bugga. If you can stomach this much defeat."

"Bugga's got *big* defeats," Blondie Boy piped happily in again.

"Shuddup, little mon," Bugga said.

"Saint Peter hopes you don't forget burnt boy," Blondie felt compelled to remind Daddy on his way out.

Kes saw Saint Peter take sudden silent umbrage with Blondie.

"Burnt boy?" Glenn asked at Daddy.

"And I'm about to tan your hide a shade darker, Blondie. Mind your own bidness, mind your own boys."

"Oopsie," Blondie Boy Bichét said, his little finger on his lower lip.

"Come on, sports fans," Daddy said, towing his entourage away from the table. "They's a criminal element in this room. We best steer clear of it."

One of the soldiers had his thirteen cards now and flipped one onto the table. Behind them, Bugga began again.

"You, mon. Me, mon—"

Going back through the striptease tent, Daddy laughed when he saw how transfixed Bettilia was by the girly doing her gyrations onstage.

"So that's Catahoula Becky, huh?" Kes asked over Daddy's shoulder.

"Right now she is," Daddy chuckled. "Whichever gal is working is Catahouler Becky. One old carcass is good as another."

Daddy was already sipping from his flask as they stepped through the front tent flap, out into the warm night air. He pulled Bettilia closer when he felt her pulled toward Hellzabub's Human Zoo, her eyes glistening.

"That ain't no place for a beautiful woman like yourself," he said, sweeping her away, toward the gospel tent.

"Who's that nasty looking lady with the cigar, Daddy?" Glenn asked.

"That'n in the overhalls? Folks call her Zeebub. The zookeeper."

"Is that *z*-zoo got elephants?" Bettilia wondered, but not really, clinging to Daddy Brass's arm.

"Naw," Daddy laughed. "Just a few polecat and one thousand-pound possum."

Bettilia wasn't listening anymore. She had moved on. She liked Daddy Brass calling her beautiful. She liked him calling her a woman. She did not believe him. But she liked it. And she felt safe. She went where Daddy Brass took her.

When they got back to the gospel tent, Chalice was still there waiting while Mama George conducted business with two well-dressed men behind the bandstand.

"Who's them two pigeons in her sights over there?" Daddy asked.

"Two promoters from Atlanta," Chalice said. "I was just waiting to drive her home."

"Come go with us," Daddy said, throwing his other arm around Chalice. "We're off on a oyster drag."

"I best wait for Mrs. Brass," Chalice demurred, slipping out of Daddy Brass's clutch. "She'll need a ride back."

"I'll drive em over, Daddy," Glenn said, taking Chalice's hand, giving a squeeze. "We'll be over soon as Mama's done her business."

"Sure thing, son. Sure thing. You got your work cut out for you."

Daddy led Bettilia and Kes away through the congregation of fair goers. The carousel still turned, the spinning sky rides and calliope still filled the night with phantasmic delights, glowing red, green, blue, purple and bright yellow amidst sounds of the same colors. Folks were starting to go home though. The Coastal County Fair was thinning out.

"Do Mama George and them know how to get wherever we're *go*-going?" Bettilia asked.

Daddy strolled along, snuggled her closer.

"Aw, that's the last of them folk we'll see tonight. Mrs. Brass ain't the oyster-eating kind."

"That's true," Kes said, smiling. "What Daddy says is true."

Bettilia smiled back at him, up at him, and took Kes's hand.

"Where's that big white puppy of yourn?" Daddy asked.

"Aw, she ain't much of a pup no more, Daddy. And she follows Bettilia wherever she goes. You oughta see it."

"I seen it," Daddy said, waving at a clown on stilts who owed him sixty bucks.

"Yeah, Sister is just a *b*-big ole polar bear," Bettilia told him. "Kes was all week building her a cage, else I never could have left to do the show."

"Yeah, and how about that show? Huh, little gal? Kes tells me you tore the roof off with that perty sound you make."

"Daddy Brass, they ain't got no roof at the *f*-fair," Bettilia said, enjoying his tease.

"She was the shining star, Daddy. You shoulda seen her."

"It did go good, didn't it?" she said up at Kes, their arms swinging along together.

"You know it did, darlin."

"Why wudn't you *th*-there, Daddy Brass?"

Daddy Brass bit the tip off a cigar, spat it in the straw.

"What? My boy here ain't told you?" he mused.

"Told me what?"

"Told her what?" Kes asked, confused.

"Me and the Governor, we try not to be seen together."

Daddy Brass's Hudson was parked in a dark corner behind Hellzabub's Human Zoo. They all three sat up front together. When Daddy pulled his big shiny Hudson out onto Montgomery Street, he told his passengers he had one quick stop to make. Just one quick stop.

"Over on Lafayette Square," he said. "A sweet little townhouse I keep. I won't be two minutes."

Then Daddy did a contrary thing. He went by and picked up Mrs. Plum. After that, Kes and Bettilia sat in the back together.

The Pirate's House was gorged with fine diners, a line of folks queued outside the door, but Daddy Brass was led straight to a table. Kes wasn't sure how that worked. He saw no money change hands. His hip was starting to hurt him, so he might have missed it as they limped through a winding maze of dining rooms, big and small. Eventually they arrived at a dark corner table in one of the bigger dining rooms.

"Once again, Mr. Malakoff, your taste in the ladies is impeccable," Percifal, the maitre de said, pulling out a chair for Bettilia. "Who, might I ask, is this princess you've escorted into our midst this evening?"

Daddy fell into his seat against an ancient, mud-bricked wall, Mrs. Plum settled beside him.

"This is my girl, Bettilia. This is my boy, Kestrel."

"Dang," Kes said, leaning over for a whiff of Bettilia's hair. "How many dining rooms y'all got in here?"

She smelled like gingermint tea.

"Oh, fifteen, twenty," Percifal replied, adjusting the carnation in his lapel. "Without a map, who can really say? Some of the oldest primitive homes in this nation have long been interconnected in this tavern. If these rooms could talk."

"If these rooms could talk," Daddy said, "You and me

could not make the bail. Could we, Percifal?"

"Assuredly, Mr. Malakoff," Percival smiled.

"Assuredly *not*, you mean."

"Assuredly *not*, Mr. Malakoff."

"I reckon you'd need a pirate map to make *b*-bail, huh?" Bettilia said, proud of herself.

"Indeed. There might be treasure buried in these walls," Percifal stage-whispered in her ear, to Bettilia's delight. He resumed his noble posture. "Now, shall we start you off with a good wine, perhaps? Or stronger spirits?"

"I'll have a Manhattan," Mrs. Plum said as she took out a cigarette.

"We'll take three Cuba Libre," Daddy said, gesturing with forked fingers at Kes and Bettilia.

"What's *th-th*-that?" Bettilia asked.

"Rum and Coke," Daddy said.

Kes and Bettilia got wide-eyed, looking at each other. Daddy drew great delight from the two of them as he lit Mrs. Plum's cigarette with his WWI trench lighter.

"Tres Cuba Libre, uno Manhattan," Percifal recited.

"And three dozen oysters on the shell, for starters," Daddy said.

"Your drinks are on their way, Mr. Malakoff," Percifal said. "Enjoy."

Percifal slipped away into the dining room maze.

"Well, Kestrel sugar, it's been ages," Mrs. Plum said with a puff of smoke. "I told your Daddy I so wanted see you again sometime."

Kes got shy, remembering how Mrs. Plum cleaned and

gutted a small town sheriff.

"It's good to see you too, Mizz Plum. Really. It is."

"Is there something betwixt you two I don't know about?" Daddy Brass interrupted, his grin-crinkled eyes cutting back and forth from Mrs. Plum to Kes. "What's going on here?"

"You've got a good man there," Mrs. Plum told Bettilia. "You best watch over him."

Bettilia felt the heat in her cheeks again.

"Well, he ain't exactly my—"

"So, where did you find this lovely girl, Kestrel?" Mrs. Plum asked.

"Up a tree."

"That ain't true, I mean—that's *n-n*-not true." Bettilia protested.

"Well, my daddy always said," Daddy Brass said, "even a blind hog will find an acorn somewheres."

"She ain't hardly never not up a tree," Kes smiled.

"Oh, really..." Mrs. Plum said, ignoring Daddy's Brass's finger diddling with her earring.

"He didn't find me," Bettilia said, "I found him. Drowning in three inches of water."

Everybody laughed at that, even Kes.

"That true?" Daddy asked him.

"Well, I wouldn't call her a liar."

"A wise decision, Kes," Mrs. Plum said. "The girl in your heart might be lied to, misinformed, or her trust abused. But never tell her she's the culprit. That's no way to chart a honeymoon."

"Bullshit," Daddy said, idly flicking sparks off his lighter. "Repeat after me. Everbody's a liar. Don't you know that? Everbody. Some's just worse than others. A dull liar is the worst. But it's the mean ones you got to watch out for. A mean lie from a mean liar's mouth. Them are the kind what will gig you. They're the scared ones. That's what makes them do it. Some don't even mean to gig you, but they do. Because they're scared. See? I don't worry so much about the others, which means everybody. I don't care if a man or woman lies to me as long as they're honest. It's fear that makes you dishonest. But if that man, that woman, has nimble thumbs and words to tell me, I figure I'm about to be lied to. Some are pretty lies. Some even have a spark or two of truth in em."

The drinks arrived and not a flick of the lighter too soon. Both Kes and Bettilia were ready to change the subject. Both quickly found they liked the taste of a Cuba Libre. Before they knew it, Daddy was buying them a second round, then a third. The trays of raw oysters arrived somewhere in betwixt it all. Daddy Brass ate two dozen. The other dozen just sat there congealing, ignored by his guests.

Still, the drinks and the freer flow of conversation and the louder jokes could not distract Kes entirely from the pain throbbing in his hip. He had spent too much time standing on that stage and walking those fairgrounds. And his shoulder hurt too, from too much time on the guitar. His head was beginning to swim a little, as the people of the Pirate's House swirled around him. Kes wasn't sure these sweet warm drinks didn't make his newly-mended limbs hurt more. He felt better in some ways. Bettilia was so beautiful, so lovely. And, oddly enough, she was hardly stuttering at all since the drinks arrived. Not that Kes cared one way or the other. But his joints ached worse.

"Where's the bathroom, Daddy?" he asked at last.

Daddy pointed.

"Little boy's room, right there behind that big fish tank," Daddy said.

"Well, sugar," Mrs. Plum was telling Bettilia, "the only way I know to keep nylons off your ankles is a good garter belt. Not these cheap rigs from the Woolworth's either. I buy all my lingerie and support garments mail order out of Neiman Marcus in Dallas."

Bettilia giggled, feeling no pain.

"Lands. I wouldn't know no mail order anymore than I know when most this town is joking half the time."

Mrs. Plum giggled back, sipping her second Manhattan from an almost empty martini glass.

"Nothing to it," she said. "I'll lend you their catalog. Neiman Marcus apparel is very fine indeed. Very smart."

"Hell, they cain't be too smart," Daddy Brass said matter-of-factly. "Ain't they the ones who coulda owned Coca-Coler before it went Coca-Coler? I guess some fellers would rather peddle panties and perfume. Come to think of it, can't say as I blame em. At least they don't rot your teeth."

"I'll be right back," Kes said, standing, trying to look steady.

Kes was glad he did not have to negotiate a labyrinth of dining rooms to reach the lavatory. The men's room was easy enough to find a few yards away, beyond the exotic fish tank. There was a ship's wheel on the door. Stepping inside, Kes took a wadded bit of tissue from his coat pocket. The paper wad held three of his mother's yellow pills. He took one, wadded the paper back, returned it to his pocket. Then he went to the urinal, stood, waited, and relieved himself. He resisted the urge to ring the brass bell over the urinal before washing his hands. When was it appropriate to ring that bell, he wondered? What might one achieve or what need might arise within the confines of a Pirate's House men's room for one to need such a bell? Maybe you were supposed to ring it when you finally got the joke.

As Kes opened the men's room door again, he heard his daddy's voice over the dining hall clatter.

"*Where's* that damn Parsifal? We need more *dranks*."

"Maybe we should order food instead," Mrs. Plum's voice advised.

Kes came around the fish tank. At the table, Chalice and Glenn were nestled in beside Mrs. Plum.

"Kestrel, I thought we would never find you in all this madness," Mama George said coldly. She did not get the joke either.

VERSE 23

The Pirate's Progress

"No, I will have a glass of gingermint tea," Mama George told Parsifal. "You have gingermint tea?"

"Not gingermint, ma'am. But mint tea, yes. We can brew you a mint tea."

"Ooooh, I just loooove ginshermint tea," Bettilia told everybody, a little sloshy.

"Yes, well, I suppose any old mint tea will do," Mama George said.

"I alwaysh loved it. Mama here was sure surprised to find out. Wudn't you, Mama?"

"Yes, dear," Mama said coolly.

"But Mama George, she brews it best. She showed me how."

"And what will you be having, Miss Dillard?" Parsifal posed, tipped in Chalice's direction.

"A Dr. Pepper, thank you," Chalice said on pins and needles. "Lots of ice."

"And you, sir?"

Glenn eyed the half-empty rum and cokes in front of Kes

and Bettilia. Mama George eyed Glenn. And Glenn knew it.

"Aw, I reckon I'll go Dr. Pepper too. Lot's of ice."

"He's driving," Mama George told Parsifal as if he required explanation.

Parsifal turned to the young black waiter standing beside him.

"That will be a fresh mint tea, Melrose. And two Dr. Peppers. Lots of ice."

"Yes, sir," young Melrose answered.

Parsifal and Melrose turned back to the table, genuflected, then slipped away.

"I'm shore gotdam glad y'all decided to show up *after all*," Daddy Brass bellowed, kicking back the rest of his drink.

"Malakoff, could you lower your voice?" Mama George said evenly, hands folded in her lap.

"I told you I'd bring em, Daddy," Glenn said, slightly peeved.

Mrs. Plum smiled at him. Glenn got stuck halfway betwixt a return smile and a weakling wince. He knew Mama was still watching.

"Mrs. Plum, our introduction is overdue, I'm afraid," Mama George said with strained pleasance. "I have long wanted to meet you."

"And I you," Mrs. Plum said. She had not touched her drink or Daddy Brass since the latecomers sat down at the table. "I feel like I know you, I've written your name on so many envelopes."

"I understand," Mama said. "As it so happens, there was a time I felt I knew Mr. Brass. I once even thought I knew my way around Atlanta, before desegregation. Where to go. And where not to."

"Now, you gals—" Daddy drawled in a drawl grown thicker.

"Now there's no telling what you'll find," Mama continued, "even in the best of quarters."

"You gals, that ain't no way to be."

"What way?" Mama George said at him from across the table, devoid of emotion. "Were we being any particular way? I was unaware."

"Leave it alone," Mrs. Plum muttered under her breath so only he could hear, not looking at him.

"My goodness, y'all was hard to find back in here," Chalice chattered, inspecting a raw oyster. "How many of these rooms does this Pirate House have?"

"Twenty or *thirty* they say," Bettilia gushed then slurped her drink.

Glenn dropped his arm around Chalice, his eyes roaming the restaurant.

"Ain't they got old tunnels under here? That's what I heard. So's them pirates could escape down to the river?"

"Yes, honey," Mrs. Plum said, returning at last to her Manhattan. "That's why we mustn't let your daddy leave the table."

Mama George laughed out loud at that. Mrs. Plum laughed too. Then Daddy laughed and everybody else at the table laughed. Kes had never heard or seen his mother laugh so free and easy in a long time.

"We'll keep our eyes on him, won't we, Mrs. Plum?" Mama George said, fully infected.

By the time her mint tea and the Dr. Peppers arrived the Governor's entourage had passed by—the Governor barely tipping his hat before hustling along at the sight of Daddy Brass—and Daddy Brass was now whispering to two stern Carmelite sisters in black habits who had approached their table. Mrs. Plum handed Daddy his checkbook. Kes started singing *Touch The Hem Of His Garment* as Glenn joined in while Kes sang and pointed at his empty Cuba Libre glass to a passing waiter. The waiter was nodding at Kes's request when four men in bowties at the next table turned and joined in singing—singing in perfect four-part harmony.

If I could just touch the hem of His garment,
I know I'll be made whole—

Kes and Glenn didn't know the gospel quartet and didn't care. As all six sang louder and louder and the crowded restaurant marveled, Mama George set down her mint tea, her hand began patting the table in rhythm. Mrs. Plum began clapping in time. Chalice looked bored and Bettilia was asleep with her head on Kes's shoulder.

When she touched Him the Savior didn't see,
But still He turned around and cried,
Somebody touched me—

Bettilia woke back up when the room gave them all an ovation at the end. She smiled and joined in, unsure why she was applauding but happy to do it anyway. She sipped some more from her glass.

Kes whipped around in his chair.

"Christ, y'all are ferocious—" he said to the four singers.

"*Kestrel*, your language—" Mama George reproached on cue as Bettilia laughed.

Kes leapt up to meet the four singers at the next table—and his hip gave out. He hit the floor.

"*Goddam it*," he yelped.

"*Kestrel*, my ears—"

"What you doing down there, boy?" Daddy asked when Kes dropped from sight.

One of the bow-tied men had jumped up to help but Bettilia beat him to it. She was already hauling Kes to his feet.

"You okay, son?" the bow-tied man said, his hair slicked and shining as his white shirt.

"Yeah. It's just my fucking hipbone," Kes snarled, his tongue cut loose by the liquor. "Goddam fucking bone."

"Kes," Daddy advised, unfazed in a haze of smoke at the far end of the table. "Your mama's about to pop a rivet. You might wanna choose your words."

"Oh, yeah—" Kes said, glancing about, avoiding his mother's eyes. "Sorry."

Mama George said nothing.

"Well, as long as you ain't hurt," the bow-tied man said.

"I never said that," Kes answered, a bit sharp.

"That's true."

The man seemed a little wounded himself now. Kes grabbed the man's hand and shook it.

"Hey, man, y'all sing fierce and fantastic. You fellers quartet?"

"We're the Fair Weather Four. I'm Del Jonquil. These are my brothers Jack, Orvy, and Ludlow."

Kes and Bettilia smiled at the table of bow-tied brothers, the brothers smiled back. Glenn shot them a salute.

"Y'all in town for the fair?" Kes asked.

"Nope," bow-tied Del said, "golf tournament. You?"

"We're the Brothers Brass. We live here. We're playing the fair all week."

"I see, well, please to meet y'all. County fair crowds are hard to hold."

"Ain't they though," Kes agreed, Del drifting back to his table.

"Break a leg," Del said.

Kes froze, Del froze, the bow-tied table winced. Del laughed nervous.

"That's show biz talk for good luck," he started to explain.

"I know that," Kes said, testy.

"Sit down, Kes," his Daddy's voice said.

Kes did as he was told. He sat and Del rejoined his brothers. Kes rejoined his Cuba Libre.

"It might be best to order some food," Mama said.

Suddenly, Saint Peter had entered the room. The elder black fellow came through the tables in his pinstripe suit and stopped behind Kes's chair. He just stood there, somber behind his freckles.

"Malakoff," he spake, in a soft honeyed voice.

Daddy Brass rose quickly from his chair and approached Saint Peter, both of them huddled for a moment behind Kes.

"What's the problem here?" Daddy said low.

"It's your burnt boy," Saint Peter said so soft that Kes could barely hear him.

Daddy Brass glanced down at the table full of eyes and ears, then pulled Saint Peter over to the fish tank, out of earshot. The two conferred briefly. Daddy began to shake his head at what Saint Peter was telling him, but Kes could no longer hear what they were saying. But—by turning to watch them—Kes could now see the doorway to the dining room. The doorframe was stuffed with that Zeebub from the freak show, the human zookeeper. She stood there in her overalls and hobnail boots, waiting, impatient, chewing her dead wet cigar.

Kes watched Daddy Brass brush lint from Saint Peter's shoulder before handing him a folded envelope. Peter nodded, impassive, then headed for the door. Saint Peter registered a trace of distaste when he delivered the envelope to Zeebub. Her stumpy fingers snatched it, she smirked, then she went away. Saint Peter followed after her, keeping his distance.

Daddy Brass returned to the table where Bettilia, newly revived, was effervescing with slurry abandon.

"Aw, I don't reckon I knew much of nothing about clothes when I got here," Bettilia was telling Mrs. Plum, "but I'm a fast learner."

"They ain't no lie about that," Daddy injected, falling back into the fold.

"Mama George, she done teached me how to walk better—"

"Taught. Not done teached," Mama whispered.

"And she done taught me how to wear these fancy shoes without falling over. I'd just as soon wear perty slippers all the time, but I think I done right well on them shoe heels tonight, thanks to Mama here. And Mizz Chalice, she taught me lipstick and eye shadder."

"It's shadow, dear," Mama whispered, "not shadder—"

"Eye shadow, that is."

Bettilia beamed, batting her lashes. Kes beamed too. She did look beautiful—for a tiny girl out of the trees.

"She's begun to shine," Mama told the table, simply, proudly.

"She sure was shining out on that stage tonight," Glenn chimed in.

"You all were," Mama said.

"Shoo," Bettilia exhaled. "I ain't been out nowheres without no big white dog at my heels since, well—"

Mrs. Plum's lips pursed.

"Since Shelfy Oak College? Where you and Kes met?"

Bettilia nodded, excited. She was liking this voluptuous Mrs. Plum with her high red hair and sexy red lips. After three Cuba Libres, Bettilia was liking everybody. She even liked singing on a stage.

"I have secured four more October bookings at even higher fees," Mama George was telling Mrs. Plum. "The Brothers Brass. Back singing bigger and better for The Lord."

"And I start *b*-back to school after Christmas. At this all girl school—"

"The Hope Ashling Academy," Mama said.

"Can you believe it? Hope Ashling. Mama George got it all worked out for me to go."

"Kes, Glenn," Mrs. Plum asked, "will you be returning to Bible college?"

Glenn locked eyes with Mama George, then looked away.

"Aw, we don't know as we will or we won't," Kes said sheepishly.

"We're undecided," Glenn told the chandelier.

"That's right," Kes mumbled. "Undecided."

"Some of us are just glad you here right now," Chalice said before leaving more lipstick on Glenn's cheek.

Mama George said nothing.

"*Chalice?* Is it?" Mrs. Plum asked.

"Yes, ma'am. That's my name."

"You and Glenn, you're so adorable together. Are you a Savannah girl?"

"Well, yes, Mizz Plum. Sort of. I grew up on the island, went to school with Kes. And Glenn. My daddy was mayor of the island until he had to step down."

"Oh?" Mrs. Plum was afraid she had stepped into something unsavory.

"Yes, my mama was diagnosed with dementia back in February. She needs him."

"Oh, I'm sorry to hear that."

"Mr. Arthel Dodson is island mayor now."

"Well, I'll be damned, if it ain't the songbird!" a voice rang out.

Kes gandered over his shoulder, a bit bleary, looking for

the voice. It was Mr. Bo Peep from the pool hall.

Mr. Bo was a bit more dapper now, breezing to their table in a linen suit like Daddy's, only Bo's was lavender blue. On his arm was a plump little woman, well dressed with salt and pepper hair.

"Darlin," he told her, "this is that canary bird I told you about. The one who sang for his supper but wouldn't stop to eat it."

Kes stood up fast again, a little too fast. His head felt as woozy as his hip. He sank back into his chair.

"Mr. Bo, it's sure *gooood* to *seeee* you," Kes oozed.

"Charmed," the woman said, extending her hand.

Kes gave her a slow over-friendly shake.

"How *are you*, ma'am?"

"This is my wife," Bo Peep told him. "Just ask her. I been rattling my tonsils about you and your high notes for some time now."

"Wolfie, with you gone who's shaving them points at that pool hall?" Daddy razzed low.

"Malakoff Brass—" Bo Peep razzed back.

"Hell, without you on the scene, somebody's bound to say he lost 'cause he had to shoot straight with an un-crooked cue," Daddy said, winking at his audience.

"I've got something for you," Bo Peep said, coming around the table, standing over Daddy Brass. Bo reached inside his coat then held up Daddy's unreleased stiletto knife. This got everyone's attention. "I told you you was out of line using it to carve my roast beef. You left it on the plate."

"Is that what you call that mess? I had to cut its throat afore I could eat it." Grinning, Daddy accepted his stiletto, laid it on his napkin. "What do I owe you?"

"More than you'll ever know, Malakoff."

"You want I should water your cactus? While you're up the river?"

"You could put a new roof on the Temple. Mikve Israel is starting to leak."

"First thing tomorrow, Wolf. Right after breakfast. I'll bring hammer and nails."

"I'll call ahead, Malakoff. Tell em you're coming."

"Set down here, son. You and the missus. Have a little drank."

Mr. Bo Peep smiled at the rest of the table.

"No, but thanks for the invite. We're meeting folks for supper. Running late."

Kes caught fragments of that conversation from his end of the table. It was too fucking hot in here now, somebody should crank the cold air. Mr. Bo Peep was waving a little goodbye at him, over the heads at the table. Kes could see Mr. Bo Peep's wife shaking Daddy's hand. Kes sure did like Mr. Bo Peep. Mr. Bo was good as gold in Kes's book.

The Fair Weather Four were leaning over Kes's chair now, their hands patting his shoulders, wishing him well. The bow-tied brother Del was taking Kes's hand again, leaning over him, shaking his hand.

"Y'all tear em up at that fair this week," Del glad-handed, saying goodbye. "Tell em the Fair Weather Four said hello."

"You too," Kes managed. "Tells em the Brothersh Brash

says hello—"

Del Jonquil did not know what that meant exactly, but he nodded politely anyway. Kes saw him nod, Kes saw Del Jonquil glance down the table toward Daddy and Mr. Bo Peep's wife and Mr. Bo Peep. He saw Del Jonquil make a wisecrack out the side of his mouth at his brothers.

"Did jew see that fancy blade knife? Scary."

Jew?

"Jew? He said *'Jew'?"* Kes sputtered at a bewildered Bettilia.

Kes flew out of his chair, landing a fist in Del's gut and a fist in Del's face. Del went down. Kes started to kick him but his hip gave out, he fell. The two took to tearing each other up on the floor.

It took Daddy, Mr. Bo Peep, and the Fairweather Three to finally pull them apart.

"Jaybird, I oughta wop you one. You ruint everthing for everbody, *go-go-*going boogernuts like that."

"I'm sorry. I thought he was being ugly to Mr. Bo Peep for being a Jew."

"Well, he weren't," Bettilia harped. "I heard ever word he said."

"You sure?" Kes winced, taking the ice-packed napkin from Mama George.

"I was right *there*, bird. He asked: *did you* see that knife."

"Oh."

Kes iced the lump on his cheek with the napkin. He reached for his Cuba Libre but Mrs. Plum swatted his hand away from the glass. Still, he was feeling no pain, not yet. The room had returned to some kind of normal, the fine diners murmuring at their tables, murmuring dark thoughts and words about him, no doubt. Asking whatever went wrong with that crazy-eyed Kestrel Brass, of the Brothers Brass, don't you know, their tongues clucking, silverware clinking, drinking down too much wine and hard spirits. Kes heard the room murmur a little louder when Daddy Brass came strolling back from the Pirate's House office.

"Well, sports fans, they ain't gonna press no charges," Daddy announced.

"How did you effectuate that, Malakoff?" Mrs. Plum asked.

"By the book. I talked at them Fair Weather Four boys a while. They's good boys, good Christian boys. The kind y'all like. Then the manager, he talked at em. Parsifal, he talked at em. Then I talked at em some more. Them Fair Weather boys, they was quite forgiving. They was more than happy to forgive, forget, and drive back to Memphis in a new Pontiac four-door. Four brothers, four doors. See how nicely that works out? Oh, and ole Wolfie Bo Peep, he said tell you Kes that he appreciated the gesture all the same."

"It was *unforgivable*," Mama George hissed, searching her purse for aspirin.

"Well," Daddy cackled, slapping the back of Kes's neck as he sat beside him. "At least I caught your second show this evening. Headliner stuff. Top of the bill. You done alright."

"He did not do all right," Mama George spat like the adder. "He did all wrong."

"He's just a fool jaybird," Bettilia sighed simply.

"This is all because of you and your subversions, Malakoff Brass," Mama said. "You insist on making our sons pay for your sins. Just look at him. Look how Kestrel is, sitting here besotted and beaten like this. You did this as surely as if you sold him to gypsies or one of those freak shows."

"He's just a fool jaybird."

Kes's eyes met Bettilia's. She hid a fleeting smile.

"I took care of the tab," Mrs. Plum told Daddy. "The drinks and oysters."

"Why, thank you, sugar," Daddy said.

"With a substantial gratuity."

"Naturally."

Bettilia took Kes's hand.

"C'mon. I'll walk you outside. Cold air will *d*-do you good."

Kes got to his feet. His hip shifted, unsteady. His hand landed on Bettilia for support.

"I'll go with you," Mrs. Plum said.

Bettilia and Mrs. Plum helped the disheveled Kes from the dining room, leaving Daddy Brass and Mama George alone at the table. Daddy took stock, resigned, watching them go.

"I figure I'm the worst thing that ever happened to you," he said.

"No. You are not," Mama said, gazing into her purse. "You're the best thing. I just can't think about it. Now, please, leave me alone."

Mama George snapped her purse shut. She rose from her chair and went searching for the others. She found Kes hobbling with Bettilia and Mrs. Plum, lost in another dining room.

"Mister," Bettilia finally asked a portly waiter, "*c-c*-could you help us sniff our way out of here?"

The waiter was happy to oblige. He led them in a left turn through a door into another dining den, then right, then left, then left, then right around a long teakwood bar and bartender. By the time they all tumbled into the lobby, they were ready to be home. Mama George pressed a dime into the waiter's palm.

"Whoa, thank you, ma'am," the waiter bemused, slipping the dime into his vest pocket.

"Let's get the hell out of this rabbit hole," Kes muttered to his mother's chagrin.

"Kestrel—"

Mrs. Plum elbowed his ribs as Bettilia laughed and pushed open the front door. They stepped outside to find Glenn sneaking a cigarette on the sidewalk.

Beside him sat a big white dog.

VERSE 24

Treehouse

"*Sister!*"

Bettilia's arms flew open for the big white dog. Bettilia tried to hug her, but Sister was too excited, barking deep, loud, her great white broom tail swishing, her front paws rearing up onto tiny Bettilia's shoulders. Bettilia was shocked with glee.

"Get down now, Sis, get down—" she tried to scold.

"How the hell she get here?" Kes said, scruffing Sister's ears as the two Carmelite nuns exited the Pirate's House.

Glenn's foot quickly crushed his cigarette, swept the butt into the bushes.

"I found her out here, just setting perty," Glenn said, leaking smoke, a smooch of lipstick still on his cheek. "Like some lady in waiting."

"So, Gaylenn," Mama George began, hugging her purse, staring at the happy dog, "how long have you been consuming these cigarettes?"

Mama's enunciation of that last word made it sound like a first-degree sodomy conviction.

"Aw, Mama—" Glenn looked off at the nuns crossing Bay Street, the songwriter in him conjuring up crows in lamplight.

"Glenn, I am very broadminded," Mama said. "If you want to die hacking out your heart and your God-given voice, that is your decision."

"Where's Chally?" Kes asked, throwing Glenn a lifeline.

"She's waiting in the car."

"This dog, she's so beautiful," Mrs. Plum cooed, joining in the scruffing of Sister's big snow-bear head. Sister panted, eyes bright, loving all this attention. "How old is she?"

"Kestrel? Are you smoking them too?"

"Nine months, going on ten," Bettilia answered.

"Fifteen or sixteen," Daddy Brass said, coming out the Pirate's House door.

"What's that Daddy?" Kes asked, his head still buzzing from rum and bruises.

"That dog come fifteen or sixteen miles to get here from Angelsprey House," Daddy said, impressed.

Bettilia sank down, hunkering at Sister's level.

"But how she find us?"

Kes squatted down, joining her as Daddy shrugged.

"Dogs been known to do it."

"Gonna be a tight squeeze, Mama," Glenn said.

"What's that you say, son? Did you cough up something? A bit of lung, perhaps?"

Glenn and Kes rolled eyes at each other.

"I was saying, Mama—it's gonna be a tight squeeze. Five of us and that big hound in your little French Renault, driving all the way back home. Cozy."

Daddy Brass let Mama process and digest that, but not for long. His keys began to rattle.

"Naw, you and Chalice, drive your mama on back. The rest of us be right behind you in my Hudson. I reckon this big white hoss will fit my backseat with room to spare for Bonnie and Clyde here."

Kes and Bettilia got nearly glad as Sister, their rum-rimmed eyes smiling up at Daddy.

"Very well. So much the better," Mama George said, clipping off across the parking lot, headed for her car. "The odor might forever permeate my upholstery."

Glenn wasn't sure if she meant the odor of liquor or the odor of the dog, but he put up no fight, trailing after her, hands in his pockets.

Daddy Brass brought his Hudson around to the Pirate's House awning. Kes and Bettilia hefted Sister into the back-seat then piled in after. Mrs. Plum's feline gaze appraised them from up front.

"My, if y'all don't look like two drowned rats behind six bales of cotton."

Kes blew a tuft of Sister's fur from his mouth as Chalice tapped on the glass with Kes's cane. Bettilia rolled down the window.

"Your hip sore as it is," Chalice said, poking the stick through the window, "I thought you might need this."

Kes nodded, wedged the cane betwixt himself and big Sister's paws. He liked the way this arrangement forced Bettilia against him, his leg against hers. He did not like the way Chalice was smiling so strangely in at them, like she could read Kes's mind. Bettilia rolled up the glass.

It was high tide below Angelsprey, waves crashing, by the time the Hudson arrived on Officer's Row. Mama George's Renault was already parked inside the dark garage.

"Bettilia Bit, wake up. We're home," Kes said.

Bettilia raised her head from his shoulder, blinking. Kes reached across her and opened the door. Seeing her way out and seizing it—Sister barreled over their laps and out onto the lawn.

"*Sister. Dang it,*" Bettilia griped, wiping her eyes. Yes, she was full awake now.

Daddy Brass and Mrs. Plum got a chuckle out of that.

"Don't forget your heels, Bettilia," Mrs. Plum told her.

"I wouldn't be in you two's shoes for all the bitter in Dixie," Daddy said, shifting around to face them in the back seat, his hand on the wheel. "Not with Hard Hearted Georgiana in there, sharping her razor. And you better get in some zees. I figure you got a bigger box to build for that big Sister dog afore tomorrow night's show."

"Oh, yeah..." Kes mumbled. He'd forgotten about Sister's cage. How had she escaped it? "Or she needs a bigger padlock anyways."

"I'll wager you find it's gonna take more than that, son."

"I can't imagine a dog like that—*locked up*," Mrs. Plum said.

"Me *n*-neither..." Bettilia murmured, still groggy.

Daddy was looking down in the backseat floorboard.

"Where'd your toe go?"

"I done bad," Bettilia yawned, eyes shut, not thinking.

"*Malakoff*," Mrs. Plum said, not wanting to embarrass.

"Nighty night, Mizz Plum, Daddy Brass," Bettilia responded, "Thank y'all..."

"Goodnight," Daddy and Mrs. Plum said.

As the Hudson drove away, Kes limped along the side lawn, an arm around Bettilia, one hand on his cane. The moss hung grey, fluttering overhead in the new autumn breeze fresh off the ocean. They could both see the silver crescent, the waning moon, afloat over the water beyond the stacked porches of the house. Ahead of them, Sister was a galloping ghost in the moonlight, bounding down to the beach.

"Ain't we going inside?" Bettilia asked as Kes kept going, limping toward the waves, pulling her past the kitchen door.

"Aw, I wanna take a look at Sister's cage. Besides, I ain't ready to go in there and get my ass chewed by my mama."

Bettilia giggled, holding tighter to him.

"Me neither."

Neither she nor Kes were prepared for what they found when they came around the corner and saw Sister's cage on the front porch—or rather, what was left of it.

"*Jeeezus wept*," Kes said as Bettilia whistled.

Two-by-fours and shreds of chain-link fencing hung alongside the front portico door, like a white bomb had exploded inside, leaving no corners or shape to what had been some fool's notion of animal control. Her water dish was upside down under the porch.

"I worked two days building that thing," Kes said, letting go of Bettilia, caning his way over to the front steps. He surveyed the damage, flipped the dish upright with his cane, then looked to the beach below at Sister playing down there, her huge paws splashing at water's edge. Kes settled on the steps, sitting, poking at what was left of the cage door in the grass. "I'll have to get started first thing in the morning. Hardware store opens at six-thirty. Maybe Glenn can help me. We'll have to make this one a lot stronger."

"Naw," Bettilia said, sitting beside him. "You won't neither."

"Huh?"

Sister began barking at something in the dunes.

"I ain't gonna leave her here again," Bettilia informed him. "She's going with us."

"In Mama's little ole car? She ain't gonna be happy."

"Mama might not be. Sister will. Drive that big copper Cadillac your Daddy give you."

"Mama won't ride in no copper Cadillac. Long story."

"Besides, Chalice won't be going to all our fair shows after tonight. She told me so."

"Oh, she did?"

"Yup" Bettilia said, watching Sister race back up the hill toward them. "Chalice says she gets bored but not to tell Glenn that. She didn't say nothing about not telling you though."

Kes blew a laugh into her hair, nuzzling it. She smelled of popcorn, sawdust, smoke, and gingermint tea. With just a hint of rum.

"Kes?"

"Yeah?"

"After this week, I cain't be singing with y'all up there. You know that, don't you?"

"Of course you can. They love you. Everbody loves you. Mama says we got four more shows coming up after the fair. So, why should I know that?"

"Because I'm telling you. Kes, I cain't be singing with y'all. Not after this week."

Kes reached up, turning Bettilia's face to his as Sister arrived and started lapping them both with her tongue. Kes shouldered the big dog away.

"Sister, get down," he said, still studying Bettilia's placid acceptance. Her mind was made up, he could tell. "What's this all about—after all our work? Even Mama wants to put you in more songs. Was it something I did? I know I acted the fool tonight. I'm sorry about that."

"Don't be daft, jaybird. It weren't nothing you did."

"Well?"

"I reckon they's something I best tell you."

"Okay. Tell me."

Bettilia breathed in, she breathed out. The air felt so sharp and salty clean and good, but did her no good now. She had to look away from Kes, at this happy dog, at that great big ocean, but none of them could help her. So she closed her eyes.

"You know how I told you I kilt my daddy, dropping that rail spike on his head?"

"Yeah. I remember."

"Well, I don't reckon I really kilt him. I just wished I did. I reckon he's still out there somewheres. Looking for me. Or maybe not. I don't know. I ain't so sure one way or the other."

"What you mean you ain't sure?"

"I hit him a good lick, I know that. I dropped that spike from a real high pine. But he was still moving when I run off."

"But you ain't sure he *ain't* dead, are you? He could be. Prob'ly be."

"Yup. He could be. Back there, through all those years with Mambly, I got where I just knew he was dead. Dead dead in the dirt. But, more and more, with each passing moon, I ain't so sure no more. Sometimes, I can feel him out there."

"But you ain't sure he is."

"If he was ever to see me up there, singing with y'all. Or if anybody else was to see me and go tell him."

"Who's gonna tell him, even if he ain't dead? Who would he know down here, him from way back in them hills?"

"That Lych."

"What's a lych?"

Bettilia opened her eyes wide and took in the stars, the moon, this great sparkling world of water and sky. Kes was right. This seemed another world from her darkling hills. This seemed like a Genesis dream.

"How can I explain something as terrible and torn as a Lych to a boy like you, a boy from down here? You've lived such a magic life."

Kes had to spit at that. It spat out nastier than he meant to let out. It splatted in the grass and Sister sniffed it.

"Bettilia, you know how you cain't swim?"

"No, I cain't swim."

"Well, even if I once could swim them waters, I couldn't swim em now. Not gimped up like I am and will be. You don't know the half of it. Mama, she had us gimped, both me and Glenn, before I ever busted a thing."

Bettilia pondered that. There was so much she wanted to tell him. Things she had never told anybody. She knew Kes had paid a price for knowing her, just like Mambly had. But knowing too much might cost him even more. Still, sitting here now, so far from the horrors of those long ago hills, Bettilia felt tempted, sorely tempted to share things she knew she should not share. Yet she wanted to desperately be with Kes, to share with him.

"A Lych is a terrible thing. Lych's is people, kind of. Scarred-up, strange folk who was rarely seen. They was sneaky. Most stayed hid most of the time, living back in the woods, keeping to their own. Their faces weren't right, they heads weren't right."

"Weren't right?"

"Most had faces like melted trees, burnt trees."

"I don't understand."

"You ain't the only one. There was no understanding a Lych. Like I said, they kept to their own. Some didn't wear clothes way we do. Didn't talk to hardly nobody. If you saw one, he'd run off on you afore he'd say a word. I reckon most didn't know no words. Except some did, I know. 'Cause they'd talk to *him*, my daddy. Tell him things they saw. I don't know what he did for em, but he had his way with em. And they was this one. Ephran Lych."

"What—what about him?"

"He wandered more than most. On his old mule. Ephran Lych was a pack rat. That mule of his, you could hear it coming from far off. Clinking and clanking from all the bottles and tin. And Ephran Lych, he wanders far, to faroff places. Like this. And my daddy, he made Ephran do for him. I think, maybe, my daddy took one of Ephran's kids and sent Ephran bits and pieces from time to time. I never knew if a Lych could feel. But maybe they can."

"What a thing," Kes pondered. "You ain't sure that Lych loves his kids?"

Bettilia shrugged.

"I know he was mighty partial to that mule. Where er that mule went, Ephran went."

Slowly, carefully, Kes wrapped her in his arms, pulling her into him.

"Don't say no more, girl. You don't have to say no more. Not tonight. Not ever about all that."

"The thing is, Kes—I think that old Ephran Lych might of been back at Mambly's place, poking around. Not long before Mambly passed."

"You think he kilt her? Hanged her?"

"No. I never knew no Lych to kill nobody. Lych's is scary of other folks. That's what makes em so scary, is how scary of you they is."

"I think I understand what you mean."

Her head fell against his shoulder, lulled by the soft rolling rhythm of the waves. The white figment of Sister drifted back down through the dunes, toward the surf ebbing in, out.

"Do you?" she asked, woozy.

"Yes," Kes said, "kind of like how you scare this boy."

"I scary you?"

"Yes, Bit, you scare me, when I see how scared you are of me."

"I ain't scary of you, jaybird..." she mumbled, yawned.

Kes watched Sister sitting down there now, Sister watching the tide roll in, out.

"Mambly said you was. She knew you was. I think she knew I was. She told me a story about a fraidy man, a kudzu man, who was afraid to let nobody close who could really see him or touch him. All the while, him longing to be seen, touched."

Kes looked down at Bettilia. She was asleep against his shoulder. As easy and unthinking as the tide, Kes leaned down and kissed her.

Bettilia came awake, lifted her head.

"What did you just do?"

"I kissed you," he said.

He cupped her head in his hand, pulling her back toward his lips.

"*J*-Jaybird..."

His lips met hers again, for just a gentle moment, before she pulled away. Bettilia got up from the porch steps.

"Bettilia—"

She wouldn't look at him. With silent resolve, Bettilia walked away in the grass, around the corner of the porch, disappearing along the side of the house. Seeing this, Sister came trotting up the hill then disappeared after Bettilia, following her.

Kes tried to get up. Falling back onto the step, he reached for his cane. Finally, on his feet, he limped quickly around the corner to see where she had gone. He had heard no door open or close. In the dimming moonlight, Kes saw Sister sitting at the foot of the great pilgrim oak, just sitting with her great white snout looking straight up into the high limbs and leaf and rippling tatters of moss.

With his hip beginning to burn again, Kes felt like that oak was miles away. But other things took his mind. Sister leapt up and met him halfway to the oak. Kes's heart was pounding by the time he reached the tree and stood beside Sister, both of them staring up at the high treehouse.

"*Bit*" Kes shouted out a loud whisper, his eyes cutting up and over toward his mother's dark bedroom window. He didn't want to wake the big house.

"*Bettilia?*"

No answer came from up this tree. Not that Kes expected one, not really. No, the tiny treehouse haven of his childhood still waited up there, high in the limbs, dark and still and unvisited by Kes since long before his fall. And she was up there in it. And she was scary of him. He knew that too.

Kes let his cane fall into the grass beside Sister. Sister's eyes met his then she returned to her Job-like fixation on the tiny trap door at the top of the tree trunk ladder. Kes's coat fell into the grass alongside his cane.

Putting the foot of his good leg on the bottom rung, reaching up, grabbing the highest rung he could reach—Kes began to climb.

If it was torture, he was unaware. It took longer than it had ever taken him to climb that tree. But he climbed it, rung by rung, one hard breath after another. When he finally pulled himself up through the trap door of the treehouse, his clothes and hair were mussed, and Bettilia was sitting cross-legged on the lower bunk. Kes pulled himself up further, into the treehouse and onto the bunk, beside her.

She seemed barely aware, like this was the most normal, every-night thing, like she need not receive him—for he had always been here. She gazed out the treetop window, beyond the spyglass, out across the endless horizon, the mysterious depths of needful but unknown waters, of wombling sea, the threat and the allure of it inward bound, together.

He leaned over, his face in her hair, the Bettilia scent of her filling him up. At last, she looked at him. She said nothing. Neither did he. In one flowing motion, Bettilia pulled her dress off over her head. Kes's fingers traveled the length of her before she had his shirt off him, kissing him again. The scent of her shoulder, her skin in the window's gingermint moonlight, these sensations took Kes in hand too.

Bettilia made no move to stop his wandering, his questioning touch, or the depths of his discovery. Here, now, he barely seemed scary at all.

VERSE 25

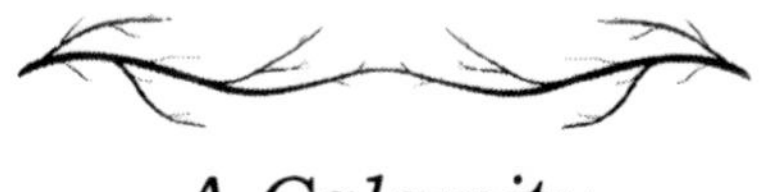

A Calamity

Mama George parked her little black Renault betwixt the big black Hudson sedan and a canvas-sided freight truck on River Street. She saw a sweat-dripping relay of mostly dark workmen unloading whatever booty and swag Malakoff was up to, the men carrying their cargo down a side alleyway. As Mama George approached the front door of M. Brass Freight & Cargo Ltd., she was displeased to see the note taped inside the glass:

Doctor appt. Back at 3. Roberta

Mama George would not be accepting this as any kind of temporary resolution, not today. All the bricks that cobbled and lined this steaming street—if they were mortared and stacked like the walls of Jericho—could not hold her back today. Mama George poked her head around the corner of the alleyway, then followed the stream of rough men, wheeled dollies, and kegs.

She found a sun-drenched loading dock at the back of the building where another truck was also being unloaded. A black goliath in a bright Tiki God shirt was manning an expanded metal lectern, eating raw peanuts from a paper bag while workers bustled past him into the warehouse.

"Malakoff Brass," Mama George demanded of him.

He took a mechanical pencil from behind his ear, scribbling figures on the bag.

"Master Brass, what? Do I know that bwoy?" he said, minding his scribbles and not her.

"You better know him," Mama George said evenly, "or my attorney will want to know what you know about my husband's assets. Such as they are. I am Georgiana Brass."

Bugga Higgin stopped scribbling, looked up, pointed the metal pencil into the dark belly of the building.

"Office, mum."

"Thank you."

Thumbing another peanut, Bugga watched the severe Mrs. Brass disappear into the inner shadows with her clutched purse, her heels echoing like rapid gunfire.

Georgiana found the office in a murky corner of the vast, high-ceilinged warehouse space. It was easy to find. Light streamed across the concrete floor from the two outer walls of glass windows, giving Malakoff an expansive view of his employees' comings and goings and his towering containers of stock. As she approached, Georgiana could see him in there, feet on his desk, talking to an elder black fellow in a pinstriped suit. She remembered the fellow from his brief visitation during that fiasco at the Pirate's House. Malakoff's feet came off his desk fast when he glanced out the glass and saw her coming. She did not bother to knock.

"Oh, hey doll, you should of told me you was coming,"

Malakoff said, one big smile as he slid a drawer shut lest she see inside it. "We woulda hosed off the porch."

"Malakoff, we need to talk," she said, closing the door.

The old fellow in the pinstripe was already out of his chair and standing.

"Darlin, this here's Saint Peter. Saint Peter, this be the missus. Hard to believe, but this is her first visit here. Ain't it, Georgiana? Your first visit here?"

Saint Peter gave a slight bow, Georgia extended her hand. Saint Peter's hesitation was fleeting, almost imperceptible, before his coffee-colored hand briefly held her soft pale offering.

"Mizz Brass," he said, his voice a warm breeze.

Then her hand was gone and he was moving for the door.

"You ain't got to go, Pete," Malakoff was quick to tell him, though Georgiana's eyes said different.

"I'll be at the Exchange," Saint Peter said kindly before slipping out the door.

With him gone, Georgiana settled in the empty chair. The chair was still warm. Behind the desk, Malakoff sat and swiveled around to face her.

"Well, that was quite the calamity you orchestrated the other night," Georgiana said, her lips barely moving.

"Aw, I wish I could accept the credit. I ain't ever orchestrated nothing in my life. You know that. I ain't the musical sort."

"Don't be coy, Malakoff. Modesty is not a suit in your closet."

"No?"

"Besides, we have another, greater calamity on our hands."

"We do?"

"Your son thinks he's getting married. I overheard him say it."

"You did, huh?"

"Yes."

Malakoff slumped back in his chair, shoving his telephone further away.

"Oh. That. Yeah, I just got off the phone from em."

"His words were few. Hers too. But any fool could decipher their code."

"They said they was scared to tell you," Daddy said. "Wanted my advice."

"Your advice? Well, I hope you told him the Brothers Brass have one more night of their County Fair engagement and a financial future to consider. Was that your advice? Tell me that was your advice, Malakoff Brass."

"Aw, doll—"

"Stop calling me that. We're not kids anymore. But they are. They're just boys."

"Yeah, and she's just a girl. A girl he's in love with, best I can tell."

"He'll outgrow it."

"Is that what you want?" Malakoff replied curtly, not so nice anymore. "You want him to outgrow love as quick as he finds it? You figure it's that easy to come by?"

This scalded her tongue. She wanted to tell him the parable of the wise and foolish virgins, but stopped herself.

They sat for a spell, stewing, not talking.

"You need some potpourri in here. It reeks of cigars."

"Ain't that serendipity?" he muttered. "I woke up thinking the same thing."

"When's the last time this rug was cleaned?"

"We didn't *know* you was *dropping by.* Wire ahead next time."

"Your Mrs. Plum. Roberta Plum? She seems very nice."

"She is."

"A nice, healthful figure. Quite the asset."

"She's capable. I figure the doc's got her up on blocks about now."

Georgiana did not flinch.

"Maybe if you took more of an interest in your sons' lives instead of staying secreted over here in the nasty smoke of this booze-filled barn—"

"Georgiana, maybe I missed it, but I ain't seen my name on the welcome mat outside your door in quite some time."

"You left."

"You booted me out *long afore that.*"

"You abandoned me, you abandoned your sons."

"Goddam you, Georgiana Kinoy. Goddam you. I never stopped being their daddy."

"Maybe if you had done the things a good father ought to do, to show a little godly guidance, they wouldn't be wanting to wallow in the world and the flesh like they are."

"Maybe if you hadn't warned em not to drink the applejack—they wouldn't be so thirsty to taste it."

"Do you realize that Kestrel and Bettilia spent the night

together, intoxicated, up in that treehouse you built?"

Bugga heard Malakoff's laugh all the way out on the loading dock.

"Naw, but I ain't surprised, precious," Malakoff bellowed. "Why you think they wanna get married?"

"What?" Georgiana sputtered, confused.

"No wonder Kes sounded so shaky about it on that phone. They was wanting *me* to tell you."

"Malakoff, what are you talking about?"

"Kes and Bettilia getting married. That's what I'm talking about. The same goddam calamity that brung you down here to River Street and planted your big girl panties in that chair."

Georgiana got very quiet as the evil grin faded slow from Malakoff's face. When she finally spake, it was a drone, a funeral incantation.

"Malakoff. Gaylenn and Chalice are planning to run off and get married. I overheard them."

"Back up. Glenn? Chalice?"

"They thought I was napping in the backseat. Driving home from your calamity the other night."

Out on the loading dock, Bugga Higgin crunched another goober and wondered what big fun Boss Brass must be having with the Mrs. Brass. Whatever they were up to, the man's laughter kept braying long and loud—loud enough to crack the glass back there in that office.

VERSE 26

Hellzabub's Human Zoo

Mama George was so distraught she rode in Daddy's old copper Cadillac that evening. She sat on the porch in a silent dither, staring at Sister who kept staring back with sad-eyed empathy, until Kes realized they were all going to be late if they didn't get up and go. He pulled the Cadillac around and Mama got in after Sister without a thought or word of protest. She finally began weeping on the drive to the fairgrounds. Bettilia hid behind Sister, sitting as far from Mama as she could in the big backseat, hearing Mama start to sniffle and sob. Bettilia felt like she had betrayed the only mother she had left, the woman who had given her the bedroom of her own childhood and opened a part of her hardened heart to a daughter she never had.

The boys did not seem to care or show it much if they did. Mama George sat offstage and wept all through the final show. But Kes and Glenn were still ecstatic—nervous but ecstatic— when Glenn took the microphone after the trio sang *How Can I Keep From Singing* for the last time. Even Daddy Brass was there to see it and hear it.

"Folks, folks, thank you so much," Glenn's voice echoed over the fairgrounds as the applause died down. "We've got a special announcement tonight, something we couldn't wait to share with all you folks we love so dear. We've been blessed in so many ways, with a good mama and daddy, good health, the joy of singing our little songs for y'all—"

The applause rose again.

"We got to cut our first record a while back—"

"*Yeah!*" a teenage girl squealed from the front row.

Kes got a kick out of that.

"So *you* were the one," he said, leaning into the mike.

It was an old joke but the audience laughed. The band laughed. Everybody laughed except Mama George. The clapping got louder, Kes and Glenn's grins got bigger. Bettilia's did too, but faded fast.

"And we got a new record coming out in time for Christmas. We ain't even recorded it yet but it'll be out before Christmas," Glenn cracked, settling the fresh laughter and applause with a downplay of his picking hand. "But tonight we'd like to share with you the greatest gift we've ever been blessed to receive. Tonight we'd like to let the whole wide world know that Kestrel and Bettilia—they're getting *married.*"

The crowd went wild as Kes's eyes twinkled, his arm around a blushing, scared-witless Bettilia.

"And, hey, you wanna know the cuckoo part?" Glenn shouted into the microphone.

"*What?*" the crowd shouted back.

"*I'm getting married too! Chally, come on out here.*"

The whoops and hollers and the pounding of hands and feet became deafening as Chalice appeared from the wings in her pink-and-white recycled Easter dress, striding to center stage, into Glenn's outstretched arm. She nestled in against his guitar, all four of them waving out at the storm of endearment and exaltation. It was a rare moment indeed.

Daddy Brass was behind the bandstand. Sister's tail went faster and faster as she swarmed around Daddy's boots. Daddy Brass was mighty pleased with himself, as if this were all his idea—his big hands clapping so slow, steady, and loud that his boys could hear him behind them, through the perfunctory clapping of the band. Kes was pretty sure he spied Saint Peter, Bugga Higgin, and Blondie Boy Bichét standing out beyond the side bleachers.

Voices began ringing out from the sea of shining faces.

"What's the date?"

"Double wedding?"

"Wanna buy my duplex?"

"Ask him if he'll carry the paper," Kes said in the microphone to Glenn.

"Aw, folks, we don't know. Double wedding? Maybe. We don't know nothing yet," Glenn said, choking back laughter. "It's all too early to tell. This is all new to us too. But y'all will be the first to know once we get any of that mess figured out. Anyway, right now, me and Kestrel here, we'd like to sing one last tune tonight, in honor of this season, this season in our hearts. Dedicated to Chalice and Bettilia."

Chalice and Bettilia waved a final goodbye to the people

as they left the stage. Kes, Glenn, and the band began a jaunty, strutting rhythm.

I'm feelin' mighty old, I've got an awful cold,
I'll soon be walkin' the streets of gold,
So I'll ask you boys,
Don't you monkey with my widder when I'm gone—

Chalice and Bettilia were already laughing in the wings. Both boys grinned sidelong at them. Kes winked. The folks out there loved it.

If you monkey round my widder I'm telling you the fact,
My big white ghost will come sneaking back,
And I'll haint you boys,
If you monkey with my widder when I'm gone—

In mid-strum, Kes reached over and tugged Glenn's britches down about six inches. Everybody howled except Glenn. The music never stopped and the pull-down stopped short of Glenn's perverts, but Daddy Brass was still howling when Bugga and Blondie Boy came to take him away.

By midnight the fair was moving on. The calliope wheezed its last, winding down. Sideshow barkers stepped aside as the autumn air took on new tones—grinding gears, truck motors, workers bouncing orders back and forth. The parading draft horses did double duty, lowering the tents while other prize livestock were locked in boxes, ready to load. Thrill rides went dark and dismantled into odd pieces of strut and tired iron, muscled by men and mules onto trailers bound for the railroad or highway.

"Don't wander far," a sniffling Mama George told the brothers. "Mr. Terrence Briney will be here shortly with his record contract for you to sign. My attorney—" she faltered, choking back a sob,"—*checked him out*—"

Chalice gave her another tissue.

"Of course he did, Mizz Brass—"

"Checked Mr. Briney's *credentials*—"

"Please stop crying, Mama," Chalice said,

"We have to be at the recording studio at seven a.m. to-to-*tomorrow mooooorning.*" Mama George burst into another crying jag.

"Aw, Mama," Glenn said, turning and walking away.

In the shadow of the cotton wagons, still wired from the show and a few hundred love offerings, Kes and Bettilia waited in the back seat of the copper Cadillac. They waited and waited until they fell into deep wet kisses. Sister was asleep in the front seat.

Bettilia had decided that she liked kissing as long as she was kissing Kestrel Brass. This jaybird was alright. Still, when his hand came up to cup her breast she gently pulled herself and his hand away.

"Don't you wanna keep him *b*-behind you?" she whispered.

"Who?" he spake into her lips.

"You know. That old Clootie you used to see."

"Since I met you, darlin, I don't see him no more."

Again, they came together, kissing deep. Again they surfaced.

"Well, just cause you don't see him don't mean he ain't there," she said.

"Oh?" Kes cared little about this dark, dumb Clootie topic.

"Cause he is."

"Girl, I'm crazy and hurtin' for you."

"I'm crazy and hurtin' for you too."

"And since we, well, *got together* the other night, what with Mama keeping you off from me and locked up like her pet parakeet—it just makes me crazier."

"Jaybird, what happened the other night—it can't happen again—not till later."

"After we're married folk, you mean?"

"Yeah. That."

"Now I know that old Cloot is real. And this is hell on *me*."

She trilled a little, nuzzling him.

"Here, I got something to show you," he breathed into her ear.

Bettilia watched Kes pull his surprise from a secret place.

"My *w*-word, Kes. You still got that pullybone?"

"About time to pull it, don't you think?"

She nodded. Kes took one end, Bettilia took the other.

"Whoever wins," Bettilia cooed, "we both win."

"Yes. That's how it is."

They both pulled in the darkness until the pullybone snapped.

"I know what got wished for," he said smiling.

"I do too," she replied gently, slipping her half in a secret place of her own for safekeeping. "*K*-Kes?"

"Yes?"

"We'll be alright. Won't we?"

"Darlin, you better know we will."

"Then there ain't *n*-nothing can't wait, jaybird."

"I suppose. Bettilia?"

"Yes?"

"You love me?"

"I do," she said, not a whit of hesitation, surprising herself most of all. "You know I do."

"And I you."

"Then, I reckon we'll always be there," she whispered, "won't we?"

"Where?"

"In our tree."

"Yes," he echoed. "In our tree."

The driver's door opened.

"Big brother, the papers is here to sign," Glenn's head said, too loud, breaking the spell.

Kes and Bettilia crawled out of the car to find Glenn and Chalice standing with Mama George and a loose-suspendered, sickly man with a briefcase. Mama made everybody shake hands.

"You Brothers Brass, you sang like twin trumpets tonight," Mr. Terrence Briney told them, spreading his briefcase and legal papers on the hood of the car.

"But I thought you wasn't here yet when we done the show," Kes said, his nightly hip ache setting in.

"Kestrel—" Mama warned. "Mr. Briney is here *now*

against doctor's orders."

Briney rallied.

"Oh, yes, but I saw your Tuesday evening performance. I'm sure tonight was as wondrous a musical event, up to your usual high standard."

"No doubt it were," Kes sniped, grabbing a pen, ready to sign. He was happier in that back seat and wanted this little girl here back in his arms. This girl. He'd stolen another pill from his mother's purse, right after the show, but it was already wearing off.

Mama George snatched back the pen.

"Wait, Kes, Glenn, let us read the contract in full first."

"Why, I would be glad to read it out loud for you," Briney said, the heel of his hand smoothing thin strands atop his head. He jittered with his tie, his glasses, then went into the briefcase. "I've brought a flashlight."

Glenn slumped against the fender.

"Aw, Mama," he groaned, wanting a cigarette, "it's four pages."

"No, five," Kes corrected him. "Five fuck-a-doodly-doo pages."

"*Kestrel.* Mr. Briney is not just a fine audio producer, he is *ordained.*"

"Ain't we all," Kes muttered, slumping alongside his brother.

Briney began to read.

"*Exclusive recording agreement* between Glory Bee Recordings Limited and the musical group known professionally as The Brothers Brass, including Kestrel James Brass and Gaylenn Wilson Brass—"

"I hate my name," Glenn said to his shoes.

"—*Henceforth* referred to in this binding agreement as the Artist. All references to Artist include all members of the group collectively and severally unless otherwise specified. The parties agree as follows—"

"I'm gonna see if they still got ice cream," Bettilia said with a wee smile and bewitchingly raised eyebrows up at Kes. He understood.

"I'll go with you," Chalice said.

Bettilia and Chalice took Sister and wandered away, forsaking the Cadillac and Mr. Briney's dull flashlight.

"I'm so happy, Bettilia," bubbled Chalice, "I hope you're as happy as I am."

"Yes, I suppose I am. I don't rightly know what happy is."

"It must be this."

"Yes. It must be, I reckon."

"I swear, you've got your work cut out for you with Kes. He seems kind of—I don't know—*surly* sometimes. These days. A streak of mean. But *nice*, you know. But not like when he and I were together."

"He ain't mean, not really. It's just, he don't suffer no fools. And he's got his scars."

"His scars?"

"Old hurts and scars. Like me. That's what I like about him. Or part of it. To tell you the truth."

"Well, that works out nicely. Doesn't it."

"I reckon you could put it that way. Nicely."

"I sure hope you and I—I hope we can get closer, be better friends. For their sake. For all our sakes."

"Well, I doubt you'll be wanting no double wedding. Considering."

"Oh, whatever makes Kes—and Glenn—happy."

"There's that word again."

"Bettilia?"

"Mind if I ask a personal question?"

"Cain't hurt to try."

"What's it look like? Up in that treehouse?"

"You ain't seen it?"

"Oh, no. I'm scared of heights."

"I ain't so sure I can describe it."

"Has it really got bunk beds?"

"Yes. And a big winder. And a spyglass for looking out to sea."

"How big are the bunk beds?"

"Big enough, I reckon."

Hellzabub's Human Zoo was still standing as they ambled past, Sister leading the way toward a rake of mules tied betwixt two trees, Sister's tail swiveling like a big white rudder. Chalice and Bettilia both fell quiet, their pace slowing along the length of signboard they were seeing up close for the first time. *The Alabama Cyclops. Bearded Penelope And Her Bearded Dog. The Thousand Pound Fat Girl. Carolina's Crocodile Twins. The Amazing Melting Man.*

Bettilia stopped, staring at the crude painting of *The Amazing Melting Man.* She moved closer to the sign. There was something about that garish, dripping, sad cartoon face.

"Hon, what is it?" Chalice asked behind her.

Arp. Arp. Arp.

A teeny little ratdog with a foot-long beard came running out from under the edge of the tent. The bearded yapper went racing away, shooting through the mules' hooves.

Arp.

Sister barked twice—*RUH-HO-FFFF, RUH-HO-FFFF*—then went bounding after the little dog.

"*Sister, stop*—" Bettilia hollered, kicking off her shoes, running after the both of them.

The mules were panicked, prancing in a flurry as Sister bounded into their midst, sailing through their flanks and out under the rope. Bettilia ran around the tangle of mules in time to see the big barking white Sister barrel past the stripper's tent in hot pursuit of the crazed terrier whose tiny legs kept tripping on its beard.

Bettilia had always been able to outrun most dogs when she wanted to. She ripped her dress on a corner of a cotton wagon but she finally caught up with Sister, grabbing her by her collar, reining the big dog to a halt—letting the little dog go wherever it had to go. Bettilia was plenty winded. She was out of practice after months spent on mostly girly stuff, sitting, primping, and walking with books on her head. Mama George had a heady stack of books for walking under.

Chalice caught up to Bettilia and Sister halfway back to the freak show tent.

"Shoo, I just knew both hounds had jumped the river by now," Chalice said, relieved at the sight of the two.

"You want me bust you one, zeeboo mon?"

An angry bullhorn voice cut through the chill. Bettilia shushed at Chalice, on pure instinct, pulling Chalice and the great white dog behind a corner of the stripper's tent. When they peeked back around the corner, they saw what looked to be three men and a blowtorch arguing in the dark behind the freak show tent—but one was actually that awful woman, Zeebub, the zookeeper.

"You just try it, you big nigger, and I'll cut you dead," Zeebub growled, tossing her cigar into the grass, ready to go at it.

"Woman, you is one muss muss ugly Zeeboo, mon," Bugga Higgin growled back, waving a plumber's blowtorch hissing blue flame. "Back on me island, yes, we hitch ox like you to sled in box mine."

"C'mon. Step closer, nig. I got me a razor what wants to kiss you—"

Bugga moved toward the broad woman in overhauls, his forehead breaking off the low slung limb of a tree.

"Zeeboo, mon, you got no bidness to let Boss Brass's boint bwoy go like dat—"

"Go easy, Bugga," Saint Peter said, off in the shadows, thumbs in his pinstripe vest. "Don't hurt no woman."

Bugga belted out a laugh at that deference to femininity—absurd to him when he sized up this blue-lit butch in her boots. And, Zeebub—she snarled back at his dumbo laughter.

"I couldn't keep Mister Long Thang locked up *forever*," Zeebub said.

"Any problem with that burnt boy," Saint Peter said

softly, "you were directed to telephone us. You've got Mr. Malakoff's private number."

"Brass ain't always so easy to reach. He still owes me for that rap I took in Statesboro and he knows it. He owes me big and I'm tired of waiting."

"That is betwixt the two of you, madam. Apparently there is a difference of opinion in that matter," Saint Peter said. "But these human oddities are your responsibility. Indisputably yours."

"Right dat," Bugga agreed. "Wha gwan, empress? Boint bwoy be your oddty.

"Fuck you. You think this be Chattahoochee or Bedlam?" Zeebub told Bugga's hissing blue flame. "You tell Brass this be sideshow. It ain't no lockdown asylum. Your burnt boy kept getting harder to handle, I tell you. Trying to take off. Kept saying he had to get back to the bobnot."

"Bobnot?" Bugga glanced back at Saint Peter. "What bobnot?"

"You agreed to drop us a dime should the need arise," Saint Peter intoned.

Zeebub began mimicking a dull dead voice.

"I gots to git back to my bobnot. Git on back to bobnot," she aped. "That's all he'd ever say, morning, noon, nighttime too. *Bobnot, bobnot.* I got plumb sick of hearing about his bobnot."

"You have been remunerated well," Saint Peter said.

"—And if ain't his bobnot, he's moaning for his Riddly Top. Whatever that is."

"Dat right, Zeeboo, mon. Boss Brass remoonate

you good."

"Yeah, well, he ain't alway on time adoing it. And he still owes me—"

Saint Peter flipped open a pocket watch. The watch glowed green from within, Saint Peter's eyes glimmering down at it.

"Mr. Malakoff is a busy man, a man on the move, even when he's standing still—"

"Bullshit and beejeezus," Zeebub grumbled, settling down, "they weren't that many paying folk who come to see no Melting Man anyhow. They come to see the Cyclops and the fat girl. Not no Melting Man."

"I be fixing to melt *you* down, Zoo Mon," Bugga said with a half-hearted wave of his blowtorch.

Fishing another bit of cigar from her bib pocket, Zeebub scratched at her tight curly hair, sloughing off Bugga's comments.

"Come along, Bugga," Saint Peter said. "Malakoff will want to realize this."

"Saint Pete? You sho?" Bugga hesitated, extinguishing the blowtorch.

With a quick click, Saint Peter closed off the glow of his pocket watch, returning it to his vest pocket.

"He will not be pleased."

"Uh-huh," Zeebub said then struck new flame from a match. "You tell him that burnt boy's mule weren't worth a bar of soap neither. Hard to harness. Couldn't pull for shit."

"You let him take the mule too?"

"It were *his mule*. I ain't feeding that swayback no more.

And I ain't listening to more wail about no bobnot."

"No, Mr. Malakoff will not be pleased in the least."

"Tell that Brass bastard I took that rap. Tell him them prison bull bitches was *mean*. Tell him I mean to *be paid*."

"Come along, Bugga."

VERSE 27

Glory Bee

At the Glory Bee recording session the next morning, Kes kept wondering why Bettilia had been so quiet on the ride back last night then still so quiet on the return ride into town today. She never got her ice cream after the show. But he doubted a cold cone meant that much to her. Bettila even wanted to stay home from the recording session—stay back at the house on the island—but Kes begged her to come along.

"We only got to cut four tracks. If we get done early and there's enough studio time left, maybe you can record our song. The one you, me, and Glenn sang in the show. Folks loved it."

"Kestrel, remember, Mr. Briney has booked two hours at Sonic Arts Studios and two hours only," Mama George advised, stirring her iced tea. "Recording studios are very expensive."

"I don't know, Mama," Glenn reasoned, jangling car keys. "You say he's ordained. Well, maybe so. But Briney sounded kind of Brill Building to me, kind of New Yorkyfried. Tin Pan Alley. Rock. Roll."

"And that's *bad*?" Kes tossed back.

"Hell, no, it ain't bad. I just bet he gets a daffodil of a deal on that studio time though."

Kes turned back to Bettilia

"Anyway, darlin, don't let Mama put you off. Glenn and me, we can cut four warblers in nothing flat. In our sleep. Ain't that right, brer?"

"You know it."

"Well, if you really want me, jaybird. I'll need more coffee."

"Mama," Glenn asked, "you got the address?"

"Yes, son. It's across from Colonial Park Cemetery."

"That figures," Bettilia sighed.

"What do you mean, dear?" Mama asked.

"Good for making records, I reckon. Quiet. No riling the *n*-neighbors."

Mr. Terrence Briney stifled his apoplexy when they arrived with a big white dog in tow at a recording studio but Bettilia was not coming any other way. The Bonafide Beats had been contracted for the session—the four players were already there waiting for them. Mama George assuaged Mr. Briney's fears. This meant Bettilia had to step outside with Sister during every take on every song, before the red recording light went on. Time was money and Sister had a tendency to let loose barking if Jack the drummer's brushes hit the snare drum real hard.

In a surprising turn, Mr. Briney would not just be producing—he would also be engineering the session himself. The pleasant queen who actually owned the facility greeted them then sat alongside the mixing board, quietly reading his Gazette.

The first song they recorded was Glenn's newly written *Mercy Is Mine.* It did not go well, not at first. Sonic Arts Studios was actually one cramped little cut-rate studio with egg cartons on the walls and patchwork quilt ceilings. Previously a dentist's office, the sound booth was the former reception desk area. Glenn and Kes were not used to playing in such tight quarters in such close proximity to the band. Since *Mercy Is Mine* was newer to their repertoire, Kes flubbed the lyrics on two takes and he had to keep shaking out his kinked left hand. He did not know these chords so well. He began to curse under his breath on the fifth interrupted take. With little sleep, Kes had a hard time waking up this morning until he popped one of those itsy-bitsy white cross pills Jack the drummer had given him earlier in the week at the fair. Now that little pill had Kes wound too tight. Glenn ignored Kes and kept smiling, coaching the band, adjusting the arrangement. Blessedly, Mama George kept her mouth shut. Kes said they needed less standup bass and the bass player obliged. On the eighth take they nailed it. It took forty-five minutes and Mr. Briney was starting to look sickly nervous again.

When the red light went off, Bettilia came back inside. She sat in the sound booth, feeding bits of Krispy Kreme donut to Sister, listening to the playback. She still seemed far-off, too quiet, her head in some other country. Kes thought maybe it was wedding bell zorros. Kes had to admit, those bells—and these pills—had him a bit skitzy too.

"It's real perty," Bettilia said after the last chords faded from the JBL speakers. Hearing her stamp of approval, Kes began to loosen up, feeling better.

Bettilia stepped back outside onto the sidewalk. The red light went on. The boys began to pick up the pace, sailing through standard tunes they'd been singing for years. They recorded *On The Jericho Road* in two takes, *Where The Soul Never Dies* in one take, and *Traveling This Lonesome Road* in four takes.

Mama George had not wanted them to record *Traveling This Lonesome Road*—especially not with heavy drums and electric bass—and *never* with that stinging electric guitar that Bonafide Beat man was now playing. She wanted her boys to spend this precious time committing only non-secular songs to wax.

"Besides, is it wise to record two *road* songs?" she asked, grasping at straws.

But Kes and Glenn insisted and Mr. Briney agreed with them, saying it could help broaden their appeal. Mr. Briney had begun to grow on the boys. Mr. Briney had a keen ear for the feel of a song and for the best take, even if it had a minor mistake or two. And Briney was highly pleased when they put the last song to bed with twelve minutes to spare on the studio clock. He was in such a jovial mood over the results that Kes felt confident when he spake into the microphone so Mr. Briney could hear him in the booth.

"Terry? Would you mind if we did one more tune real quick? One take? Two takes max? Promise."

Terrence Briney smiled, switching on the intercom into

the studio.

"Sure, boys. Go for it."

With his guitar around his neck, Kes went hustling out into the hall, to the front door. He opened it, stepped out onto the gloomy sidewalk, and found Sister sitting there waiting for him.

Bettilia was nowhere to be seen.

VERSE 28

The Graveyard

Bettilia stepped outside the studio with Sister. The little red light went on by the door. She heard the faint chords and driving bassline of *Traveling This Lonesome Road* throb from within the walls of the building.

She and the dog had already walked up and down this block of Abercorn Street twice, Bettilia keeping a wary eye on that moss-draped graveyard across the way, Sister's nose flexing in high gear at all the new flora in this unfamiliar air. The clouds hung heavy and dark this morning, promising rain, the air a thick vapor like so many early autumn days in these parts, the new season haunted by the last vestiges of summer. It reminded Bettilia of those too hot Indian summer days back on Riddle Top, reminding her of those hills, those mountains, in ways her mind was forever trying to resist.

Ever since last night, Bettilia felt like she was floating, floating in a heavy fog of fear.

With the pulse of the studio at her back, the muffled musicians *Traveling This Lonesome Road* began to fade as Bettilia crossed the street, she and Sister meandering into the cemetery. The tiny young lady and her great white dog drifted through the gravestones and crumbling burial vaults. They made passage through the dead until they reached a long high wall of vaulted tombs with etched stone markers denoting each ancient ancestor. Bettilia had never seen such a wall of dead. This was almost as strange as the Tree Of Hands or some of the other human-forged testaments to death which could be found back in the hollers and crags around Riddle Top. No doubt, the remains of the folks deposited within this cemetery wall were now bits of bone and particle fused with these bricks like mortal's mortar. Thousands of sweltering damp days would have baked them in their brick ovens, thousands of frigid nights turning them brittle, until they finally let go of all they had ever been in life.

Bettilia heard the clopping of hooves. Behind her.

The clink of tin and glass.

She turned to see.

Through the weave of oaks, stone markers, and dripping moss, Bettilia saw a dark tattered man on a mule. The mule was hung with bottles and tin. The terrible, scarred stringbean of a man sat on his mount out on Abercorn Street, gazing into the cemetery, gazing in at her.

It was Ephran Lych.

Bettilia fell back against the wall of tombs, like the air itself was pressing her hard against them, into the brick. Sister barked, far off, somewhere in the back country of Bettilia's head.

Lych turned his melted face away, railman's cap pulled low. He and his slow mule went clopping, clanking away, down the street, disappearing behind a skein of dead stones and live oak.

"Mr. Briney says we ain't got but seven or eight minutes left on the clock," Glenn said, coming out of the studio behind Kes. "They got a chamber orchestra coming in at nine-thirty."

Kes and Glenn stood on Abercorn Street, guitars across their backs, looking both ways. The early morning street was empty. Dew still glistened on the brick pavement, mostly undisturbed. If he had looked closely, Kes might have detected the smear of a cat's paw, of a skittering chipmunk or mule shoe—or the small pair of footprints leading across to the Colonial Park cemetery. But Kes did not look that close.

"I can't figure where she'd go," Kes said, the fog of fear beginning to float in and lift him up too.

Then, Sister—who had been watching the two brothers and their wasted motions—went striding up to Kes, pretty as you please. Kes heard her approach. He looked down at the great white head, the almost human eyes with those delicate dusky lashes.

"Sister? Where'd she go?"

Sister turned, walking purposefully across the street, into the cemetery. Kes and Glenn watched as the dog continued through the markers and mouldering vaults until, a short way in, Sister reached one particular oak among the many.

Sister stopped, her tail wagging. Then she sat on the grass and stared up into the high limbs.

VERSE 29

The Hobnails Coming

Bettilia slipped away and took the last bus from the island, all the way into Savannah by herself. She left Sister behind and, for a change, Sister let her. Bettilia was glad to see how Sister had started sticking to Kes as much as the big dog had always stuck to her. Sometimes folks forgot: Sister was always meant to be Kes's pup, to take the place of the one he never had.

The bus driver kept whistling *Angel Band* as they rolled through the moss-swept tunnel of dead azaleas and antebellum mansions folks around here called Victory Drive. Bettilia kept thinking how there were no streets, no drives, boulevards with names where she came from and the bus driver kept whistling *Angel Band.* She wished he would stop it. She was antsy enough as it was and those *Angel Band* words she knew too well kept streaming through her head.

My latest sun is sinking fast, my race is nearly run...

It was almost two weeks since Kes and Glenn had

coaxed her out of that tree in Colonial Park Cemetery. They pestered her all the way home from the recording studio, asking why she was hiding up in that strange oak. Trapped betwixt Sister and Mama George in the back seat of the Renault, Bettilia tried to throw them a bone or two so they would leave her be while her mind raced.

"I just wished we hadn't run out of studio time. I surely wanted some wax on that trio song, for the wedding guests maybe," Kes said at the steering wheel, his eyes on her in the rearview mirror.

"Listen at you," Bettilia said, "talking like you been in Nashville playing that Opry all your life."

Kes smiled back at her in the mirror. Bettilia tried to.

"Well, if somebody hadn't gone to counting oak limbs and colored leaves—" Glenn teased from the front seat.

"Glenn, Kestrel, hush," Mama George injected.

"I told you," Bettilia mumbled. "I done got bored."

It was a weak excuse after coming all the way to town with them just so she could maybe sing that dang song. But it was the best she could muster under the circumstances. The more folks talked about weddings the more Bettilia felt protected by Mama George. Still, Mama George was as trepidatious about this wedding business as Bettilia, maybe more. Definitely more.

That did not stop Mama George from trying to take the reins as usual or fighting for control of coming events. It was too much in her nature for that to ever change. There was also an irrepressible strain of society hostess bred into her which Mama George could not suppress, a gracious strain which forever lured her, tempting her pride and her debutante's ego.

"We've got bookings piling up after the first of the year," she said. "And folks will be wall-to-wall with parties and spiritual events between Thanksgiving and Christmas. If we are to plan a grand affair and expect people to RSVP with a yes, we need to stage it before mid-November, while it's still fair enough for a ceremony and reception on the lawn. It's that, or wait until next summer."

Kes did not want to wait until next summer. Neither did Glenn. Their energies were raging. Bettilia did not want a grand affair at all. Chalice just seemed to want whatever Kes wanted, and whatever Glenn wanted too, of course.

Betwixt the other three and Mama George's hand on the throttle, Bettilia felt like she was on a runaway train. She took to spending more time hiding in Mama George's childhood bedroom, with the dresses, books, and bits of jewelry Mama George had given her. Kes had a hard time stealing moments with her in the upstairs hall, kissing and cuddling away from prying eyes. He whispered beautiful, lyrical things to her, the sweetest things. Things Bettilia knew she would never forget. She knew he wanted more from her, in every way, again. But she could not give him all those things, not yet. Bettilia caught herself wondering, for fleeting moments, if their night together in the tree-house had been a mistake. But most of the time she did not wonder, she just lost herself in him. She only knew that Kestrel Brass made her feel things she had never felt for another creature in all her crooked and winding life.

Kes almost made Bettilia forget the vision of Ephran Lych she had seen in the cemetery. She began to think maybe that Lych had come riding out of the overwrought fog of her memory, a hallucination borne out of only three hours sleep, out of a morning spent fretting over things said the night before by that terrible woman, that Zeebub zookeep, when that woman spat out that name. It was a name Bettilia knew she would never forget. Bobnot. That cigar-chewing Zeebub, had she really uttered it over and over again? Bobnot, Bobnot?

Kes could only help her forget so much. There were things Bettilia knew she could never tell. She was raised not to tell. Thankfully, despite Kes's questioning bent, he did not question her much about such things. He was smart that way. She loved him for that. Besides, his energies were raging, like he had taken a pill or something.

So Bettilia was not really surprised—she was along for the ride—when Mama George hung up the telephone before sitting down to supper a week after Bettilia dropped from that graveyard tree.

"Brother Dub has put us on his calendar for November 15. We've reserved the church also, in case it rains."

Bettilia ate her pork chop and decided she could live with that.

Then she saw those bootprints this morning. She had seen those bootprints before.

She awakened early to the sound of Sister barking. Sister did not usually start barking at crack of dawn like some dang rooster. If that dog kept it up, the neighbors would be writing letters and calling the island patrol. The rest of the house was still asleep, hopefully, so Bettilia risked Mama George's wrath and stepped outside onto the porch, still in her night dress. She filled Sister's dish as the bright-eyed snowhound bounced excitedly then shoved her nose into the kibble, crunching and gobbling it up. Bettilia yawned, watching Sister eat for a spell, then started back down the porch for the kitchen door, dragging the Alpo sack as she went.

When she saw the faint mud of bootprints on the porch Bettilia stopped in her tracks. Hobnail boots. She could even see a distinct trail of prints up and down the steps, through the dew atop the grass. The dark outline of footsteps in the dew came and went, from the porch down the embankment to Cedarwood Drive in back of Angelsprey. Those boot soles were bigger than that Zeebub's feet. Bettilia was sure of that.

She slipped inside the house quickly, peeking back out the window at an empty yard.

"Hallelujah, darlin," Kes cried out, grabbing her later that afternoon. "Mama done set up a private showing with a jeweler on West Broughton. We pick out rings *tomorrow*."

Kes kissed her well then ran out the front portico door to play with Sister on the beach. Bettilia ran out the back door and got on the last bus into Savannah.

She got off the bus on Bay Street.

She remembered where River Street was, below, under the bluff of Bay. She knew where Daddy Brass's office was. She had been here last Thanksgiving night. This is where she first found Daddy Brass. Bettilia and Sister had walked in through his open loading dock, knocked on his office window. Later, she figured he had been too drunk to get the bay doors closed against the storm on his own. She was never sure why he came in that way with it sleeting and blowing—but Bettilia was glad he had. In the storm that night, the soft light from those big bay doors was welcome, warm refuge, inviting the girl and puppy approaching down the frigid alley.

And Bettilia just knew Daddy Brass would be there now, today. Daddy Brass would know how to stop this runaway express.

As the bus pulled away, Bettilia crossed to the opposite curb, headed for the Drayton Ramp down to River. She had barely stepped up onto the curb before she heard hobnail boots behind her.

Click, click.

Hobnail boots on the brick streets of old Savannah.

That clicking, that tackety-tack sound, was unmistakable to Bettilia. It was a sound she had hoped to never hear again. Back in the hills and steep hollers around Riddle Top, hobnail boots helped a man grip the earth, bust a mouth, grind a bone. On a bedroom floor at midnight—or here in the waning sunset on streets of Savannah—hobnail boots ricocheted like a terrible pistol's report.

Click, click. Click, click.

Bettilia dared not look back. Her body wanted not to breathe, but she had to breathe to move, to move fast.

Click, click.

She heard the hobnails over her right shoulder, so she veered left, walking faster, faster, away from the Drayton Ramp. She was almost running—in a panic, trying not to run—as she headed for an iron stair railing up ahead, stone steps down to River Street. Stone steps down to Daddy Brass.

Bettilia reached the top of the steps and almost fell forward, catching herself on the rail. Looking straight down, she saw that these stone steps were so steep—they were almost like a ladder. Their long vertical descent to the alleyway below was treacherous.

Click.

Bettilia started to drop down the steps, gripping the rail, faster and faster her feet took the next step, then the next, the hobnails growing louder above her. Her heart pounded, she fought for breath—she dropped down another step—her hands smearing sweat on the sheer iron stair railing. This was no tree.

Click, click, click.

Hand over hand, the iron rail nearly straight up-and-down, she descended, too fast—

Her hands slipped, her foot missed a step, and Bettilia *fell*—

Bettilia tumbled—a pummeled ragdoll tumbling, bruising, down the last of the stony flight—landing *hard* on the bricks of the alleyway.

Click. Click. Click.

Click.

Click.

The hobnails were coming down the steps. Brutalized by the stones, the bricks, Bettilia rolled over onto her back, her eyes tried to focus. A dark figure against red sky overhead was descending the granite stairs. Bettilia couldn't see the dark face but knew it was *him*. Yes, it was *him*. After nine long years, Bettilia had been found.

She didn't have time to think. Not about *him*. Not about anything.

Bettila leapt up and ran down the alleyway, along the back of the warehouses that faced River Street. She ran under one meshed iron walkway after another—walkways that entered the warehouses up on the Bay Street level overhead.

Clickety, clickety, clickety, clickety.

He was behind her, approaching, the sound of his boots bouncing off iron walkways above, off the tight walls of brick on each side of her.

Up ahead, Bettilia saw the light of another alley down to River Street, down to the water.

To evade those hobnails picking up speed behind her, Bettilia rounded that corner, running faster than any runaway dog—running down to the waterfront, circling the front of Vetter & Co. and the Chatham Paperworks. If someone had seen Bettilia at that moment, in the brighter reddening light along the front of the warehouses, they would have seen a tiny girl, her knees and dress torn, racing headlong in abject terror. They would have seen her turn back up another alley, running back into the darkness, trying to baffle and lose the terror advancing fast behind her.

Her panic cut deeper. Bettilia didn't even know where she was now. She was turned around three different ways in her head. She didn't know which way to go to find Daddy Brass, to escape those *clicking* hobnails back there. Still, her feet flew, deeper into the dark.

The hobnails were about to catch up, that *clicketyclick-etyclick* behind her like a haywire teletype machine, gone crazy, relentless.

Heart bursting, almost spent in her mad despair, Bettilia turned into the black alley behind the buildings again.

She *collided* with him. She ran into his arms. She *screamed.*

Bettilia looked up from those arms, the *clicking* still behind her.

It was Glenn. It was Glenn Brass and Glenn had a gun.

Bettilia whipped around under Glenn's left arm as his right hand held the gun ready, both of them looking back at the light streaking from the side alley. They both saw the running, clicking shadow of her hunter in that streak of low sunlight, that clicking shadow coming, still unseen, about to come from around that corner.

Glenn's thumb *cocked back* the hammer of his pistol. The *click* of the hammer was unmistakable in this echo chamber of brick.

Bettilia and Glenn both saw the clickety-clicking shadow *stop.*

The shadow stood in the streak of sunset red, her hobnailed hunter still unseen, around that corner—stopped by the hammer cock of Glenn's gun. Then they heard the *scrape* of the hobnails as those boots began to retreat, slowly, those hobnails taking that long shadow with them.

Quicker now, the clicking retreated and hurried away.

VERSE 30

Freak Orchestration

Sister's bark—*RUH-HO-FFFF*—resounded in the cavern of the warehouse, mingling with the click of her claws and Mrs. Plum's high heels on concrete. Mrs. Plum had met Kes at the front door. His thumb stopped riding the buzzer when he finally saw her through the glass.

"Is she alright?"

"Yes. I think she is," Mrs. Plum said, twisting her finger rings nervously as they walked.

Inside the dark warehouse, Sister ran ahead to the open door of Daddy Brass's office, like Sister knew who she would find within its soft light.

Sitting together in front of Daddy Brass's mahogany desk, Glenn kept pressure on a cotton swab against Bettilia's cheek. The first aid kit lay open on the desk. Glenn was relieved to see Kes as Kes rushed in and sank down beside Bettilia's chair. She wouldn't look at him, her eyes on the thinning carpet. She lay a hand on Sister's great white head. Sister's chin settled into Bettilia's lap.

"Sister..." she murmered in her daze.

"Bettilia?"

Kes wanted to sweep her up, hold her close, pull her inside him to a safe place. But she was somewhere else now, he could tell.

"She's jist a crazy ole Sister..." Bettilia was telling her petting hand,"...ever family's got one."

"Thank you, Glenn," Mrs. Plum said as Glenn surrendered the chair. Mrs. Plum sat and went back to dabbing the cotton on the Bettilia's worst outer wound, the big oozing scuff on her cheek. "Looks like the bleeding's almost stopped."

Dropping the blood-sogged cotton ball into a wastebasket, Mrs. Plum took another clean cotton ball from the first aid kit. Bettilia flinched when Mrs. Plum began to treat the weepy scuff with alcohol.

"You got here fast, big brer," Glenn said, peering through the open blinds, out into the warehouse. "From the house to here in under half an hour? You fly TWA?"

Kes gave a wan smile, his gaze never leaving Bettilia.

"What you doing down here on River Street?" he asked her softly.

She said nothing.

Glenn turned around, slumping back against the window, crushing the venetian blinds, studying Kes as much or more than Bettilia.

"I was walking down the sidewalk, headed here to Daddy's office, when I saw her run around the front of the Cotton Exchange—I think it was—then cut back up the alley. Looked like somebody was after her. I ducked around the back way to catch her."

Finally, Kes looked up at his little brother, in the shared understanding only they could ever know.

"I'm glad you were there. Here."

"Me too. What did Mama say—you scrambling over here like this?"

"She don't know," Kes said, brushing Bettilia's arm with the back of his hand. She seemed to accept it. "Mama's down for one of her naps. Or she was when I dropped the phone and took off in that dang Renault of hers."

"You should call her," Bettilia said, forming words of awareness in a weak voice, at last. "Let her know everything's all right."

Kes turned her chin toward him.

"*Is* everything all right?"

Her eyes met his. Again, she fell silent.

The room became aware of loud footsteps. Daddy Brass and Saint Peter came through the office door. Daddy had his .357 Magnum in his hand.

"Well, I tell ya," Daddy said, flipping open a desk drawer, putting the gun inside, "Bugga, me, the boys, we done checked ever alleytrap and slop bucket on this waterfront, up and down the street. Up and down. We ain't seen nobody didn't belong here. I got em still out there looking. I don't know. Too dark to see much out there now. Maybe the sumbitch's head will pop up." He eyed Bettilia, dropping back into his big chair behind the desk. "Whoever the sumbitch might be," he said at her, evenly, quietly.

Her eyes flit over at Daddy Brass then looked away.

"So who is he?" Daddy didn't leave much wiggle room.

"My *d*-daddy maybe. I dunno," she mumbled.

"Your *daddy*?" Malakoff Brass growled back, a little too loud. "Kes, you—you both told me your daddy was *dead*."

Bettilia shrugged, brooding into her lap of white fur, white ears.

"Well? Is or ain't he? Dead, I mean?"

"I reckon he is. He was the last time I seen him."

Daddy laughed a little at that. Just inside the door, Saint Peter smiled back at him. Mrs. Plum took passing note of the two men as she peeled a bandaid.

"Knew an old gal in Nixburg like that," Daddy cracked. "She lay there dead most the time too."

Mrs. Plum rolled her eyes.

"Turn around here, honey," she said.

Bettilia turned her head as Mrs. Plum taped the bandaid on Bettilia's cheek. Kes gave Bettilia's arm another little stroke then got up and joined his brother at the window into the warehouse, leaning alongside him, flattening the venetian blinds.

"Bettilia," Kes asked again, having given her a little space, "what was you doing down here on River Street?"

"I come to see Daddy Brass."

Daddy Brass leaned forward against his crossed arms on the desk blotter, trying to be closer to her.

"Darlin, what was you coming to see me for?"

"I—I wanted you to stop everthing," she said.

"Stop everthing? The wedding?" Kes asked, faster than he would have liked.

"Shuddup, Kestrel. She didn't say that." Daddy Brass held Bettilia in his sights. "Stop what, darlin?"

"They's this melted man," Bettilia began, "his face looks like it got burnt but it ain't really—"

Daddy Brass fell back again, exasperated.

"Oh. *Him.*"

"He weren't who was after me. Or I don't think it was him. Whoever chased me done it in hobnail boots. But, that melted man, from the freak show—I know him. I seen him outside the graveyard that morning."

"While we was inside cutting records," Kes said to himself, grimly.

"So she climbed herself a tree," Glenn said to Kes—Kes who was already nodding, understanding now.

Drumming his big fingers hard on the blotter, Daddy Brass was weighing his options, like he might or might not let you see his freaks.

"Look," he said slowly, keeping his eyes to himself, choosing his words, "I done what I had to do. That melted feller, him and his clanking mule, well—that feller was peeking in the windows out at the house, out on the island. The morning after Bettilia showed up here. Sneaking around, snooping. I finally catched up with him that night when his mule come clanking and clomping back by. Well, once I catched him—I had to do *something* with him."

Roberta Plum was not amused:

"So you sold him to the *freak show*?"

"Aw, hell no," Daddy said, throwing up his arms. "You cain't sell nobody for cash money. Not no more. Them days is gone. Don't you know that?"

All eyes in the room were staring at him. Daddy began shaking his head in a ridiculous way.

"It weren't like I had him *kilt* or anything," he insisted. Something within him drooped. "I just took that burnt boy out of circulation for a while. That's all. Worked me out a little *orchestration*. A little tit for tat. That's all."

"With that Zeebub," Bettilia murmured. "Or zookeeper. Whatever she is."

"Yeah. Her," Daddy sighed heavy, looking anxiously at an impassive Saint Peter.

Glenn tipped his head back against the blinds, taking in the ceiling.

"That Zeebub," he said. "She wears hobnail boots."

"Yes, she do," Bettilia agreed, flat, without color.

Avoiding the evil eye Mrs. Plum was giving him, Daddy Brass saw an escape route and took it.

"Look, you let *me* take care of that Zeebub," he said boldly, sweeping his arm over the desk like a grand city planner. He threw a quick smile at Bettilia. "And you ain't gotta worry about no burnt boy. He's long gone by now. And if he comes back I'll put a bullet betwixt his horns. Don't worry. I'll uncirculate him for good."

"Don't go killing nobody, Daddy," Kes said firmly. "It'd spoil the wedding."

"But I knew him—*know him*," Bettilia sputtered, bursting from her shell, "he's another weird Lych that I knowed of, back on Riddle Top."

"Lych?" Daddy drawled. "blithering idgit if you ask me."

"Them Lyches, they's like that. In them hills, them Lyches, well—his name is Ephran Lych. He could of got back to Riddle Top by now. A body could of got to Riddle Top and somebody else could of got back here by now. Ephran Lych used to sneak and snitch for my daddy."

"Who's this daddy? What he do to you?"

Bettilia fell silent, said nothing.

"Don't make her say," Kes's voice scratched softly.

"And your father is dead," Mrs. Plum reminded her, trying to leave off the question mark. Bettilia still said nothing.

But Daddy Brass was already tapping his forefinger on his breastbone.

"You just leave it all up to Daddy Brass," he said, in a way that made you know that you could. "You ain't got to worry about no burnt boy. You ain't got to worry about no Zeebub. That Zeebub, I'll have a word with her too. Nothing fancy, no uncertain words. You just got to worry about planning the biggest, most go-to-hell, rambunctious hillbilly wedding that island's ever clapped eyes on. The kind that gives a whole new twist to a double-barrel wedding."

Bettilia couldn't help but smile. Lightening up a little, she looked up at Glenn.

"Glenn, thank you for being there when you was. I don't know what would have become of me if you hadn't been there with that gun of yours."

"You welcome, Bettilia," he said. "Besides, I cain't let this Kestrel here be a widower when they ain't even got a word for one what ain't married yet."

While Bettilia was giggling at that, letting go a little

more, Kes was staring at his brother.

"You got a gun?"

Glenn got sheepish.

"Well, yeah, I do. Daddy bought it for me."

"That's right," Daddy said at Kes. "I bought him a .38 Special when I had to leave you all unprotected out there at that Angelsprey after our peeping Lych come around. I figured I'd leave a gun with my prodigal that weren't the one that was so hotheaded. Why? You want one? Okay. I'll buy you one. I'll buy you a biggun. Take it on your honeymoon."

"No," Kes said glumly, his eyes off in thin air. "I don't like guns."

"As you will, son."

"I want me a knife. A fancy stiletto sticker like that one you got."

Daddy smiled easier.

"You got it."

"And I want—" Kes said.

"Yes, son?"

"I wanna know what Glenn was doing down here on River Street."

"Oh, that's easy," Glenn answered. "Daddy Brass, he asked me to come."

Taking up a mechanical pencil, Daddy doodled a note pad as his mood shifted. His momentary reprieve had vanished. He looked like a man who had reached the end of his road.

"Yes, Kes. Yes, I did invite Glenn down. I was gonna talk at him first. But, since you here, I might as well talk at you both, at the same time."

Nobody moved.

"Well?" Kes asked, studying his suddenly strange father—strange by even Daddy Brass's standards.

Without emotion, Daddy Brass looked at the others.

"Could y'all leave us alone for a few minutes?"

Mrs. Plum took Bettilia's arm, squeezing it.

"C'mon. I'll show you that Neiman Marcus catalog."

Bettilia and Mrs. Plum got up and left the office with Sister leading the way, tail wagging. Saint Peter slipped out behind them, closing the door. Alone in the room with his sons, Daddy Brass stared at his doodles for quite a spell.

"Have a seat," he said in time.

Kes and Glenn sat. Across the desk, they watched Daddy Brass heave a fatal breath, like a bull trapped and dying in an arena.

"Boys," he began, "I didn't want you set up for no surprises."

He fell dark again, opened his desk drawer, glanced at the .357, closed the desk drawer.

Kes didn't know what to think.

"What's the deal, Daddy?"

"Well, the deal is—I didn't want you set up for no surprises. See, I fuckered up things a lot in this life. I done things. Things a man ain't proud of. I'd like to say I wouldn't do most of em again. But, truth be, I might. But, one thing I'll never regret is falling for your mama. And, father forgive me, I fell in love with her hard. So hard I didn't dare show it to her. Not that she made it easy. See, it's differnt for a man. A man ain't supposed to show it, his heart can't chance it. Men's hearts ain't as strong as women's. You'll see what I mean in time. So, whatever you do, boys, don't show it too much. Don't show em you love em too much."

Women's faraway laughter echoed out there in the warehouse, looking at lingerie, no doubt. Kes and Glenn exchanged furtive glances.

"Is that what you wanted to tell us, Daddy?" Kes asked.

Daddy Brass sat there blinking at them, walleyed, like they were both leprechauns that just crawled from under his desk. He was in his rarest of states: Daddy Brass was at a total loss for words. Finally, he got up and went to the door, sticking his head out.

"Step inside, will you?" he was heard to say.

Silver-haired Saint Peter came in, his pinstripe suit neatly pressed, his freckled-brown skin smooth as a baby's. He seemed pleased to see them.

Standing alongside him, Daddy Brass turned to the boys, squaring his shoulders.

"Saint Peter here, well boys—y'all ain't been properly introduced."

"Yes, we have, Daddy," Glenn said.

"Naw, naw, you ain't. Boys," Daddy Brass said, locking onto Saint Peter's coffee brown eyes. "I'd like y'all to meet big brother."

"Big brother?" Kes fumbled.

Daddy Brass gave Saint Peter a go-ahead nod. Saint Peter stepped forward, smiled down gently at the boys.

"Gentlemen," Saint Peter said, "well, Kestrel, Gaylenn. I'm your Uncle Pete."

VERSE 31

Bugga's Hands

Bugga must have walked the length of River Street and back a half dozen times or more. He lost count. Bugga had two of his warehouse men armed with shotguns still searching the alleys. Bugga worked the front side, the dock side. He tested the doors and windows of the other darkened warehouses and the closed factories.

Bugga pocketed his pistol when he stepped inside the faceless supper clubs and piano bars that hid behind facades of windowless brick and unmarked doors. What was this, 1960 or 1961? Bugga wasn't so sure, but he sure knew how the River Street had started to change. It was a dozen years or more since he first arrived as an engine man on a Singapore freighter, when the River Street was a dark and often dangerous place to walk the bricks on a night like this, back when Bugga first hired on with Boss Brass. Now, in the last few years, it had gotten safer to walk the River Street after a few clubs and pubs opened down here. But it was still mostly dark, so quiet you could hear your own footfalls, like a secret street for secret rendezvous and things you do in the night.

Most of the clubs were discreet, muted places with well-dressed folks sipping drinks at candlelit tables with white tablecloths. When he stepped inside with all this soft-talking Savannah gentility this evening, Bugga knew he looked out of place, big and shiny black in his bursting shirt of tropical colors, whispering questions to the head-waiters and hosts. But play was play and business was business for Bugga. Boss Brass didn't import Bugga from all the way across the sea for nothing but big fun.

So Bugga trod the bricks. For the umpteenth time, he was approaching the Drayton Ramp which curled up to Bay Street when he saw the headlights of Boss Brass's old copper Cadillac pull away from the front of Brass Freight & Cargo. Before turning up the ramp, the Cadillac slowed to a stop in front of Bugga. The window rolled down.

It was Gaylenn Brass at the wheel, alone in the car. He looked shook up and boo-eyed, a little scary, even for a fluffy little white boy. He looked like somebody done wopped him upside the head.

"Mr. Glenn. How you dis evening?"

"I'm awright. I think. And you? How are you?"

"I be good, yes."

"You're Mr. Bugga, right?"

"Yes sir, Mr. Glenn. I'm Bugga."

"Mr. Bugga—you mind if I ask you a question? A personal question?"

"I do not, no. What's on your mind, Mr. Glenn? We ain't turned up no hobnail man, if that's what you asking. But ebry ting awright."

"No, it ain't that, Mr. Bugga. Well, uh, Bugga—you and Saint Peter back there—are you kin?"

"Kin?"

"Yes, you know. Are you two related? Are you family or cousins or anything like that?"

Bugga chuckled like a steel drum.

"Dat gillygog? No, my word. We ain't no kin, mon."

The boy looked a little relieved.

"Oh. Okay. That's all I wanted to know, Bugga."

"Hello, goodnight-night, Mr. Glenn Brass."

"Goodnight, Bugga. And thanks."

The window rolled up. The old copper Cadillac drove up the Drayton Ramp, disappearing around the bend. Bugga was still a little walla walla and confused by his chat with Glenn when he spied the headlamps of the little black Renault driving toward him. The Renault came to a stop, the window rolled down.

"Good evening, Mr. Bugga," Kestrel Brass said.

"Evening to you, Mr. Kes."

"Everything alright?"

"Oh, yes, Mr. Kes. Eby ting A-okay."

Bugga bent down and saw Bettilia in the passenger seat of the Renault, her pale little face mooning out at him.

"Evening, mizz boopsie."

"Hi," she said.

"Hope you ain't too shook, mum."

"No. I'm alright, I *th*-think. Thank ye *f*-for asking."

"Don't you worry, eby ting A-okay. Bugga ain't gone let

nobody hurt you."

She smiled weakly.

"Thank you kindly."

Kes was staring intently at Bugga, looking almost as shell-shocked as his little brother.

"Bugga, would you be offended if I asked you a very personal question?"

"Mr. Kes, I ain't no kin to Saint Peter."

"Oh. Okay. But that wasn't my question."

"It wudn't?"

"Bugga—have you accepted Jesus Christ as your personal Lord and Savior?"

"Why, yes, Mr. Kes. Yes I has."

Kes looked relieved.

"That's good. I reckon."

"Yes, me mama teach me Beble ebry day."

"But that's a good question, ain't it?"

"Yes, sir. Dat's a real fine question."

"Well, that's why—why I done asked it."

Kes was floundering. Both Bettilia and Bugga could see that.

"You two lubbers have berry nice evening."

"Thank you. Goodnight, Bugga,"

Bugga leaned down again, looking past Kes, into the car.

"And don't you worry none, mizz boopsie. Ain't nobody hurt you now. You in Bugga's hands now. Safe in Bugga's hands."

"I feel *b*-better already," she said.

Kes rolled up the window and drove the Renault up the

ramp onto Bay Street.

He had so much to tell Bettilia, so much he was afraid to tell her now. He didn't know where to begin. So he began. Like that moment in the vamp, he knew to just jump in and go, no looking back. He was still talking and she was still listening when Kes accelerated out of Victory Drive onto the causeway, out over the marshlands, headed home to the island.

"So that's the long, the short of it," he was saying, both hands gripping the wheel, afraid to look at her. "Or the black and the white of it, I oughta say. Daddy and Saint Peter, their daddy was a dirt farmer. Back in Bama. A white man. They mama weren't." Kes felt tears start to well in his eyes but fought them back. "I'm sorry, darlin. About the wedding. All that mess. I know this changes everything."

Sleepy, Bettilia slipped over, nestling in under his arm. Yawning, her eyes closed, she gave his sore hip a little jab. She had to be sure he felt it—to be sure she was getting through..

"You fool jaybird. And Mambly, she was *my* mama. This don't change nothing."

She slept the rest of the way to Angelsprey.

VERSE 32

Days of Schiffli Lace

Mama George must have received a telephone call from Daddy Brass. Almost certainly she had. When the boys and Bettilia arrived home late that evening with her car and their daddy's car, looking worse for wear, Mama George asked politely if she could fix them bowls of Brunswick stew (they declined) then she went back to bed. Nobody was ever sure what Daddy Brass told her over the telephone while their two-car caravan was heading her way—but, whatever tale he wove was expertly designed not to further aggravate her fears or upset her plans.

Kes kissed Bettilia goodnight then watched the door close on his mama's childhood bedroom, once again. Returning to his own room, collapsing on the bed, Kes decided that he had missed an opportunity to ask his daddy what his *real* secret was—the secret behind Daddy's biggest card trick—the most mysterious power his daddy possessed. Kes wanted to know how Daddy Brass always managed to land on his feet, no matter how cockeyed his predicament. It was a skill Kes knew would come in handy in these busy days to come. No doubt, Glenn would like to acquire such cat-like prowess as well, since he must be lying awake down the hall, wondering how and what to tell Chalice. Kes could tell when they stumbled out of Daddy's warehouse—both brothers shaking hands goodbye with Saint Peter after so much hard conversation—that neither Glenn or Kes would be sleeping much tonight. Not with so much to plague their minds through the witching hours.

The next morning, Glenn's bleary eyes across the breakfast table confirmed this. After breakfast, Kes and Bettilia and Glenn and Chalice drove into the city where they all chose simple gold bands.

Autumn winds began to blow a little harder, faster. Autumn leaves turned more quickly after that. A little too quickly, perhaps. Colors changed. Even Bettilia began to shed her fret and woes and got into the spirit of things. Less than a week after discovering their hidden racial heritage, the Brothers Brass played a benefit for the Bethesda Orphans' Home. For the first time, Kes and Glenn drove to an event by themselves, in their new old copper Cadillac, accompanied only by their two guitars and Glenn's mandolin in the back seat. Bettilia had all but decided her moment in the spotlight had come and gone before that fateful evening she took the last bus into Savannah. The sound of hobnail boots on River Street pretty much sealed the deal. She would not be joining the boys on stage anymore. She felt so exposed in so many ways up there that what fun and thrill there had been was now gone, stolen from her forever. But Daddy Brass's presence and Daddy Brass's assurances always seemed to have a profound effect on Bettilia. Slowly, she began to regain a sense of haven inside Angelsprey. The almost hourly passage of one of Daddy Brass's men in the same two-tone blue Ford—cruising the tight lane of Cedarwood Drive behind the house—helped increase Bettilia's sense of safe haven. Sometimes the driver was Bugga Higgin and he would smile, he would wave.

On the afternoon of the orphans' benefit Mama George, Bettilia, and Sister all went shopping for Bettilia's wedding dress. The lady clerks at the boutique never blinked or uttered an ounce of protest when Bettilia Whissler and Mrs. Georgiana Bass swept into their shop led by a big white dog. It seemed the most natural and regal thing somehow. Big, white, and grand with grace were things these bridal wear clerks understood.

"You were right to choose the Schiffli lace, dear," Mama said. "My own wedding gown had Venetian lace, but I always thought it too busy."

"Yes, Mama George. I think the Schiffli lace will do best."

"I wish you could have worn my dress, dear. We could have stitched it with Schiffli. But it was simply impossible. Your figure is too petite. I envy you."

"Yes, Mama George. Thank you *k*-kindly, Mama George."

"Of course, you know I was fond of those darling open-toed D'Orsay shoes with the satin rose flourishes. But I can understand your reticence to wear them. Naturally."

"Natcherly."

"The gold satin slippers will do fine."

"I believe they will, Mama. Gold slippers is *n*-nice."

The cash register rang.

"Madame, it's been our pleasure to serve you ladies and your heavenly Pyrenees this perfect day. And how shall we settle the account?"

"Yes, send the bill to Brass Freight and Cargo on River Street. I believe arrangements have been made? You should have a registration on file. Mark the envelope: Attention Mrs. Plum."

"Yes, Madame. Will there be anything else?"

"Yes, my sons will be in tomorrow for their fittings. Send their bill to the attention of Mrs. Plum also."

"Yes, Madame."

Engraved invitations began to arrive in mailboxes across the island and in townhouses throughout the city. The cakes (there would be two, matching), the flowers, the gold and white color scheme and decorations were chosen and put in the pipeline for the big day. Mama bit her tongue, with Pirate's House memories roiling in her head, as the four young betrothed insisted upon a limited amount of champagne and hard cider, along with the obligatory punchbowl. The Bonafide Beat Band was providing the reception entertainment on the lawn, along with a few other folk troubadours who had become friendly with The Brothers Brass in recent years.

After much whispering in Bettilia's ear, Chalice convinced her that the two of them should corner Mama George in her master bedroom the night before the wedding, for some motherly pearls of wisdom. The two girls waited until the right moment, when the boys were out on the front porch nervously looking at their toes, picking their guitars.

"Mizz Brass? Bettilia and myself, well, we've been anxious to find an opportunity to sit with you in private like this and ask your advice. As you can imagine we are at sixes and sevens about what to expect, well, not only tomorrow night—you know—in regards to our wifely duties. But, Bettilia and myself, we were wondering if you might have some morsels of insight, some dos or don'ts or any kind of design for living you might offer us, you know, for newlyweds like we're gonna be."

"Yeah. What you got, Mama George?" Bettilia asked.

This put Mama George at sixes and sevens herself. For the first time in all these weeks of addressing minutiae never too small and endless scrupulous planning, she was caught short, staring at the two pie-eyed, expectant young ladies seated across from her. She was stuck. But not for long.

"Girls, when it comes to making a marriage, I've made a complete botch of it all. I really don't have anything to tell you."

Then she got up and left the room.

Bettilia and Chalice just sat there, looking at each other. So this is how it would be. It was almost showtime and they would have to fend for themselves. At least Chalice had her own fading mother with whom to seek counsel. At least Bettilia was used to fending for herself.

The Brothers Brass did not bother asking their mother for advice in such matters.

Considering the rough and reckless nature of recent

events—and after the Pirate's House debacle—even Daddy Brass did not think it wise to chance the fallout of a traditional bachelor party the night before such an ostentatious and precarious occasion. Instead, he dropped by late in the evening, then sat up till well after midnight with Kes and Glenn, talking comic books and telling jokes that Daddy told racier as the night wore on, and frying up fried egg sandwiches with lots of black pepper.

In the wee hours, unable to sleep, Bettilia found Kes down on the beach gazing across the sea at a reddening harvest moon. Neither of them had much to say. They walked hand in hand for a time, their thoughts lost in the roar of the surf. After a while Kes began to sing and Bettilia joined him, softly, barely heard amidst the wind and rushing water. Later, in years to come, it was hard to remember what song they sang. Kes sometimes thought they had sung the *Shenandoah.* Other times he was not so sure. The remembrance he would be most sure of was the sound of Bettilia's voice against his own, her odd, comforting, ethereal harmony weaving its way into him, inside his truest timbre, the very heart of his melody.

VERSE 33

Observance

It was raining the morning of the Brass wedding. Mama George was beside herself for about ten minutes after she awoke to the sound of raindrops. She came downstairs in her housecoat where she paced the kitchen, arms folded, plucking nervously at her top button whilst expressing her concerns to all who would listen. With that part taken care of, she folded up her frets and put them in a tiny drawer in her head for safekeeping. She began to make telephone calls.

The ceremony would be moved to the church. The reception would now be held in the church fellowship hall. Daddy Brass made a noise from his bedroll on the parlor couch.

"But darlin, the Bugga and his boys will be here to set up the bandstand any old minute now."

"Malakoff, stop your shouting. You'll awaken Bettilia. Your sons and I can hear you quite well without you wail-hailing like an ill-bred oaf."

He talked softer.

"Bugga and the boys—"

"I heard you. No need to repeat it. Your Bugga and his boys will just have to see if they can fit what they can of the bandstand into the church hall. Or we will do without a bandstand."

"Mama," Glenn interjected, "with this many folks coming, the Bonafide Beats will never be able to squeeze all their amps and drums into that tiny chapel. And then to have to move all them wires and that tangle into the reception hall right after the ceremony—"

"No, there will be no room for them in the chapel," Mama said firmly. "I have already addressed that in my mind."

"Might you address some of it to us, doll?" a tired Daddy said, shuffling into the kitchen, favoring his morning sore knee.

"But what about the wedding march, Mama?" Kes pondered, dazedly shifting his coffee cup like a chess piece to different stations on the tabletop.

Glenn just sat looking catatonic.

"I will be playing the wedding march myself, on the Hammond organ," Mama George announced.

It was all taken care of. The wedding was at two o'clock.

As the morning progressed, Mama George checked names off her guest list, calling each to inform them of the day's adjustments. She was on the last page of her address book when the skies began to clear and the sun came out.

"A buttload of sunshine now, your ladyship," Daddy Brass said, returning from outside. "Bugga's out on the porch with the boys. They ain't unpacked any gear yet. He's wondering which way to jump."

"Tell them to proceed as originally planned," Mama said without hesitation. "The ceremony will be in the chapel. The reception will be here on the lawn, after. The Beats need not attend, I will still play the march. Now, I'm going upstairs to check on Bettilia."

"Tell Bettilia good morning for me, doll," Daddy said, making a widening motion with his hands as he watched her rump head up the kitchen stair. He almost got a chuckle out of those somnambulist sons of his, still sitting bewildered at the table.

"I will tell her, Malakoff."

Mama George kept Bettilia sequestered inside her childhood bedroom as the hour of reckoning approached. It would be bad luck to see the groom before the ceremony. Bettilia ate the biscuit and marmalade from her breakfast tray, parting the curtains and watching the production unfolding on the lawn. Two stories below, under the spyglass of the treehouse, Sister galloped about the glistening wet lawn, excitedly greeting the arrival of flowers, caterers, cakes, and musicians. The bandstand took shape, bright white tablecloths were spread over a phalanx of tables under a soft autumnal sun.

There was lots of laughter down there, joshing, talking, people. Bettilia felt certain this was all being assembled for somebody else's day, not hers. But she liked the calliope of people down there all the same, it reminded her of the fair. As long as they were far off, down there, like they would appear to her from high up a tree, they were okay. Bettilia had never liked folks much—especially not lots of folks in the same place at the same time, until now. But this was okay.

By noon the gold and white streamers were strung from the trees to the bandstand to the eaves of shining Angel-sprey. The decorations were all but done.

By one o'clock Bettilia was sitting on the tiny child's bed in her wedding dress, hands limp in her lap, staring at the Noah's Ark wallpaper with her tinkerbell eyes, her eyes made up special for this day, just like Chalice taught her. She was thinking of how much she had learned and grown in this little room, with the help of Mama George, with the help of the family Brass. She might or might not know what love was, depending upon when she asked herself. But mostly she was thinking of what Chalice had said that night outside the freak show about happiness, about how this surely must be it.

Bettilia wondered how that Chalice was holding up over at her own house in her wedding dress as their last minutes of childhood ticked away. Chalice was surely in a swarm of aunts right now, with her father hovering, her half-daft mother of little help. Poor Chalice—she still loved Kes. Bettilia knew that. But that was okay too. Bettilia did not mind really. Besides, soon, they would all be family.

As Bettilia was squeezing her wedding dress into the back seat of Mama George's little black Renault to drive the two blocks to the chapel, Sister came barking and bounding up to the open door, trying to climb in with her.

"Will one of you men come collar this dog?" Mama George commanded out her window, from behind the steering wheel.

"Aw, let her come, Mama George," Bettilia begged. "Besides, she'll *j*-just follow us to the church anyway, soon as they let her go. Unless Kes or me is here, she'll just follow us."

"But, dear, her big ole paws will muddy up your dress."

"Bettilia, sugar, you come sit up front with Mrs. Brass," Mrs. Plum said from the front seat, opening her door, getting out. "I'll sit in back with Sister."

Mama George had no choice really. The brothers and their father had already left in the Hudson, accompanied by Saint Peter. Besides, Mama asked herself, how could she refuse this wee girl anything on her wedding day?

"I just wish that photographer would arrive. Where *is* he?" Mama asked instead.

Sister got in the car.

Sister also trailed after Bettilia's gold slippers as Daddy Brass led her up the aisle, giving her away to Kestrel Brass. Then, in a well rehearsed move, he sidestepped into place to serve as Kes's best man while Chalice's daddy did the same for Glenn. By that time, Mama George had given it all up to God and was too busy leaving teardrops on the keys of the Hammond organ to question the mystery of His ways, even if His ways did involve big white dogs. She finished playing the march, sniffling into her hanky as she took her place in the front pew.

The vows began well, with Glenn and Chalice taking their vows first. Bettilia wasn't sure where she was half the time, this seemed like a dream, but she was bearing up.

Kes had never looked more handsome than he did right now in his tailored black silk tuxedo and bolero tie. Still, Bettilia's mind began to drift as the preacher asked:

"Chalice Dillard, do you take this man to be your lawful wedded husband, to have and to hold—"

Behind the preacher, behind the Hammond organ—

Bettilia saw the rectory door *crack open* slightly, just a few inches, like somebody was behind it listening. Bettilia felt all the air leak out of her.

Then Sister barked. Loud. *RUH-HO-FFFF.* Sister *dashed* toward the rectory door. Half the pews were trying not to laugh, the preacher tried not to ruffle.

"*Sister—*" Bettilia scolded in high whisper. Hiking her wedding dress, she scuffled after the dog, grabbing Sister's collar and dragging her back to the front of the altar. All the while, Bettilia's eyes kept darting back at that cracked open rectory door. The door clicked shut as Bettilia resumed her position beside Kes, smiling Kes. Bettilia's hand gripped tight on Sister's collar for the duration of the ceremony. Yes, she saw that door click shut. The rest of the vows were a blur to Bettilia. She must have said yes. She must have said with this ring I thee wed. The next thing she knew Kes was kissing her and they were headed back down the aisle, Bettilia, Kes, and Sister—Chalice and Glenn—through row after row of glowing, happy faces.

Because his car was the biggest, the two newlywed couples rode in Daddy Brass's Hudson the few blocks back to Angelsprey.

"With all this gotdam rice y'all done shed in here, I just

need a pot of red beans," Daddy joked, cocked sideways in his seat. He steered the island-length of Butler Avenue with one hand, waxing nostalgic to his four numbed captives, full of thorny life lessons with his philosophic emphasis on lessons of the heart.

By the time his Hudson arrived back at the gold streamered house on Officer's Row, Daddy Brass had succumbed to his own reflections, consumed with poetic regret:

"We loved with a love that was more than love in this kingdom by the sea—"

"You quoted it *wrong*, Daddy," Chalice laughed.

Daddy Brass didn't care.

Bettilia's door opened for her.

Bugga's massive black hand reached in to take her tiny hand, his head leaned in after his hand, his magnificent white smile lit up the car. Bettilia saw the holstered pistol under Bugga's coat. Kes saw it too.

"Congratulation, Mizz Boopsie, Mister Kes. Much food, much drink. Be lovely. Be joyful, yes. You in Bugga's hands now."

Bettilia had to admit that Bugga's reassurances in tandem with his size sixty-two tuxedo coat did wonders after she sipped a bit of champagne. Mostly, Bugga kept his distance, hovering at the edges of the party as she and Kes stood in the reception line on the porch alongside a growing table of gifts. But Bettilia felt there was big magic in that Bugga man.

"So pleased to finely meet you, yes, you *are* the beauty. And *that dress*," Aunt Jewell mewed. "And you're such a tiny thing."

"Thank you kindly. I'm strong *f*-for my size."

"Of course you are, you little china doll. Kestrel? Will you and your new bride be honeymooning in Florida?"

"Naw, Aint Jewell, we're booked pretty tight through the holidays," Kes said, pulling at his tight collar whilst shaking hands with a solemn Uncle Bee Joe. "Brothers Brass got gigs outside Atlanta next week. So, Daddy fixed it for us to spend tonight and tomorrow night at the Marshall House Hotel in town. Glenn and Chally are staying there too. We hope to do a proper honeymoon first of next year. Florida maybe. Honolulu."

"Gigs? What is gigs?" Bettilia asked up at Kes as Aunt Jewell moved on.

"*Mrs.* Chalice *Brass*, yes, so pleased to finely meet you. And *that dress*."

Now that this Aunt Jewell mentioned it, Bettilia realized she did feel like a little doll. Like a frilly dressed-up doll on display as she got handled and touched and fawned over by a parade of folks she had never seen before—more human flesh than Bettilia had touched in all her days put together. Even Kes seemed unfamiliar with half of them and ready to fly away, up to that treehouse. Or that Marshall House Hotel he kept telling everybody about. She knew he was ready for the Marshall House Hotel. And they still had not solved the problem of what they should do with Sister tonight. Right now, as Kes, Bettilia, Glenn, and Chalice stood lined up receiving this endless chain of Mama George's old society friends, Sister was frolicking amongst the guests in front of the bandstand while the Bonafide Beats segued from *A Summer Place* into the plaintive twangs of *Sleepwalk*.

When Saint Peter came down the reception line with his two modest gifts in hand it almost seemed welcome relief amidst all these unfamiliars. Kes and Bettilia had begun to warm to Saint Peter and he was most gracious. Glenn was less warm, less easy as he shook Saint Peter's hand. Glenn still had not told Chalice.

Inside the house, with a few drinks in him, Daddy Brass was trying to tell Mama George. For reasons fathomable only if you were Daddy Brass, he decided to corner her alone when he saw Mama George head to the kitchen for more napkins.

"Darlin, they's something I gots to tell you. Something what's troubled me for years. This ain't easy..."

"Malakoff, please count your cocktails. Remember this is your only sons' one and only wedding."

"Georgiana, I—I am of a racial mixture."

"Oh, Malakoff, of course you are. I would call that *hardly news*. I've known you were octoroon since I was pregnant with Gaylenn and Mama made me put the detective on you after you fed me all those fiddlesticks about your hereditary madness which never really existed."

"You've known all these years?"

"Of course I have. One of the last things Mama told me was it doesn't matter as long as he loves you."

"She did? Meaning *me*?"

"Yes. And I would like to say *at least you were not crazy*. I would like to be able to say that. But such is life."

"I was afraid to gamble on more children with you, darlin. I was pushing the odds and didn't want no surprises."

"Yes, so you did your gambling elsewhere. Now, get out of my way, Malakoff. They are waiting on the napkins."

"Gotdam. I'm feeling mighty relieved. Like a new man."

"I'm very happy for you, now let me by. We are about to cut the cakes."

About an hour later, as moonrise began to bloom amber over the ocean, the Beats were playing *The Evening Star Waltz.* Folks mingled more freely, more jolly, many full of more hard cider punch than soft. Blondie Boy Bichét was unofficial barkeep at the speakeasy operating from the open trunk of Daddy's Hudson parked down on the street behind Angelsprey. There was a steady flow of folk back and forth to the Hudson. Glenn and Chalice were holding each other, a bit tipsy, sometimes waltzing, sometimes just swaying. They were both thinking about the Marshall House Hotel. Bettilia didn't know how to dance any better than she could swim and Kes's hip wouldn't let him dance. They clung to each other in two chairs under the great spreading oak, him sipping hard cider, her sipping gingermint tea. The champagne made her too hot she said. But they were sharing much the same thoughts as Glenn and Chalice.

Suddenly the band stopped playing as Daddy Brass staggered drunk onto the bandstand, knocking over one of Jack the drummer's cymbals, dragging an ill-at-ease Saint Peter with him.

"Boys, boys, stop your playing for a minute," Daddy bellowed so all could hear. "That's some perty music, but I got something to tell everbody here."

The entire lawn stopped swaying, looked at the stage. Daddy Brass grabbed the microphone stand for support, his other arm holding Saint Peter close.

"Folks, everbody. I got sumpin to say and I'm agonna say it," Daddy's voice echoed at the crowd. "I want y'all to meet my brother. That's right. I'm colored. I'm a nigra."

This sank in for a moment, a short moment. The wedding guests blinked.

Then they all went back to talking, swaying, and the Bonafide Beats went back to playing *The Evening Star Waltz.* Saint Peter resurrected the drummer's cymbal. Nobody gave a damn.

Mama George was unimpressed and went on telling Marybelle Wiggins how to make her cinnamon red hots gelatin dish. Kes and Bettilia were about to fall out of their chairs laughing. Glenn was mortified until he found out Chalice already knew too. Bettilia had told her before the wedding, for good reason. Chalice did not give a hoot (not too much) at this point, and for good reason: she was almost two months pregnant. Sitting on the porch, Mrs. Plum sipped her Blondie Bichét Manhattan from her paper cup, raised a private little toast in Malakoff's direction, then she went back to whispering in the island mayor's ear.

"Wait here," Bettilia told Kes once they finally stopped chortling. "I almost forgot. I've got a special present for you. Your mama, she suggested it."

"I can't wait."

Her tinkerbell eyes looked wise.

"I know you can't. Just a *b*-bit longer, Kes. We'll get out of these clothes and slip away to that hotel in town."

"I like that slip away sound. Especially that first phase."

She cooed like the evening dove—and left him, going into the house.

Inside, Bettilia climbed the quiet stair. Slipping quickly down the hall toward her little bedroom alongside Mama George's room, she only hoped Kes would love the gift she chose as much as she did when Mama George spake it. Yes, that Mama George, she had her moments. As Bettilia approached her bedroom she saw little pockmarks. Little pockmarks in the rug outside her door. The kind of marks that hobnail boots might make in a hook rug. Bettilia was trying not to let her head run away with her today of all days.

She opened the door and went in to get Kes's gift.

Not long after that, Mrs. Plum came up the stairs then started down the hall, her high heels clicking, headed for Mama George's room. Mrs. Plum had left her fox fur coat on the bed in there and she was about ready to go. She had a late supper date at Johnny Harris's with a young oilman from Odessa.

Coming toward Mrs. Plum, coming barefoot from her bedroom, was little Bettilia in her gown—moving toward the stair with a strange little smile on her face. To Mrs. Plum, Bettilia's tinkerbell eyes looked odd as she passed in the hall.

"Bettilia? What's wrong, sugar? Can I help you?"

Bettilia stopped at the top of the stair, turning her quizzical little smile back at Mrs. Plum.

"But if you try to help me, he will harvest you. He'll always harvest you."

Mrs. Plum stood in the dark hallway, watching Bettilia disappear barefoot down the steps.

Under the great pilgrim oak, Kes was showing off Sister to The Bonafide Beats. The Beats were taking a smoke break whilst Raynard Erry, an old local fiddler, played the *Shenandoah* up at the microphone.

"You'd never know she looked like a round and fat snow bunny when she showed up here," Kes told them.

Sister stood quiet in the circle of players, basking in all their admiration.

"Them big white hosses that pulled my mother home," Zeb the bass player said, flicking ash off his wedding cigar, "they looked a lot like this'n here."

*"J-*Jaybird?" she said soft."

Kes turned and saw this girl, Bettilia, standing a few feet away from the circle of players. This girl, now his bride. Still nursing his cider, Kes stepped away to talk sweet with her, slipping an arm around her waist.

"It's almost dark, darlin. I never knew you could look so beautiful under paper lanterns," he said, leaning into her, smelling her.

"Thank you. For everthing."

"Thank me? I'm supposed to be thanking you. Where's that present you promised?" he asked, hinting quietly, urgently, at more. "And where's your slippers?"

"Oh. I *f*-forgot."

"Your head going south on me already?"

"I'll go back and get it," she said.

"I can't wait."

"Kes?"

"Yes, darlin?"

"You love me?"

"You know I do, darlin."

"Then, I reckon we'll always be there, won't we?"

"Where?"

"In our tree."

He smiled. She stretched up on her toes and kissed him.

"Wait here," Bettilia said, looking at him, looking at Sister.

"I'll try," Kes said.

Bettilia slipped from his hand, drifting away, passing barefoot in her white wedding gown through the crowd of people, across the lawn, not moving toward the house at all. Kes watched her as she went, passing like a tinkerbell vision under the paper lanterns, passing to the fiddler's tune. He saw Bettilia turn slightly as she went. He saw her give him a little far-off wave before she disappeared into a crowd of folk beyond the bandstand.

Kes never saw Bettilia again.

VERSE 34

Riddle Top

The next six years were unkind to Hellzabub's Human Zoo. They were even more unkind to the zookeeper. Zeebub's operation had dwindled to only four sorry freaks and the girly show. By the time the tiny carnival Zeebub ran with now made camp across from the country store at Hayden's Crossroad, Zeebub had a nasty black tumor the size of a gumball on her lower lip. The tumor had been growing for two years, maybe more. Having to give up her cigars only made this carny life more of a graveyard crawl with calliope instead of jazz band. Half the time anymore Zeebub didn't know if the full moon sounds of madness she heard whilst lying besotted on her cot after midnight were real or imagined.

"Don't y'all worry," she told her mules, pouring water in their buckets. "You'll get fed just soon as we get some cash in the door tonight. Hopefully."

Zeebub patted the neck of her oldest mule, Katy Bee, watching the beast drink thirstily. Zeebub loved Katy Bee. Katy Bee had been with her since Zeebub was a young gal just getting started, working as a part-time barker and full-time roustabout down in Florida. But Katy Bee was over forty years old now and worn out.

"Don't drink too fast, Kates. You'll bloat," she said, then gave a shout to the ferris wheel man over there inside his truck. "Watch my babies for me. Be back in a few minutes."

The ferris wheel man gave Zeebub the high sign then went back to swapping slobber with the Snake Woman.

As her hobnails pockmarked the gooey hot asphalt crossing the highway to the gas station store, it hurt Zeebub to think she might have to have Katy Bee put down and rendered for a paltry few shekels. Old friends were hard to come by.

Zeebub could trace her biggest downturn of fortune to that day she had to pull up tent stakes and abandon that one-ring circus outside Camp Stewart without giving the circus owner proper notice. Zeebub knew she was never going to get her money out of Malakoff Brass. So what choice did she have? It would not have been wise to linger within a hundred miles of Savannah, Georgia after that bastard's daughter-in-law went missing. Yes, Zeebub, knew one thing after all these years: Malakoff Brass did owe her. And Zeebub could use that money about now, what with this runny black thing growing on her lip. Doctors had looked at it and every doc wanted to just cut it out and leave Zeebub looking like one of those specimens back there in her zoo tent. Well, folks didn't know it—how could they when they always saw Zeebub in her overalls and thick-soled boots?—but Zeebub had always had a streak of vanity about her looks. She did not want the bottom half of her mouth looking like the Royal Gorge with missing teeth. If Zeebub just had that money now that Brass owed her back then for eighteen months spent behind grey stone walls on his behalf, why, Zeebub could afford to see one of those specialists at that hospital in Texas.

No, Zeebub wasn't sorry she had done what she had done when she ducked out of sight from Savannah in the middle of the night. She just wished she could duck out of these weird hills now the same way and get her bad lip down to that hospital in Houston before this tumor got much worse.

Inside the country store, Zeebub waited her turn at the counter behind a couple of sun-dried girls and their hick daddy who were mighty excited about the carnival across the road. They couldn't wait until tonight, they told the old nigger tending the cash register.

"If you don't mind me saying, ma'am, you ought get that goiter looked after," the old nig said as he handed Zeebub her change for the pint of Three Roses. "A proper doctor might could help you with that lip. They got a Nursey Jane over in Cayuger Ridge. She's a white lady."

Zeebub grunted back at him. He had a lot of nerve.

"I had it looked after. Nothing they can do," she told him. "I reckon it'll go away its own afore long."

"Yez'm. I reckon."

Zeebub could tell the old nig didn't believe her. Yes, he had a lot of nerve. The things you had put up with from nigs these days.

“Where is this Cayuger Ridge anyhow?” Zeebub asked, not really sure why she was asking.

“Up the road a piece, ma’am. About ten mile on past that roadhouse. Now, them new doctors—if you don’t mind me saying—they don’t know everthing. They don’t know the old ways.”

“Old ways?”

“Yez’m. They’s an old root woman hereabouts. I seen her rid a gentleman of a black egg like that he had on his forehead. After she give him one of her salves, that nasty cancer just come off in his hand one day. Left his forehead looking right pink and perty.”

Zeebub snorted with distaste, heading for the Rainbow Bread screen door, her boots clicking the planked floor. She stopped suddenly, looked back at him behind the register.

“Where’s this old woman, you say?”

“Just up the Riddle Top road, bottom of that mountain. But don’t go too far up that road though.”

Riddle Top? Where had Zeebub heard that name before?

“And this Riddle Top? Where the hell is *it*, boy?”

“Just past that roadhouse, ma’am. Bull’s Gladiola. Betwixt here and Cayuger.”

“I’ll think on it. You still be here after supper?”

“We is, ma’am. We’s staying open late for your carny tonight.”

Nodding, Zeebub fingered the tumor, mulling her options as she turned to go. Then, before she could kick open the screen door, Zeebub got stopped in her tracks like a train wreck. Yes, Zeebub had her a good and nasty laugh when she saw the wall poster by the door. She was still chuckling over that damn playbill by the door as she crossed back over the highway, tucking her pint inside her overalls. It was the first time Zeebub had laughed in days. It almost took her mind off her lip for a little bit. It almost made her forget her bottomless craving for another cigar.

For One Night Only. The Brothers Brass at Bull's Gladiola Lounge.

Yes, even Katy Bee would get a mule shiver and a good hee-haw out of that.

VERSE 35

Go Back into That Land

He kept looking for her. Of course he did. Almost six years later—even in a backcountry, dirtwater hill town like Ewe Springs—Kestrel Brass was still looking for her. There was no stopping him. He still wore her ring.

The Brothers Brass were playing the Cassandra Ballroom in Ewe Springs on a Friday night. If you asked Kes where Ewe Springs was he couldn't tell you. He had been drunk so long on the drive up that he couldn't remember how they got here or the name of the hotel where he passed out standing upright in the lobby. He was carried to his room, where he slept it off until it was almost showtime. Glenn managed to rouse him, but Kes did not bother to shave. The safety razor was rusty. It scared him. And Kes could not hold it steady.

The Ewe Springs show turned out to be a weird mix of church folks and roadhouse folks. Some of them overlapped of course. But a lot of them didn't and did not mix well.

"Thank you, folks. Brother Glenn and me, we 'ppreciate ya," Kes slurred into the microphone, mostly sober. "This next number is a stupid little doggerel we first learnt back in kindergarten. Actually, come to think of her, I reckon it ain't doggerel at all—it's a little birdrell. Ain't that right, Glenn?"

Glenn managed a wan smile under the bright lights. The audience didn't laugh much at that because they didn't get the joke. Kes muddled on, unaware.

"Anyhoo, it's called *Little Birdie*," his voice echoed. "Some y'all might know it."

Kes and Glenn launched into *Little Birdie*, with Kes's left hand cramping, struggling to keep up.

Little birdie, little birdie, what makes you fly so high?
It's because I'm a true bird, and do not fear to die—

Kes's hand cramped more when he was coming off the hooch, when he had the shakes like this. If it weren't for the pills, Kes doubted he could get through a show. But a little nip before curtain time would make it a whole lot easier for big brother and help oil out the kinks. He kept telling his little brother, but brother was not listening any-more. No, Glenn couldn't understand Kes's need to drink before every goddam show. And after the show. And every waking minute betwixt the shows. Glenn could could not understand that only drink kept that Clootie's hooves from dancing on Kes's heart, in Kes's head, dancing more gleeful than ever before.

Little birdie, little birdie, what makes your wing so blue?
It's because I am a-grievin', grieving after you—

Goddam it. Kes just missed that A chord, turned it into a bad E-Minor, then jumped to the D chord ahead of the beat. Kes felt it, heard it. He knew Glenn heard it. Glenn didn't show it, but he heard it. Kes knew little brother didn't miss a beat. Little brother heard it all, but—

But now, suddenly, tonight in his upright dream, Kes was hearing something new. Old and new, borrowed and blue. Where was that voice, *her* voice, coming from? Kes wondered if little brother—who heard it all—was hearing that strange harmony Kes was beginning to hear, or nearly hear. That descanting harmony singing with them from out in that foggy crowd. Then Sister started *barking*, very loud, back in the dressing room. Little brother must be hearing her too, barking. Still, Glenn Brass soldiered on.

With little brother's able support, despite the barking of the dog, the Brothers Brass almost made it. Two more songs and they would have been off the stage, into the darkness, and Kes back inside his bottle. They nearly made it. But when Kes chased that little birdie past that A chord again, his fingers fumbled again—and some drunk joker on the front row knew a dry drunk when he saw one.

"Stop beating on that bucket, buster—she's had *enough!*" the hillbilly kid hollered.

Kes kept playing, singing, throwing the bucktooth kid a queer but fast grin. But the kid had rattled him. And Sister kept *barking* back there. Kes was missing more chords.

"I said let that bucket *be*. Ye done knocked a *hole* in it!"

Kes stopped playing, squinting down at the kid he could dimly see at the edge of darkness. Glenn played another couple of bars then fizzled, forced to a stop too. The room was simmering.

"Whoa, mister," Kes said to the edge of darkness, "why don't *you* drag ass up here and *do it*? Think you can do better? *Huh*? Come on, *Jethro*. Play this fucking song for these hillbillies."

The bucktooth heckler pushed closer to the stage, into the light where Kes could look down and see him clear.

"I just might—" the kid sassed back. "I can *pick*. I can *sang*. I might just climb up there and teach you what *your mama* shoulda learnt ye."

That snapped it. Kes flipped the kid a big tall bird with his middle finger.

"Yeah? Climb this, Tarzan!" he said, and not nicely.

Kes *leapt* off the stage, onto the kid.

There wasn't much different about this fight. It was like a lot of fights betwixt two drunks in a roadhouse. And Glenn had gotten good at grabbing for Kes's guitar before it could get busted in another fight.

It was pushing three a.m. before the deputy let Kes out of his cell at the Ewe Springs jail. Bedraggled and aching, the deputy led him in cuffs to the front desk where Glenn was counting out cash from the cigar box he kept for such occasions. Whilst the deputy unlocked Kes's handcuffs the bailiff double-counted the money, out loud, before handing Glenn a receipt.

"One seventy-five," the jug-eared old bailiff intoned. "That covers all fines, so no court appearance necessary."

Glenn thanked him. The bailiff seemed friendly enough.

"My old lady's got several of y'all's records," the bailiff—a Sergeant McGee—said. "You boys are alright. I ain't much into the music. But she is. She's real involved with church work. You know how it is."

"Thank you, Sergeant," Glenn said. "You tell your wife that the Brothers Brass sent her bright blessings and a Holy Ghost howdy-do."

Kes tried not to roll his eyes. There went little brother running on auto-pilot with his cutesy slick horseshit.

"I will tell her that, sir," Sergeant McGee replied, smiling gently. He looked past Glenn, eyeing Kestrel's wasted shape. "I'll tell her I run into you two out on street patrol, though. Not in here."

"We appreciate your goodness and mercy, sir," Kes said. Little brother wasn't the only grease merchant in the family. "Can I have my cane back now?"

The Sergeant gave Kes his cane tied to a sealed manila envelope that held his personal belongings. He made Kes sign a receipt.

"You git on and offstage without your walking stick?"

"I'm good for a couple of hours these days," Kes said. "My hip ain't what she used to be. If I stand with my leg cocked just right—I can get through a show without falling on my ass."

"Or if you don't *jump* nobody? You might want to clean up your act, Mr. Brass," the Sergeant told him.

"Yes, sir. Working on it. Say—Sergeant?"

"Yes, son?"

"You mind if I pin up a wanted poster of my own, over on your board here?"

The Sergeant took the rough, damp page Kes produced from inside his coat. Unfolding it, the jug-eared baliff studied the pencil sketch, the words at the bottom.

"Who is this girl?" the Sergeant asked.

"My wife."

"Oh? How long is she missing?"

"Look at the bottom of the paper," Kes said, trying not to go testy on this good man. "It's all there. She been gone over five years now. Going on six."

"Son, are you sure—well—are you sure she ain't deceased?"

Kes locked eyes with Glenn for a moment.

"We ain't sure of nothing," Glenn said.

The Sergeant's hard hands flexed the sketch on the paper, the sweet button of a face and the sad eyes. His brow creased with real concern.

"Sure, fellas. I reckon it'd be alright to pin this on the board next to the others. If you don't mind me asking—how'd you come by this sketch of her? You ain't got no photo?"

"Naw, sir, never got no photo," Kes said, his gaze lost in the whirl of the ceiling fan. How many times had he heard these questions? "You might find this to your amusement. But I had a police artist sketch that. I described her to him, best I could. Tried to pay him a hunert bucks but he wouldn't take it."

The bailiff was ready to change the subject.

"Say, would you boys sign something for my wife? The two of you? If I bring home some Brothers Brass autographs she might even put out without it being my birthday."

"Sure, Sergeant."

"No problem, Sergeant."

Glenn was already pulling out a forty-five r.p.m. record from his mandolin case. Kes had to admit—Glenn was smooth, Glenn was ready. Glenn was always loaded with those forty-five revolvers. He dispensed those little discs like payola.

Kes stepped forward to the front desk, trying not to shake too bad as he attempted his jittery signature alongside his brother's inky flourish on the record sleeve. On the sepia record sleeve they looked like saintly sons, posed with their guitars against a heavenly lit backdrop of dramatic clouds.

"So where you boys booked to play next?" the Sergeant asked, watching Kes's hand struggle with the pen.

"Some joint up near a boondock called Cayuga Ridge," Glenn said. "We're booked tomorrow night—well, tonight really—into a Bull's Gladiola Lounge."

"Bull's Gladiola?" the Sergeant brightened. "Bull Hannah's place? Why, Bull and me, we go way back. He's County Sheriff up there. Some rough hills, but he's a good fella. He and me went to training academy together down Roanoke. We wudn't much older than you two."

"Bull's Gladiola is owned by a sheriff?" Kes grumbled, caught himself, smiled.

Glenn gave Kes the walleye, closing the near empty

cigar box.

"Well, Golden Gloves, you might be forced to go the night making music instead of mayhem," Glenn said. "Good evening or morning to you, Sergeant. And say howdy-do to that wife."

Sister slept all the way to Cayuga Ridge, a back seat full of white fur. They didn't get away from Ewe Springs until mid-morning. Kes made Glenn wait around until the store opened so he could buy another bottle. Glenn went back up to his hotel room for a nap, but Kes was too close to the D.T.s to sleep. He walked Sister around and around the hotel parking lot, then up and down Main Street. Kes was still walking it when Glenn had the copper and black Cadillac packed and ready to go. Once the package store did open, Glenn was actually glad to see Kes get that first drink in him so big brother would settle down and give that big dog some rest.

Despite the hotel clerk's directions Glenn got lost on his way up to Bull's Gladiola Lounge. Worn down, snoring in and out, Sister was barely aware, yet fully aware. She was listening in two places—one place a deep piney wood inside her great white head, the other being the backseat of this groaning car. She heard their voices up front, she felt the road winding and turning as her copper carriage climbed higher into hills unknown.

"You sure you on the right road now, little brer?"

"I'm happy with it. That was the crossroads back there that hotel man described. I'm pretty sure."

"My money says you still lost," Kes snickered, nipping bourbon.

"You ain't got no money," Glenn said, unamused. "That Dutch Masters box is near empty. We're losing more money than we make this trip, keeping you out of jails and into your hooch."

Glenn looked over at Kes. Kes was gazing dull-eyed out at the blur of trees, his head against his window glass.

"We didn't get paid last night," Glenn added, but Kes kept saying nothing. "I thought you might give a damn."

Kes tapped the window glass with his bottle.

"I wouldn't wanna get lost in them woods," he said. "Don't like the look of em."

"Me neither."

As it turned out, Glenn had found the true road to Cayuga Ridge, if there was such a thing. Indeed, he had. They swung through the tiny community, past the rock schoolhouse, then connected to another road out of town, heading toward a looming dark mountain—toward Bull's Gladiola Lounge, if all went well. Lately, things seldom went well. Kestrel grew pensive as they passed the white steeple of the First Reconstructed Baptist Church of Cayuga Ridge on their way out.

"I remember, time was, we'd of been playing there tonight. Not Bull's Gladiola. Not some roadhouse."

"Yeah," Glenn muttered, "if Mama'd had her way."

"If Mama had her way we'd be celibate boy missionaries in Cambodia. Strumming our banjos for a bunch of gooks and geeks, feeding em Bibles with thick gravy."

"Naw, she wouldn't," Glenn said. "Not unless we could do it and her still tuck us in bed at night on Officer's Row."

"Well, little brer, all I know is—she'd ruther us diddle each other than to have wandered so far from the fold."

Even Glenn got a laugh out of that, then his laugh fell away as the hills, the woods, and that dark mountain up there consumed them again. He tried to hide the resentment that was lodged in his throat.

"No telling what she'd say if she knew how many church-folk won't even book us no more," Glenn said, finally.

"You blaming me for that?"

"I ain't blaming. I'm just saying."

"Yeah, well, Mama ain't saying much these days. Now is she?"

"No. She ain't."

"We go where the money be. They's bills to be paid."

Glenn's whelp rang nasty in Sister's ears. Eyes closed, half awake, Sister buried her nose under Kes's coat in the back seat. Sister didn't like it when they made cruel sounds at each other up front.

"Well, ain't no bills getting paid this trip," Glenn said.

"Sure they is, little brer. We gots to support the municipalities we frequent, help ease their tax burden. Ever one of these towns got light bills, sewage, infrastructure to consider. That's what them hefty fines help pay for."

"You ain't funny, Kes. We barely had money for gas up here."

"I ain't trying for funny."

"Why don't you take one of your goddam pills and another pull?" Glenn fumed. "Gimme a goddam breather. Go back into that land inside your head you live in."

"Just singing my parts is all."

"That looks like that Gladiola up there. Put that bottle away."

"I wish you'd make up your mind."

Kes slipped his bottle under the seat as the copper Cadillac eased into the gravel parking lot of Bull's Gladiola Lounge. It was a long, lowslung building with tin roof and rusty sign, lonely out here alongside two-lanes of cracked asphalt. The rear bumper of a police cruiser nudged from behind the far corner of the roadhouse. By the time Kes opened the Cadillac's backseat door, Sister had perked up and was glad to get out of the car. Her tail working, Sister ran around the parking lot sniffing at oil spots, dandelions, and the scents of a thousand other creatures that had passed through here before her. Finally, she squatted and peed in the gravel whilst Kes and Glenn stood in the sun with their instruments, waiting for her. Then they all went into the cool, dark place together.

Sheriff Bull Hannah was back in his office and turned out to be a big, decent, white-haired fellow. He greeted them heartily, showed pity when Glenn spake of their plight in finding his far-flung establishment.

"I copy that," Bull said. "But you with us now. And that's the thing. Ain't it? Feel free to use my office here for your dressing room."

Bull had no problem at all with Kes putting one of his Missing Woman handbills on the posting board behind the bar. Kes tacked one to the board then went out to the car for a nap. The bar was still closed and they had several hours until the show.

"You ain't got no photo of her, you say?" Bull asked later, leaning over his upended beer mugs and decanters, inspecting the sketch in the murk of the unlit dance hall.

"No photographs," Glenn said, sitting on a barstool, tuning his mandolin. "None that we know of."

"Over five years? Hell. That cain't be good," Hannah said. "Generally, from my professional experience, if we ain't got em back within the week, we don't get em back."

"Yeah."

"Savannah, you say?"

"Yeah."

"Ain't that somewhere's by the sea?"

"It is that."

"Yep, well, this here's a long ways from the sea."

"Don't I know it."

Bull Hannah picked up a dish towel but couldn't keep his eyes off the sketch on his wall.

"Not even no wedding photos?"

"Naw sir. The wedding photographer, well, he never made it. He met final misfortune. A three-car pile up. Chalice—my wife—she and I got studio portraits later. But they's just a few folks' Polaroids took at the reception. The ones with Bettilia, she's mostly a blur or too far off to recognize. Seems like everbody—even a dim stranger or two—got into a snapshot that day except her. And what a day it was. Turned out, Bettilia, she seen some things that day.

Things we didn't know about till after."

"After what?" Hannah asked.

"After she went gone."

"Hmmm. Where'd your brother get off to?"

"Now? Or back then?"

"Now. Today."

"Aw, he's out catching him a nap in the car."

"Awful hot out there," Bull Hannah said, flipping on a lamp to see the sketch better while he polished a shot glass.

"He don't notice. He's used to it. Hell, he still don't know they shot Kennedy."

"Didn't nobody tell him?"

"Oh, we told him. But he still don't know."

"Ever get any leads on this girl? From this here picture?"

"Not really. Oh, a nibble or two, but nothing that went anywhere. Hard to believe, ain't it? My Daddy, Mama, ain't neither of em ever be the same. Hard to say which took her hardest. Bettilia—you see, sir—she was one of us. And Kes? I reckon Kes's tacked up a few thousand of them sketches. Two, three thousand of em over eight states over the last six years counting. There's a Savannah printer's kid we've put through college. But, Bettilia, it's like she got swept off the edge of the world. Vanished. She couldn't swim, so she might of drown. I doubt it. Some even said a gator might of got after her, back there on our island. But we got mighty small gators. Even Bettilia was bigger than one of them gators, tiny as she was. Or is."

Bull Hannah met Glenn's uncertain eyes for a moment before the boy went back to tuning his string. Bull let it go.

He didn't want to shatter any delusions. This sheriff had seen too much sorrow, too many grieving kinfolk in these hills, to ever want to rob one of what hope they could hold onto. He'd comforted so many folk over missing kids and loved ones lost hither and yon—why, Bull often thought he missed his true calling as a preacher. Besides, this Glenn Brass didn't look like he had many delusions left. His brother was a drunk and, no doubt, this Brass brother sitting here knew it.

"I copy that," Bull Hannah said, trying to make conversation. "It happens. More often than you might think. It's like another world just swallers some folks up and they're gone. Hell, I even seed kids I didn't know existed come out of nowhere then go back into nowhere without ever knowing who they was."

"What you mean?"

"Aw, when you're sheriffing in these parts, you see things you can't explain nearly ever week, once a day even. In fact, they was a tiny little child—this gal in this picture makes me think of her somehow—they was this tiny little child, not much more than a babe, I used to see up around Elda Ninzly's place years back."

"Elda Ninzly?"

"Yeah. Old gullah gal. Ninzly. The Piney Woman. Lives just up the Old Top road, near the foot of Old Top. Folks go to her for their herb serums and conjures, the old time doctoring. Them folks that don't trust that County doc over the new clinic. Nursy Jane. I'm telling you, lots of kids go missing around here. You lose count over the years. Just like I seed Elda Ninzly walking the roads with that teensy pale child a time or two, years back, then never saw the child again. Thought I knowed all the kids around here, I always have. But I never knowed that one. One day I asked Ninzly and she don't know who I'm talking about, she say. You see how it is? Gone, then here, then gone again."

"What you figure happens to all them missing kids and folks?"

"Oh, I figure, most just run off, on their own. Lots got good reason to run. Some folks say wolves git em. Some say gypsies. Some say it's just boogery old bobnot. Ninzly, that's what she done. She started jabbering under her tongue about bobnot. So I let it go. Have to let em go sometimes. Seeing how it is."

"Did you say *bobnot?*" Kes asked from the shadows.

Glenn and Bull Hannah looked toward the sound of Kestrel. Kes had slipped inside without them being aware. His face looked white, like he was just floating over there, suspended by something Bull Hannah had said.

"Did you say bobnot?" he repeated.

"Did I say bobnot?" Bull Hannah let out a jangled little chuckle, clicking off the light beside the pencil sketch. "When you git to be my age, the mind starts to wander. Don't pay no attention to me. Or no bobnot nonsense neither. I could of said mister cloots or scratch. It wouldn't make no difference. In hills like these, folks needs their spooks and horn gods chasing after em or they cain't get out of bed of a morning. It's all boo smoke. Keeps their minds off all the sickness and half-nekked Lychs what plagues these hills."

Bull Hannah stepped into his office and closed the door before Kes could ask him anymore fool questions.

"Lychs?" Kes asked the closed door.

That night, in the middle of Bull Hannah's packed Gladiola Lounge, in the middle of the first verse of *Life's Railway To Heaven*, Kes heard her harmony seeping in again—coming out of the spectral ether, finding passage through the brother's voices.

Life is like a mountain railroad
With an engineer that's brave—

Hovering out there, over glistening eyes, in a listening darkness, her ghostly vibrato returned. Sister began *barking* from behind the door of Bull Hannah's office at the other end of the hall from the stage. His tenor rising, Kes saw Bull smile and look toward his office door. Sister barked some more in there. Bull served up two mugs of beer and did not seem upset about her barking. He took it in stride, a tad amused.

Kestrel Brass was not amused. Kes was vexed, haunted, grim as a defiled grave. Glenn Brass kept plucking his mandolin and singing, eyes squeezed and lost in song. Kes held on, held on, held on, and sang along.

There was more fighting that night during the show. Two fights, in fact. Fortunately, Kes did not partake in either of them. Sheriff Bull settled both fights with a wood mallet he kept under the bar and that was that. The Brothers Brass even got to keep their pay for a change. But Kes could see how all this nastiness was taking its toll on Glenn. As usual, Glenn did not complain when they bedded down once more in the Cadillac with Sister in the rear floorboard for the night. Glenn even had a little taste—and allowed Kes three pulls on the bottle—so they both might sleep. Kes knew Glenn slept poorly in the *car*, though they had often slept there lately, for lack of funds. Besides, there were no hotels or lodgings to be had around here and Sheriff Bull couldn't be expected to haul every string band and brother act home with him.

"I'll be by, check your pulse in the morning afore you go," Bull told them.

"Forgive us if we're long gone," Glenn said. "We got over three hunert miles to clock tomorrow."

"I copy that," Bull Hannah said, getting in his police sedan.

Glenn watched Hannah's headlights rake onto the moonlit highway, his headlights soon blotted by hills and trees. No, Glenn did not complain. At least he had a car to sleep in.

But Kes could tell his brother was feeling the strain. Just as Kes felt the strains of a gingermint harmony in his ears, reverberating as he lay in the back seat alongside Sister, longing for a dreamless sleep that eluded Kes night after night—nights when morning sat at the wrong end of a long tunnel.

But morning did arrive at last. Breakfast was crackers and cheese and aching joints at crack of dawn. Sheriff Bull had sacked up the first two, out of kindness, before locking up and leaving.

Glenn had slept little and Kes not at all. Kes was wide awake.

"I could do with coffee black," Glenn said, carving off a cheese wedge with Kes's stiletto.

"That, my little brer, is a given," Kes said, stomping his foot into a boot on gravel. He sat sideways behind the steering wheel, all four Cadillac doors open wide. "We'll git you gassed up first chance."

Seated sideways in the passenger door, his back to Kes, Glenn spat stale cracker into the gravel betwixt his own feet. He was thinking about Chalice warm in bed about now, the fresh talcum smell of her, the feel of her against his rod and staff. Her eager mouth on his. Glenn was tired of looking at his brother every sorry morning of his life.

"You ain't tired?" he asked.

"Naw, I ain't," Kes said so lowly that Glenn could barely hear him, then: "Sister. Git in the car."

In this first dim light of day, Sister looked like a white figment floating along the depthless treeline over there, at the edge of the parking lot. Winged things and skittering sounds of life had Sister on full alert to whatever lurked within those woods. Kes had been watching her white snoot and tail scout up and down the trees for a good half hour or more.

Kes chose not to tell Glenn about the one time he almost dozed off last night—only to awaken to the squeak of those two girls' faces against the window glass, looking in. They wore bonnets and their faces looked terrible, melted, eyes almost webbed shut. Kes sat up and saw them run off into those night woods over there. They ran off bare breasted and barefoot, wearing only long skirts and bonnets. Sister slept through it all, her white fur rising and falling steady in the floorboard. Kes was all but certain, now, in this pearly light of dawn, that those girls were just another delirium, like that new old harmony inside his head.

"Sister—" Kes called again.

This time Sister wheeled and ran back to car, leaping into the back seat. Kes fed Sister his crackers and cheese. She had eaten the last of the dog kibble the morning before. With Sister barely breakfasted, the brothers closed the doors on either side of her before sliding back into their front seats.

"Sure you're okay to drive?" Glenn asked, cranking down his window.

"Why wouldn't I be?" Kes said blankly, eyes ahead.

"You take one of your white cross pills?"

"Maybe."

Kes cranked the engine.

The truth was, Kes had not taken one of his uppers. He didn't need any upper right now. Driving back down the road toward Cayuga Ridge, there were too many things troubling his mind, keeping him too wide awake—things Kes did not want to explain to brother Glenn dozing in the seat beside him. Kes did not want to jaw about things he wanted to jaw with Bull Hannah about but never got the chance. Kes wanted to forget these new old harmonies he was hearing. His attic had bigger haunts, with little time for ruminations over that carnival flyer with all those carny attractions he saw on the wall when he tacked Bettilia's handbill on the wall beside it. *Hellzabub's Human Zoo.* Kes would not know how or where to begin to flesh out the hellish flock of memories flapping through his heart right now

So Kes tried to keep to himself as these hills wound around the tired Cadillac. Still, try as he might, some things would not keep.

"You hear what that Sheriff Bull said? About Lychs?"

"Did he say Lychs?" Glenn mumbled, eyes closed, arms crossed, his head pillowed against the passenger door. "Them pills make you think too much. Don't go south on me again."

Glenn was soon snoring. He was still snoring when Kes drove past a sign pointed up a side road. **<<Riddle Top.** The road it signified appeared to wind up that dark mountain that loomed above. **<<Riddle Top.**

Where had Kes heard of such a place before? Hadn't Sheriff Bull said something about Old Top? Could Old Top be Riddle Top? Kes wanted to know more. But, looking over at his brother snoozing against the glass, rocking with the rhythm of the road, Kes knew he didn't dare brook the subject. They had a revival booked in Roanoke tonight—one of the few church gigs they managed to book on this trip since word of Kes's wastrel ways and motel sink Bible burnings had swept through gospel circles. Then, after the revival tonight, they had four more shows booked next week in the Carolinas and North Georgia. The Brothers Brass needed that money, bad. And they needed every church date they could get if they were ever to get back in good graces on the gospel circuit. No, it would not bode well to pull a no-show on tonight's Roanoke revival. Kes had plenty of doubts at the moment, but none about that. If they missed this Roanoke gig, Brother Glenn would gig Kes with his own knife.

Knowing these things did not mean Kestrel Brass could get Lychs or topless girls in old-timey bonnets or that Riddle Top sign back there out of his head. They were still nagging at him as he steered his big sleeping white dog and sleeping brother through Cayuga Ridge then out the other side of that tiny mountain village. The blacktop road kept winding tighter and tighter as Kes prayed for descent. The deep ravines and mountainsides that flanked the road kept him edgy, fretting over things best forgotten. It felt like these mountains were edging in on him, eating at him.

A couple of miles outside Cayuga Ridge, with one hand steering the wheel, Kes leaned over quietly, reaching under the seat—under his brother's sleeping legs. Kes unscrewed the cap with his teeth then began nipping at the bottle as he drove. Parking it betwixt his seat and the door, out of sight from Glenn, Kes kept revisiting the bottle as he fought to tame his fevered brain.

Without the benefit of his white cross pills or a night's sleep, Kes must have been more tired than he first realized this morning.

It was not long before Kes's eyes and head got heavy. It was not long before the copper Cadillac careened off and over the ledge of the road. The car flipped twice on its way down the ravine before hitting bottom—landing upside down with a splash.

VERSE 36

Ain't No Brothers Brass No More

It was a miracle.

The wheels were still spinning at the sky when Kes pulled Glenn out of the passenger window, dragging his brother through the shallow water to the creek bank. When Kes had first come around, after the Cadillac tumbled, Sister was already splashing in the creek, barking and tugging at him through the driver window. Either Sister had been thrown clear during the crash or she had scrambled out as soon as the car landed on its roof.

Glenn did not cuss him. Kes appreciated that, at first. Once he came around and realized what had happened, Glenn was too stunned and determined to survive to indulge himself by cussing out his brother. Glenn had much to survive for and he knew cussing out Kestrel Brass would be a waste of good dirty words at this point.

They were both banged up pretty bad, but neither brother was cut much even though all the windows shattered when the car crunched upside down. This new world they emerged into seemed unreal. They began to move about numbly, like robot men, as Sister watched their mortal efforts. The first thing to do was take inventory. No words had to pass betwixt them for Glenn and Kes to know that. Wading in the ankle-deep glass and water, using Kes's cane, Glenn managed to pry open the car trunk. Inside, the news was not good. Their suitcases had exploded, filling the trunk with dirty laundry. But even all that unwashed cushioning had not been enough for their instruments. Only Glenn's Martin guitar survived. Kes's guitar and Glenn's mandolin were hard to even recognize—just splintered wood and steel strings, broken and unbroken.

Kes's cane was a godsend that day. With Kes's cane, Glenn snagged his wallet from the wet rubble inside the flattened cab, then—with the help of his cane and his brother—Kes managed to climb all the way out of the ravine, up to the road.

They all began to walk, two ragged men and an unruffled white dog—Kes limping with his cane, Glenn carrying his guitar case, Sister trailing after them, watching them. They walked in descent, in the direction of Ewe Springs. They said nothing. They saw no cars. So Glenn began to cry which made Kes start to cry too.

"Kes—" Glenn finally blurted, still walking. "I got a wife and a new baby. I got a sick mama who's had a stroke. They all need me. I got to be there for em because you ain't."

"I know," Kes said, tears coursing his cheeks, dripping on his torn shirt.

"I cain't go killing myself like you."

"I know."

"Even Daddy ain't what he used to be. Not since that day. Not since he seen what we all seen in that room of hers."

"I know he ain't. I cain't get what we seen outa my head neither. That's why, the dranking, it keeps Clootie away."

"Yeah. But he don't keep away. When you drank the way you drank, Cloot becomes you."

"I know, brer." Kes's head sagged, looking down at his shuffling feet and cane, looking at himself hobble this road like a cripple. "But I cain't stop thinking about her. I swear I cain't. She comes to me in dreams ever night. Like she's out there, somewheres. Like she needs me. And back there, what that Sheriff Bull said about Lychs and that old woman and little girl, and I seen a sign what said Riddle Top, while you was asleep. Maybe I never told you about what she said, about this place called Riddle Top. I'm sure that was the name—"

Glenn stopped walking and got angry.

"Goddam it, Kes. *Stop that.* Stop your wallering. Cain't you see how it is? Cain't you see?"

Kes stood staring back at him, blinking, scared.

"See what?"

"She's dead, goddam it. Bettilia is *dead.*"

Kes struck Glenn with his cane.

Sister *barked,* but Glenn was already punching back. Kes and Glenn fell into the dirt, punching, gouging, kneeing, both of them breathing hard, both voices locked together in desperate silence. Sister kept *barking* at them.

Then, as suddenly as their fight had started, they stopped. Both began to hear Sister's barking and came to their senses. Wiping away the tears and smears of dirt and blood, they both got back on their feet.

Kes had not taken three crooked steps before he had to say it.

"You don't know she's dead, brer," he said bitterly.

"Yes, I do."

"No, you don't. How could you know?"

Glenn stopped again, this time looking at his lost brother with eyes more gentle.

"I know because she loved you. She loved you. And if she was alive she wouldn't let you do this, be like this. She wouldn't have tolerated it in you. Jaybird. She wouldn't have flown off on her own. She would have come back or sent word or—*something*. That's how I know, brother. She's gone. For good."

"I don't know that I can accept that," Kes quivered, the tears coming again.

"You got to accept it. And there's something else I know—that all of us who loved her know."

"What?" Kes braced himself, wishing he hadn't asked.

"Whatever happened—whatever in the clear blue Jesus it was—it ain't her fault." Glenn finally caught his brother's weary eye for a moment and held it. "It ain't her fault."

Kes began to nod, slowly, when a truck honked behind them. A small flatbed truck loaded with melons and chickens pulled alongside, idling to a stop. The red-faced young farm wife smiled. Her plump husband smiled too, leaning against the wheel to see the brothers better.

"Y'all need any help?" the woman asked.

"Well, see," Glenn said, turning on his poker-faced charm, "we had a little spill with our sedan. I figure it's a total. No saving that paint job now."

"Yeah, we saw that flipped-over mess back up the road," the farmer said. "You lucky you ain't in pieces."

"Ain't we though," Glenn allowed.

"We're on down to Beaufort, for First Monday market day tomorry," the woman told them, her arm hanging out her window, stout fingers tapping the outside of her door as the wheels turned in her head. "If you don't mind the bugs, you're welcome to ride in back as far as Roanoke or Beaufort."

Glenn sized up the couple then sized up Kes. Kes offered no objection.

"That's real nice of you," Glenn told the woman with a dry smile before smiling past her at her husband. "We'd appreciate that."

Kes followed Glenn around to the back of the truck where he watched his brother slide his guitar case in betwixt two chicken cages.

"I won't be going with you," Kes said.

Glenn squared himself against Kes, genuinely surprised. "You ain't?"

"No. Besides, just like my guitar, your mandolin—this trip's a bust."

"Yeah, I reckon it is at that," Glenn said. "But we can work it out with everybody. Always have. When they hear about the Cadillac they'll understand."

"No, they won't. They'll know it was me. And they'll

be right."

"But, what about the Brothers Brass?"

Kes looked his brother steady in the eye.

"Ain't no Brothers Brass no more. They's just me. They's just you. And your wife and your baby. You're right. They need you. And leaving you be is the best gift I can give em."

The truck horn honked, the farmer revved his motor impatiently. Glenn saw the farmer looking back anxious in the side mirror. Glenn bought a few moments with a nod and thumbs up at the mirror. Quickly, he took out his wallet, counted out the bills, then handed half the cash to Kes.

"That's one hunert twenty-two dollars. That's half. Without no guitar you're gonna need it."

"Thanks."

"Is there anything else I can do, brother?" Glenn asked. "Anything I can do for you?"

"Yeah, there is. Gimme that gun of yours."

Glenn had no time to hesitate. He unlatched the guitar case, reached in, then slipped Kes the gun without letting the farmer in the mirror see.

"I'll try to get it back to you. Someday, maybe," Kes said, leaning on his cane, pocketing the gun in his coat.

Glenn climbed onto the truck bed as it was pulling away, giving his big brother a thousand yard stare.

"Goodbye, Kestrel."

"Goodbye, little brer," Kes said loud, watching Glenn and the truck rumble off down around the curve. "Tell Mama and Daddy I love em. Always love em."

Kes stood rooted in the middle of the road for a long

time, trying to think of the next right thing, the sound of the truck fading. After the truck was well gone, Kes pivoted on his cane then started back toward Cayuga Ridge with Sister walking beside him.

VERSE 37

Magpies Ascending

"She ain't nowheres for ye to be."

These words kept circling his head like magpies as Kes and Sister started up the Riddle Top road, the road up the dark mountain.

The asphalt played out and gave way to a steep grade threading up through thicket, trees, and scouring leaves. It felt too late in the day—later than it should—like evening tide was already brooding in, blowing Kes's way. His hip was a hellish grind but he wanted to save his last few pills. His pains would creep on him, they would fester, they would grow. Kes knew. Later, he would need his ruby red pain-killers to give him sanctuary. So he abided his dread, his agony, leaning into his cane, working his cane up the road into a rising hot tempest of black and thrashing treetops.

Sister trod steady at Kes's crooked heel.

"Sis, did you know magpies don't migrate? Most spend their lives winging it within ten mile of where they's hatched? That is true. I read it in a book."

Kes had not gone this long without a drink of spirits in

over three years. His body was starting to remind him of that, reprimanding him for his neglect. His body wanted its spirits.

"And a magpie will carol all night."

By the time Kes had climbed a half mile or more his chest had a strap of fire across it. And he had still seen no sign of a shack or hut or any mossy old women.

It was Sunday so the country store in Cayuga Ridge had been closed. Everybody was in church. Without any real plan, Kes, his cane, and his dog, were headed out the highway—heading back toward Bull's Gladiola Lounge—when two large middle-aged sisters in men's khaki chugged by on a tractor pulling a hay wagon. They offered, he accepted, Kes and Sister hopped up on the hay wagon. The strawberry blonde sister hopped from the back of the tractor onto the wagon with Sister and Kes to keep them company. The dark-haired sister steered the diesel beast toward Bull's Gladiola.

The wide strawberry blonde did not say much at first. She spread out on the hay bales, petting on Sister and smiling a lot. The tractor roar and wind were too loud to hear very well or make easy conversation. Kes heard her say something about hauling hay to the carnival livestock. Kes wanted to ask if it was the carnival that featured Hellzabub's Human Zoo. But he did not ask. He did not need to. How many carnivals could there be in these hollows at any one time? Kes finally took the leap and asked if she knew an old woman named Nimzly or Ninzly or some elder like that.

"The darky? The Piney Woman?" she asked loud above windy racket, brushing a spider mite off her collar.

"I suppose," Kes said, wondering if the other sister—the tractor driver—could hear any of this. "Some kind of root doctor?"

The blonde sister nodded without color, betraying nothing. It was a mask, Kes was sure of it.

"That's her," she said finally.

I hear she lives up near some whatnot called *Old Top*? Where's that?

"Can't rightly say. Ain't never visited that Piney Woman. I only know she ain't nowheres for ye to be."

"No?"

"How'd your perty suit git so tore up?" she asked.

She obviously did not want to discuss Piney Women or Old Top so Kes was forced to let it go. He told her about the upended Cadillac. That seemed to amuse her. The urge to ask more questions began pulling at Kes again as the hay wagon chugged past the **Riddle Top>>** sign. The dark haired sister steering the tractor cut her eyes back at the blonde sister on the wagon. The blonde sister looked away, glanced up at the mountain, then quickly looked away again. But Sister—Sister did not look away. Sister raised her head fast as they passed the sign and the turnoff. Kes heard Sister's D Sharp whine keening over the rumble of wind. The Riddle Top turnoff was soon behind them. Eventually, Sister dropped her chin back down on the hay betwixt her big white paws.

Kes was glad to see Bull Hannah's patrol car parked

outside his roadhouse. The two wide girls in khaki dropped the stranger and his white dog in the parking lot, told him he was welcome, then chugged away. Kes was already knocking at the roadhouse door.

When Bull Hannah finally opened the door he was quite different from the night before and not in a good mood. He grouched some about balancing ledgers on Sundays. Hannah's mood turned blacker when he heard Kes's first questions, the questions this picker had come back to ask. Sheriff Bull finally slammed the door in Kes's face. Kes heard the deadbolt slide inside, hearing it lock with a last muffled protest from the Sheriff in there—telling Kes to leave that nigger woman be.

Kes wondered if Bull Hannah would care—or care to know—how much nigger man there was in Kestrel Brass. Kes doubted the Sheriff would care much. Kes wasn't so special in that regard. Not here or anywhere. Kes was beyond feeling that kind of sting anymore. Wasn't he? Hell, by standards of the day, Kes had it easy and knew it. Hell, some might even say he was passing. Kes also knew he had long stopped passing for anything that mattered. He couldn't even pass for present, accounted for, or sober on his best day.

Back home, Saint Peter tried to help Kes dry out more than once. At one point Saint Peter even drove Kes secretly to a sanitarium for folks in Kes's condition, so word wouldn't get around. Even Daddy Brass and Mama George didn't know about Kes's side trip with Saint Peter. Kes left that snake pit the next morning, discharged himself and got no good out of the visit. By then, Kes and Glenn had taken to oft calling him Uncle Peter. Not uncle like an Uncle Tom. Uncle like an uncle uncle. Uncle Saint Peter was a good man and, as it turned out, the Brothers Brass warmed to his presence. He was a great help to Glenn after their mama went into decline.

But even his Uncle Saint Pete with all his warmth and mercy could not save or help Kestrel Brass now—not here on this bent mountain road counting these magpies when this was nowheres to be.

"One brings sorrow, two bring joy, three bring girl, four bring a boy. Five bring want, six bring gold. Seven bring secrets never to be told. Ever hear that one, Sis?" Kes asked. "You ain't? I'm surprised at you."

Sister looked up at Kes as she padded quietly alongside, listening and panting, saying little herself. Sister was used to Kes's deranged gibber. She took her Kes in stride, just as she took in stride this ghostly gloam which now befell this Riddle Top. No, she did not break stride, but even Sister knew there was nothing Holy Ghost about this place. Still climbing, climbing—Kestel felt less and less certain of his next move, whether it be righteous or wrong or all that was left him.

"Eight bring wishing," he groaned, breathing hard, "and nine bring kissing—"

Kes had no water, no food, no bourbon. His mouth was dry. He was sweating profusely, his feet sloshing in his boots. Salt burned his eyes, making this harder in such dimming light.

"Ten bring a bird your own heart's missing..."

His body shook, shivered, climbed. The magpie and other nightbred wings kept shrieking. All the while, Kes kept thinking darker things. Yes, this quest was in flurried disorder and mental chaos, the stuff of a boy with bad blood. That's what Kes kept thinking. What we gonna do? That's what he kept thinking, thinking.

"What we gonna do, we even find this old piney woman?" he asked Sister, he asked his poking cane.

Kestrel and Sister were passing beneath a rocky crag when they heard the first *gggrrrrrrrrrrrrrrrrr.*

Sister did not bark.

Sister stopped. She looked up. She backed up two steps—then she began *growling* back.

Kes raised his salty eyes.

What he saw was not good.

Grrrrrrrrrrrr.

A big, lanky, bad-looking hound with pointed ears stood overhead, a stone's throw above them. The hound's paws clumped at the edge of the wooded crag, as if that mottle-skinned hound might jump them any moment.

Grrrreeerrrrrrrr.

Sister's eyes gleamed up into the dark hound's eyes, their growling throats joined in fearsome, tenuous duet.

Then Kes saw red. He saw reddish splintered light in the woods behind the hound. In the black depth, just inside that treeline, Kes could see what looked like a red railroad lamp shifting, moving within the pines. He glimpsed a man's face, the edge of a lantern jaw, but only a glimpse.

The red sliver of a face stopped just inside the trees. Whoever it was, he did not emerge, could not to be fully seen.

"Judah—ho now," a guttural voice spake.

Looming over them, growling down at Kes and Sister, the behemoth hound hesitated. Kes had never seen hate in the eye of any beast. But he saw hate in that hound's eye.

"Judah."

The hound withdrew slow at first from the edge of the crag, then wheeled and bounded back into the high dark wood. Faint rustling trailed the red light as it began to decay, swallowed by those pines up there. Kes saw a last fleet reflection of red splinter deep inside the trees, splintering into nothing—then it was gone.

Kes and Sister were alone again in the dark. Or so it would seem.

Christamighty, Kes could hear his insides rattle. *Who and what* went there? Were there more, waiting to pounce, waiting hereabouts? Unnerved, Kes felt suddenly weak, naked, his body revolting against him. Yes, this was a bone-rattling failure of nerve, failure Kes had come this far to find. He was ashamed for Sister to see this.

Kestrel turned. Kestrel started back down the road—back, from whence he came. Sister trailed after him. Sister was reluctant. She followed slow, well behind as Kes stumbled and faltered.

Soon Kes knew. It was too dark to go on. He could hardly see. He was bound to take a spill with his cane on this rough grade in such brackish light. Kes did not fancy leaving the road or being without some open space, some zone of safety around him. So, despite the aggressive onset of spasms, Kes gathered dead limbs and tinder from the embankment and built a fire in the middle of the narrow roadbed. He wasn't worried about blocking traffic. Not on this nightwinged road. He had seen none. He had seen no recent wheel ruts or tracks of any kind on his way up.

As the fire crackled, Kes curled in its cold warmth, his body in anarchy, withdrawing from all the poisons he'd been feeding it for so long. His arms and legs jerked, jerked *hard* at random, out of his control. He kept shivering, sweating. All the while, through most of the night, as Kes worsened his big hearted white dog worked in a circle around him, facing off against the trees, barking from time to time. If she were not here, everywhere, Kes knew he would surely die. Ever alert, Sister padded and pawed the edge of a perimeter of her own making, barking at steady interval, sounding warning to those woods, to cloven hooves, to whoever might dare come near. Stay away.

One brings sorrow, two bring joy—

Kes kept singing those same sounds over and over.

One brings sorrow, two bring joy—

It was a very old song. Yes, Kes was shiveringly surprised that Sister did not know it.

In the earliest morning hours, well before daybreak, the dark wind began to settle and Kes began to feel a bit better.

"Sister, please come here," he said, his eyes lost in the coals of the fire.

He coaxed her to his side. Sister lay down, at last, beside Kes. She was weary and soon asleep. They must have passed an hour like that, Kes holding Sister in the fire's fading glow. Then Kes heard the clinking, the clanking.

The last of his shivers and shaking stopped. He lay there frozen, eyes wide.

The clanking grew louder, with a shuffling coming down the road toward him, coming from the last vestiges of night. Sister kept sleeping, unaware.

Into the remains of firelight came a grey creature, a man in a long rough coat and railman's cap, with clanking bottles and tin cans hanging on wire and string from his hunched neck and shoulders. Under his tattered cap, the man's face was a horror. A mass of melted flesh, charred, long wrinkles ingrown the length of his long face. There were no eyebrows, no eyelash left. Kes knew the moment he saw this melted man—this was Ephran Lych.

And, seeing this creature clearly now, conjuring up that name, Kes suddenly felt no fear of this Lych. Kes felt only sorrow for him. One is for sorrow.

Ephran Lych lingered a moment, his tall body clinking softly at the rim of the light. This Lych seemed to barely register Kes's existence or the fire or the sleeping white dog.

"Bobnot," the Lych spake in low dead voice, barely-heard, "bobnot."

Kes kept waiting for their eyes to meet—Kes's eyes and Ephran Lych's eyes—but they never met. Still staring at the ground, Ephran Lych finally shuffled on out of the light, on down the road, taking his sad clink and clank with him.

Stranger still, after a night of standing sentry, Sister slept through this entire Lych interlude. For all his thoughts on it later, Kes would never understand the unearthly how of that. Yes, Sister slept through Lychs.

Another hour passed and then some before the sky began to brighten. Sister was awake by then, Kes knew she must be hungry. Yet Sister seemed hesitant to leave. She kept glancing up the road, higher up the road.. Kes felt bad that he had nothing to feed her. If only that damn country store had been run by money-hungry pagan idolators who kept Sunday hours. It did no good to wish for such things, but wish he did. Eight bring wishing.

Kes pitched red pills in the coals, kicked dirt over the fire, then the two started back down the road, retracing their steps from the day before. Sister trailed behind. Kes's mind was still slithering about, lost. He yearned for wisdom, for lessons learned. For this bristle-backed mountain was nowheres for ye. Was it?

At this moment Kes only knew one thing. He wanted to find Sister some breakfast.

They had not gone far in their descent, not even a quarter mile, when Kes saw the smoke and the door. First he saw smoke trickling from the sod overhead, drifting up out of the earth atop a low bluff—a bluff choked with roots and rock.

Then he saw the small door inset in a cave-like hollow

beneath it.

It was not hard to see how he had missed the leather-hinged door the day before. He must have climbed the road right past it, adrift in his own fever and suffering. Without any tell-tale smoke, without looking at the door head-on to see it, this door would be easy to pass unseen. Even Sister had shown no notice of this place upon passing—or none Kes was aware of at the time.

After his wrenching and restless night—after his encounter with Ephran Lych—Kes was feeling strangely unafraid. He felt curious, weary, perplexed—but unafraid. Sister pressed close against Kes's leg as he caned his way under the awning off roots. Kes knocked softly on the low arched door.

Shortly, Kes heard movement within the earth, from behind the door. Then he heard a latch. Then the door swung inward and open.

There, inside, stood a bent old black woman.

It was Mambly Whissler.

VERSE 38

Is Dark, Is Red

"They's some herb and a powder in this tea. Ought help ye with that bone shaking that ails ye," she said. Her arthritic hand stirred a blackened tin can nestled in the coals of her tiny fireplace.

Kes's spoon scraped bottom on his second bowl of corn mush. Corn mush had never tasted so good, even though he'd never tasted corn mush.

"Thank you, ma'am," he said, wiping his mouth with his coat sleeve.

Kes set down his empty bowl on the crude table. He watched Sister, beside the door, devouring the pile of potato skins and animal offal dumped on the dirt floor for her. Kes did not care to ponder what kind of animal innards those were, but Sister seemed to enjoy them. The scent of those fresh guts mingled with the earthy smells that filled the dugout room—oddly smells to Kestrel's nose. With no window and only the scant fire for light, it was like a cave in here. Once again, Kes took stock of the shelves of clay urns and murky bell jars, the dried roots and the milkweed, jimson, and sassafras hanging from the low ceiling—so low that when Kes stood his head would brush through them if he didn't stoop down like the old woman tending that hot can of tea. Once again he gaped at her resemblance.

"I woulda swored you was Mambly Whissler," he repeated.

"Yez, we used to git that, when we was baby twins. I oft wondered what come of Mambly. Now I knows. One be sorrow, two be joy."

Kes couldn't believe his ears. Did he really hear this Piney Woman wheeze out those words?

"Funny thing," he stammered. "Mambly said she used to sing that."

"That be true. That'n we sung together."

"Your name is Ninzly then?"

"That it be. Them days, o'course, I were Young Ninzly. Now I be Elda Ninzly."

Squatted over the flame in her long dress, whatever this Ninzly was waiting for finally transpired inside the tin can on the coals. With a pair of pliers she lifted the hot can and poured its tea into another tin can then brought that can to Kes. Ninzly sat on a three-legged stool on the other side of the table. The red pockets of her rheumy black eyes peered into him. Kes had already told her what brought him here. Or most of it.

"Drink yer drink afore it gits too cool," she croaked, her gaze falling on an unlit tallow candle betwixt them on the table. "It'll work ye best while it be warmly that way."

"Thank you, Mizz Ninzly."

Kes sipped the brew in the tin can. It was nasty stuff.

He did not let on or allow his feelings about this nasty stuff show. Kes was not raised that way. He kept sipping it, looking at the two other tin can cups over there, together on her fireside bench. The two cups this Ninzly snatched off this table quick as he came inside.

"You best be heading back to your people after ye had your fill," she said weakly. "This ain't nowheres for ye to be."

"That's what the big woman on the hay wagon told me."

"She were right."

"Y'all don't understand. I think Bettilia might be here. Somewheres."

Kes could never be sure, but he thought he saw Ninzly bristle slightly at the mention of Bettilia's name, like an icy breeze blew across her leathery brown skin. Knowing Ninzly was Mambly's twin made Kes think maybe Bettilia had not told him the whole truth or the whole story of how she made her way to Mambly's door in that farflung pasture, outside Newdundy, a thousand school days ago.

"You sure you don't know her?" he pressed. "Ain't seen her hereabouts?"

"I told ye. No."

"She's tiny. Real small."

"No."

"She's pretty."

"You'll get over your heartbreak, son. Or find a place to keep the heartbreak off ye, in time. That is, you will do if you can go without going back to drankin'. These hills, they's full of drankin'. That drankin', it seem like it makes them pains go away. It do for awhile, I reckon. But it's really watering em and making em grow. Like them heart pains is being watered with wine."

"My brother, Glenn, he says it turns me devil. Turns me into Clootie, he says."

"Maybe, a little. But you ain't really no Cloots. I know me a Cloot or two. And you ain't one."

"It's the not knowing that kills me," Kes said, then finished the dregs of the strange tea in his can. He spit bits of loose leaf back into the can then rested it on the table. "For her to just disappear like that. Like she was a pale vapor that just blew away that day."

"Hit might not seem so. But some things it's best not knowing."

"I know something or somebody had to of got her. She wouldn't have just run away—or run off on her own. Not like that. Not without letting on to me."

"Mr. Kestrel," Ninzly spake slowly, weighing her thoughts. "Ye ever stop to think maybe that sweet gal was trying to protect ye? Trying to save ye from something? Or somebody? Trying to save you and yourn?"

"Save us from what? Who?"

"Din't you say she seen things that day? Weren't they things you say she seen you din't know till later?"

Sister had stopped eating, she now sat watching Kes. All the offal was gone. Sister sat terribly still, staring back at Kes's terrorized eyes in the firelight.

"No, we didn't know till later. They was this big man named Bugga. He was a big black man. Black like you and me."

"Like me—and you?"

"She must of found him in her room, like we found him. Somebody left big Bugga laying dead on Bettilia's tiny bed."

"Dead?"

"Yes. But that weren't the worst of it."

"It nary is."

"Bugga, well—Bugga's big hands was gone. His hands was chopped off."

"His hands?"

"Yes'm. Bugga kept telling her she was safe. You in Bugga's hands, he'd say."

"Anything else carved off him?"

"No. She left her gold slippers is all."

"You figger your gal took his hands? To keep her safe?"

"Of course not."

That thought had never crossed Kes's mind in all these years. What an insane old woman this was. He was beginning to want out of her hidy hole here. But where would he go if he were to leave her right this moment? Which way would he turn? Kes decided to go for broke.

"Mizz Ninzly?"

"Yez?"

"What's a bobnot?"

This time there was no mistaking it. Ninzly's crooked fingers splayed out, both hands pressing against the table. Kes had struck a chord.

"Where you hyear about bobnot?" she whispered slowly, her eyes galvanized, riven upon her own hands.

"Your sister, Mambly, she told me that's the first word

she ever heard Bettilia say when she was a little girl. Then that Sheriff Hannah, he said it. Then, in the wee hours this morning, a burnt-looking, melted-looking man come by me in the road. I think he was a fellow Bettilia told me about. I saw some burnt-looking young girls like him the night before outside Sheriff Hannah's roadhouse. I think they was what Bettilia called *Lychs*—"

Ninzly gave Kes a hard appraisal. She seemed more cautious of him, more measured, like she did not trust what Kes had brought in here to her table.

"Yez. We got Lychs lurking around these parts. They cain't help what they is. Leave em be."

"Well, this Lych who come by me last night, this morning, if he was the one—Bettilia said he always rode a mule hung with scrap tin cans and bottles."

"Ephran Lych."

"Only last night, all that scrap was hanging off of *him*. It was all wired and strung to his body. Like somebody strung him with that jangled mess. He didn't have no mule."

"Ephran Lych always rides him a mule—"

"Well, he didn't have him one last night, Mizz Ninzly. And, that Lych, he only said one thing when he passed. Bobnot. He said bobnot."

"Well—"

"Sister never waked up, and Sister always wakes up when anybody comes near. But she never waked up when that Lych come by saying bobnot. And they was another man—"

"Another—?"

"Yes. Me and Sister, before that, last night about nightfall, we saw a man in the wood who had a big damn dog. Biggest damn motley dog you ever did see."

"Judah."

Elda Ninzly looked numb, almost dead herself.

"Yeah, I think that's what he called out to him. Judah. I couldn't get a good look at the man before he disappeared with his red lamp."

"Were his arms scarred up? Scarred tattoo arms like he tried to carve them tattoos away?"

"I don't know. Like I said, I couldn't see him too good before he disappeared. Took his Judah dog with him."

"Well, son, there ye go. That be he. There's your answer."

Ninzly looked a tad relieved, like a secret burden had lifted from her sloped shoulders.

"What you mean? Who be he?"

"That man you seen. He's your bob not. Boogery Old Bob Knott some calls him. Bob Nottingham."

"Bob Nottingham?"

"Yez. Now, son, I'm gonna ask ye not to say his name no more in hyere. It don't do to say his name too much in hyere."

Kes swallowed deep.

"Yes, ma'am. I'll try not to."

"If I was you, son, I wouldn't say that name nowheres else around hyere neither. Heed my words. He's why this Riddle Top ain't nowheres to be."

"No, ma'am. I mean—yes, ma'am. I'll try to heed em." Kes skidded his tea can back and forth on the table top, afraid to ask the next needed question. "Ninzly? Is he Bettilia's daddy?"

"I couldn't say."

"But, she said, her daddy's dead."

"Maybe he is, maybe he ain't."

"I don't understand."

"Some say, whatever he is, that Bob has always been hyere in these hills, always been up hyere on Riddle Top. Some say he's almost human. Some even say he's a horn god."

"A horn god?"

"Shhhhsh."

"A horn god. Is that bad?"

"He ain't good, he ain't bad. He is. That's all. I doubt he feels much about it. He's a soul reaper. He harvests folks. Some he keeps, some he throws back. Your man back there—the big man with his hands carved off? That's the kind of thing Old Bob Knott would do."

"Ain't you scared of him? Living on this mountain with him?"

"Oh, he don't fool too much with *old* womens, like me, living all the way down hyere. I ain't fresh enough for him. He likes young'uns and children. The fresher the better. He takes em. Some say, was a time, he even skint black babies. And what's his is his."

"His?"

"That red lamp he carries? He took a shine to that lamp. A young railroad jasper was found smoked and quartered, wrapped in newspaper. It's said that railman tried to help a girl he seen. A girl up the mountain."

"A girl?"

"They's nights in these hills, you can still hyear that railman's screaming, locked inside your smokehouse."

"My god."

"Brer Bob, he kept that red lamp. He made Ephran Lych wear that rail jasper's cap. To keep Ephran reminded."

"Right there on his head? All the time?"

"Your god, he cain't help ye hyere, son. Him, that Bob, he don't answer to none of them gods down there. He be his own. That's why folks, well—some folks—they still comes to me for the old roots, or when they needs some goofer dust, or a spell, or they got a mouth cancer. I'll mend an ox or a magpie wing. Some folks around hyere, they don't fancy no chrome doctors like that Nursy Jane in the town. So they comes to me for the old ways. But they never comes too far up this Riddle Top where he roosts and dwells mostly. They's got danger enough back home nights in they own beds. They comes just far enough up hyere to get what they needs from me, only by light of day, then they goes. That's 'cause they knows. This ain't nowheres to be."

"My mama never told about none of this," Kes said, boggled by all Ninzly just planted in his own guts and offal. He watched Sister sniffing at those two cans together on the fireside bench.

Ninzly gave a soft cackle.

"I doubt ye mama knowed. Or, maybe she did. And that's why she din't tell ye. Or maybe she told ye but you weren't listening. Son, I think you best go now. Now ye been foretold."

"Yes, ma'am," he agreed, hurriedly rising from the table.

Forgetting the nature of the place, Kes found his head engulfed in the hanging roots and herbs. He ducked back down as Ninzly led him to her dwarfed door. He stepped outside with Sister then looked back to thank the old woman.

But Ninzly already had her door half closed.

"Mambly—" she was saying in a quivery tone.

"Yes? Mambly?"

"That Bob Knott, he set his eye on Mambly, he did. Took a shine to her. That's why she had to run. Don't ye see?"

"Yes," Kes said, wanting to understand. She seemed to beg his understanding. "I reckon I do."

"You go home, Mr. Kestrel. You been foretold. You go home. Where folks don't know you's black as me, black as all us be."

"Am I supposed to wear a sign? An I-ain't-lily-white sign?"

"Brer Bob, he ain't one to care. All our hearts in the dust is dark, is red."

"Yes, ma'am. But, ma'am?"

"Yez?"

"Bettilia said she dropped a rail spike on his head. Said she kilt him dead."

"Did she?"

The door creaked shut. He heard her latch it from inside. That's when Kes noticed for the first time: Ninzly's door had no outside knob or handle.

As Kes caned his way back out into the road—Sister at his heel—he kept thinking about all the strangeness this

Ninzly had told him. He wondered how much was true, how much was old wife women boo smoke and gossip. Wasn't that what Bull Hannah called it? Kes wondered if Ninzly really knew nothing of Bettilia. Taking a few steps downhill under the canopy of pines, Kes wondered if the best thing to do wasn't exactly what Ninzly warned him to do. Maybe he should go home now. Kes's feet and cane began to move down the road.

But Sister did not follow.

Sister still stood in the middle of the road outside Ninzly's door. The great white dog stood staring up the road, ignoring Kes as he hobbled away, descending this mountain. Kes was well aware of Sister, yes, he was well aware of she.

Kes took a few more steps downhill, well aware and forewarned. Then he stopped. He pivoted on his cane. He started climbing back up the road, climbing Riddle Top. As he climbed past Sister—she fell in step with him, walking beside him, the two together.

"Seven bring secrets never to be told..." he began.

Soon the old woman's hovel was far below them and behind.

VERSE 39

Nowheres for Ye to Be

Kes heard screaming. The rain was glaring, it fell hot in the bright burning sun without a cloud in the sky. Moving out of the hot rain into deep woods, Kes heard short cries—cries which led to longer tails of screaming.

He could feel little of the rain's sting now. Little of anything penetrated the thick green canopy overhead. The death hanging behind him gave Kes dread of what he might find ahead. In here, in these woods, it smelled of rotting fruit, festering rind and vegetation, in a fetid heat so brutal it seemed to muffle and dampen the screaming Kes heard hanging on this thick air.

He and Sister descended to the rain-splattering creek, what there was of it. Kes doubted these fat raindrops would last long enough to help this boiling little creek much. The creek was pitiful, a trickle in a deep creek bed that had obviously seen much flooding in longer, colder, rainier seasons. Kes and Sister leapt across the bright sizzling trickle, heading upward and deeper into the trees again. Kes was glad, he supposed, for these thick tall pines that helped them keep less damp. But, as Kes and Sister moved toward those high-pitched, almost inhuman wails which sounded so dire in their pain—he was beginning to wish he had never left the odd comfort of the road. Even in here, in these trees, things were about to get worse.

In mournful bass harmony, a lowing began, joining with those screams in sickly call and response, moan and scream.

What a terrible day this was.

Still weakened by his night spent shaking and jerking, withdrawing from the demons in his flesh, Kes had begun his long climb up Riddle Top this morning with little strength to sustain him. It was not a hot rain then. Not yet. It was not hot rain in the sunlight.

Somehow, Kes found reserves within himself as he pushed up the mountain from Ninzly's door. And the higher Kes and Sister climbed the hotter and hotter it got. Crackling hot. The primitive road was sometimes hardly visible beneath the overgrown grass. Faint ruts curled out over chasms of treetops below, then burrowed back into suffocating stands of timber where little moved save the flies and other insects, where little was heard except the insects and unseen birds.

Unsure of what he was looking for, Kes avoided certain side spurs and paths that left the main grass-clotted artery. He saw no reason to pursue them and was often carried along by Sister's instinct as she led him past those side trips and detours without apparent concern. The pain of his hip and the thump of his cane worked in tandem as

Kes dripped sweat—sweat he was surprised he still had. He was thirsty, so awful thirsty. He wanted to take off his suit coat but did not want to carry it or leave it. So his clothes soon plastered to his skin, soaking, his feet sloshing in his boots again. He tried to distract himself from the struggle, trying to factor how far they had come as they went. Had they come three miles winding in and around this mountain? Could they have climbed four or even five miles now? Yet still no shacks, no houses?

This game gave way to a kind of delirium that no longer cared about *how far*. Kes didn't even know why or what for anymore. How far became the least of his concerns.

"Ten bring a bird your own heart's missing..." he despaired to Sister, "*missing...*"

Much of the way, Sister kept her head down, the fur fringe of her tail lazing back and forth before Kes like a white rudder moving up a rut river of grass, moving back and forth slow as the morning eked away, as the sun scorched higher into the sky. Kes was inclined to pity her, thinking Sister must be suffering terribly in this heat under her cotton-white coat.

But, to Sister, all suffering seemed to be his, Kes's, not hers.

"Eleven bring health, twelve bring wealth..."

Sister was unbothered.

"Thirteen, beware, brings the devil hisself."

The rotting flesh found their noses before they saw it.

Certainly, Sister must have smelled it first. Once it was upon them, the smell was the kind Kes wanted to retreat from without ever seeing the origin of this putrid blanket in air that did not move. The pines were chokingly tight along this cut of road but Kes could barely see a white sandy side road just ahead, two ruts of mountain sand catching the glint of sun.

For the first time, Sister left the main trail. Her nostrils flexed again and again as her senses led her up the sandy side road, Sister's head lifting, seeing.

The moment Kes saw what Sister saw, Kes knew it was Ephran Lych's mule. There was no doubt in Kestrel's mind although Kes had never seen the mule alive.

The long hooved carcass hung heavy from a high pine bow. It hung on a long strand of barbed wire. The wire had been wound twice around the poor mule's neck then twisted into a barbaric noose. Thick flies had already set upon her blackening hide. She had once been grey, a day or so ago—or so Kes supposed. Her shiny black tail and hind hooves dangled only a foot, maybe two, off the sandy ruts.

Mixed with the stench came a heavy undercoat of something burning—a burned tar smell that did none of this any good.

Sister slowed, approaching the two fly-infested hooves with caution while Kes threw up his corn mush in the grass. Sister looked back at him for a moment, seeing the mushy slobber heaving from Kes's lips. Then Sister pointed her snoot upward, looking past the four dangling legs to the mule's blasted eye sockets and longears against the hot sky. High up there, with barbed wire cranked under her jaw, the chin of Lych's mule hung open, her long yellow teeth screaming silently at the heavens.

Then Kes and Sister heard the faint scrape of a real scream. It came and it went. It came from somewhere far ahead, up this strand of sandy road. Both of them heard it. Both of them looked when they heard.

Sister moved on past the hanging mule, up the road. Kes wiped his sour mouth with his sleeve and followed. He gave the stinking, sad, hanging thing a wide birth as he passed.

Several yards farther, the road bent a bit and they came to the remains of a bridge over a deep creek bed. The bridge's creosote-soaked timbers were still smoking. Someone had burned it. It had been a short bridge, no more than twenty or thirty feet across. Now only smoking stumps and a few blackened timbers jutted from each side of the span, reeking an oily smell that was relief from that rotting mule behind them. Outside of a war, why would you burn a bridge? Kes knew what his daddy would say. Daddy Brass would say there were only two reasons to burn a bridge. To stop somebody coming. Or to stop somebody from getting away.

Then, as if to quell Kes's creosote thoughts, without thunder or word one the white and cloudless sky began pelting hot rain.

("*Aaaaeeeeh.*")

There was that far off scream again.

Once more, it came scraping into Kes and Sister's ears, leaving them little choice. They entered the trees that flanked the burned bridge, descending the wooded embankment to the dry sandy creek bottom. After leaping the trickle, Kes spat and blew flies from his lips as he followed Sister up through the dense misting wood toward that terrible sound on this terrible day.

There was a clearing ahead. By the time they reached it, the screams no longer rasped out at them. Stopping short of the well of sunlight, just inside the pines, Kes sank down hugging his cane, pressed against Sister's fur.

Out there, in bright rainfall under uncloudy sky, a twisted barn sagged off to Kes's right. Centered in the clearing was a primitive house with rock chimney and a stagnant pond. Beyond the house and a dead elm stood an upright, coffin-sized smokehouse in a clog of iron drums and rusting junk. The house itself was rough log, porched on three sides, steps slumping up the front. All windows and the front door were wide open, orifices as blasted and empty as that dead mule's eye sockets. This house did not look abandoned, no. Kes wished it did. That bottomless moaning came from inside there. The moan was not constant. The moan would tremble from those open windows, that door. The moan would go for a spell—then stop—then start up moaning again.

From where he crouched, Kes spied chairs inside one long window's frame, a blue wooden pull toy on the side porch beside a couple of old truck batteries. Yet, that house stood unbearably still, too still out in all that wet glare.

Aaaaeeeeeeeeeee.

There it went again. Another short scream, piercing the day. The scream cut through the rain.

It did not come from the house. It came from that sagging, twisted barn.

Sister had not barked, not yet. Kes was relieved that she had not. Sister seemed as cautious as he. Together, they crept inside the treeline, toward the barn. But, before they could get very close, they froze. Kes ducked his head, pulling Sister's head down with him.

A man in gray factory work clothes emerged into the hot deluge. Kes could not see the man's face clearly. The man hung his head, thumbing the blade of the harrow tooth in his hand. Even in this thick rainfall Kes could tell there was something odd about the man's forearms. His hobnail boots clicked up the steps, then clicked inside the house through the gaping front door.

Moments later Kes heard another scream—then the moaning—both from inside the house this time. Or he thought he did. They were muffled sounds, dampened by this bright sunlit torrent. The house stopped screaming. The mournful moan from the house stopped again too.

Kes realized he might not get a second shot at the contents of that twisted barn any time soon. Inside the trees, Kes and Sister moved closer, the barn's tin roof a drumroll in the rain, snaring louder upon approach. Kes said nothing to Sister. He leaned his cane against a tree trunk and left it.

Throwing a last glance at the house, Kes dashed out into the bright downpour. He felt exposed by the sunlight but tamped his fears and bore the pain of his hip as he skipped quickly over to the parted door of the barn, slipping inside the twisted hulk. Sister stayed back in the trees, watching that barn swallow Kes.

Inside the barn drum was sudden dark, rumbling, sweltering, a dull red glow leaking from the far end. Kes stood a moment while his eyes made sense of the scant light. The barn smelled of mildewing straw and motor oil. There were dim red tools hung on the wall to Kes's left. He ventured farther into the belly, leaving the door sliver of sunlight. Kes did not know what he expected, what he was looking for. Did he hope to find someone helpless but breathing in here? A heartbeat, a whimper? Or did he hope not? His foot brushed the edge of a saddle and blanket lying in a heap. He could see the snipped bits of string and wire glinting red where they still hung from the saddle horn and harness rings, wires once attached to glass bottles and tinbits, no doubt. Ahead of Kes, three livestock stalls lined into a rear corner of the barn. The last stall—the stall at the back of the barn—that was the stall that glowed red. Kes was creeping closer to it, to see, when he heard bootfalls splat in puddles outside.

Kes sidestepped fast into the first stall, out of sight. The man reentered the barn. Kes dared not breath, his heart pounding, hoping this man could also not see well in such sudden darkness—just as Kes could not see well coming in from the bright outside. Kes pressed back into the shadows of his hiding place as the man's shape went past him, headed for that reddish glow back there—back in the last stall of the barn.

The *screaming* began again, loud.

Kes flinched, but in the same reflex realized how—up close, in here—it didn't sound so much like a scream anymore.

The sound stopped. Then started. Then stopped.

Kes detected a soft, rhythmic creaking, rasping, behind the screech, a steady whir. No, these were not screams at all.

What made Kes do what Kes did next? He would never be sure. But, everything he had ever been and done in this life felt like prelude to this moment. Quietly, Kes emerged from his hiding place. He moved toward the glow. As he approached that last beastly stall he began to see more clearly.

In there, by red lamplight, the man sat peddling a grinding wheel—hunched over a sharpening wheel—his back to Kes.

The sweat-stained back of the man's work shirt, the cords of his muscled, tattoo-scarred arms, moved with the rasping rhythm of the wheel. His head was bent forward, Kes could not see it. The man's meaty hands held a harrow blade to the grinding wheel as he pedaled, giving the harrow a fresh gleaming edge.

No more than a penny pitch from the grinding man, Kes was betrayed. It was Kes's bad hip that betrayed him once again, causing his foot to rake the floor, disturb the rhythm.

The man heard this. The man rose from grinder, harrow tooth in hand. The man turned to see.

But it was Kes who saw most.

The tall, heavyset man's face had deep cavernous eyes, a raftered brow, widow's peak, a lantern jaw.

He also had a spike through his skull.

Even in the barn darkness, by dull red ember, Kes could clearly see where the rail spike's flattened head had rusted at the top of the man's skull—the spike's head nested like an iron mushroom in the black backswept hair. The spike had shot down into his brain, entering at a sharp angle southbound behind his right eye. The spike's tip exited downward beneath his left cheekbone, sticking out of his upper lip, at the far left corner of his mouth like an extra fang of iron. The man's right eye looked slightly skewed, yet it twitched at Kes like it could still see him.

Kes took another step.

Kes spake the words.

"Are you Bob Nottingham?"

The man began to simmer in the murking heat—nay, he almost glimmered red under the pummel of tin rain. The voice came deep, like late thunder.

"Who wants Bob Nottingham?" the man asked.

And Kes knew. Of course he was he.

"I am Kestrel Brass."

VERSE 40

Bobnot

"Do I know me a Kestrel Brass?"

"I believe you do."

Overhead, the tin roof got louder as Bob Nottingham stepped away from the grinder, backlit now by the red lamp-light. Still, Kes could see the flint of Nottingham's eyes.

"Where you be from, Kestrel Brass?"

"Far from here. By the sea."

"Uh-huh. I remember now." The deep voice had its own rasp, almost metallic, like his throat vibrating with the spike through his brain. "You out of that big house. Down by that sea."

"Yes, our house is big."

"Big house. Big pile of a place."

"Yes."

"Piled with porches. Built like a wedding cake."

"I believe you've seen it."

"You the one went messing with her."

"Bettilia?"

"Bettilia? She ain't no Bettilia. She's just Button

around hyere."

"Button?"

"My Button."

Kes could not help it. He could not keep his eyes off that spike through Bob Nottingham's skull.

"How can you live like that?" Kes had to ask.

"Oh, this iron?" Nottingham's eyes rolled up, trying to look through the top of his skull. "Button done this. Dropped it on me. From high a tree. High, high a tree."

"Does it hurt?"

Those eyes rolled back down, one ahead of the other, a bit annoyed at such suggestion.

"Me? Hurt? I don't mind it so much."

"How can you not mind it?" Kes asked, incredulous.

"My friends, they say they seen change in my personality."

"You have *friends*?"

"They say I'm sweeter than before."

"Mr. Nottingham? How sweet was you *before*?"

"So, Button, I really got her to thank."

Over the rumble of the rain the mournful moaning sounded again outside. Kes threw fretful eyes toward house.

"What's that sound?" he asked, on guard.

"Hard to say," Nottingham said like he had rust in his head. "Judah prob'ly."

"Judah?"

"Judah. Dog."

"Your dog?"

"Ain't nobody's dog. Judah runs with me. When he so chooses."

The moan strangled, stopped.

"Where is she?"

"Who she?"

"Bettilia. Button. Whoever. Where is she?"

"You ain't knowing?"

"No. I do not."

"Well, I ain't so sure where she be. And you, you ain't meant to be at all. But I ain't got no truck with you now."

"You ain't?"

"Not no more. Now she's left ye. Now that you left her be."

"She wasn't took? You didn't take her?"

"Naw, she left ye. Left ye good. Now ain't that right, Kestrel Brass?"

"Ain't nothing right about it."

"You best be glad she did. Else you wouldn't be here. You wouldn't be nowhere—"

"And what does that mean?"

"—Not you or none of that sorry shitting bunch what birthed ye."

"Do you hurt people, Mr. Nottingham?"

"Me? Who told you things like that?"

"Bettilia. Other folks."

"Button and me—we always got along fine. I give her things. She give back. I even give her one them song players. Victrola. Went 'round and 'round. Don't you know? I'm plumb gentle. With Button."

"Then why did she drop that—that *thing* on you?"

"Whut, whut, why, whut, where, yez, whut, no, no, don't do it—" the man uttered, stuttered, eyes rolling back, his brain a stuck needle on a Victrola, then: "Who know why? You'd have to ask her. Now wouldn't ye?"

Something wrong and restless in him made this Bob Nottingham move. Kes cleared a way, limping backward as Nottingham moved past him now, toward the wall of tools and cutting implements.

"Where is she?"

"I ain't knowing where she be neither," Nottingham told, his back flexing as a tattoo-tortured arm reached up toward the hanging tools. "She might be around here somewheres. Ain't likely though. Not no more it ain't."

The back of Nottingham's head tilted toward Kes as the man looked up, giving Kes a direct view of the spike's head, nested like a crusty jewel in Nottingham's black hair. Kes watched the red-hued forearm shift upward—riddled with hairy snatches of scar amid a butchered maze of blue tattoos. Nottingham's hand brushed across the hanging tools.

"You nailbrain trash," Kes spat suddenly, "if you ain't knowing. Who is?"

Kes hated hearing himself use this man's rhythms, this man's gist of words. He also didn't give a damn anymore.

"You kiss your mama with that mouth?" the back of the man's head asked with no real concern.

"If you ain't knowing, who—"

"Hard to say. But I ain't seen her. Ain't seen that tail in quite a while."

Nottingham found what would serve him. He took an axe from the wall, turned for the barn door.

"I want my wife back, Bob Nottingham."

Nottingham stopped, ratcheting his head toward Kes with a bit of difficulty A terrible grin crept across Nottingham's face. The extra iron fang under his left cheekbone punctuated the grin, not so nicely.

"Your *wife*? Boy, I been walking these hills, these woods. Many's the night I been looking for my Button. Looked everwhere. Even down to the sea."

"And you expect me to believe—"

"I ain't never expected *nobody* to believe *nothing*," Bob spake quick, without grin. "You make me sound like your notions of a human critter's *god* or something. I don't never expect. Never."

"You cain't keep me back. I aim to find her. I aim to take her."

"You got your work cut out," Nottingham said, then went out into the white hot rain. "I oughta know."

Kes followed him into sunlight. Nottingham walked easy in the glare, like slow swinging beef, unfazed by the heavy rainfall. But he did not walk toward the house, no. With axe and harrow tooth in hand, Nottingham lumbered straight for the edge of the woods—straight for the spot where Kes had left Sister back in there, just inside those pines.

Kes limped after him, trying to keep up.

"She told me tales about you—" Kes shouted at Nottingham's rippling back.

"Juicy ones, I hope. Button was always juicy."

Nottingham entered the trees, disappearing.

"I thought she didn't talk when she was little—" Kes chided after him.

“She did not,” the man’s voice said in there. “Not when she was little.”

By the time Kes caught up to him again, Nottingham was standing square in front of Sister inside the misting wood.

Sister stood, four paws planted, her muzzle damp, looking up at the man. Sister did not growl or whimper or take her eyes off him. There was no wag or life in her sogged tail. Nottingham stared back down at Sister, like he expected to find her here.

Kes slowed, twisted tight as a sawbones’ tourniquet. He ached to yank Glenn’s gun out, kill this man, now. But Kes had this girl he feared was hurting or gone to dust. This girl he was supposed to have, hold, keep. Yes, brother Glenn was right, it was likely she was no more but if Kes killed Nottingham here, now, Kes would never know and Kes could never let go.

“She *never* talked?”

“Not much, she din’t. And she’s still a little’un I reckon. Gitting smaller ever day.”

“What’s that mean? I reckon it means you know what’s come of her.”

“Yes, nigger, and you reckon wrong. You reckon dead and you reckon wrong.”

Bob Nottingham showed nothing, eyes dull. He watched Kes unlean his cane from the tree then lean himself on the cane. Nottingham took note, but his spiked brain was elsewhere. He spake to himself, with peculiar nostalgia:

“She always hid from me. In them trees...”

“Who hanged that mule back up the road? *You?”*

"They's a mule hanged up the road?"

"You know there is."

"How high that mule be hung?"

"You tell *me*. Enlighten us, *Bob*."

"I am unaware of this. This troubles me. I got bidness to tend. Then I'll give her a gander."

"That Lych didn't hang his own mule."

"Might of done," Bob mused, "I told him not to do it. But he don't never listen to nobody. He disappoints."

"I don't know how you done it, but I hope you put a decent bullet in that poor thing first."

"Decency? I never shot nothing in my life. I don't like guns."

The strangled *moaning* came again.

Kes looked in time to see the big mottled hound trot out the house's front door, squelching and moaning low in his throat. Judah stopped at the porch's brink. Judah quit moaning. Judah stood, black eyes staring through walls of rain toward these woods where Kes and Sister stood with Nottingham.

Kes jabbed his cane at the house.

"Why are all them doors and windows open up there like that?"

"Aw, I got to air it sometimes. Needs to breathe."

Nottingham moved to leave, dragging his dullard's gaze off Sister.

"This your house, Nottingham?"

Nottingham turned back. His right eye twitched upward. With the harrow tooth he flicked a wet fallen leaf off the head of his rail spike. The eye twitched back at Kes, the left eye followed a split-second later. He seemed grievously amused.

"Whose house would it be?"

Nottingham's eye twitched toward the house, at Judah, then back down at Sister. Then he ratcheted himself around, taking leave of them all, taking his cutting tools with him.

"Who is in that goddam house?" Kes demanded.

"See for yourself."

Kes and Sister watched Nottingham stride off through the depths of the rain-misted forest, toward the creek and road and hanged mule.

"Judah—" the bull voice echoed as he went.

Judah shot off the porch of the house. The clumping paws scrambled through the pines until the mighty Judah reached Nottingham. Together, they both disappeared into thistle and pine.

Whipping around, Kes caned his way to the edge of the clearing. That house sat wide open, waiting. Kes flew out into the rain, moving faster, faster toward the house, his hair and clothes plastered to him by sweat and scorching downpour.

Kes's cane hit the house's bottom step—*Judah shot out the front door* to the top of the porch—barking thunder, growling, eyes ablaze.

Sister barked, leaping from the trees, into the rain—barreling toward Kes—toward Judah.

"Sister—*no,*" Kes yelped back, plenty shaken but the

flat of his hand out to stop her.

Sister stopped. She watched, ready to charge again, as Kes kept stumbling backward.

With Judah still growling from the porch, Kes retreated through the rain, Kes returned to Sister. Had they not stood and watched Judah heel when Bob Nottingham commanded? Had that man and hound not gone off together? And there was only one Judah. Kes had no doubts about that. There was only one Judah. Yes, Kes just might have to kill that brute—after he killed Bob Nottingham. Yes, Kes decided, then and there, it was time to make Bob Nottingham talk him—*really* talk to him—so Kes could get on with the killing.

Kes charged back into the woods, taking out Glenn's pistol as he went. Gun in hand, Sister keeping pace, Kes caned his way through trees and thicket, chasing down his torment, gunning for his tormentor.

"Nottingham—" he yelled, hobbling fast.

The hot rain began to ease, tapering off as Kes and Sister advanced through the woods. By the time they splashed across the steaming trickle of creek then back up the wooded bank, the rain had stopped. By the time they reached the road it was a mudstretch of rising steam. Looking both ways, neither Nottingham or hound—or the hound's damned doppelganger—were anywhere to be seen.

Lych's mule still hung by barbed wire down the road, dangled there in steaming vapors, the mule's carcass dripping in the sun. The high pine bough the bloated corpse hung from seemed to sag worse under the rain-soaked burden,

Then a sunglint caught Kes's eyes. Something new had been left there in the road, under the mule.

Kes and Sister went to see. As they drew near, Kes saw the speckled glint of hobnails. Sister held back, keeping her distance. Kes did not.

The mule's two hind hooves hung directly above a pair of boots. The boots were hobnail boots. The boots were upside down, with two feet and legs in them, sticking straight up out of the ground. The mule's hooves dripped rainwater onto the hobnails, the water slithering down the pant legs, puddling on the ground around two kneecaps.

"Nottingham?" Kes asked the boots, the legs.

Kes stepped closer, gun in hand, testing each new link in this chain of aberrations. But Kes was losing interest and patience with such inhuman oddities. Why, if Kes didn't know better, he might think Nottingham took a deep dive into this road, from high, high up a tree—trying to dive back into the hell from whence he come from. Yes, it looked like this putrid road had sucked Boogery Bob up, swallowing him to his knees.

Kes bent, balancing on his cane handle, his face studying those riveted thick soles. With his pistol barrel, Kes tapped one of the hobnails.

The boot didn't like that. The boot *moved*, flexed, flicked away the pistol.

Kes leapt up and back, eyes wide. Sister barked a warning to the boots. Magpies began to chatter.

Magpies from above.

Kes's unhinged eyes floated up from those upended

boots—up the mule's carcass, as the magpies chattered louder—up to the mule's wire-noosed head screaming silent at the sky. Only, now, the tips of those long mule ears were golden, shining in the sun.

Kes stumbled back farther, arching his neck to see what all this chatter was about—

High up there, the dead mule's long ears now wore Bettilia's golden wedding slippers.

Kes's knees began to buckle—

Her golden wedding slippers. And, hanging over those slippers, the tree hosted hundreds of chattering magpies.

"Shuddup, shuddup—"

Back, Kes stumbled, falling flat on his back in the mud, the gun firing a shot. *BLAM.*

"Shudduuuuuuuuup—" he cried at the magpies.

Her slippers gleamed hot and gold up there. *BLAM*—Kes fired again into the air. But the magpie tree kept chattering, taunting him.

A squeeze-doll pain blew out of Kes's throat as he twisted away from the gleaming, stinking fetish—this fly-blown altar. Kes flipped onto his belly, losing gun and cane, burying his face in the slime,

Sister *whimpered* and kept *whimpering* as her Kes tried to claw his way into the earth, into mudbound oblivion.

The sound of heavy footfalls on timber hit Kes and Sister's ears at the same time. Kes stopped clawing, he looked up. Sister spun around, her white paws ankle-deep in the muck.

Bob Nottingham was up the road, crossing that bridge.

Judah was already across the bridge, loping away. Nottingham's boots clicked across the timbers of the burned bridge that was now there again—the bridge back intact, spanning over the creek, reeking smoke into the miasma of steam.

Kes threw a mud-faced backward glance. The two hobnail boots were still stuck in the earth beneath the mule, the magpies still chattered and chittered, and Kes knew if he looked up he would still see her golden slippers. So he did not look up. Instead his eyes came back around, boring into that hateful figure of something like a man crossing that bridge. Kes shouted loud so Nottingham could hear.

"What you done?"

In the distance, Nottingham paused, turned, unmoved by one more bit of insignificance named Kestrel Brass, sniveling back there in that mud.

"What's that boy?" Bob echoed.

"What you done—to her?"

"She's dead," Bob said, a little shrug, a little smile. "Must be. You ain't got her. Now I ain't got her. She outfoxed us both. Didn't she, brer?"

Nottingham turned away, continuing over the bridge.

From behind Kes and Sister came a chorus, a chatterbox hosannah. In a whirlwind of flapping wings, the great tiding of magpies swept out of the tree, flapped fast up the road, disappearing in a black flume over Nottingham's head, over Nottingham crossing that smoking bridge.

With cane and gun, Kes scrambled to his feet. His cane slipped. He fell again, face down in mud again. Sister could only watch him and wait, coiled to go forth. Kes ached back up onto his feet and hurried after that spike-headed specter.

"Nottingham—" Kes screamed, bandying the gun as he reached the bridge's black smoking timbers and began choking on the smoke.

His cane clattered onto the bridge, starting across.

But there was no bridge, no more, never was. And Kes was gone.

VERSE 41

Angel's Prey

"Open ye eyes. Your time is come," Elda Ninzly said.

Kes opened his eyes.

Here was Ninzly squatted alongside him by the trickle of creek, her grizzled black face leaning over him, peering into him. The hot wind was risen, dark was falling.

Kes's mouth hung open, parched, thirsty. His lips worked at the air, trying to draw breath from it as he lay there, trying to focus on Elda Ninzly and the deep purpling sky above her. Somewhere in the faraway, Sister barked.

Ninzly's gnarled fingers lay a button of toadstool on Kes's tongue.

"Swaller this," she told him. "Hit'll help carry ye."

"What is it?"

"You ask too many questions, *j*-jaybird," Ninzly said.

"Yeah. Yeah, I do," Kes heaved, words coming like great stones he had to lift from his chest. "I know I do. Always have."

"He's *cl*-*cl*-close. Nearly here," she spake into his eyes. "And you be *t*-too close for too long."

"Ninzly, I'm—I'm glad you're here. I'm glad you come to me."

"I aint hyere. Not really. I'm inside ye, but I ain't hyere. I'm in that tea ye drank, that tea I give ye thiz mawnin."

"I'm glad you did."

"It's time for you to know hit—"

"Know? Know what?"

"For ye to know what become of her, so ye can go on with the living."

"Yes, Ninzly. Please. What come of her?"

"Bear southly through the wood—the wood betwixt here and that house. You'll see. Bear southly. You'll know. Then leave this mountain."

"What will I see? And what about all them others? Them he's hurt and will hurt?"

"You should have stayed away from him, like I told ye. Brer Bob, he don't keep giving ye no second chances. He'll say things, do things, he don't really give a hoot about. He goes after whatever's in ye that will git ye."

"But—but I had to find him. To find her. And here is where he is."

"Brer Bob, he ain't just hyere. Thought you knowed that by now, boy. Brer Bob, he everwhere."

"He is? Everwhere?"

"He nests up here is all. Roosts up here. Then he go out into the world. They ain't a child who don't know him."

"But, when Bettilia first told me about him—"

Ninzly scowled fierce in a way that stopped Kes's fool jabber. Her long dress ruffling, Ninzly forced her face down into his until he could smell the tobacco-stained ages of her ancient breath.

"She din't first tell ye. You knowed Bob Knott all your life. Ever child has. She put another name to him, that's all. And even then, it's just one name. They's lots of gods with lots of names. They come. Go. Some dawdles around too long, long past they day. But they's *always* been Bob Nottingham."

They's always been Bob Nottingham.

They's always been Bob Nottingham.

They's always been Bob Nottingham, she said.

And his hurt will forever be, she said.

Bear southly.

Kes opened his eyes again.

He was breathing hard, his arms and gimp leg muscles straining. He was climbing the roots and rocks up from the creek as he had climbed so often before. If it was torture he was unaware. Sister was up there—looking down at him, panting, waiting for him at the top of the burnt bridge.

It was nighttime. And the hot wind blew crazy.

Kes took the woods, he and Sister, moving quickly but southerly of where they had passed through these trees before. Elda Ninzly was right, had been right all along.

The bit of graveyard was not hard to find, even by hot moonlight through wild pines. There were eight graves in the moonlit clearing, some long, some small. Most of the graves were marked by stacked stones. A couple had rotting shards of wood where a headstone would go. Lych graves, most likely.

And there was a ninth grave. Small enough to be a child's grave.

Sister's throat moaned high and sad when she saw it. A wooden stake was driven into the earth at the head of the tiny grave. A yellowing shred of Schiffli lace was tied around half a pullybone—tacked together into that wooden stake.

Kestrel fell slow to his knees before this grave, hers, and wept for all the world. Elda Ninzly had foretold, yes, he wept. Ninzly knew all along. He wept. Kes knew he should have listened but, being a songbird, listening did not come easy to him. Kes forced his swollen eyes open, to see the pullybone and Schiffli lace again—to see Sister's soft chin flat upon her grave—Kes saw as all moonlight suddenly faded, taken from him, stolen like she was stolen. That hot moon went out like a thumb smudged it from the night sky.

The woods were pitch black as Kestrel Brass crashed through and into the trees. He followed the white figment of Sister moving fast through the forest ahead of him. Kes began to slash at the trees ahead of him with his cane, feeling his way blind at times. All around him, the towering pines of this mountain thrashed in the wind, dead falling limbs crashing to the ground around him.

He could smell the tar smoke. Then he smelled the woodsmoke.

When Kes finally stepped into the clearing he saw the flickering hulk of the twisted barn. Then he looked up at the house and he saw her. There she stood blazing bright in this night.

It was Angelsprey.

No, Angelsprey was not resting on the faraway seashore, no. Angelsprey House stood in this clearing, alongside this twisted barn on this damned mountain, where a split-log house once stood. And all of Angelsprey's windows and doors were open wide with light, her porches all aglow.

Kes and Sister climbed the front steps. They went in the open portico door.

There, sitting at a crude wooden table in his mother's parlor, sat the wide-eyed, dead-eyed corpse of Zeebub, the human zookeeper. Zeebub sat beside the table in a ladderback chair. Zeebub's entire lower lip had been slit off. Zeebub's legs were missing, cut off at the knees, both legs gone—gone along with Zeebub's missing hobnail boots. Missing and off stuck in the mud, no doubt. On the wall above Zeebub was scrawled: **THeR WaY Of ALL FLeSH**.

In the dining room, alongside the broken crystal on the floor, Kes found his mother. Given time, his mind would blessedly destroy all memory of the things that had been done to her.

By the time Kes stepped into the kitchen, it was the lamplit kitchen of an old split-log house. On the plank floor of that kitchen were the flesh remnants of a bare-breasted Lych mother in a long skirt lying beside two Lych girls—the bare breasted girls wore bonnets like those girls who peered through the glass of a copper and black Cadillac so many long mornings ago. These Lych girls had been violated, slowly violated, in ways Kes's brain could only beg to devour and purge in time, whilst knowing their dark residue would ever linger. There was no way of telling anymore if these were the same Lych girls, not after all that had been done to them. But there was one thing Kes could tell. One of these butchered Lych girls—she wore patchwork bits torn from Bettilia's wedding gown. Yes, Ninzly was right. Kestrel Brass had been foretold. But Kes would not listen.

Kes stumbled out the back door of the split-log house, down the creaking steps, watched over by Sister sharp at his heels.

Out in the yard, beyond the dead elm tree, Bob Nottingham was stepping out of the smokehouse. He left the smokehouse door open, night wind whipping away the gray billows. As Kes approached, Nottingham tossed something into a nearby burn barrel. Flames flickered high from the fifty-gallon drum. The fire danced on Nottingham's face, danced on the spike driven behind that fearsome face. His cavernous eyes lit up when he saw Kes coming. He picked up an old truck battery from an upended drum and began pouring the cloudy acid from it into a mason jar.

"What would you say," Nottingham said, "if I was to tell ye that I can spy a thief, a spoiler, a whoremonger when they's just babies in the cradle?"

"I'd say I come to put an end to you, Bob Nottingham." Kes kept coming.

"Didja now? How unkindly." Nottingham watched his jar as he poured, spilling a bit. The spilt acid bubbled away the rust, eating into the iron barrel. "But who's gonna snatch them babies and save em when they call out for me come the night?"

Judah came out growling from behind the billowing smokehouse. The dark and giant-boned hound began advancing on Kes and Sister.

Kes and Sister stopped coming, stood in place, alert.

"Ho, Judah," Nottingham rumbled.

Judah stopped advancing. Setting down the battery, Nottingham picked up the mason jar, moving easily, dreadfully toward Kes. Bad Judah fell into step with him.

"I can also spy a fool who cain't hold onto his baby brother's shoot-em-up when he needs it," Nottingham said. "Now what kind of little cowpoke is that?"

Revelation struck behind Kes's eyes. Wildly his hand ransacked his coat pockets. The gun was not there.

In grim amusement, Nottingham raised the jar to his lips, sipping the acid, swallowing.

"Why you think baby brother left his shoot-em-up hung there on that tree?" he asked.

That's when Kes saw the gun.

The pistol was hanging upended betwixt Kes and Bob, dangling on a low-hooked limb of dead elm.

Kes began to move slowly toward the dead elm limb, toward the gun. So did Nottingham, his jar, his hellhound.

Kes knew this Bob now well enough to know—the gun was likely empty. But Kes had to try.

"You'll kill for what you love?" this Bob was saying. "You think loving it gives you rights to it? Killing rights? Kill if you must. But don't never kill for love. Love might leave ye, run out on ye. But dead is done for good."

Nearing the elm tree and dangling gun, Kes finally

spake again.

"There's a house full of dead folks behind me."

"They is?" Nottingham asked, coming to a standstill, the gun and tree limb dangling in front of his face. He sipped some more battery acid from the jar. "I am unaware of this. I got bidness to tend. Then I'll give her a gander."

Nottingham and Kes stood to face to face, both within reach of the pistol, Judah growling soft, low, but ever growling.

Nottingham fingered the spike tip under his left cheekbone for a moment, mulling this conundrum, looking down at Sister. Sister was coiled, but calmly, her eyes fixed on the man, her eyes never wavering.

Nottingham saluted with a tip of his mason jar, arching an eyebrow at Kes.

"Have a little taste?"

Kes shook his head with a slow no.

"No?" Nottingham said, dryly. "Too bad. It's a good year. Delco 1949. They don't age em like that no more, do they?"

Kes said nothing, seething.

"Don't wanna get one too young, do we?" Nottingham asked, shaking his spike a little at this stubborn little cuss. He took another taste. "Cain't believe you'd pass on good spirits like this. But that's a nigger for ye."

"Nottingham?"

"What you want, boy?"

"*I* just got one question for *you*."

"Shoot."

"Have you accepted The Lord Jesus Christ as your personal savior?"

The man's headspike tipped back. His grin cracked wider.

"Naw," Nottingham chortled low. "But that's a good goddam question. Now *ain't it?*"

Kes's hand came up with the stiletto knife. Kes's thumb pushed button, the blade shot out.

Judah *growled.*

Sister *growled.*

Judah *lunged* at Kes.

A white dervish, *Sister sprang* for Judah's throat—sinking her teeth into the bad hound.

Nottingham grabbed the gun and shot Sister betwixt the eyes. Blood red exploded from her great white head, a whimper, she fell gone on the ground, a heap of snowy fur.

Sister's blood splattered Kes—

"BOB*GOTDAMNOTNOTNOT—*" he *screeched.*

Kes *flew* at Nottingham—

Nottingham flung the acid in Kes's face.

Searing fire curdled Kes's eyes as Kes *grabbed* Bob's railspike and started *slugging.* The last thing Kes's eyes ever saw was his left hand holding the top of Nottingham's head whilst Kes's right hand kept *slugging, slugging,* Nottingham's unfeeling, heavy-lidded stare faded into black abyss as Kes hit him again and again and again, punching blind, a death grip on that spike's head—

—until the pistol butt *smashed* into Kes's skull.

The hard iron hammered Kes's temple *once, twice, thrice.*

Kes lost his grip on the railspike, fell back, and was out of this world before he hit the ground.

VERSE 42

The Holy Oaks Beheld

Kes became dimly aware of hard hands dragging him up the rickety steps, across the porch, into the kitchen. His eyes and face felt like fire itself. His tongue burned. Some of the acid had made it into his mouth. Then he lost consciousness again.

He could never know how long he was out, but when Kes surfaced once more, he was still blind. His eyeballs were in curdled torment, about to pop from their sockets. Too weak to move, he felt like half his brain had been blotted, his motors cut. He could hear hobnail boots moving around the house. Clicking. Clicking. He smelled kerosene and heard it splashing the floor in other rooms, then here on this floor, in this room around him. Kes tried to speak, but his throat did not seem connected to his blotted brain. The fight in him, the hate in him, his black heart and spirit, was almost gone.

Faintly, Kes heard the whoosh of flame when the match was tossed. He heard those hobnail boots click down the steps, into the night.

All around Kes the flames crackled and popped, consuming the house. Kes knew his fitting end now. He would return to the ashes, to the dust, along with all these other human vessels, these freaks in these other rooms, in this burning zoo. Soon he would be forgotten, never to be found in the charred horrors of this mountain, this Riddle Top. Kes began choking on the smoke, fighting to breathe as his eyes and face stung from the acid and the encroaching hellfire. It was getting easier now, he was ready—he tried to breathe in the smoke and thrive upon it—ready to let go of this life thing, succumb to whatever hell or heaven or nothingness might have to offer. Kes only wished there had been one more night in that tiny house up that tree, but 'twas not to be. No, now that the smoke rolled over him like a strangling blanket, Kes quit trying, quit even wanting to see. His last thoughts were of his brother, Glenn. How would little brother ever forgive him?

Suddenly, in the smoke and heat of the room, Kes heard more clicking, fast clicking. Like claws clicking. Kes felt a wet nose, a tongue tasting him. Blindly, he reached up his hand. He felt the great head, the thick long fur.

It was Sister. And Sister was whimpering, biting into his collar, dragging him.

There was a moment, a reflexive moment, when Kes struggled *against* her. Then Kes began to rally, vaguely, to struggle *with* her. He did not question how Sister could have come to him, how she could still be alive. Still, even as she fought to tug him out the door—fought with all her great strength—Kes could feel the life oozing out of the big white dog, dripping off her nose, smearing his cheek with wetness.

Outside the house, free of fiery death, Sister kept going.

Kes could never know or calculate how far they went in that windstorm. It felt like an endless black thicket of briars and brambles tearing at Kes as he half crawled and half stumbled through the swirling woods, holding onto Sister as she weakened. It felt like long hours. But she kept on going, on through night forest unseen by Kes's blind eyes. Only the relentless pull of the dog kept Kestrel Brass half alert, among the living. He tried not to let his mind wander or dwell on what might be the next right thing or the next wrong thing that might be. Yet, all the while, he was grimly aware as his hand and Sister's fur became more and more soaked, her big heart pumping out of her.

Then, as suddenly as Sister had arrived in that fire, as suddenly as she had sniffed out his salvation, Sister collapsed against a great tree.

Kes fell against the tree alongside her. He tried to sit up, he tried. It was too troublesome so he slumped, lost in blackness, the wind and woods howling around him. He smelled his hand, he smelled Sister's blood. He could not see it. He could not see anything. But he knew it was blood, he knew the scent. He dropped his hand back down onto her, losing his fingers in her fur. Sister did not move anymore. She was spent.

So was Kestrel. He felt cold, so comfortably cold. His back began to slide from the tree trunk. He fell over, into white oblivion, oblivion at last, his face buried in Sister's wet and wind-ruffled fur. Buried here, he heard only white wind now, beckoning, white wind from a comforting and cold dark grave.

Then the strangest thing happened to Kestrel Brass.

There was this girl.

This girl, she dropped barefoot out of the tree. She landed barefoot alongside Kes.

This girl, Kes heard her, the soft thump when she hit the ground. Kes knew she was there, felt her there, beside him.

This girl, she pulled Kes up again, her hands holding him upright against the great oak. Then he tasted her lips as she kissed him. She kissed him and she tasted of gingermint tea. Later, Kes would remember that too. He was sure of it. Gingermint.

He knew little, remembered little, after that.

With no time to waste, she grabbed his collar with her left hand, the hand that wore the ring. She worked her right arm under his arms, around his chest, and began to move him, drag him. Kes had slipped into deep coma by then, or so it seemed. She was not sure, she could not tell.

She knew little these days. She only knew she had a long way to go, that this boy was in sad shape, skin and bones, but that made him easier to haul through this hainted wood. She only knew how she missed him, ached for him. She only knew he was a fool jaybird and would never learn.

Fortunately, she had always been strong for her size.

VERSE 43

Afterlife

Kes's journey in total darkness only began that night. There was little else he would recall in years to come, but he swore to one and all that he remembered a voice, no, two voices. One old, one young. Somewhere in his first hours or days of willer wisp abyss he remembered hearing Mambly's old voice or Ninzly's old voice. One of those two whispered, "We can tote him together."

The other voice he heard in his darkness was hers, forever hers.

Away, I'm bound away...

He wandered for ages in the black oak forest of his fevered brain. He even met some folks he knew there. All the while the sound of this girl's voice kept sifting in soft from unseen places around him.

Away, I'm bound away...

Then, the sound of a mandolin took up the tune and began to noodle around in that forest, off in depths of the trees. As he wandered over the ages, then days, then hours, that mandolin trilled closer and closer to him, circling him as he dwelt in the nocturne. A morning of the mind arrived, in time, when Kes could feel the bed beneath him, and hear the mandolin in the chair beside the bed. Kes tried to sing with the mandolin, in a soft croaking voice. The mandolin stopped.

"Kestrel? It's Glenn. Can you hear me?"

Yes, Kes could hear him. He could not see, he would never see again. But he could hear.

"You're at the clinic in Cayuga Ridge," Glenn confided. "Nursy Jane's been taking fine care of you. You look good."

"How *y*-you *g*-get here. How you *f*-find me?"

"Aw, I got back home and—Daddy Brass—he hands me his new El Dorado keys, his .357, and two thousand dollars. Tells me I better go drag my brer's ass back home else he'd do it hissself after they say the prayers over me."

Kes discovered that he had been wandering his black oaks, here in this bed, for over a week. An old woman named Ninzly had brought him to Nursy Jane's door in the middle of the night. He was fortunate enough to be in one of only two hospital beds the tiny clinic had, they said. Yes, he was fortunate, Kes agreed.

While they were waiting for the eye specialist to return from Roanoke for a follow up, Kes began to tell his brother everything, in torn bits and short pieces. Mostly, Glenn listened. After hearing the story a few times, Glenn expressed a smidge of skepticism. Kes got so agitated—banging his head against his headboard—Nursy Jane had to come in and help Glenn restrain him, lest he mess up his bandages or do more damage to himself.

"Go ask Elda Ninzly. She must of took me to Ninzly."

So, Glenn went looking for Elda Ninzly. He got Sheriff Bull Hannah to take him to her door. Having heard of Kes's journey to Nursy's clinic—and knowing Kes's current condition—the Sheriff was more agreeable than before, enough to brave the last of a summer storm and that unpaved Riddle Top road.

When Glenn returned to Kes's hospital bed, he did not come with news Kes wanted to hear.

"She says she don't know no Bettilia or Button or nobody like that," Glenn said, drumming his fingers on Kes's room window, gazing out at the climbing hills, that dark mountain out there. "She said you just showed up blind, half crazy, half gone already at her door, middle of the night. Said you must of stumbled there."

"I ain't believing it."

"That Elda Ninzly, she's a bent one alright. Weird. But she seemed righteous enough to me. She figures maybe Sister got you most of the way to her hut, then give out, or dragged herself off somewhere to die."

"I ain't believing it. Sister, she got me, she gave—well, Sister gave all her heart had in her. But she couldn't get me all the way down that mountain."

"That's what Ninzly said, Kes. You don't believe me—ask Sheriff Bull. He'll tell you."

The eye specialist finally arrived the next day and looked at Kes again. The damage to Kes's corneas was irreparable. There was little hope he would ever see again. Kes just sat there and took it. He was still back on that mountain, on that windy night, tasting a gingermint kiss.

He tried to pester, then badger Glenn into going back up and looking around the mountain some more. But Glenn wasn't game for any of that. Then Kes tried to guilt him.

"I see how it is," Kes said. "You got you a wife, kids. It's no more burden to you. You got them to think about."

"You living prick. You're lucky to be alive."

"Yeah, ain't I lucky though?"

"That Elda Ninzly told me she don't know nothing about no Bob Nottingham or none of them other folks you keep raving on about. Or Bettilia neither. She said maybe you got a bad lick to the head. Hell, brother, you said that old crone slipped you something in her witchy tea. Maybe you dreamt it all."

"It weren't no dream," Kes insisted. "It weren't no fucking dream."

He kept saying so in the car all the way back home.

Naturally, once Glenn got his brother back to the safety of Angelsprey House, his mother insisted he see a proper specialist in Savannah. Atlanta if need be. Despite the limitations Georgiana now suffered on the left side of her face and body, she was adamant. So Kes saw a specialist in Savannah. After that didn't pan out, Kes went to a specialist in Atlanta. Then another specialist in Atlanta.

Then Kes went home to sit on the front porch of Angelsprey, listening to the tide come in and go out. He sat there, listening, as summer turned to fall and the smell of burning leaves mingled with ocean air, nagging at his bitter memory.

He did not drink. He did not take pills. He did not want to see anybody. About the only person he could tolerate was Saint Peter who would come by, sit on the porch with Kes, and read out loud to him. Saint Peter would often read *The Gazette,* Jack London, even old songbooks. He kept his sermons short or not at all.

"Kes, only the untruthful claim to know more than this here, this now," Peter said once. "What you've been or done is no longer in question. The only question be, what will you make of this here, this now."

"Maybe you, Uncle Peter. Hell, you might be right, probably are. But I know one thing more than this here now."

"And what would that be, son?"

"I ain't telling."

At that, Saint Peter smiled, returning to his page. Mostly Kes liked the sound of Saint Peter's sonorous voice reading passages by a Mr. Cervantes and a Miss Nin. Uncle Pete got downright nervous sometimes, reading that Miss Nin. But Kes made him read her out loud anyway.

Chalice had her second baby. She and Glenn struggled with the usual young married couple woes. Money was always a problem. Her daddy let them live rent-free in one of his rental houses on the island. But Glenn still had to accept checks Daddy Brass pressed upon him, since Daddy knew those stray studio and backup musician gigs that came Glenn's way weren't going to keep anybody in diapers or chops.

Meanwhile, Kes sat around and poked around Angelsprey, bitching when he did speak and learning to use his cane for new purposes until Mama George was ready to warehouse him or forever banish him to that treehouse where he couldn't get down.

"I declare, poor Kestrel will unleash another stroke upon me," she said, in that lopsided but mind-your-peas way she spake these days.

After a particularly dreadful Christmas dinner with Kes on his worst behavior, Daddy Brass finally pulled Glenn aside and told him:

"He's gone Looney Tune. You better get that man back out there working that sumbitch of a road before he kills hisself and takes us all with him."

So, with surprisingly little push, Kes agreed to try playing shows again as the blind half of The Brothers Brass. He was bored and most of his outer scars had healed by then. He tested his voice. The acid had changed it. He could sing, hit all the notes, but he hit them with a touch of fine sandpaper. The Brothers Brass started playing around Savannah again, then began to branch out, accepting bookings farther afield as Kes got his rhythm rebooted in the ass. His hip still gave him hell, but he hardly noticed it anymore with fresher afflictions to focus on.

When he was back home at Angelsprey betwixt bookings, Kes tried to teach himself piano on the old upright in the parlor. Glenn told him he was lousy at it and he was. On occasion, to kill some time, Kes would take the bus downtown and shoot a few games of blindman's pool with his cane. Wolfie and the boys at Bo Peep's Pool Hall always got a big jocular out of that. The following Christmas, with

New Years on the horizon again, Daddy Brass asked Kes half-jokingly what he wanted for his birthday. Kes knew exactly what he wanted.

"A straight razor," he said without a smile.

"Straight razor? Why don't I get you another of my stiletto pig stickers?"

"Nope. I want me a barbershop-to-barroom straight razor."

"You sure that's a good idea?" Daddy Brass said in all seriousness, his smile waning.

"Yes sir, I want me a nice quiet razor. I wanna know I'm only here because I wanna be. I wanna know I can leave out of here anytime I wanna go. So I might as well wait around and see what happens next."

This unsettled Daddy a bit, he laughed a little queasy. But he bought Kes a gold-plated straight razor.

Not long after his birthday, in early February, Kes and Glenn were riding the train down to Mobile, Alabama on a particularly cold winter's day. They had ridden for a long time in silence as Glenn grew more and more pensive, looking out the glass at the bare trees clicking by. Something was weighing on his mind.

"Kestrel..." he began, at last.

"Yeah?" Kes pulled himself up straight in his seat. Train travel always made him dozy or lovey. One or the two. "What's going on with you, brer?"

"There's something I got to say. Something I ain't been square with you about."

"Oh?"

"Yeah. You know when you was back at that clinic in

Cayuga Ridge and I told you I went with the sheriff to see that Elda Ninzly?"

"Yeah, I remember." Kes began to pay attention, shifting in his seat. His dark glasses tilted at his brother.

"Well, I never told you this, but I never believed that Ninzly. Not really. I got this feeling she wasn't telling me true. I just knew in my bones, she knew more than she told when we asked what happened that night. She didn't want us there. But she played it cool. But she couldn't hide it, not all of it. That was one scared old woman. Maybe not scared for herself, but scared for somebody. And truth be, who knows how long she doctored you or kept you before you got to that Nurse's clinic. And Sheriff Bull, he kept telling me it would take two folks at least—to get you off that Riddle Top, to that Nursy Jane."

"No, you never told me about your doubtful bones. Thanks for the telling."

"Naw, brer. That's not what I have to tell you."

"Well?"

"Remember how you said it was raining hot and hard that day? That day all that hell happened with you? Well, it rained more the morning the Sheriff took me to talk at that old Ninzly. Sun come out while we was up there. Anyway, we said our goodbyes and, that old woman, she couldn't close her toadhole door on us fast enough. Then I seen something. There in the wet mud. Outside her door."

"What you see?"

"I seen little barefoot prints in the mud, from feet nearly small as a child."

A magpie chitter ran through Kes. He tried not to show it or shake.

"Another lost child come around, maybe..." he said, his voice a husk.

"Yes, but brer, there was fresh dog tracks too. Everwhere in that new morning mud. The paws of a big, big dog."

"A dog."

"A dog. Alongside them tiny footprints. And that right foot—"

"Yes?"

"That little right foot was missing a toe."

VERSE 44

Altar Call

Yes, Nurse Nightingale was true too.

How strange for a blind boy like Kestrel not to have no dog. Why, anyone could see. The boy needed guidance, never listened, never learned. Anyone could see why Kes did not like to drive Cadillacs of copper much these days. If he went to drive one, he might jump the tracks, flip once, twice, then go spashity-splash. Then he might crawl out and go do it again. This was true. Yes, he was better off a wayfarer, a wayfarer bound away.

Instead, Kestrel was sitting here hot tonight with gospel cooking out there. And, yes, Kes knew damn well what scent lingered inside this Elgar Hill dressing room.

This trailer did not smell of gingermint. This Airstream smelled of dead roses.

Kes opened the book his brother left in his lap. He could not have seen the words, even with a light. But Kes knew the words written inside the front cover.

Two Kestrel, Love Bettilia

It was Bettilia's old schoolbook, the hornbook he found when she ran away that first day they met back at the Bible school, when she first saved him. Later, after she was gone, Kes found the hornbook again. He found the book wrapped in ribbon and pretty paper inside her room on their wedding day. So her hornbook always made him feel better, when his temper ran high. He always learned a lot from it.

How often had he read her handwritten inscription? How many times had he read her last words to him before he could never read her words again? No matter. Even now, after all these years, he could still see these words. He knew them by heart.

Two Kestrel, Love Bettilia

Glenn opened the door of the trailer.

"Any Looney Tunes alive in there?" he asked the dark within.

"Still vamping."

Yes, her book made Kes feel all the better.

"Showtime, brer Brass. They got the dogs out alooking for us."

"Them's just weavers in your melon, child," Kes said.

Kes put away her book and his razor, finding his feet. He left his cane on his guitar case and found his way to the door. Dropping out of the trailer, the sounds and smells of The Elgar Hill Full Gospel Jamboree came flooding back at him. He wondered how that sad wart-covered elder was fending over at Baptist hospital with his wife.

"Just got off the phone from mama," Glenn said morbidly. "Some scary news."

"What happened?" Kes asked, adjusting his dark glasses.

"She's buying her grandkids swimming lessons."

"That's a fine fucking notion. Day is come."

"Needless to say, Chalice approves."

"You tell that girl you love her?"

"Damn right I did."

"That's good, too. I'd allow that Mama ain't so uneasy about her Kestrel no more neither," Kes said.

"Well, you ain't so easy to take sometimes. You know that?"

"I do know that," Kes allowed, his hand on Glenn's elbow. "See, brer, I don't do too good with scary-scared folk and they don't do too good with me. That fear blights your everloving soul, I tell ye."

Shuffling toward the stage, Kes heard the Holy Mountain Orioles warming up in their dressing room. He heard the grating noises of Rebecca Frang telling a very old story to the Blackwoods.

As he navigated through all this backstage electricity, bumping into bodies and pressing against flesh his snoot did not recognize, Kes kept remembering the first words he spake after his brother told him of the dog prints in the mud, the tiny foot prints, the missing toe.

"Glenn, you said you knew she was dead because she wouldn't let me suffer so thinking otherwise. All that time I was on that mountain I kept telling myself I must be fifty kinds of a fool and Glenn was surely right. That's the part I couldn't figure. Why she let me suffer so, thinking otherwise. But now I see."

"You see what?"

"She knew this jaybird, see? She knew me. She knew if I got wise to what she'd done and why she did it, I'd come looking for her up on that Riddle Top. I'd come for her, in the land where that man dwelt."

Kes listened for his brother's take on what Kes just told him, but Glenn took his time. Kes waited. Most of life was about waiting, vamping, Kes had learned. Knowing when to jump in and when to just let the waters flow your way. When the time to jump comes, you'll know it, if you're listening. You'll know when to make your move. Wasn't that what Bettilia had done?

"She always was a wise one, that girl. Wiser than the rest of us, I'm thinking," Glenn said, finally. "Cain't say she didn't try. She loved herself enough to try for the normal things a girl wants, the things of the heart that she never had. She went as far as she could go with us, until she knew she had to turn back. Not to save herself, but to save you and them she loved. That's how much she loved you. That's how much she loved us."

"That's why I got to go back for her."

"No, you ain't going nowhere, Kes. Not like you are. Look at you. You're a blind cripple psalm-singer, now ain't you? What would you do was you to even get back where you think you want to go?"

"I could tell her she didn't have to lock so much inside

her. Even a dumb and blind psalm-singing bird like me coulda understood."

"Brer," Glenn said gently, "I figured that one out a long time ago. We're all fool birds. We all got devil. We're all psalm-singers. And everybody's got two psalms in them. That song they sing out loud, for others to hear. And the song they sing only to themselves."

Holding his brother's elbow, Kes passed through the Elgar Hill Jamboree gaggle of good-news, ready-to-testify psalm-singers, quartet singers, and family gospel groups. He waited patiently outside the promoter's tent, smelling fresh-cut lilies from within, whilst Glenn picked up the brothers' pay envelope. Then they shuffled through more folks until they reached the stage where Kes waited patiently some more in the wings, holding his guitar while that fat Preacher Furl Rainey finished reading prayer requests into the microphone. Both brothers waited, vamping, as they had waited thousands of nights for the proper introductions to be made.

Suddenly, Kes snapped his fingers twice.

"Gimme fifty of my pay, brer."

Glenn looked askance.

"Furl's about to call us out there—" Glenn protested.

"Then hurry up."

Quickly, Glenn fished the envelope from inside his coat. He tore the envelope open and handed Kes a new fifty-dollar bill. Kes sniffed it, held it to his ear, listening to the crisp snap of it in his fingers. Then he reached over, fumbling for Glenn's breast pocket, finally poking the fifty in behind the silk pocket square.

"What's that for?" Glenn asked, perplexed.

"Buy you some swim lessons. Past time one of us did. Your hip ain't boogered. You might have to save one them kids from our moon river one day. Or from that clear blue sea."

Trapped, searching for an out, Glenn searched Kes's shuttered eyes.

"Don't be too scary, little brer," Kes's blind eyes told him. "Daddy was right. The scary ain't honest."

"But I am, I think. I'm scared."

"Don't think, don't worry, don't vamp. Don't think. Jump in. We might make a mistake or two, but we'll get there."

"We will?"

"Even a blind hog will find an acorn somewhere."

Glenn was still searching when they heard Preacher Furl finally speak his pearly words.

"Folks, let's have a big jamboree welcome for Glenn and Kes—*The Brothers Brass.*"

The ocean of applause washed over them as Kes held onto Glen's elbow, letting his brother lead him to the center stage microphone, hiding his limp, abiding the pain, both brothers waving and smiling at the crowd.

For Kes, it was a familiar and familial ocean—a clapping and cheering faceless sea of color-blind love, exaltation, and endearment. Waters that sprang from true affection and many a deceit. But Kes never swam in it. He could only stand here, crippled at this microphone, on these golden shores, listening to the waves rushing in and out while he sang his psalms and his heart out to those waters.

Kes locked his gimp leg into place, took a wedged pick from his guitar neck. His dark glasses caught the spotlight like double-black suns as he blindly looked to his brother. Without a wasted word, the Brothers Brass began strumming hard, their voices locking together as they launched into *Jericho Road.* Then they sang *Bosom Of Abraham* for Mrs. Carl Mosby over in Baptist Hospital tonight. They sang Glenn's song *Mercy Is Mine.*

As Kes hoped, once again tonight, in the middle of *Little Birdie* her voice came stealing in to sing with him, sharing in song.

Little birdie, why do you fly so high...

Again, he heard Bettilia's voice in sweet, unearthly harmony, rising and falling and wending her way like a sister through the brotherly voices. Surely everyone within sound of this holy revival must be gifted by her harmony tonight, as Kes had been both gifted and haunted by her voice, her presence. If they would only listen, her gift would never leave them. Kestrel believed this. He truly believed as he believed in little else in these waters of life. He believed in a brother standing here, rooted like a tree beside him. He believed in a mother, a father, the waters that birthed him. He believed in bobnot.

But mostly he believed in the healing power of her close, entwining, gingermint harmony, dreaming or awake. Yes, she was close, forever close, yet faraway hiding high in their tree, lest he who hunted her come hunting her love and the one, the ones, who would forever hold love for her. For they, she gave it all away.

So Kestrel did not just believe his psalm he sang, he knew. He knew one more thing true. Kestrel knew that soon, any elder day now, sure as a hot rain will fall, he would wend his way back to that wicked and unholy mountain and kill that bobnot bastard, just for her.

Other Riddle Top Tales by Randy Thornhorn:

WICKED TEMPER
(prequel to *The Kestrel Waters*)

HOWLS OF A HELLHOUND ELECTRIC
Riddle Top Magpies & Bobnot Boogies

THE AXMAN'S SHIFT
A Love Story

Visit Randy Thornhorn online at
www.thornhorn.com

CPSIA informati
Printed in the US
LVOW07s20232
415835LV